the bookstore
on the beach

brenda novak

the bookstore on the beach

mira

ISBN-13: 978-0-7783-1138-6

The Bookstore on the Beach

Printed in U.S.A.

To Emily. You are such a beautiful woman—inside and out.
It's hard for an author to switch editors after sixty books,
but you made it as easy on me as it could be. I appreciate
your inherent kindness, your measured approach to life, your degree
of empathy for others and your hard work on this novel in particular.
No one can "trim the fat" quite like you can. Thank you.

the bookstore on the beach

For whatever we lose (like a you or a me),
It's always our self we find in the sea.

—e.e. cummings

1

Tuesday, June 8

Today her daughter was returning for the summer. Mary Langford gazed eagerly out at the street in front of her small bookstore, looking for a glimpse of Autumn's car and, when she saw nothing except a large family going into the ice cream parlor at the end of the block, checked her watch. Three-thirty. Autumn had called at lunchtime to say that she and the kids were making good time. They probably wouldn't be much longer.

"You've been quiet today," Laurie commented from where she sat behind the counter, straightening the pens, tape, stapler and bookmarks.

Mary turned from the large front window she'd recently decorated with posters of the hottest new releases. "I worry when she's on the road for so long."

"She'll make it, and it'll be great to see her and the kids. They haven't been back since Christmas, have they?"

"No." She picked up the feather duster and began cleaning shelves—a never-ending job at Beach Front Books, which she and Laurie owned as 50/50 partners. Autumn lived in Tampa, Florida, far enough away that it wasn't easy to get together when Taylor and Caden were in school. "And I doubt they'll come back for the holidays this year." Fortunately, they were more consistent about returning for the summer—except for last summer, of course, which was understandable. Mary hoped she'd be able to count on that continuing, but with the kids getting older, nothing was certain. Taylor had only one more year of high school before heading off to college. Caden had two. Mary feared this might be the last time, for a while, they'd all be together in Sable Beach.

"You could go visit them," Laurie pointed out.

Autumn had invited her many times. Remembering the arguments her refusal had sparked over the years caused Mary's stomach to churn. She wanted to go to Tampa, wanted to make it so that her daughter wouldn't have to do *all* the traveling. Autumn had been going through so much lately. But the thought of venturing into unfamiliar territory filled Mary with dread. Other than to go to Richmond occasionally, which was the closest big city, she hadn't left the sleepy Virginia beach town she called home in thirty-five years. "Yes, but you know me. This is the only place I feel safe."

Laurie rocked back on the tall stool. "Well, if the fear hasn't gone away by now, I guess it's not going to."

"No. I don't talk about it anymore, but the past is as real to me now as it's ever been."

Although the store had been busy earlier, what with the influx of tourists for the season, foot traffic had slowed. When that happened, they often talked more than they worked. Beach Front Books wasn't Laurie's sole source of income. Her husband, Christopher Conklin, was a talented artist. He painted all kinds of seascapes, and while he wasn't in any prestigious galleries, he sold his paintings in a section they reserved for him in the store as well as online.

But Mary, who'd never been married, had no other support. Beach Front Books didn't make a large profit, but no one loved the escape that books provided more than she did, and the store garnered enough business that she could eke out a living. That was all that mattered to her.

"Autumn gets so mad that I won't go out and see the world. Visit. Travel. That sort of thing," she murmured, wishing she didn't have the scars and limitations that had, at times, put such a strain on their relationship. "She keeps saying I'm too young to live like an old lady."

"She has a point."

Mary sighed. "I'm not young anymore."

"What are you talking about? You're nine years younger than me. Fifty-four is not old."

That was true, but she'd had to grow up far sooner than most people. "I feel ancient."

"Next year, you should go to Tampa, if they ask you."

She shook her head. "I can't."

"Maybe you'll prove that you can."

Mary couldn't help bristling. She didn't like it when Laurie pushed her. "No."

"Autumn doesn't understand, Mary. That's what causes almost every fight you have with her."

"I know. And I feel bad about that. But there's nothing I can do."

Laurie lowered her voice. "You could tell her the truth…"

"Absolutely not," Mary snapped. "Why would I ever do that?"

"There are reasons. And you know it. We've talked about this before," Laurie said, remaining calm, as always. That was one of the many things Mary liked about her—she was steady and patient, and that steadiness somehow helped Mary cope when old feelings and memories began to resurface.

In this instance, Laurie might also be right. Mary could feel the past rising up from its deep slumber. Maybe it *was* time to tell Autumn.

But there were just as many reasons *not* to—compelling reasons. And the thought of revealing the past, seeing it all through her daughter's eyes, made Mary feel ill. "I can't broach that subject right now, not with what she's been dealing with the past year and a half. Besides, it's been so long it's almost as if it happened to someone else," she said, mentally shoving those dark years into the deepest recesses of her mind. "I want to stay as far away from that subject as possible."

Laurie didn't call her out on the contradiction her statement created. And Mary was glad. She couldn't have explained how it could be real and frightening and always present and yet she could feel oddly removed from it at the same time.

"Except that it *didn't* happen to someone else," Laurie responded sadly. "It happened to you."

The scent of the ocean, more than anything else, told Autumn she was home. She lowered her window as soon as she rolled into town and breathed deeply, letting the salt air fill her lungs.

"What are you doing?" Taylor held her long brown hair in one hand to keep it from whipping across her face as she looked over from the passenger seat.

Autumn smiled, which was something she knew her children hadn't seen her do enough of lately. "Just getting a little air."

"You hate it when I roll down *my* window," Caden grumbled from the backseat.

"I'm hoping I won't be so irritable anymore." For the past eighteen months, Autumn had been mired in the nightmare that had overtaken her life. She almost hadn't come to Sable Beach because of it. But when her children had each pleaded with her, separately, to ask if they could spend the summer with "Mimi" like they used to, she knew they needed some normalcy in their lives—needed to retain at least one of their parents. Her grief and preoccupation with her husband's disappearance had probably made them feel as though she'd gone missing, too—at least the mother they'd known before. She hoped by returning to the place that held so many wonderful memories for them all, they'd be able to heal and reconnect.

It wasn't as if she could do anything more for Nick, anyway. That was the ugly reality. She'd exhausted every viable lead and still had no idea where he was. If he was dead, she had to figure out a way to go on without him for the sake of their children.

The second she spotted the bookstore, the nostalgia that welled up—along with memories of a simpler, easier time—nearly brought her to tears. When she was a little girl, she'd spent so many hours following her mother through the narrow aisles of that quaint shop, which looked like something from the crooked, narrow streets of Victorian London, dusting bookshelves or reading in the nook her mother had created for her.

She'd spent just as much time at Beach Front Books when she was a teenager, only then she was stocking shelves, ordering inventory, working the register—and, again, reading, but this time sitting on the stool behind the counter while waiting for her next customer.

God, it was good to be back. As hard as she could be on her mother for her unreasonable fears and idiosyncrasies, she couldn't wait to see her. Until this moment, she hadn't realized just how much she missed her mother. So what if Mary was almost agoraphobic with her unwillingness to leave her little bungalow a block away from the sea? She was always there, waiting to welcome Autumn home. Maybe Autumn had never had a father, or the little brother or sister she'd secretly longed for, but she was lucky enough to have the enduring love of a good mother.

"There it is." She pointed to the bookstore as she slowed to look for a place to park.

"We're not going to the beach house?" Caden asked, looking up from whatever he'd been doing on his phone.

"Not right now. First, we're stopping to see Mimi and Aunt Laurie. Then we'll take our stuff over to the house."

A glance in the rearview mirror showed her his scowl. "I hope it won't be too late to go to the beach," he said.

"I'm sure we can manage to get there before dark," she responded as she wedged her white Volvo SUV between a red convertible and a gray sedan and grabbed her purse.

Taylor spoke, causing her to pause with her hand on the door latch. "You already seem different."

"In what way?" Autumn asked.

"Less uptight. Not so sad."

"Coming here makes me happy," she admitted.

"Then why were we going to skip it again?" Caden asked.

Autumn twisted around to look at him. "You know why."

A pained expression claimed her daughter's face. "Does this mean you're letting go?"

"Of Dad? Of course she's letting go," Caden answered, the hard edge to his voice suggesting he considered the question to be a stupid one. "Dad's dead."

"Don't say that!" Taylor snapped. "We don't know it's true. He could be coming back."

"It's been eighteen months, Tay," Caden responded. "He would've come back by now if he could."

"Stop it, both of you." Autumn didn't want them getting into an argument right before they saw her mother. They were at each other's throats so often lately; it drove her crazy to constantly have to play referee. But she could hardly blame them. They'd lost their father, and they didn't know how or why. And she had no explanation. "Life's been hard enough lately," she added. "Let's not make it any harder."

"Then *you* tell her," Caden said. "Dad's dead, and we have to move on. Right? Isn't that the truth? Go ahead and say it— you *are* letting go."

Was she? Is that what this trip signified? If not, how much

longer should she hold on? And would holding on be best for them? She couldn't imagine her kids would want to spend another eighteen months swallowed up by grief and consumed with seeking answers they may never find. Taylor was seventeen, going to be a senior and starting to investigate colleges. Caden was only a year behind her. Surely, they would prefer to look forward and not back.

Regardless, Autumn wasn't sure she *could* continue to search, not like she had. She was exhausted—mentally and physically. She'd put everything she had into the past year and a half, and it hadn't made a damn bit of difference. That was the most disheartening part of it.

"I'm continuing to hold out hope," she said, even though everyone she'd talked to, including the FBI, insisted her husband must be dead. It was difficult to see the idyllic, two-parent upbringing she was trying to give her kids—something she'd never had herself—fall apart that quickly and easily, and the heartbreak, loneliness and frustration of looking for Nick, with no results, created such a downward spiral for her. She knew it had been just as painful for her children. That was why maybe she *should* let go—to provide the best quality of life for them as possible.

"What does that *mean*? Are you going to keep looking for him?" Caden pressed. "Is that how you're going to spend the summer?"

He could tell something had changed, that coming here signified a difference, and he wanted to reach the bottom line. But Autumn wasn't ready to admit that she'd failed. Not with as many times as she'd tried to comfort them by promising she'd have answers eventually.

She opened her mouth to try to explain what she was thinking in the gentlest possible way when she spotted her mother. Mary had come out of the store and was waving at them.

"There's your grandmother," she said.

Thankfully, her children let the conversation lapse and got out of the car.

"Hi, Mimi." With his long strides, Caden reached Mary first. Although he wasn't yet fully grown, he was already six-one. And Taylor was five foot ten. They were both tall, like their father.

Mary gave each of the kids a big hug and exclaimed about how grown-up they both were and how excited she was to see them before turning to Autumn.

"You've lost weight," she murmured gently, a hint of worry belying her smile before they embraced.

"I'm okay, Mom." Autumn could smell a hint of the bookstore on Mary's clothes and realized that was another scent she'd never forget. It represented her childhood and all the great stories she'd read growing up. She'd once hoped to read every book in the store. She hadn't quite made it, thanks to new releases and fluctuating inventory, but she'd read more books than most people. She still considered books to be a big part of her life. "It's good to be home."

"Laurie's dying to see you. Let's go in and say hello," Mary said and held the door.

As soon as the bell sounded, Laurie hurried out from behind the register. "There you are! It's a good thing you came when you did. I was afraid it would drive your mother crazy waiting for you. She's been so anxious for you to arrive. We both have."

Taylor allowed her aunt to give her an exuberant squeeze. "I'm glad we got to come this year. Where's Uncle Chris?"

"Probably on the beach somewhere, painting. You know how he is once the weather warms up—just like a child, eager to get outdoors."

They took a few minutes to visit the small section of the store dedicated to Christopher's work so they could admire his latest paintings. Autumn was especially enamored with one he'd done of the bookstore that portrayed a child out front, hanging on to her mother with one hand and carrying a stack of books with the other. That child could've been her once upon a time. She almost wondered if his memory of her had inspired it, which was why she decided, if that painting didn't sell before she left, she'd buy it herself and take it back to Tampa.

Fortunately, she had the money. As a corporate attorney, Nick had always done well financially. After the first few years of their marriage, which he spent finishing school, they'd rarely had to scrimp. But it was what he'd inherited when his father passed away that'd really set them up. After Sergey's death, Autumn had quit working as a loan officer for a local bank and, for the past ten years, had focused on her family, her home, gardening and cooking. Her financial situation was also one of the reasons she rejected the idea that Nick might've left her for another woman, a possibility that had been suggested to her many, many times. Why would he leave his children, too, and walk away without a cent? Sure, they'd had their struggles, especially in recent years, when his work seemed to take more and more of his time and attention, but neither of them had ever mentioned separating.

"This is amazing," she exclaimed as she continued to study the little girl in the painting. "I love Chris's work."

"The last original he donated to charity went for six thousand dollars," Laurie announced proudly.

"Who bought it?" Autumn asked. If whoever it was lived in Sable Beach, chances were good she'd know him or her.

"Mike Vanderbilt, over at The Daily Catch. He was drunk when he got into a bidding war for it, and now it's hanging in his restaurant. I think he's glad to have it, but I imagine he also sees it as a reminder not to raise his paddle when he's been drinking."

They all laughed to think of the barrel-chested and good-natured Mike letting alcohol bring out his competitive nature.

"His wife must be doing well, then," Autumn said. "She's still in remission?"

Laurie shot Mary a surprised glance, and it was Mary who answered. "I'm afraid not. She was when he bought that painting, but they received word just a couple of months ago that Beth's breast cancer has come back."

"Oh no," Autumn cried. Everyone knew the owners of The Daily Catch. They did a lot for the community. And it was her favorite restaurant. When she was home, she ate there all the time. "What's her prognosis?"

"Not good. That's why Quinn has moved home from that little town in upstate New York. He helps his father with the restaurant these days. I'm sure he's also here to spend time with his mother before…well, before he has to say goodbye to her for good."

"Quinn's home?" Autumn said. She wasn't expecting that; the mention of his name knocked her a little off-kilter. When he was a senior and she was a junior, she'd given him her virginity in the elaborate tree house that was in his backyard, even though he hadn't been nearly as interested in being with her as she was him. And then he'd broken her heart by getting back together with his girlfriend, the same woman he married five years later. "So his wife and kids are here now, too?"

"No, he doesn't have any kids," Laurie said, chiming in again. "And he and Sarah—what was her maiden name?"

"Vizii," Autumn supplied.

"Yes. Vizii. They divorced almost two years ago. You didn't know?"

"How would I?" She'd seen nothing about it on social media, but then, Quinn had never been on social media, and she'd never been able to find Sarah, either—not that she'd checked recently because she hadn't. "I haven't seen him since he was working as a lifeguard at the beach after his first year of college and he had to swim out and save me from drowning." She didn't add that she'd faked the whole episode just to get his attention. She was mortified about that now and cringed at how obvious it must've been to him.

"I'm surprised the gossip didn't reach you all the way down in

Tampa," Laurie said. "For a while, it was about the only thing anyone around here could talk about."

But who would tell her? Her mother wasn't much for gossip, which was ironic, considering she'd lived in Sable Beach for so long. The town where Autumn had been raised took talking about their friends and neighbors to a whole new level.

"Why would his divorce be such big news?" she asked. Besides being one of the most popular boys in school, Quinn had been handsome, athletic and at the top of his class—undoubtedly one of Sable Beach's finest. But still. Divorce was so commonplace it was hardly remarkable anymore. And Quinn was thirty-nine. He'd been gone from this place—except for when he visited his folks—for twenty-one years. How could what was going on in his life be such a hot topic?

Laurie tilted her head toward Taylor and Caden in such a way that Autumn understood she was hesitant to speak in front of them. "There were some…extenuating circumstances. Have your mother tell you about it later."

"*I* want to hear," Caden protested.

"Why? We don't even know him." Taylor jumped in before Autumn could respond, then Caden snapped at her to shut up and they started arguing again.

"Don't make Mimi regret inviting us." Autumn rolled her eyes to show how weary she was of this behavior.

"Should we go over and get you settled in?" Mary asked. "Laurie offered to close the store tonight, so I'm free to start dinner while you unpack."

"Sure," Autumn said. Once Caden and Taylor got to the beach, maybe they'd mellow out and fall into the same companionable rhythm they usually achieved when they came to Sable Beach.

Her mother's house seemed the same, except that its shingle siding was now white instead of green. It had needed a fresh coat of paint, and the white looked clean and crisp. But as much as she loved the update, Autumn was relieved to find that nothing else had changed. Visiting Mary was like going back in time. Not many people could do that twenty years after they'd left home.

Because it was such a small cottage, Caden had to sleep on the couch, Taylor took Autumn's old room next to Mary's, and the three of them shared the only bathroom, which was off the hallway. Autumn slept above the detached garage, where she had her own bed and bath, thanks to Nick. Because he'd typically had to work when she brought the kids, he'd never spent more than a few days at a time in Sable Beach. That had caused more than a few arguments over the years, so she'd readily agreed when he'd insisted they have their own space for when he did come. She'd thought it might mean he'd accompany them more often, or stay a little longer when he did. It made no difference in the end, but he was the one who'd hired an architect to create the plans to finish off the top of the garage, even though it had been Autumn who'd picked out the finishes and colors.

A wave of melancholy washed over her as she left the kids with her mother to get settled in at the main house, let herself into the garage and climbed the narrow stairs at the back to the apartment, where she'd be living for the next few months, by herself. As often as she'd been here over the years, it felt strange to know that Nick would not be visiting. At times, she was still so lost without him.

"Where are you?" she whispered as she walked around, touching the things he'd touched. She'd come for Christmas without him, but she and Taylor had shared her old room in the house. They could do that for a week or so but not for three months— not without wanting to turn around and head straight home.

She stopped in front of the dresser, where her mother had put a picture of her family. She'd known her husband was getting involved in something secretive, that a friend who was with the FBI had recruited him for his knowledge of Ukraine. Because his parents had emigrated from there, he'd known the language, was familiar with the customs and still had a few relatives in the country. That made him useful in what had become a very troubled region.

Although he couldn't tell her exactly what he was doing for the government, she guessed he was working in counterterrorism, probably trying to infiltrate various radical groups. She'd read that the FBI sometimes used civilians who were particularly adept with computers, or had some specific knowledge or ability, to assist them.

Maybe he'd become a full-fledged spy, and whoever was on the other side had discovered his activities. The FBI claimed they hadn't sent him to Ukraine to begin with, but she'd discovered that he'd flown into Kyiv before disappearing and had no idea why he'd go there if not at their request. If he wanted to reacquaint himself with his uncle and cousins, he would've told her. Besides, the family he had there claimed they hadn't heard from him. She'd traveled halfway across the world to speak to them face-to-face—not that the long, tiring trip had accomplished anything.

She lifted her suitcase onto the bed and was unpacking her clothes when her mother came up. "The kids would like to go to the beach before we have dinner, but I told them I'd rather they not go alone."

"Mom, they're sixteen and seventeen," she said. "Kids that age go to the beach by themselves all the time."

"Still. I don't mind walking down with them."

That was her mother's polite way of saying she was afraid they wouldn't be safe and felt the need to watch over them. Mary had always been overprotective. But Autumn managed not to say anything. What would it hurt for their Mimi to walk down to the water with them? There was no need to transfer the suffocation she'd felt to her children, especially because they'd had to put up with so much less of it. "Okay."

"Would you like us to wait for you?"

"No, I'll find you in a few minutes."

With a nod, her mother turned to leave but paused before descending the stairs. "It can't be easy for you to stay out here, knowing that Nick won't be coming. Would you rather we make other arrangements, like we did at Christmas? Have you stay in the house with us?"

Unless Nick suddenly showed up, she'd have to brave it at some point, wouldn't she? It might as well be now. "No. There's not enough room. Taylor and I both need our space."

"If you're sure."

"Mom?"

She looked up. "Yes?"

"Before you go, tell me what Laurie was referring to at the bookshop."

"About…"

"Quinn and Sarah," she said.

"Oh. No one really knows exactly what happened," her mother said.

"There must've been a story circulating." And she was eager to focus on something besides her own troubles for a change. She could see Nick's rain boots in the corner of the room and knew there would probably come a time—in the not-too-distant future—when she would have to make the difficult decision about what to do with them.

She couldn't even imagine that. But she had a whole houseful of his belongings in Tampa, and if he didn't come back, she'd have to decide what to do with all of it. Should she box it up and put it in storage? Stubbornly continue to wait? And if so, for how long?

Her mother seemed as reluctant as ever to repeat gossip, but she must've understood that what'd happened to Quinn might create a good distraction, because she finally relented. "Sarah claims he was having an affair, which caused her to fly into a jealous rage and stab him."

This was not what Autumn had expected. "Did you say *stab* him?"

Her mother frowned. "I'm afraid so."

"But…he must be okay. Laurie said he was here, helping his father run the restaurant."

"She didn't hit anything vital, thank goodness. But I heard he spent a few days in the hospital, so his wounds weren't superficial, either."

Autumn whistled as she imagined how bad their marriage must've been for something like that to happen. "I thought they'd be happy together. They dated for so long before they got married. It's not as if they didn't know each other well." She sank onto the bed next to her suitcase. "Did he admit to cheating?"

"Not that I know of."

"But you think he did—cheat, I mean."

"I wouldn't be surprised. *Something* had to have made her react so violently."

Mary never gave the benefit of the doubt to a man. Autumn had noticed this before and assumed her father was to blame. Although Mary refused to talk about the past—went rigid as soon as Autumn mentioned her father—there were times, more of them as she got older, when she found herself wondering who he was and what he was like. Before Nick went missing, she'd told her mother that she was tempted to try to look him up, and Mary had been so appalled—that Autumn would have any interest in him when he was such a "bad person"—that she'd dropped the idea.

It was something she thought she might like to revisit, though. Times had changed. Nowadays, a simple DNA test could possibly tell her a great deal. And there were moments when she felt she should be allowed to fill in those blanks.

But she hated to proceed without her mother's blessing. She owed Mary a degree of loyalty for being the parent who'd stuck with her.

Finished unpacking, she put her empty suitcase in the closet while trying to ignore Nick's snorkel gear, which was also in there, changed into her bathing suit and cover-up, slipped on her flip-flops and grabbed her beach bag. She was on her way down the stairs when she heard her phone buzz with an incoming call.

Assuming it would be her mother or one of her children, wondering what was taking her so long, she dug it out of her bag so that she could answer. But according to Caller ID, the person attempting to reach her wasn't a member of the family. It was Lyaksandro Olynyk, the Ukrainian private investigator she'd hired to look for Nick.

It was seven hours later in that part of the world. Why would he be calling her in the middle of the night?

2

Taylor stretched out on her towel. It was late in the day, so it wasn't as warm on the beach as she would've liked, but she was glad to be out of Florida, to have a break from her regular life. She was tired of being the girl whose father had gone missing. Tired of how everyone acted because of it. Tired of seeing her mother show up at school for one of her volleyball games with dark circles under her eyes, her mind thousands of miles away. Tired of the constant arguments with her brother because they suddenly couldn't get along.

Tired of it all.

Losing her father was bad enough without the other stuff. She just wanted to run away or be someone else for a while.

Thank God her mother had agreed that they could come to Mimi's. Sable Beach was better than Tampa. For one, she could breathe here. The place was so small she wasn't quite as invisible as she wished she were, but most of the people in town only knew her as Autumn's daughter or Mary's granddaughter, so she could hide behind her mother and Mimi most of the time. And when they weren't around? She could handle the occasional superficial interaction. It was the constant pretense that was so

hard. Smiling. Getting up and going to school every day. Feigning interest in conversations, events and high school drama that
no longer interested her.

Now she could save all her energy for the acting she had to
do for her own family.

Before she left, her friends had said she'd probably get bored
and start begging to come home. They'd been joking, but she
hoped they were right. Maybe if she did get bored, *really* bored,
she'd be able to make herself go back to Florida after the summer was over. Otherwise, she was going to ask her mother if she
could move in with Mimi and finish high school in Sable Beach.
She hated to hurt Autumn. But she couldn't seem to relate to
anyone anymore. She had to escape the past eighteen months.

Her phone chimed, but she didn't bother to pick it up. She didn't
want to hear from her old friends, who cared so much about stuff
that seemed stupid to her. A man had gone missing. A husband, a
father and a good lawyer. How could life go on as if that was nothing? Couldn't they see that he'd taken a huge part of her with him?

Caden leaned around Mimi, who was sitting between them.
"Can't you hear that?" he said, obviously irritated.

Rather than admit that she'd heard the ringing of her phone,
too—because then he'd only demand to know why she wasn't
answering—she picked it up so she could see the screen.

She'd missed a call from her best friend, Danielle Kent, who'd
followed up with a text message.

Answer your phone! You're not going to believe
who I just saw at the mall.

Who?

Oliver Hancock.

She didn't want to talk about Oliver. Danielle and her other
friends assumed she liked him—he probably did, too—because

she'd had sex with him at a party two weeks ago. But that incident held no meaning for her. She'd simply been trying to shock herself into feeling *something*.

Too bad that night hadn't fixed anything. Even when she'd been with him, she hadn't felt anything. She'd just stared at the ceiling, totally numb, wishing he'd hurry up and finish. Although she'd been vaguely aware that they hadn't used a condom, she'd also been too reckless to do anything about it—couldn't bring herself to care—and now she had to worry about the possible consequences.

Can't talk right now. What'd he say? she wrote back, acting interested only because she knew Danielle would expect her to.

He wanted your number!

Taylor grimaced.

Did you give it to him?

I did.

"Shit," she muttered.

"Something wrong, honey?" Mimi was wearing a long turquoise beach dress, her knees pulled into her chest and rope-like sandals on her feet. Taylor had always thought her grandmother was beautiful in an ethereal, almost untouchable way. With silver hair, light blue eyes that slanted slightly upward and high cheekbones, she could've been a model. She was definitely prettier than the grandmothers of Taylor's friends, but Mimi was also a lot younger than most of them. She'd had Autumn when she was only sixteen.

Taylor hated that she might be following in her grandmother's footsteps and having a baby when she was way too young. She knew better and should've been more careful. "No. Nothing." Why say yes? Where would she even begin to explain?

This was where the acting came in...

Caden got to his feet, caught her eye and jerked his head toward the water. "Want to go for a swim?"

She knew part of the reason they fought so often was because she'd withdrawn from him. But she couldn't help it; she was hurting too badly to try any harder than she was. "No."

She could tell he was disappointed. Even Mimi glanced over as though she wished Taylor would change her mind. So she forced herself to relent. "Okay," she said grudgingly. "Go ahead. I'll be out in a sec."

"Are you excited for your senior year?" Mimi asked as they both watched Caden run into the ocean and dive beneath the surf.

Taylor turned off her phone and slipped it into her bag. She didn't want anyone to touch it, including her grandmother and especially her brother, if, for some reason, he came out of the ocean before she did. He'd be disgusted if he learned what she'd done with Oliver. Since she wasn't even attracted to Caden's ex-best friend, she was disgusted at herself. "Yeah," she lied. "I'm looking forward to it."

"Where would you like to go to college?"

Her grades had fallen so much she wasn't sure she'd be able to get into college—although she had done surprisingly well on the SAT. That could save her, providing something else didn't get in the way, like a *pregnancy*. She wished she knew when to expect her period, but she hadn't been paying any attention to her monthly cycle. Since she'd broken up with her boyfriend just before Christmas and had gone off the pill, there hadn't been any reason to. "Mom said that Old Dominion is only two and a half hours from here. Maybe I'll go there, so I can drive over and see you whenever I have the time."

"I'd love that," Mimi said. "It would be great if Caden chose Old Dominion, too."

She stood and dusted the sand off her legs. "He's hoping to

get a water polo scholarship, so I doubt we'll go to the same college." That was another reason she was pulling away from her brother. They were going to be separated soon, regardless, and she couldn't face another loss, had to be more prepared for the next one.

"Of course." The bangles on Mimi's wrist jangled as she shaded her eyes. "How's your mother been doing?"

Taylor could tell by the tone of Mimi's voice that this wasn't a casual question. "I couldn't tell you. She doesn't talk to us about how she's feeling."

"Because she doesn't want to make what you're going through any worse," Mimi explained, always quick to defend her daughter.

Caden came to the surface, threw back his hair and went under again.

"I think Mom's decided Dad's not coming back," Taylor admitted.

Mary blinked several times before speaking. "Do *you* think he might?"

Taylor's chest suddenly felt as though it was buried beneath a thousand pounds of sand. "No," she admitted for the first time and ran down to the water.

Mr. Olynyk had a thick accent, making it hard for Autumn to understand him. She'd spoken to him many times since she'd hired him over a year ago, before she went to Ukraine. But it'd been months since he'd had anything of substance to report. Although he claimed he was working with various contacts inside the SBU, the Security Service of Ukraine, she was beginning to suspect that whatever he could do had already been done. So many people—from various governmental agencies, as well as chat rooms and forums she'd visited while trying to get help online—had warned her about her vulnerability and how easy it would be for an unscrupulous person to take advantage of her. After all, how would she know if he was telling the truth?

Now that she was no longer in the country, she felt so out of touch, so helpless. But she couldn't go back. It had been hard to leave her children, who each went to stay with a friend while she was gone so they could continue going to school. Not only had those three weeks seemed interminable, she also hadn't accomplished anything. She had a face to put with Mr. Olynyk's name and had spent some time with him. But that certainly didn't stop her from lying awake at night, imagining that he'd proved Nick was dead months ago but had decided not to say anything.

Meanwhile, she couldn't tell her children what'd happened to their father, and she couldn't bring Nick's body home, where she could give him a proper burial and be satisfied that, even though his life was over, she'd done everything she could. While she hoped that he was alive and would come back to her, if they found him dead, that would at least put an end to the questions that nearly drove her mad. Not knowing when to quit, when she'd fulfilled her duty to the love they'd shared, was one of the worst parts of what she was going through.

"Say that again?" she said, when Olynyk mentioned something about the Donetsk region, which was held by separatists.

"A friend of the man I told you about last time, Ananiy Kushnir, recognized your husband's photograph. He believes he saw him."

She clutched the phone tighter. It was dangerous to get her hopes up. How many times had she been through this? But she craved news of her husband so badly she simply couldn't avoid taking the bait. "How long ago?"

"Months. Many months. Nick was in the company of known rebel forces."

"You think he came to your country to infiltrate the separatists." This was a theory they'd floated before, but there'd never been anything to suggest it was actually true.

"Possibly."

He'd called her in the middle of what would be his night to tell her *this*? Apparently, she'd imbued his timing with more meaning than she should have, because this sounded like more of nothing to her.

"You want me to keep going, yes?"

That was his way of asking if he should spend more time. And more time meant more money. Should she continue with this? Was he on the right trail, or was this "friend" fictitious?

"What could've happened to him?" she asked for the millionth time. This was always how their conversations went—she pummeled him with questions and he danced around in his efforts to answer them.

"He could be working somewhere. I am looking. But it's very dangerous. The Russian government has sent many sabotage groups—you understand? Sabotage is the correct word?"

"Yes. I know what that means."

"These groups, they work…um…how do you say…independent."

"Independently," she said.

"Very dangerous," he repeated. "Maybe…maybe they don't like your husband."

"Are you suggesting that Nick might've become a target of one of these Russian groups?"

"Could be. If they deem him an enemy, they could…do anything," he finished weakly.

Had they murdered him? It sounded like something out of a movie, not her *life*.

She gripped the railing as she sank down onto the wooden steps. "Can I ask you something?"

"Of course."

She let every bit of the longing she felt fill her voice. "In your *honest* opinion, do you believe Nick's dead?"

He hesitated as though uncomfortable with the question. Then he said, "I think...yes. Otherwise, I find him long time ago."

It was one thing for her to say Nick was most likely dead. It was another thing entirely to hear it from someone who knew the area and the situation far better than she did. This one response sounded completely frank—so frank that along with all the other emotions zipping around inside her, she felt a degree of guilt for suspecting Olynyk of trying to cheat her. Maybe she just hadn't asked the right questions.

"Where could his body be?"

"Anywhere. But you want me to keep trying to find it, yes?"

Squeezing her eyes closed, she let her head fall back. Now they were searching for a body?

God, what should she do?

Tears trickled from her eyes and rolled back into her hair while she struggled to decide. For the most part, she'd quit weeping at random moments. Having Nick gone had become normal. What was new was the realization that she'd come to the end of the road. It was time to give up no matter how difficult it was to let him go.

She thought of those rain boots in the corner upstairs. The fact that he would probably never come back to wear them made it almost impossible to speak. "I'll send you another two thousand. That should take you through June. But if you can't provide something concrete by then—something that shows you're on the right trail—that will be the end of it. Do you understand?"

"*Tak.*"

After the past eighteen months, she'd learned enough Ukrainian to know that meant yes. She also knew how to say thank you: "*Dyakuyu tobi.*"

"*Nemae problem.*"

No problem. She shook her head as she disconnected, but another call came in before she could finish going down the stairs. It was her mother.

"Are you coming?" Mary asked as soon as she answered.

"Yes. I'll be right there."

After Mary ended the phone call with Autumn, she leaned back, feeling the soft sand give slightly beneath her palms as she watched her grandchildren bodysurfing in the ocean. She loved this small part of the world. Living in Sable Beach had brought her peace and safety. She walked down to the water almost every night to visit the sea and be heartened by its constancy and beauty. It was more of a mother to her than her own mother had ever been—her *real* mother, anyway. She loved watching the gulls swoop and land and study her as curiously as she studied them.

One gull who visited this beach quite often was missing an eye. He would cock his head and look at her with the eye he had left, but he wouldn't venture close, not as close as the others.

She felt a certain kinship with him. Although hers were less visible, she had scars, too. They both clung to the sanctuary Sable Beach provided and weren't willing to trust too much.

Would the peace she'd found here last? Or was everything about to change? For so long, her secret had felt safe. But thanks to the interest Autumn had shown in finding her father—right before Nick went missing—and the technological advances that made DNA testing commonplace, she was on edge again, like she'd been in the beginning, always wondering what might sneak up from behind.

Taylor had mentioned something only two weeks ago that indicated Autumn had been talking about her father again. Mary could remember the exact words and even the tone of her granddaughter's voice: *I think it bugs Mom that she doesn't know more about her father's side.*

Mary had glossed over that statement by saying she didn't know anything, either, but she felt that was a harbinger of doom. The subject would come up again—this time with Autumn—

and probably before the summer was over. Mary desperately wanted to stick with her story, to keep everything status quo, but she knew she couldn't get away with that, not when a simple DNA test could give Autumn the means to track him down and prove her a liar.

And if she came out and told her? What would Autumn do with the information? Mary was afraid she'd reach out to people she didn't want her to have any contact with—and was loath to allow back into her own life.

The thought of that nearly caused her to pump her fist at the sky and scream, "Over my dead body!" It was the fight in her that had carried her through those terrible years. But despite all she'd done to protect Autumn and create a new life for them both, and despite all she might do to keep the past from catching up with her, in the end she might not have any say in it.

Secrets had a way of coming out.

"There you are!"

Mary turned to see Autumn trudging toward her and waved.

"Taylor and Caden are having a blast," she said as soon as Autumn arrived and let her bag drop onto the sand. Sometimes Mary marveled at the banal things that came out of her mouth when there was so much more going on inside her head.

Autumn slid her sunglasses higher on the bridge of her nose as she turned to watch her children out in the waves. "For once they're not fighting." Pulling a towel from her bag, she prepared a spot where she could sit down. "Sorry it took me so long to get here. That private investigator I hired in Ukraine called."

"Did he have any news?"

"Not really. Just more of the same. He's found someone who might've seen Nick. He's taking more pictures to show this contact or that contact. A friend in the government might be able to help. He's managed to speak to the person he told me about last time, so we can at least cross one more potential lead off the list. That's all I ever get."

Mary could see why she'd be discouraged. "He has to be methodical, I suppose."

"That's true, but it's been so long. Is this investigator doing anything that will make a difference?"

"Who can say?"

It was difficult to watch her daughter suffer. For a long time, Autumn had been so intent on finding Nick that Mary could scarcely reach her. She was up night and day, always on the internet or the telephone, trying to get more information, to push the government to help her, to speak to people who might have more power, to circulate his picture around various groups in Ukraine, to find someone over there who might be capable and willing to look into his disappearance. It terrified Mary to think that Autumn's efforts might draw the attention of the wrong sort of person or persons. What if Nick had indeed infiltrated a terrorist group, and they were so bothered by Autumn's dogged efforts to track him down that they decided to put a stop to her nosing around—by putting a stop to *her*?

When Mary mentioned the possibility to Laurie, Laurie had said she shouldn't let her imagination run away with her. The odds of something that terrible happening were one in a million.

But Mary didn't care how remote the chance might be. The odds of what'd happened to her were just as slim—and yet she'd been that one in a million.

"Do you trust him?" Mary asked.

"I did at first. He's the one who gave me that fuzzy photograph taken by a security camera at the airport in Kyiv, remember? That was how I knew Nick made his flight and landed in Ukraine, which was huge."

Mary remembered. Autumn had made a big deal of that picture, calling out the FBI on social media, claiming they were trying to sweep her husband's disappearance under the rug. His "handler" had finally reached out and admitted that Nick had been doing a few "low level" things for the bureau but only online. They wanted her to accept that he'd gone to Ukraine on his own and pipe down, but she kept saying she couldn't believe he'd do that—not without telling her he was going out of the country.

"Isn't there something more that could be done to track Nick's cell phone?" Mary asked. "I know I've asked before, but they can do so much more now than they could even a year ago. I see it all the time on those forensic shows."

"His cell phone should've yielded more information," Autumn replied. "Believe it or not, if it were an older model, it would've had a baseband processor that powers up every ten minutes or so to retrieve text messages—although not phone calls—and I would've had a chance."

"But he didn't have an older model."

"Of course not. He relied on his phone a great deal, always had the latest and greatest. He loves—" she frowned and cleared her throat "—*loved* technology."

"But most people have new technology these days. And I've read about the NSA being able to track cell phones, even when they're turned off."

"The new phones have a unibody design where the battery can't be removed," she explained. "As long as there's a battery, a phone can be tracked even when it's turned off." She grimaced. "But only if it's infected with Trojans. According to everything I've been able to find, that's how the NSA does it. Anyway, I've tried. There's nothing more I can do in regards to his cell phone. And everything Olynyk provided of any real significance was almost a year ago. Yet, I keep paying him."

"Because you're hoping he'll eventually find a thread you can use to unravel the whole mystery."

Autumn bit her lip. "Yes. But am I letting my attention be diverted when I should be giving it to the kids instead? Am I throwing away money on a dream that will never come to pass? I need to know whether I should be chasing it."

Mary heard the anguish in her voice. "I wish I could answer that for you. But only you can decide. It's whatever you can live with, right?"

Autumn adjusted her sunglasses. It was too late in the day for there to be much glare, but she probably felt safer behind them. Mary understood the need to have a buffer of some sort once in a while. "I told Olynyk to continue to search for the rest of the month. Then I'm done. I have to make myself let go, have to stop letting Nick's disappearance tear our family apart."

"You've done all you could," Mary said softly. "You've worked night and day, investigated every lead, spent a fortune."

"I have, and yet…is it enough? There's always more I *could* do. The items that remain just don't come with much likelihood of being worth the time, angst or money. And my children deserve to have at least one parent fully present. At this point, to continue searching almost seems—" she wrinkled her nose "—selfish, I guess. That I'll be indulging my own broken heart and thirst for the truth over what would be best for them."

Mary studied her daughter. The golden brown of her eyes, hidden behind those sunglasses, as well as her long, dark hair came from her father. But the oval shape to her face, the way her eyes turned up at the outer edges and her prominent cheekbones were Mary's. So was her thin build. She looked far more delicate than her own children. Taylor and Caden had Autumn's eye color and the same thick, wavy hair, which Taylor also wore long, but those features were paired with their father's stubborn jaw and sturdy build. "What would Nick want you to do?"

She folded her arms atop her knees, rested her chin on them and stared glumly off for a while, presumably at the ocean and her children—although it was hard to tell because of the sunglasses. "He'd want me to take care of the kids. He was generous that way."

"But…" Mary could hear the hesitancy in her voice.

"As soon as I decide that's the course I should take, I think…

what if he's alive? What if I'm giving up just a few weeks or months too soon? What if I could've found him if only I'd kept searching?" She gestured emphatically. "The possibility nearly drives me insane, keeps me chasing my own tail."

Mary adjusted her dress while taking a moment to decide how best to approach what she wanted to say. "I can't tell you how he'd feel," she admitted. "But I can tell you how *I'd* feel if I were him."

Autumn looked so tragic and forlorn sitting there on the beach with the wind whipping at her hair. "How's that?"

"I wouldn't want you to be sad, lonely or filled with regret. I'd want you to rebound and embrace the life you have, enjoy every moment of it. And I would want you to be available to Taylor and Caden."

A tear slid from beneath Autumn's sunglasses. She dashed it away with notable impatience, but then she sniffed and said, "Thanks, Mom. I'm glad we came."

Mary smiled at the one person who had, once upon a time, been her only reason for living. "So am I."

3

Is everything okay?

Nick? Are you there? Can you answer me?

I thought for sure you'd check in by now. Are you all right?

Please, babe. I'm going crazy. Answer me.

Seriously? You can't even let me know that you're okay?

WTF?????

What do I tell the kids? They're asking about you, can't reach you, either.

This can't be happening!!! Where are you?

Unable to sleep, Autumn sat in the window seat of the dormer that served as the only window in the small studio above her mother's garage, scrolling through the text messages she'd sent to Nick a year and a half ago. They started out conversational and friendly, quickly turned frantic, then angry and insistent before hitting heartbroken. The last one she'd sent: Please, babe! I can't live without you.

But she *was* living without him. She had no choice.

She sighed. It didn't matter which kind of text she sent, they'd all gone unanswered. So had hundreds of others over the months since then.

You bastard, she wrote to his FBI handler. She hoped having his phone suddenly light up or ding in the middle of the night might at least wake Richard Jenkins. He deserved it. He knew more than he was saying; she felt it in her bones. Whatever the FBI had asked her husband to accomplish had gone terribly wrong, and now those who were involved in sending him to Ukraine were worried about the liability. She didn't think they knew where he was *exactly*, but she believed they could've provided information—in the beginning, anyway—that would've given her some direction in her search. And that might've made all the difference.

Because she saw no evidence that her text had been received, she assumed Richard was sleeping soundly, as unconcerned as ever. "Psychopath," she muttered and tossed her phone onto the cushion beside her. Even after he got her message in the morning she wouldn't receive a response from him. He'd quit communicating with her months ago.

In order to get her mind off Nick, so that she might be able to sleep at some point, she crossed to the bed and opened her laptop. She was curious enough about Quinn and Sarah Vanderbilt to want to learn more. No one could have predicted this wrinkle in his life; she was completely blown away by it. And thinking about his problems made her own a little easier to bear. She felt guilty acknowledging that, but "misery loves company" was a cliché for a reason. She felt less alone in her own suffering.

Quinn and Sarah had lived in upstate New York, where she'd heard on one of her many trips to Sable Beach over the years that he worked as a structural engineer. Because some areas of upstate New York were quite rural, maybe the stabbing incident had been remarkable enough to be reported in the local paper.

Sure enough, after about ten minutes of searching, she found a short article in *The Villager*, which touted itself as "Ellicottville's Official Newspaper," dated nearly two years ago.

Wife Stabs Husband Over Purported Affair

Last night police were summoned to the home of Quinn and Sarah Vanderbilt on Longwood Drive where they found Quinn Vanderbilt, a male in his thirties, suffering from multiple stab wounds. He was taken by ambulance to Olean General Hospital, where he was admitted and treated.

A spokeswoman for the hospital has reported that he is now in stable condition and is expected to recover. Mrs. Vanderbilt was no longer at the scene when police arrived, but one officer found her at a neighbor's house. When asked why she stabbed her husband, Mrs. Vanderbilt claimed he was sleeping with another woman.

Mrs. Vanderbilt will be arraigned on Friday. Her lawyer was not available for comment at the time of this printing.

Autumn scrolled through several other links, hoping to find more information, and located an even shorter article in the same paper, three days later.

Woman Who Stabbed Husband to be Arraigned

Sarah Vanderbilt is being charged with attempted murder in the stabbing of her husband, Quinn Vanderbilt, who was taken to Olean Hospital three days ago. Mr. Vanderbilt has since been released from the hospital but has yet to make a statement.

Katherine Wilson, a neighbor, claims Mrs. Vanderbilt showed up with a kitchen knife covered in blood, screaming that her husband didn't love her anymore. "She said she'd rather have him dead than lose him to another woman," Mrs. Wilson reported.

Mrs. Vanderbilt is expected to plead not guilty. If convicted, she could serve twenty years to life.

Twenty *years*? "Wow," Autumn said on a long exhale as she continued her search and found one final article, written a year later.

Vanderbilt Gets Ten Years

Sarah Vanderbilt was sentenced today for the attempted murder of former husband Quinn Vanderbilt. Her defense lawyer argued that she was not guilty by reason of insanity, but the prosecution had several witnesses to testify that she was aware of her actions, including a neighbor who claimed she said she'd rather see him dead than let him leave her.

It took the jury only three hours to return a guilty verdict.

Quinn Vanderbilt attended the trial but refused to testify against his ex-wife. In a surprising move, he asked the judge for leniency during the sentencing phase of the trial, claiming Sarah needed psychiatric help.

Sarah Vanderbilt wept as she heard her husband read his prepared remarks. She called out, "I will always love you," as he left the courtroom.

The judge sentenced her to ten years.

Autumn set her computer on the nightstand and leaned against the headboard. Did Quinn's actions indicate he had some culpability in what happened? Maybe he *had* been cheating. It wasn't legal to stab an adulterer, but if he had gotten involved with another woman and broken Sarah's trust, the argument could be made that he'd wronged her first.

She slid down beneath the covers. She'd wanted him so badly when she was in high school that she couldn't help wondering how different things would be if he'd been interested in return.

Maybe they'd both be living different lives.

Mary jerked awake, skin clammy, heart racing.

Breathe. It was only a nightmare, she told herself. It wasn't as though this was the first one she'd ever had. But it had been a while since she'd remembered the details so clearly.

She looked around her bedroom, searching for movement or anything that might be out of place. Although she saw nothing alarming, she got out of bed and went through the house to double-check that all of the doors and windows were locked.

The wind tossed the chimes on the back porch and caused the screen door to creak. Those were familiar sounds during a storm, and yet, tonight they raised the hair on the back of her neck.

Did she also hear footfalls?

She moved the drape aside to peer out into the backyard. A jagged bolt of lightning lit the sky. Thunder boomed several seconds later.

She couldn't see anyone. But occasionally, on nights like this, she thought she saw his face at the window—

"Mimi?"

She jumped and dropped the drape. Taylor had come out. "Yes, sweetie?"

"Sorry. I didn't mean to startle you. I just wanted to see if you were okay."

"Of course I'm okay." Mary spoke softly so they wouldn't wake Caden, who was in the living room on the couch, and clasped her hands in front of her to hide a slight tremor. "It's only a little bad weather."

"I know that. I thought I heard—"

"Someone trying to get in?"

As soon as Taylor's eyebrows snapped together, Mary regretted answering so impetuously. She hadn't given herself enough time to get over the residual effects of the nightmare.

"What? No! It sounded like you were crying out for help. I thought maybe—" she fell silent, raked her hair back off her face and drew a deep breath before finishing with a reluctant "—you were having a heart attack or something."

No one had ever accused her of crying out in her sleep before, not even when Autumn lived with her. But like Caden, Autumn had been a deep sleeper. Mary had always been grateful for that. Things would've been much worse if that hadn't been the case.

Mary gestured at the window. "Are you sure it wasn't the thunder?"

"I'm positive. I've been up watching the storm. I heard the thunder, too."

Since she was unable to convince Taylor that it wasn't her, she could only try to minimize the truth. "Well, then. I must've been having a bad dream. Because I'm fine."

"You thought someone was trying to break in?"

"No." She waved her granddaughter's concern away. "That must've been what I was dreaming about. Don't mind me. I'm still a little groggy."

"Oh."

Mary peered out the window again, this time craning her neck to be able to see the detached garage. "I wish there was room for your mother to stay in here with us."

"I do, too. But she's okay where she is, if that's what you're worried about. I just texted her to see what I should do, and she told me to get up and check on you."

"She's awake? It's after two. I worry about her getting enough rest. But it's daytime in Ukraine, so I guess that makes sense after all the late nights she's put in the past eighteen months."

"Are you saying she's still searching? She's not giving up on finding my father?"

Mary hated seeing the pain in her granddaughter's eyes. "I'm saying her internal clock has got to be a little mixed-up. That's all."

"Then she *is* giving up."

"Without new information, fresh leads, there's only so much she can do, right? And she's torn. She still loves your father very much, but she feels as though you and Caden have lost *two* things—Nick and the normal life you were living before he went missing. She can give one of those things back to you, if she lets go of the other."

Taylor walked to the window and gazed out for a long time. "Have you ever felt so helpless you wanted to rant and rave and tear everything apart around you?"

Mary was thinking about her own nightmare—not the one that had awakened her tonight but the one she'd lived through at twelve years old—when she went over and pulled her granddaughter in for a hug. "Absolutely."

"How did you get through it?"

"I decided I wasn't going to let anything destroy me."

Taylor pulled back to look at her. "And that worked?"

Mary cupped her cheek. "Sometimes determination is all we have."

Autumn slept in for the first time in ages. With her kids having finals and the many events involved in ending the school year, they'd all been especially busy. She'd just come off several weeks of early mornings to go with her late nights, so although she'd slept until ten, she was still too tired to drag herself out of bed. It was a relief to know that her mother was with her children. Even if she didn't go in right away, they'd be greeted with a smile and offered something to eat. Coming home meant she had some support. She could always count on her mother, and she was eternally grateful for that.

She told herself she'd walk over to the house in a few minutes. She wanted to lie in bed, hearing nothing and feeling no pressure, for just a little longer. But she fell back to sleep, and it was after noon when she stirred again. She might've continued to nap the day away except she heard footsteps on the stairs coming up to her room.

"Hello?" she called out and shoved both pillows against the headboard so that she could sit up and lean against them.

Her mother appeared, carrying a tray of food. "You're still in bed?" she asked in surprise. "Should I come back later? I thought you might like something to eat."

"No need to leave. I am hungry. But you could've called, and I would've come in. You didn't have to bring breakfast all the way out here."

"I don't mind. I bought this little tray at an antiques shop not long ago and wanted to use it. Isn't it cute?"

The white wicker tray held a china teapot and teacup with sugar and cream as well as a plate with a metal cover to keep whatever her mother had made warm.

"This is fancy." There was even a vase filled with roses and the local newspaper had been tucked into one of the side receptacles.

After settling the tray over Autumn's lap, Mary went to open the drapes.

Sunlight flooded the room, and Autumn closed her eyes and turned her face eagerly toward it. She felt as though she was rising from the dead—coming back to life after a long, dark period during which she hadn't even noticed if the weather was good.

"It's a beautiful day," her mother commented.

"I love summers here." Drawing a cleansing breath, Autumn opened her eyes and took the embroidered cloth napkin off the tray. Mary put such a nice touch on everything. Autumn was less whimsical and more practical in her approach to life. She was all about getting things done. But maybe that was why she admired her mother's careful attention to beauty and detail. Coming to stay in Sable Beach was almost like visiting a bed-and-breakfast. She'd been so busy being a responsible mother to her own children she'd forgotten how wonderful it was to be her mother's child—which, once again, brought a wave of guilt for wanting to find her father. Searching for him would feel so disloyal, which was why she hadn't done it yet.

"Why aren't you at the bookstore? I'm not keeping you from work, am I?"

"No. Laurie insisted I take the day off to spend with the three of you."

"Where are the kids?"

"Taylor's reading on the couch, and Caden's already down at the beach."

"Without you there to save him from drowning?" she asked wryly.

A scowl indicated her mother wasn't amused. "I offered to go watch him swim, and he laughed at me. He said he can't take me with him every time he goes to the beach or there wouldn't be a girl within fifty miles of here who'd even look at him."

Autumn lifted the lid off her plate to reveal her mother's sour-dough waffles with fresh-cut strawberries and whipped cream. "So you're allowing him to risk his real life to save his love life?"

"One has to have priorities."

That her mother had decided to join in on the joke made Autumn chuckle. "He's a strong swimmer, Mom. He'll be okay." And even if there was trouble, she doubted her mother would be capable of pulling such a large boy—the size of a man, really—out of the crashing waves. "This looks delicious. I bet the kids were excited."

"Fortunately, I had a feeling they'd request my waffles, so I was prepared." She sat on the edge of the bed while Autumn ate.

"I found an article last night on what happened to Quinn," Autumn told her after she'd swallowed a few bites.

"You searched for more information?"

She took a sip of tea and felt a sense of satisfaction as the warm brew hit her stomach. "I did. It kept my mind busy so that I couldn't focus on other things."

"Then I'm glad I told you about it. What'd you learn? Did I leave out anything important?"

She was teasing with that last question, but Autumn didn't react to it. "You didn't mention that Sarah went to prison for ten years."

"I knew they convicted her, but I don't remember hearing the length of her sentence." She crossed her legs. "That seems excessive, doesn't it?"

"According to what I saw on the internet, it could've been twenty to life. That's the sentence for attempted murder in New York State. The only reason it was shorter was that it seemed to be a spontaneous act—and even Quinn pleaded for leniency."

Mary smoothed the coverlet. "I feel so bad for her parents."

"Do they still live here in Sable Beach?" Autumn used her fork to slide the mint leaves her mother had added for garnish off to one side.

"They do. Her mother's a big reader, comes into the bookstore quite often."

"Has she ever mentioned her daughter?"

"Not since the stabbing. But I'm guessing Sarah isn't an easy subject."

"And you prefer to mind your own business."

"I wouldn't want to make her feel worse. I imagine things are bad enough. It can't be comfortable having Quinn back in town."

"Do they blame him for what happened?"

"Who can say? Maybe. It's hard for a mother to see any fault in her own child."

"It's always easier to make a villain out of the in-law. I got a taste of that with Nick's mom. She was so afraid of losing the number one spot in her son's heart that she did whatever she could to drive a wedge between us—complained about me constantly."

"That could've been a big problem had she lived much longer than she did."

"It was hard enough putting up with it for the first five years of our marriage. She almost managed to break us up. It drove me crazy how Nick allowed her to manipulate him."

"He was just trying to be a good son," her mother said mildly.

"It was more than that. He defended her against me because he couldn't see how intentional it all was." She shoved another bite into her mouth. "So some people are blind when it comes to their mothers, too."

"Not necessarily," her mother said.

Autumn was surprised that Mary had disagreed with her. "You and Laurie have always gotten along well with Nana, haven't you? You've never said a bad word about her and love having her and Poppy come all the way from Montana to visit every Thanksgiving."

Mary stood and crossed back over to the window.

"Mom?" Autumn lowered her fork. "Has something happened between you and Nana?"

When Mary turned, she looked tired and drawn despite her beauty. "No, of course not."

"So what's wrong?"

She lifted a hand to her head. "I didn't sleep well last night—because of the storm—and woke up with a headache. That's all."

"Then *you* should be the one in bed, and I should be bringing you breakfast."

"Oh, stop. It doesn't hurt that bad. But I'd better take a pain-killer before it gets any worse."

"Okay. I'll bring the tray over when I'm done."

"That'd be great."

She started down the stairs, but Autumn called after her. "If something was wrong, you'd tell me, wouldn't you?"

Her mother's footfalls came to a stop and Autumn imagined her turning to yell back up the stairs. "Of course I would. Don't worry, honey. Everything's fine."

4

Mary took a second to compose herself before opening her own back door. That had been her chance. She could've explained what her mother was really like, why Mary had no contact with her, how Laurie, Laurie's son Jacob, who was ten years older than Autumn, and the woman Autumn thought was her Nana had come to be her family instead.

But Autumn didn't need her world to be torn apart right now. She was pale and had lost weight, and she was so exhausted that she had dark circles under her eyes. What she needed was peace, love, consistency, support and plenty of rest so that she could heal.

Once again, Mary had chosen to keep her mouth shut. But she knew Autumn was curious about her father. What if she got it in her head to take one of those ancestry tests that were advertised on TV all the time?

Mary was about to go back when the door swung open and her granddaughter came out wearing a visor, sunglasses and a bikini with an orange sarong tied around her hips.

"There you are," Taylor said when they almost collided. "Mom up yet?"

"She's having breakfast."

"It's not like her to stay in bed. Is she sick or something?"

"No. She's lost a lot of sleep over the past eighteen months and is catching up, that's all."

"Okay." She anchored her bag on her shoulder so she could pull her ponytail tighter. "Caden just texted me. Said he's met a group of kids our age at the beach and wants me to come down."

"Sounds like fun."

"We'll see." She didn't seem completely convinced. "They need me to make the teams even for volleyball."

"It's always nice to meet new people."

"Except… I didn't come here to make friends. I just want to be left alone."

Obviously, Autumn wasn't the only one who needed to heal. "That's understandable. Grieving makes it hard to socialize. But the right friend can help you through the worst of times." Mary was speaking from experience. She had no idea what would've become of her had she not met Laurie when she did.

"That's hard to believe," she grumbled. "I'm so tired of the friends I have."

"You've known a lot of them for years. What don't you like about them?"

"Everything they say and do seems lame."

"They haven't experienced what you have."

"I guess. Anyway, will you tell Mom where I am?"

"Of course. She'll be in before too long."

"Thanks." Her ponytail bounced as she whirled around, clutching her beach bag, and Mary had to wonder how the secrets she'd guarded for so long might impact her grandchildren.

She battled a sinking feeling as she went inside to finish cleaning up. She was convinced they were all better off not knowing, which was why she hadn't told them.

Hopefully, they'd have at least one more summer just as they were. After what'd happened to disrupt their lives already, she thought they deserved it.

★ ★ ★

The group Caden had met consisted of three girls and three boys. Taylor could see them lounging on the sand not far from one of the volleyball nets strung across this portion of the beach. The ball itself sat next to a tall, skinny dude with red curly hair and turquoise swim trunks.

Caden was far more outgoing than she was, so he was usually the one who made new friends and then introduced her. Although she'd never admit it to him, she appreciated that she had someone to make that process a little easier, but she still hated the part at the beginning, when she didn't know someone and it was awkward and uncomfortable.

Once she realized that she'd be meeting more kids than she'd anticipated, she probably would've chickened out and turned back, except her brother spotted her right away, jumped to his feet and came jogging over.

"These guys are cool," he said as he reached her and took her bag. He knew from experience that she was often resistant when it came to unfamiliar settings and people, that he had to ease her into it, so he'd gotten good at it. She guessed he'd taken her bag as a way of committing her, since she'd have to ask for it back if she changed her mind.

"How do you know?" she grumbled, eyeing them warily. "You've barely met them."

"We've already played one game."

She slanted him a glance. "Really? One whole game?"

He ignored the sarcasm. "You never like anyone until you get to know them. Give these kids a chance, will ya?" He lowered his voice. "Besides, the girls are hot. I could really use you as a wingman. Chicks always feel more comfortable when a guy's got his sister around."

"Remember that you owe me a favor the next time we're arguing over who will ride shotgun," she muttered under her breath and braced for first contact—for her, the equivalent of having a bucket of ice water thrown in her face.

· "You can have the front seat for the entire summer," he said magnanimously.

She would've made a wisecrack about the fact that he hadn't even bothered to negotiate—she would've settled for two weeks—but the others were getting up and coming toward them, and she was afraid they might hear.

"Hi," she said, feeling self-conscious as they drew close.

"This is Penn." Caden introduced the guy with the curly hair before indicating a much stockier boy, about her height, with blond hair and blue eyes. "Shawn—and Chester."

Chester had dark skin, brown eyes and a ready smile. Something about his apparent friendliness helped make her a little less anxious. "Nice to meet you," she said as Caden moved on to the girls, who were bringing up the rear.

"And this is Adrienne, Shawn's twin sister. Don't let her size fool you. She's got a wicked serve, so be prepared for it. I've been bragging about how good you are. You can't let me down," he joked.

Blond like her brother, Adrienne was maybe five foot two and weighed less than a hundred pounds. For some reason, Caden was always attracted to that sort of girl—the petite kind that made Taylor, at five-ten, feel like Sasquatch. So Taylor guessed Adrienne was the one he was most hoping to impress. Until she looked into the face of the next girl—who was called Jasmine, she was told. Her name fit her well. She looked as though she was of Mediterranean descent and was so gorgeous with her long black hair, olive-colored complexion and liquid brown eyes that Taylor assumed she couldn't also be nice—then felt guilty for making such an assumption when the girl smiled and said hello.

"I'm Sierra Lambert." The last girl introduced herself before Caden could even get to her.

Sierra was attractive, too, but in a completely different way.

She had short, spiky blond hair with dark roots, several piercings going up each ear, a nose ring and an intricate and very large tattoo of a tree climbing one arm. She wasn't especially tall, only about five six, but she was lean and well toned. She reminded Taylor of how she'd imagined Lisbeth Salander in *The Girl with the Dragon Tattoo* back when she'd read it. Bold. Smart. Determined. Self-sufficient. And somehow...exciting, probably because she seemed so daring.

"I like your tattoo." Taylor was being honest; the artist had done a fabulous job.

"Oh yeah? That nearly got me kicked out of the house," she said with a careless laugh.

"Why? Did you have to lie about your age to get it?"

"I did. But I'm seventeen, so it's not as if I had it done when I was twelve or something. I don't think waiting five months would've changed my mind."

"It's new?"

"I've had it for a while, but my birthday is coming up in August."

"What'd your parents say when they saw it?"

"It's just me and my dad. And you should see how tatted up he is! But with him it's 'do what I say, not what I do.' He doesn't consider tattoos to be feminine. Says I'll never be able to catch a husband."

"What do you say to that?" she asked, intrigued in spite of herself.

"The truth. I don't think I want one. Do you?"

Caught off guard, Taylor stepped back. "Um, I don't know."

They all laughed at her answer but she'd never considered a future any different than her mother's. She thought she'd go to college, meet someone, get married and start a family. What did Sierra plan to do that would be so different?

"Let's start another game," Penn said, tossing the ball in the air and catching it.

Taylor was eager to do that. She'd much rather play than stand around trying to talk to people she didn't know. Sports created a sense of camaraderie with her teammates, which made things easier.

She took off her sarong as Caden dropped her bag near the spot where they'd left their own belongings.

"You're over here with me, Jasmine and Chester," Caden said as the others ducked beneath the net to go to the other side of the court.

Because Taylor wasn't warmed up, she wasn't able to contribute a great deal to the first game, but she did much better in the second. She loved volleyball, but that wasn't the only reason she was having fun. The longer she played with Caden's new friends, the more she began to agree with him. They were nice.

The only person she wasn't sure she liked was Sierra. She was different. But it wasn't only her piercings, tattoo and cocky attitude that set her apart. It was the way she watched Taylor that put Taylor on edge. Every time she looked up, she found Sierra staring at her with an inscrutable expression. What was she thinking? And why the interest?

When they finally dropped onto the sand where they'd left their towels, sweaty and exhausted from battling out a close three-game set in which her team had finally eked out the win—on her serve—Taylor was slightly relieved when Sierra didn't join them. She ran down the beach and plunged into the waves by herself, and eventually Penn and Adrienne joined her.

Taylor told herself that this was her chance to relax and get to know the others. But every few seconds she found herself glancing toward the ocean, searching for one person in particular.

Autumn enjoyed being at the bookstore anytime, but especially when she could be there by herself. On her second day in town, as soon as her mother and Laurie went to the bank, where they were hoping to secure a business loan to put in a coffee shop upstairs, she stood behind the counter and smiled. Being there, gazing out the large front window at the town where she'd been raised, reminded her of when she was in high school. In the afternoons she'd drive her mother's car over, spread her homework on the counter and complete her studies between serving customers. Sometimes her mother and Laurie would be gone, taking care of various errands, but more often one or the other would be there with her. She didn't mind either way. She liked the atmosphere and the customers who frequented the store, and she was always excited when she finished her homework, because then she could read for pleasure.

She'd never forget wandering down the aisles, touching the spines of the books she'd already enjoyed. As an only child, the fictional characters they contained were her first friends, and even though she had plenty of real friends as she grew older, she was always eager to retreat into the imaginary world created by a good storyteller. She loved deliberating on which novel to choose next and felt such wonder at the possibilities. Each shipment they received had her rushing to unpack the boxes, especially if one of her favorite authors had a new release.

Maybe she should move back to Sable Beach, she thought. She hadn't fully realized how suffocating she'd found Tampa lately, but the freedom and happiness she felt here contrasted sharply with the miserable experience she'd been through. She wanted to leave all the upset and negativity behind and start over. It was possible that the only way to let go of Nick would be to leave the home they'd shared and embrace a change of scenery as well as a change of pace. She was certain her mother and Laurie would welcome her help with the store. Since they already had their hands full, she could run the coffee shop, once it became a reality. Then they wouldn't have to hire someone else.

She'd always planned on coming back, anyway. She'd known Nick wouldn't be happy to give up the big city. At times, she couldn't help resenting the fact that he was so resistant to the idea and figured it would only be fair for her to have her way at some point. After all, she'd gone with him to Florida and stayed for the past sixteen years.

She belonged *here*.

The only thing stopping her from putting her house on the market right away was her children. It wouldn't be a smart decision to uproot them before they could finish high school. She had a feeling Taylor wouldn't mind. Since Nick's disappearance, her daughter seemed listless, as though she'd lost her anchor and was drifting this way and that. Autumn couldn't help worrying about her. But even if Taylor was willing to move, Caden relied on his friends a great deal, and he was doing well in water polo. She wouldn't take that away from him.

Two more years, she told herself. She only had to last a little longer. If Nick wasn't back by then, she'd sell the house and move home as soon as Caden graduated.

She was pulling the stool closer to the counter so she could sit down and dive into a book when the bell sounded over the door.

Autumn didn't immediately recognize her first customer. The woman came in wearing a wide-brimmed hat and sunglasses with a flowing cotton dress covering her ample bosom. But as she lifted her head, Autumn came to her feet. It was Mrs. Vizii, Sarah's mother. She'd aged since Autumn had seen her last, and she'd gained quite a bit of weight, but that beauty mark on her cheek was unmistakable.

"Oh!" Mrs. Vizii sounded slightly startled when she realized it was Autumn behind the counter. "Is Mary here?"

"No, she and Laurie had to take care of something, so I'm filling in. What can I help you with?"

The bell rang over the door before she could respond, and two more women, talking about sharks and whether it was safe to go in the water while they were visiting the coast, walked in. Mrs. Vizii seemed as shy of them as she was of Autumn, but the moment she realized they were just tourists, she visibly relaxed.

"Your mother told me she was waiting for more copies of Neil Gaiman's new book to come in. I was wondering if they had arrived."

She hadn't removed her sunglasses. Maybe she felt the need to hide behind them. After all, her daughter had been sentenced for stabbing her husband less than a year ago, and the scandal had to be pretty front and center again now that Quinn was back in town.

"Let me see." Autumn checked the computer. "Yes. They should be out on the floor." She walked over to the G's in general fiction and pulled a copy from the shelf. "Here you go."

"Thank you."

They returned to the register where Autumn started ringing her up.

"Where have you been living?" Mrs. Vizii asked.

Autumn gestured for her to insert her credit card. "In Tampa."

"Oh yes. Your mother mentioned that to me. Did you ever find your husband?"

"No."

"What happened to him?"

"I wish I could tell you," Autumn said and indicated that it was time for her to remove her card.

She took off her sunglasses and lowered her voice. "Do you think he could've been seeing another woman?"

Autumn's spine stiffened. She hated that everyone jumped to that conclusion. "No. Even if he was, I imagine he'd want half our assets, wouldn't you? Without money, he'd have to work somewhere, and that should've made it possible for me to find him."

"Have you hired a private investigator?"

"Yes. One here and in Ukraine, where Nick was last seen."

She put her sunglasses back on. "Still," she said, clearly unconvinced, "I've heard of crazier things. Your mother told you what happened to my daughter, didn't she?"

She hadn't said, "Your mother told you what my daughter did." She'd said, "What *happened* to my daughter" as though *Sarah* had been the victim. "Just the basics," she said so that Mrs. Vizii wouldn't feel as though Mary had been gossiping about the incident.

"Well, be careful. As long as your husband's been gone, you'll be looking to start dating again soon, and there aren't a lot of single men in this small of a town."

Autumn put the Gaiman book in a bag with the receipt and handed it to Mrs. Vizii over the counter. "I'm aware of that— and I'm not in any hurry to start dating. I don't even know if…" Her words fell off before she finished with, "If I'm free to start dating or still married." Knowing her husband could be alive and going through hell halfway around the world made it impossible to say that. It sounded so cavalier—as if it would be easy for her to walk away from everything they'd built together.

"If he's coming back?" Mrs. Vizii said.

A lump rose in Autumn's throat. She'd thought she was through with tears, but coming home and facing what felt like the final loss of her husband of eighteen years was dredging up all the pain she'd experienced in the early months—as well as the suspicion that maybe he *was* alive and well somewhere, enjoying life while she struggled to carry on without him. Was it possible he'd had a secret bank account? That he'd stockpiled enough money that he could seemingly drop off the planet?

She would've noticed that something was up, wouldn't she? He'd never given her any reason to doubt him. And she knew he loved Taylor and Caden, even if it was possible that he'd fallen out of love with her and she hadn't realized it. But insecurity could twist the clearest of evidence. "Yes."

"Well, if you *do* start dating, be careful. After what my daughter has been through, I wouldn't want you to get caught up with a certain gentleman who lives here."

The two women who'd wandered into the store left without

buying anything. "Quinn's back?" Autumn asked as though she didn't already know.

"He is. And all the single women are flitting around him because he's so handsome. But fishing lures look awfully attractive to the poor fish they hook, too," she replied and walked out with her purchase.

Autumn sighed as she sat on the stool. She wondered what Quinn thought about his ex-mother-in-law going around town saying such terrible things about him. She was willing to bet he wished he could leave this place. But with his own mother stricken with cancer and his father in need of help with the restaurant, there probably wasn't much he could do.

5

"What is it?… Hello?… Hey, I'm talking to you."

Mary finally heard Laurie over the pounding of her own heart. But it wasn't until Laurie touched her elbow that she lifted her eyes from the article she'd been reading. As soon as she'd walked out of the bank, and Laurie had gone into the store next door to get some allergy medicine for Chris, the headline had jumped out at her from one of the newspapers in the bins by the door. "What? Oh, it's nothing," she said and tucked the paper under her arm.

Laurie followed her to the car. "It's obviously something. You seem upset even though our meeting went well. They're going to give us the money. Aren't you excited?"

Mary was hopeful that putting a coffee shop in the bookstore would bring in more business, but she was too worried about her family to focus on the progress they were making toward that goal. "I was just reading an article that… Never mind. It's no big deal."

Laurie didn't let her get away with the evasion. "What was it about?" she asked after they climbed into her Honda Accord and snapped on their seat belts.

"What was what about?" Mary tried playing dumb in hopes that Laurie would let it go in her hurry to get on with the day.

"That article!" Laurie responded in exasperation.

Reluctantly, she handed over the newspaper she'd purchased, and before starting the car, Laurie read the heading that had caught her attention. "DNA Reveals Daughter's Only Parent To Be No Relation."

"Can you believe that?" Mary said. "Some poor woman took a DNA test because she wanted to learn more about her mother, whom she'd never met, and found out that the man who'd raised her wasn't even her father. He's dead now, so she can't ask him what happened, and she has no idea how she came to be in his custody."

"Poor thing. That would be a real mystery, wouldn't it?"

"I don't think these DNA tests are a good thing."

Laurie frowned. "I can see why you wouldn't."

Mary rubbed her forehead. "Stories like that are popping up all over the place."

"Which is why I think you need to get out ahead of the problem. If Autumn takes a DNA test, how will you explain the results?"

"It won't be easy. But I'm not sure I want to guarantee she finds out by telling her, either. The truth won't impact just her life. Or mine. Or yours. It'll impact Taylor's and Caden's. I doubt that's what she'd want."

"Then let *her* decide whether to share it with the kids."

Mary adjusted her seat belt, which suddenly felt too confining. "But once she knows, she can never *not* know. Should I really put her in the same position I'm in now, trying to decide whether it would be best to bury the past or drag it into the present?"

Laurie folded the newspaper, put it on the console and started the engine. "There are no easy answers, Mary. You could be right. I was talking to my mother this morning, and she thinks you'd be crazy to bring it all out into the open. So maybe I should quit encouraging you to do it."

"You're just trying to help. I know that." She waved at Joann Hunter, who'd come out of the grocery store. Joann owned an alterations business in town and brought her granddaughter into the bookstore two or three times a month. Mary liked her but was grateful when she didn't stop and expect Mary to lower her window so they could chat. "What, exactly, did Nana have to say?" she asked as Joann got into her own vehicle one row over.

"That it's behind you, and we should let it stay that way. That it doesn't have any bearing on the present. She also mentioned that Autumn has been through enough and insists that talking about how you came to be who you are, and she came to be who she is, won't serve any good purpose. There's no reason to look back."

Mary desperately wanted to agree with Nana, but... "Did you mention how easy it would be for Autumn to find out the truth without me?"

"Of course. She said to let that make the decision for you. If Autumn finds out, then you'll *have* to address it."

Mary tried to imagine how her daughter might react to the news. "She matters more to me than anything, Laurie. She always has."

Laurie put the car in gear but hesitated before backing up. "You've proven that time and again. You've done an amazing job as her mother, have always tried to protect her."

"Maybe now what I have to protect is our relationship. That's what frightens me."

"Does that mean you're going to tell her?"

"It does. I just... I want to enjoy one final summer with her and the kids first—one summer in which everything still feels the same. Do you think that's too much to ask?"

Laurie glanced at the newspaper as though it were a ticking time bomb. "I hope not."

★ ★ ★

When Taylor's phone rang, all of her new friends were swimming with her brother except Sierra, who'd come out of the water and was lying on a towel beside her. Sierra must've heard the buzzing, because she opened her eyes, leaned up on her elbows and gazed out to sea while Taylor dug her phone from her bag.

The caller had a Tampa area code but didn't have a number Taylor recognized. It could be Oliver—Danielle had told her he might call—but it could also be someone else, like her high school with news about the yearbook, which hadn't been ready on time this year, or registration dates for fall.

She'd been monitoring her calls and would've waited to see if whomever it was left a message. But Sierra glanced over as if she was surprised Taylor wasn't answering, and that made Taylor impulsively hit the talk button.

She regretted doing so the second she heard Oliver's voice. "Hey."

Conscious of Sierra watching her, she tried not to show her sudden panic. "Hi."

"What's up?"

"Not a whole lot. I'm at the beach with some friends."

"Did Danielle go to Virginia with you?"

"No. These are just…some people I met."

"For the first time?"

"Yeah. Two of them are twins." She wasn't sure why she added that unnecessary detail, except that she was nervous. "They live here year-round."

"I live here year-round, too," Sierra volunteered. "My dad and I moved in just after Christmas."

Taylor glanced over. "Three of them live here. The rest are visiting for the summer, like me."

"How'd you meet them?"

"They were here at the beach when Caden and I arrived."

"Oh."

He didn't say anything else, so she scrambled to fill the silence. "What are you doing?"

"Babysitting my little brother. He's such a pain in the ass," he added under his breath.

"How old is he?"

"Eleven."

"My brother's quite a bit older than that, but he can be a pain, too." She said that automatically, with a laugh, but regretted it right away. Oliver knew Caden—they used to be friends—so he might have something negative to say, too, which she already knew she couldn't tolerate. *She* could say what she wanted to, but if anyone else put Caden down, she'd defend him to her dying breath.

Luckily, Oliver didn't comment on Caden, and managed to gain a little of her respect.

"When will you be back?" he asked.

"Not until school starts." She was glad she had almost three months before she had to face even the possibility of running into him. Except…if she was pregnant, she would almost be showing by then.

She grimaced at the thought of going through her senior year carrying a baby. *What* had she done? If she was pregnant, her mother was going to be *so* upset.

"Okay. Well, call me if you get bored," he said.

"I will."

"Um, Taylor?"

She caught her breath at the more somber tone of his voice. "Yes?"

"That night at the party…"

Knowing Sierra was watching her closely, she tried not to react. "What about it?"

"I keep thinking…"

She waited.

"We didn't use any protection, did we?"

"No," she replied and heard him sigh heavily through the phone.

"I didn't think so."

They'd both been a little drunk.

"Is that going to be a problem?" he asked.

She could hear the anxiety in his voice, and it almost made her angry. He thought *he* was scared? The worst that could happen to him was he'd have to pay child support for eighteen years. As bad as that sounded, especially at their age, it would be much worse for her. Not only would she have to pay at least as much, she'd also have to carry the baby, deliver it and raise it—unless she had an abortion or gave it up for adoption. "I hope not."

There was a long silence. "Does that mean you don't know?" he asked at length.

She glanced over at Sierra, who was adjusting the straps on her swimsuit. "That's exactly what it means."

He said nothing for a moment. She wanted him to comfort her, to reassure her that she wouldn't be in it alone. But she knew that was asking too much. He wouldn't be there for her; they weren't even together. "Will you let me know when you find out?"

"Yes."

"I'm sorry if you're scared," he said. "If it comes to that, we'll…we'll figure it out, okay?"

Not only did his words surprise her, they also came off as sincere, dissipating some of the tension, fear and anger she'd been feeling. "Okay. Thank you."

"Sure thing," he said, and then he was gone.

"Who was that?" Sierra asked as Taylor put her phone back in her purse.

"A guy from Tampa."

"Your boyfriend?"

Taylor saw Caden coming toward them and wanted to stop

talking about Oliver before he overheard and started asking questions. "I'll tell you later," she muttered under her breath.

Sierra's eyes moved from Taylor to Caden and back again. "Your secrets are safe with me," she said.

"Let's go over to The Daily Catch for dinner."

Ever since her mother and aunt had returned from their errand at the bank, Autumn had been curled up on the antique red velvet couch in the corner, deeply immersed in Kristin Hannah's latest book. She couldn't remember the last time she'd been relaxed enough to read for pleasure, so it felt familiar in the way coming home felt familiar—cathartic, healing, right. "Tonight?" she said to Laurie, who'd been the one to suggest it.

"Why not?" Laurie put several pens into a drawer as she straightened the register area. "Chris is dying to see you, and he loves that restaurant almost as much as you do."

Autumn's mind reverted to her encounter with Sarah's mother and what Mrs. Vizii had had to say about Quinn. "I can't wait to see Uncle Chris." She was about to suggest they go somewhere else, though. She wasn't eager to run into Quinn, given her embarrassing behavior when they were younger and then his awkward situation now.

But as she opened her mouth to continue, Laurie spoke again. "I try to give them my business whenever I can. I heard that one of Beth's cancer medications costs eight thousand dollars a month. Can you believe that?"

Using one of the bookmarks they gave away for promotional purposes, Autumn closed her novel and sat up. "No way! That's outrageous. How could one prescription cost so much?"

Laurie shook her head. "I have no clue. It's a crying shame— that's what it is. And, apparently, it's not the only medication she needs, so there are other bills piling up."

Mary had just carried a box of books that hadn't sold into the back so that she could make room for all the new releases. "There was talk around town of creating a GoFundMe campaign to help cover her treatment," she said as she returned, keeping up with the conversation while she worked. "But Mike and Quinn wouldn't hear of it."

"Why not?" Autumn prompted.

Mary glanced toward the front, apparently to make sure someone wasn't about to walk in and catch them talking about the Vanderbilts. "They won't accept any help," she said when she found that the coast was clear. "They don't feel right asking others to sacrifice on their behalf."

"They insist they'll cover everything themselves," Laurie concurred.

With so many people asking for handouts on the internet, Autumn couldn't help but admire their determination to remain self-reliant. That wasn't very common these days. But if they were already falling behind, how would they ever catch up? The restaurant seemed to make a decent living—it was popular—but the Vanderbilts had never been considered *rich*. "That's admirable," she said, changing her mind about what she'd been so eager to suggest before. She couldn't ask to go somewhere else, not if the Vanderbilts needed money to help finance Beth's cancer treatments.

"They're fine people," Laurie said.

Autumn wondered if that statement extended to Quinn. His parents were well-respected in the area, but with Mrs. Vizii running around, intimating that Quinn was no better than Satan himself, Quinn's reputation couldn't be as sterling as his parents'. Even if people discounted what Mrs. Vizii said—after all, he was the one who'd been stabbed—Mrs. Vizii had cast a shadow over him by making people wonder if he was partially to blame. "I've always liked them," she said.

"Good. I'll call Chris and have him meet us as soon as we close up."

"Should I call the kids? We could swing by the cottage and pick them up on our way."

"Sure. They like The Daily Catch, don't they?" Mary asked.

"Taylor isn't big on seafood. But she might be willing to have some shrimp. And Caden will eat anything."

She tried her daughter's cell phone but couldn't reach her. She was about to call her son instead when Taylor's face lit up her screen.

"There you are," Autumn said as soon as she answered. "I thought you and Caden might stop by the store this afternoon when you got home. Don't tell me you're still at the beach."

"No, we're at the cottage now, but we're getting ready to go to a friend's house. You don't mind, do you?"

"What friend?" she asked in surprise. Finding their summer friends usually took a few weeks. It had never happened so soon before.

"Just some kids we met playing beach volleyball," Taylor said.

Autumn asked for the details, and fortunately, Laurie could vouch for some of the kids' parents, so she felt comfortable letting them go. "I guess that'll be okay," she replied. "As long as you think it'll be a good environment."

"You worry too much," her daughter said.

"I'm a mom. It's my job to worry."

"Well, don't. Their parents will be home. We're just going to have pizza and play some video games."

Autumn could easily detect the eye roll in her daughter's voice but felt instantly better. "Great. That's what I needed to hear. I love you. Make good decisions," she said and disconnected. "Looks like it's just us," she told her mother and aunt.

"I'll call over and get a reservation for four," Mary said.

Make good decisions.

Her mother's parting words seemed to mock Taylor as she dropped her towel and examined her naked body in the mirror. Was there any change in her stomach? Were her breasts getting bigger?

She didn't feel nauseated. Or maybe she did. A little. It was tough to tell. When she thought that she might've destroyed her life, she felt slightly ill. Was that regret and fear, or morning sickness?

She'd never been around anyone who was going to have a baby, so she had no idea what it would be like—if there'd be obvious signs before she missed her period or if the changes in her body would be too subtle to notice.

Her brother banged on the door, causing her to jump. "What's taking so long?" he called through the panel.

She scrambled to put on a pair of panties and a bra so she could dry her hair. "Mom called when I was getting out of the shower," she said.

"What'd she say?"

"We can go."

"Good."

She heard his footsteps move away from the door, but she knew he'd be back if she didn't emerge on her own in the next few minutes. She rarely wore makeup. He wasn't used to it taking her very long to get ready. But for some reason, she wanted to look good tonight.

"Hey, where are you?" Caden yelled from the living room fifteen minutes later.

"Almost done!" She swiped more mascara on her eyelashes and stepped back to evaluate the effect before putting on some lip gloss and perfume.

"Taylor! What the heck?" he cried, a whine to his voice. "Are you kidding me? We're going to miss the food!"

"I'm coming!" She shoved twenty dollars into the pocket of her skinny jeans before grabbing her cell phone off the bathroom counter.

When she came down the hall, he lifted the remote to turn off the TV but forgot about that the moment he saw her. The video game he'd been playing droned on in an annoying loop as he said, "What's going on?"

"What do you mean?" she asked.

"You never wear makeup."

"I do *sometimes*."

He peered closer at her. "Why tonight?"

She locked the screen on her phone so that she wouldn't accidentally pocket dial someone—and also because it gave her something she could do to appear preoccupied. "No reason."

"You didn't even want to meet them. And now you want to impress them? Who? Which one?"

When she didn't answer, he went ahead and turned off the TV, tossed the remote on the couch and stalked closer. "Shawn?"

She gave him a get-real look. "No, not Shawn."

His eyes narrowed. "Don't tell me it's Chester. Dude's nice, but he mentioned having a girlfriend back home."

"I'm not trying to hook up with Chester!"

"Then it has to be Penn. But when he tried to talk to you, you shut him down so fast I felt sorry for the guy."

"I didn't *shut him down*," she argued. "He had no clue what he was talking about, so I let him know I wasn't buying his bullshit, that's all."

"Well, can we not mention climate change? Or Greta Thunberg or any of that when we get there tonight?"

"*I* didn't bring it up. He did," she said as she searched for the key to the cottage Mimi had given her earlier.

"Doesn't matter. Smile and nod next time, okay? Can't you let someone else feel like the smartest person in the room for a change?"

"If they are the smartest person in the room, yeah. But the dude *literally* told me that humans are not responsible for climate change, which is…stupid. Obviously, he hasn't studied the evidence."

"So? His dad probably owns shares in ExxonMobil or something."

"It matters," she snapped. "If we don't do something to stop global warming, Earth could soon be as hot as Venus."

"How hot is Venus?" he asked in spite of himself.

Taylor moved from the table to the counter and lifted the mail piled on top of it. "Hot enough to melt *lead*."

"Just…stay away from Penn tonight," he said in exasperation. "I don't want you screwing up our summer."

She still hadn't come up with the key. "I'll do my best, but if he starts in on *that* subject again, I won't be able to stop myself."

"Let Sierra handle it, then. She's even worse than you are. She told me the meat industry is causing global warming."

At last, she spotted the key. It had slid off the counter onto the floor. "It is," she said matter-of-factly.

"I don't care. I don't want to talk about that," he said and walked out ahead of her. She knew he was frustrated, but she was relieved. At least he'd quit pushing to find out who she wanted to impress.

There was no way she'd ever tell him.

There was no way she'd ever tell *anyone*.

6

Autumn glanced around the restaurant as they sat down. Uncle Chris had met them out front, where he'd given her a big hug. Now he was telling her about the loggerhead turtle he'd found on the beach early this morning and quickly sketched, and she was listening to his plans to paint it. But she was also wondering if there was any chance she could get through this meal *without* having to see Quinn. After all, that he was helping his father with the restaurant could mean many things. He could be doing the accounting, the food sourcing, the prepping or the cooking—none of which would necessarily put him into direct contact with diners. He might even have the night off.

She breathed a sigh of relief when a young woman approached their table and said she was Erin and would be taking care of them tonight. Quinn wouldn't be waiting on them, at least.

"Thank you," Autumn murmured as Erin handed them each a menu and began to rattle off the nightly specials.

"Oh, the scallops sound divine," Laurie gushed. "I think I'll have those."

Mary lowered her menu. "You're not going to get the blue crab?"

"Not this time. They do a great job with the crab, especially in the salad. But I'm in the mood for scallops."

"The salmon looks good to me," Uncle Chris announced. "What about you?"

Autumn felt his gaze, but she didn't have an answer. She'd been too busy searching out the people who were working at the restaurant and hadn't been completely focused on selecting her meal. "Um… I'll probably stick with the crab salad. I've been looking forward to it for months."

Someone besides Erin brought them water, but their waitress returned after a few minutes. "Are you ready to order?"

They all stuck with what they'd initially mentioned, but Aunt Laurie stopped Erin before she could leave. "Is Mike in?"

"He is. He's cooking tonight."

"What about Quinn?"

Autumn tensed.

"He's here, too," Erin said, "helping out in the back."

"Can you let him know Autumn's in town and would like to say hello?"

No! Autumn felt her stomach drop. *Damn it!* Her outgoing, gregarious aunt was just being nice. Laurie probably didn't know, or remember, that Autumn and Quinn had a bit of history. But Autumn wished she'd mind her own business.

"Of course," Erin responded. "I'm sure he'll be out in a few minutes."

"Quinn's here!" Laurie announced as if Autumn hadn't heard the entire exchange and it was going to be *such* a treat for her to see him.

Autumn forced a smile. "It's busy in here tonight. I'd rather not disturb him."

"He won't mind taking a few seconds. You two went to school together, didn't you?"

Her mother sent her an apologetic look. No doubt she could tell Autumn wasn't excited about what Laurie had just done.

Mary would never have made the same mistake. She listened to the subtext of a conversation and watched those who were speaking. In most instances, except those when her own fears and limitations kicked in, she knew what to do and what not to do, while her far less intuitive sister bowled ahead, regardless.

Autumn reminded herself that Laurie's intentions were good as she confirmed that she and Quinn had indeed attended the same high school, one year apart from each other. But Laurie's intentions didn't make it any less awkward when, shortly after their food arrived and right when she had a mouthful of crab, Quinn appeared at their table—*as requested*.

"Hello. It's nice to see you," he said, greeting them all before focusing on her. "Wow, it's been a long time, Autumn. How are you?"

The food in her mouth went down as a hard lump. He hadn't aged at all. His dark hair, with the cowlick in front that swept it up off his forehead, looked as thick and silky as ever. Between that, his dimples and his straight, white teeth, he looked so much like JFK Jr. she couldn't help thinking he should've been born a Kennedy. Except that his eyes were blue and not brown. "I'm doing great. You?"

"Hanging in there. Are you here for the summer or—"

"Just for the summer." She wondered if he'd heard that her husband had gone missing—and, if he had, whether he'd mention it. To show they cared, most people she knew, especially here, asked her if she'd heard anything, and she had to explain, over and over, that there'd been no news. But if Quinn brought up that subject, it would be natural for her to inquire about *his* partner, or former partner, and she had a feeling he'd try to avoid that.

Sure enough, he asked about her children instead. "Did you bring the kids with you? Or are they old enough now to be working for the summer at home?"

"They're still in high school and here with me. They're seeing some friends tonight." She was afraid she had a piece of salad stuck in her teeth but there wasn't anything she could do to check.

"They must love coming to the beach."

"Yes, they were really looking forward to it this year. I'm sure they'll be swimming in the ocean almost every day."

"Will you be at the beach with them?"

"Sometimes. When I'm not helping out at the bookstore."

His lips curved in a faint smile. "You always had a book in your hand."

She'd left the novel she'd been reading in his tree house the night she gave him her virginity. She remembered doing it on purpose, so that he'd have to bring it to her, and was now embarrassed about that, too. She still remembered the title: *Prodigal Summer* by Barbara Kingsolver. "I love to read."

"Like your mother. She must be glad to have you back."

"I am," Mary piped up.

"How's your mother feeling?" Laurie asked, jumping into the conversation.

"Some days are better than others," he replied.

Laurie lowered her voice, giving her next question a deeper reverence. "Do the treatments seem to be working?"

"We won't know until her next blood test, which isn't for two more weeks."

"Tell her that I'm praying for her," Laurie said. "We all are."

Mary set aside her fork. "How's your father holding up?"

"Mom being sick is hard on him, of course, but he never complains. Keeping busy helps. Fortunately, this is our busiest time of the year, what with all the tourists coming in."

Autumn could imagine how much they were juggling to keep up and hated that Laurie had disturbed him on her account. "I'm sorry to have interrupted you at work. The kitchen must be slammed right now."

"It's no problem," he said. "I'm glad I had the chance to see you. But I'd better get back." He looked at her aunt, uncle and mother. "Thanks for stopping in."

"Autumn has always loved this restaurant," Mary said. "Especially the carrot cake you have on the dessert menu."

"That's a special recipe of my mother's," he informed them.

"I'm glad you still serve it," Autumn said. "I'll have to order a piece tonight, if I have room."

"I hope it's as good as you remember it." He flashed those dimples at her, and she felt mildly guilty for finding him every bit as attractive as she had back in high school. "Hopefully, I'll see you again soon," he added as he started to walk away.

She doubted he wanted to see her again at all. He was probably as uncomfortable as she was that he'd been summoned to their table. But like him, she played along and pretended otherwise. "That would be nice."

"I feel so bad for him and his father," Laurie murmured when he was gone. "What they're going through is terrible."

Autumn exchanged a look with her mother. She sympathized with the Vanderbilts, too, but Autumn felt—and guessed her mother agreed—that drawing Quinn away from the kitchen hadn't made his night any easier. He had to be tired of responding to the well wishes of the community.

"I hate to ask this," Laurie said, "but do you think you'll ever start dating again?"

"Laurie!" The tone of Uncle Chris's voice was a rebuke for asking such an indelicate question.

Laurie winced. "I'm sorry. But surely you must've considered what happens next if...you know, if Nick doesn't come back."

"Nick probably isn't coming back, but I haven't quite let go. So I don't think I'll be dating anytime soon."

"You'll know when the time is right," Mary said.

Autumn hoped the fact that Quinn was now single hadn't provoked the question, but the timing certainly suggested otherwise. "I hope so."

★ ★ ★

Penn liked her; Taylor could tell. No matter where she went at the party, he followed, trying to talk to her. If he wasn't driving her crazy going on and on about his disbelief—or denial—of climate change, he was dissing veganism, which bothered her almost as much. She wasn't a vegan, but she respected those who had the self-discipline to care that much about animals and the Earth, and it bothered her that he was giving Sierra, who *was* a vegan, such a hard time.

Fortunately, Sierra was more than willing to spar with him. He'd said vegans don't get enough B-12, and she'd snapped back that B-12 doesn't come from animals, it comes from the soil adhering to the grass and other vegetation eaten by animals, that meat-eaters are usually deficient in B-12, too, and that the fat and cholesterol in animal products has been tied to heart disease and some forms of cancer.

Taylor had learned a lot just listening to them. "I'm sorry there isn't more here you can eat," she said to Sierra when Penn finally went over to play a game of pool and she noticed Sierra eating only the corn chips and salsa.

"I'm used to it," she said with a shrug.

"Are you ever tempted to break down?"

"Not really. I feel better eating the way I'm eating. When I'm working out, I'm stronger and recover more quickly."

"How often do you work out?"

"Whenever I can. I like to do yoga on the beach as the sun is coming up."

"You seem..."

Sierra stiffened and narrowed her eyes. "What?"

"Older than the rest of us," Autumn said, and the tension in Sierra's face disappeared.

"I get that a lot. I've been told I have an old soul. Even the music I like to listen to is a throwback."

"What are some of your favorite bands?"

"Bob Seger and the Silver Bullet Band. Bread. The Beatles. Pink Floyd. Queen. Bruce Springsteen. The Eagles. The Doors. Mostly seventies stuff. And I prefer vinyl."

Taylor had heard of only a few of those bands. "How did you start listening to them?"

"My dad introduced me to them."

"Do you like rap?"

"Hardly."

As Taylor sipped her Coke, she couldn't help noticing that Sierra drank only a glass of water. She wouldn't accept a plastic bottle because she said plastics were part of the problem. "How long have you been vegan?"

"For almost a year."

"What made you decide to stop eating meat?"

"I watched *Game Changer.* Have you seen it?"

Taylor felt kind of lame because Sierra acted as though she should be familiar with it, but like some of the bands Sierra had named, Taylor had never heard of it. "No."

"It's on Netflix. You should check it out."

"I will."

The billiards game Penn had been playing ended, and Caden called over to them. "Hey, you two want to get in on the next round?"

Taylor held her breath. She was afraid Sierra would agree and the conversation would be over, but Sierra said, "Not right now."

"I'm fine, too," Taylor said.

Sierra popped a few peanuts into her mouth, which was about the only other food on the table she could eat. "So what type of things do you do when you're in Florida?"

"Hang out. Shop. The usual."

"Do you miss Tampa?"

She looked down into the dark liquid of her soda as she said, "Not really. I'm glad to get away. Things have been...weird the past couple of years."

"In what way?"

She'd promised herself she wouldn't tell anyone in Sable Beach about her father. Having to respond to everyone's curiosity about it was like rubbing salt in the wound. She didn't want to start that up again. And yet, she found herself wanting to share her pain with this unusual girl. Sierra approached life so differently than any other friend Taylor had met. She hoped Sierra might have some answers for her, some way to cope that she hadn't figured out for herself quite yet. After all, Sierra seemed to have had plenty of her own problems, not having a mother and trying to get along with a father she described as difficult and demanding. "My dad went missing eighteen months ago."

Her eyes widened. "*Really*? From where?"

"Ukraine. We think," she added with a frown.

"You don't know?"

Taylor shook her head.

"Were your parents married when he disappeared?"

"They were. My dad went on a business trip one day and never came home. My mom's been searching for him ever since."

"What was he doing in Ukraine? Is that where he worked?"

"No. We believe he went there because he was doing something for the FBI, but we're not sure what, and no one will say."

Sierra studied her thoughtfully. "So he was here one day and gone the next."

"Pretty much."

"That sucks. I'm sorry."

Her empathy somehow made a big difference. "Thanks. My mom's about to give up. She's talking like it's time for us to move on."

Sierra reached for more nuts. "You're still hoping he'll come back?"

"I'll *always* hope. But I don't know if I can expect her to keep going. So far, she's devoted eighteen months of her life to finding him. Where does it end?"

"You should get a tattoo," she said simply. "Your father's name. The date he went missing. A symbol or saying he loved. Whatever is significant to you."

Although Taylor had never considered a tattoo before, she found the idea to be comforting, as if Sierra had suggested a way to reclaim a small piece of her father, one she could carry with her always. But she knew her mother would never allow it. Although she'd never asked for a tattoo, Caden had asked several times, and her mother always said he couldn't get one until he was old enough to do it without her permission. *Tattoos are too permanent to decide when you're still in high school,* she'd said.

"I can't," Taylor told Sierra. "Not yet, anyway. I'm only seventeen."

Sierra finished her water before looking over at those who were playing pool. "I know someone who would do it for you," she said under her breath.

"You do?"

"If you're *positive* you want it. I wouldn't want you to regret it and then blame me."

"I'd never blame you even if I did regret it. But…my mother will freak out."

"Get it somewhere your mother will never see—maybe on your hip. You could hide that easily enough."

"True."

"Think about it and let me know. It's not a decision you should make quickly," she said and popped a final handful of nuts into her mouth before going over to play pool.

Taylor would've followed. She was fascinated by this girl who seemed old beyond her years, strong and wise and willing to forge her own path through life, even if it meant facing the judgment and criticism of others.

Most kids wanted to fit in. Sierra bravely stood out.

Taylor thought of a saying one of her teachers had put on the chalkboard and left there for the entire semester: *Courage is as contagious as fear.*

Now she believed it.

Autumn's phone dinged with a text as she climbed the stairs to her apartment over the garage.

I'm sorry that Laurie embarrassed you at the restaurant. She probably doesn't remember that you used to talk about Quinn so often.

Her mother hadn't mentioned Quinn since he left their table, not even after they arrived home and Laurie and Chris were no longer with them. But she knew how Autumn had felt about Quinn, because it had been impossible for Autumn to hide it. She'd had such a crush on him in school she'd doodled his name on all of her notebooks, cut his pictures out of the yearbook and put them up all over her room, lingered at the field whenever he had baseball practice so she could watch him play—and have him walk past her to get to the locker room. If Laurie didn't remember those antics, it was because her mother had protected her from looking like a lovesick fool by purposely not passing along those details. Since Quinn had been going out with another girl—except for brief periods of time when they were broken up, like the one during which she'd been so forward with him in his childhood tree house—she probably hadn't seen any reason to embarrass either one of them.

Now Autumn was grateful her mother had always been so reserved. If Mary was as much of a talker as Aunt Laurie, the whole town would know how Autumn had felt about Quinn and would be coming up to tell her he was now available.

Thanks for not reminding her, she wrote back.

He looked good tonight.

He'd always looked good—was easily the most handsome man she'd ever known. All that thick, dark hair paired with his light eyes was striking. But she recognized her mother's response as a subtle attempt to discover her reaction to him, and she wasn't going to let on that seeing him had affected her more deeply than she'd imagined it would. It was probably normal to feel a little breathless when confronting someone you'd once craved that badly.

I feel terrible for what he and his parents are going through, she wrote back and couldn't help smiling. Nothing too meaningful could be gleaned from that.

Nice dodge, her mother replied with a winking emoji.

She was mildly surprised that Mary had called her out on her response. They typically allowed each other to parry when necessary. I'm married, she wrote as though they shouldn't even be discussing another man.

But *was* she still married? Or was she widowed?

I'm not putting any pressure on you, her mother wrote back. Good night.

Autumn sent her mother a kiss emoji but sighed as she plugged her phone in to charge and left it on the nightstand. How long would her life be like this? She felt suspended in time—unable to reclaim her husband and reunite her family and yet unable to move on without him.

She climbed into bed, frowned at the empty spot beside her, then reached for her laptop. After eighteen months, it'd become a habit to go online and search for Nick's name. If he'd been killed and his body had been found, maybe an article would pop up before she heard from any authorities about it.

She clicked on a couple of new links, but the person involved wasn't her husband, just someone with the same name. After that, she read everything she could find on what was going on in Ukraine. A Ukrainian woman she'd met in a chat forum a few months after Nick went missing knew English and had been willing to translate various articles from the daily paper so she could have more specific and detailed news. Her name was Yana, and she sent it via a voice mail on WhatsApp. But she hadn't sent anything in over a week. The articles she translated had been growing fewer and farther between over the past several months. She'd been doing it for so long—with no results as far as finding Nick—that she was probably losing interest.

Autumn covered a yawn as she surfed to her Facebook page. She couldn't help hoping that even if Nick no longer had a cell phone, he could somehow reach her through social media.

But there was nothing new there, either.

She was about to close her computer so she could get some sleep when she received a friend request—from Quinn Vanderbilt.

Her mouth fell open as she stared at it. He'd never been on Facebook before. Why now? And what did he want? She was in town for only three months. She had two teenage kids and a missing husband. He had an incarcerated ex-wife, angry ex-in-laws who happened to be local and a mother who was battling cancer. They were both in a mess when everyone else their age seemed to be cruising along.

She could use a friend, and he could probably use one, too. But what she'd felt when she saw him at the restaurant—that twinge of guilt for being attracted to him in spite of her love for Nick—had frightened her. The last thing she needed was to complicate her life by once again becoming infatuated with Quinn Vanderbilt.

She thought of that encounter in his tree house when she was a junior in high school and shook her head. He'd treated her kindly, had been gentle. She remembered almost melting when he first kissed her. But he'd definitely tried to talk her out of stripping off her clothes. *She* was the one who'd insisted they go so far. He'd just finally given up and indulged her.

She cringed. God, she'd been so young and naive. She wished

she could go back and erase the whole incident. She hoped he'd forgotten about it. If it hadn't meant anything to him, why would he have any reason to remember it?

Although...on second thought, it couldn't be every day that a girl followed him home and acted the way she'd acted. No way would a guy ever forget that.

She raked her fingers through her hair as she continued to stare at that friend request. *Damn it.* Even if he couldn't forget it, she wished she could. She told herself sex with Quinn didn't mean anything to her now—not after Nick. And yet, in this moment, when she was lying in bed alone and it felt as though it had been an eternity since she'd felt a man's arms around her, the thought of making love with Quinn Vanderbilt filled her with a sudden and very acute desire.

"No way," she muttered, horrified by her own reaction, and closed her laptop without accepting him.

7

The next two weeks passed so peacefully and uneventfully that Mary decided she'd been right to leave the past in the past. Taylor and Caden had taken up with a group of friends they really enjoyed, and Autumn appeared to be catching up on her rest and settling into a healthy routine. She was quicker to smile than at any time since Nick had gone missing, and she'd quit talking about him all the time. She hadn't yet boxed up his belongings—Mary was waiting for that. But had Mary listened to Laurie, her family would not have had this chance to recover.

Although Autumn spent mornings with her kids, making breakfast, doing yoga on the beach—something Taylor had insisted they try—and tending to the garden Mary had planted before they arrived, she usually came into the store after lunch.

Having her help was nice, especially because a third person in the store enabled Mary and Laurie to leave together, if they wanted to. They met with the architect they'd chosen to explain how they wanted the coffee shop to look and began vetting contractors, trying to determine who would do the best job for the most reasonable price.

Mary was worried about going into debt. She'd always been

conservative, cautious—afraid if she wasn't cautious she'd lose everything she'd so painstakingly established in Sable Beach. Laurie was much more of a risk taker. She insisted they were doing the right thing—that having a coffee shop in the store would keep them relevant—but she had her husband and her family to fall back on if it turned out to be the wrong decision. While Laurie and Laurie's family had done a lot for her, Mary wasn't truly related to them and knew she couldn't depend on them quite to the same degree.

Still, during this golden period when the summer was just getting into full swing, it was easy to believe that all would be well. Everything seemed to be going right. Mary had even been sleeping soundly, hadn't had a nightmare since Autumn, Taylor and Caden's first night.

She was feeling so good she found herself humming along with Sister Sledge's "We Are Family," which was playing over the stereo system in Mabel's Food and Drug, while Mary was waiting in line to check out. She eyed the racks of gum and candy near the register as the man ahead of her spoke to the cashier, Lenore Graybel. For only purchasing a soda, he seemed to be taking a long time, but Mary wasn't in any hurry. Autumn was at the bookstore with Laurie, so Laurie could leave if she needed to; Mary didn't have to worry about the time.

She dropped a couple of candy bars into her basket, thinking Taylor and Caden might like them, and the man wearing chinos and a red golf shirt finally grabbed his Dr Pepper and strode confidently out of the store.

Lenore always greeted her with a smile. They'd known each other for years, since before Lenore's mother, Mabel, passed away last September and Lenore took over the store. But she was too preoccupied to look up as Mary took her purchases—paper towels and garbage bags they needed at the store, along with the two candy bars—out of her basket and set them on the counter.

"Well, that was weird," Lenore mumbled as she stared down at the business card she held.

Mary pulled her wallet from her purse. "What was weird?"

"That guy." Lenore jerked her head toward the door.

Mary caught one last glimpse of the man who'd been in line ahead of her before he disappeared. About six feet tall, he had short, dark hair streaked with gray, and she remembered that he wore glasses. He looked about her age, but nothing else stood out about him. "Who was he?"

"A private investigator from Atlanta, according to this." She handed his card to Mary, and Mary read the name on it, printed in a black professional font with embossed letters.

Drake D. Owens. Private Investigator. "What'd he want?" *Mary had been too busy with her own thoughts and enjoying the music to eavesdrop on their conversation.*

"He's looking for someone. Wanted to know if I'd ever heard of her."

A chill ran down Mary's spine. "Who?"

"Someone named Bailey North," she replied with a shrug in her voice.

Mary dropped her wallet, and her change scattered over the floor. She kept Mr. Owens's card in her hand, couldn't have released it even if she'd wanted to, as she bent to gather up the coins.

Lenore leaned over the counter. "Need some help?"

"No, no. It's just a…a few nickels and dimes," she managed to say despite the fact that she could hardly breathe. She hadn't heard that name in over thirty-five years.

"What does he want with her?" she asked as she stood up again.

"With Bailey North? I have no clue. He said she was once abducted by a man and his wife and held captive for years. I don't remember hearing anything about that on the news, though, do you?"

"No." She slipped Mr. Owens's card into her purse, planning to say she'd done it without thinking if Lenore happened to ask for it back, but Lenore didn't seem concerned about it. She just started to ring Mary up.

"There are some sick people out there," she said, shaking her head as though she'd never understand what made some people do what they did.

Mary's mind flashed back to the day Nora Skinner stopped to ask her for directions, and Mary had been kicking a rock as she meandered home from school.

She remembered being so willing to help. A woman alone seemed safe—which was how she'd walked right into a trap.

Autumn glanced at her watch and then checked the back door. She hadn't expected her mother to be gone for so long. Where was Mary? Normally, Autumn wouldn't care that her mother was late. She was fine handling the store. But assuming Mary would be back any minute, Laurie had left to go to the dentist, and Autumn had an appointment to get a pedicure that she was about to miss. She'd heard that an old girlfriend had moved back to town and opened a nail salon, and Autumn wanted to see her. She also couldn't remember the last time she'd done anything to pamper herself—unless she counted sleeping in, which she'd done a lot of since she'd returned to Sable Beach.

The bell went off over the door while she was on the phone with Melissa Cunningham, saying she wasn't going to be able to make it, after all. The store had been fairly busy today, but for every person who made a purchase, she had a handful of browsers, and she was on the phone, so she didn't even try to see who it was.

It wasn't until she heard a man clear his throat that she realized the person who'd come in had walked straight to the counter. She told Melissa she'd call her back to reschedule and turned to find… Quinn.

"Hey," he said, treating her to that Hollywood smile of his. She caught her breath. What was he doing here? "Hello."

He turned in a circle, making a point of taking in everything he saw. "It's been a while since I've been in. The place looks great."

"It should. My mother and aunt pour everything they have into this store. My mother loves it almost as much as she loves me," she quipped.

He faced her again. "I doubt that. Your mother thinks you hung the moon. Have you been spending a lot of time here since you've been home?"

"Quite a bit," she admitted. "I help out most afternoons, once I've spent some time with my kids and have finished gardening."

He held a sack in one hand but leaned casually on the counter with the opposite elbow. "I didn't realize you were a gardener."

"My mother planted it. I just tend it. It gives me something to do while I'm here besides helping out at the store, and I like feeling the earth between my fingers, watching things grow and eating what I produce."

"You make gardening sound fun," he said wryly. "I wouldn't have believed anyone could do that—other than the eating part, of course."

She laughed. "You don't like getting your hands dirty?"

"I don't mind that. I've just never had the burning desire to plant anything, I guess. What types of things are you growing?"

She was tempted to cut straight to the part where she asked him if he needed help finding a book, to save him the effort of making small talk. But if he was going to be polite, so was she. "Watermelon. Sweet potatoes. Zucchini. Tomatoes."

"I have to admit there's nothing better than a homegrown tomato. If I was tempted to grow anything, it would be that."

"I make my own spaghetti sauce every fall—bottle it for the winter, leave some for my mom and take the rest back with me.

So we raise a lot of them. I'm growing some basil and other herbs, too, that I use."

Now that he'd spent a reasonable amount of time chitchatting with her—a nod to the fact that they'd gone to school together—she assumed he'd tell her it was good to see her again and ask where he could find the cookbook he'd come to purchase. Or maybe he was looking for a book on how to better manage a restaurant or survive a divorce. She was already wondering if they'd have what he wanted when he said, "I sent you a friend request on Facebook a while back, but I'm not on there very much, and now I'm guessing that you're not, either."

She was on every night, hoping for some word from her husband—or from someone who could tell her what'd happened to Nick. Each time she logged on, the little symbol that signified she had a friend request waiting drew her eye again and again. But she didn't own up to having seen it. "Not since I've been here," she lied.

"Well, you mentioned how much you like our carrot cake, so I brought you a slice." He lifted the sack he'd been holding and put it on the counter. "I hope you enjoy it."

Shocked, she glanced at the logo of the restaurant before meeting his gaze. "Thank you. That's...really nice."

"No problem," he said and, with a parting wink, started to leave.

He didn't need a book? He'd come just to deliver this cake— *to her*?

Fortunately, there wasn't anyone else in the store at the moment. That was the only reason she allowed herself to call out to him. "Quinn?"

He had his hand on the door when he turned.

"I'm really sorry about your mother."

"Thank you. I appreciate that."

"And..."

He waited patiently as she drew a bolstering breath.

"And I'm also sorry for how I behaved when we were in high school."

The words tumbled out so fast she wouldn't have been surprised if he needed her to repeat them. Fortunately, he seemed to have heard and understood. "You didn't do anything wrong," he said magnanimously.

"I did."

"When?"

She was tempted to say, "Never mind," in case he had really forgotten. But she was the one who'd brought it up. "You know…when I did what I did in the tree house that day."

"What *you* did? I'm pretty sure we both participated."

"But I was so forward even though you tried to tell me you weren't interested."

The glimmer in his eyes suggested he was tempted to laugh. Once she caught that, she suspected he'd been teasing her since she mentioned it. "I don't remember those being the words I used."

"Whatever you said, you were right. I was out of line. I apologize."

His lips curved into a sexy grin. "Is *that* why you won't accept my friend request?"

Damn. He'd guessed she'd seen it, and he was right, so she figured there was no use continuing to lie. "Partially."

"I promise you—that's the last thing you need to worry about," he said, and the door swung shut as he walked out.

"I've decided what I want to get," Taylor announced to Sierra. They were at Sierra's house binge-watching *A Handmaid's Tale,* a series Taylor hadn't seen. Caden and the others hadn't wanted to watch it. They were at the twins' house playing pool, Taylor supposed. She didn't know exactly where they were, and she didn't care. While she liked the others, Sierra was the one who mattered to her. She'd never been quite so taken with anyone.

Regardless of what question Taylor asked or what happened when they were together, Sierra's response was always unexpected and unusual. Sometimes it was even inspiring—or witty or wise or just plain supportive and nice.

"Get for what?" she asked, moving the bowl of popcorn they'd been eating to one side as she paused the television and sat up.

"For the tattoo."

"Oh! What are you thinking?"

"Daddy's girl." Just saying the words made Taylor smile. The idea of having that as her tattoo felt right and seemed to soothe some terrible upset inside her.

"In English?"

She felt her eyebrows go up. "I was thinking in English, but now that you bring it up, maybe I'll go for Ukrainian. That's his heritage, what I associate with him—and that's where he went missing, so I feel like he must still be there, somewhere."

"I could see that. Where will you put it?"

"I'm going to have it written right here in small letters." She indicated the inside of her wrist.

Sierra sat up straighter. "Are you kidding? Your mother will be able to see that. Everyone will be able to see it."

Taylor was well aware of that. "I've decided I don't care," she said, emboldened by Sierra's example.

"Are you going to ask for permission, then?"

Taylor nibbled at her bottom lip as she imagined how that conversation might go. Considering the reason she was getting the tattoo—the significance of it—she felt she might be able to talk her mother into giving her permission. But she was afraid to risk asking in case she was wrong. "No," she said with some conviction.

Sierra lowered her voice. "Will you get into a lot of trouble?"

"That's hard to say. I might." Taylor was nervous to find out, but she'd never been more committed to the idea than she was right now. "Whatever she does to me will set the precedent for Caden, and he also wants to get a tattoo, so there's more to think about than how close I am to turning eighteen and being able to decide for myself."

"Your situation and Caden's are very different."

"He's only a year younger."

"A year is a year. I just… I don't want you to get grounded for the rest of the summer or something. Your mom would never do that, would she? Because I would hate it if I couldn't see you. If there's any chance of that, I think you should wait. Nine months isn't really very long."

It was the first time Sierra had indicated that she was special in any way, and that made her feel so good she couldn't help reaching out to grab her new friend by the arm. "I'd sneak out, if I had to."

Sierra's eyes dropped to Taylor's hand. "You don't mean that."

"I do," she said earnestly.

"I don't believe it," Sierra said, pulling away. "It's only because you don't know me very well yet."

"We've been together every day for two weeks! That's a lot of time."

Sierra looked as though she was about to say something important, but the door opened before she could, and Sierra's father came into the house, yelling her name at the same time.

Sierra nearly spilled the popcorn she jumped to her feet so fast. "What is it?"

Dennis Lambert looked from his daughter to Taylor and back again. "Get her out of here," he snapped.

Sierra's face turned bright red. "But…we're right in the middle of watching a show."

His eyes were bloodshot, his clothes rumpled and he reeked of alcohol. It wasn't even dinnertime yet. "I don't care. Do what I say."

A muscle moved in Sierra's cheek. "You've been drinking again. Just go into your room. We won't bother you."

He moved so fast that Taylor fell back to avoid getting stepped on, and the next thing she knew, he'd doubled up his fist and was brandishing it an inch away from Sierra's nose. "Oh yeah? You're going to talk back to me? You know what happens when you do that."

Taylor nearly twisted her ankle she was in such a hurry to get up. She didn't want to give Sierra any reason to continue arguing with him. She was too afraid it might land her friend in serious trouble. "I'll go, Sierra. No worries. Just…call me later, okay?"

Sierra didn't look scared like a normal girl would. She looked angry, the way she tilted up her chin and glared at her father.

"Don't. Please," Taylor whispered, but it didn't do any good.

"You're a drunken ass," Sierra told him. "A poor excuse for a father."

Mr. Lambert's eyes narrowed until they were barely slits as they slid to Taylor. "What are you waiting for?" he ground out, but now Taylor was afraid to leave. She was terrified Sierra had pushed her father too far.

"I—I—I'm sorry," she stammered, trying to make it better. "Sierra didn't mean that. I know she didn't. What if…what if we cook you something to eat? Are you hungry? Because I know how to make the best spaghetti you've ever tasted." Taylor swallowed against a dry throat as her mind cast about for something she could say that might defuse the situation. "My—my mom, she makes this incredible spaghetti sauce. I swear she could be a millionaire, if only she started selling it in stores." She laughed, but it was too high and shaky to be believable.

"Get out of here. Now!" he shouted, unfazed.

"Go," Sierra said without looking at her. "I'll call you later."

Taylor couldn't move. It was almost as if her feet were glued to the floor. If she didn't go, she might only make matters worse. But if she *did* go, she was afraid something terrible would happen to her new friend, and she wouldn't be around to help. "I shouldn't have stayed so long. It's my fault. Please don't be mad at Sierra," she said to Mr. Lambert, but he ignored her and so did Sierra. Their eyes were locked in what looked like a laser beam of hatred; it was chilling and almost as if she didn't exist, except as a nuisance.

"I can't believe you'd embarrass me in front of my friend," Sierra bit out.

"Your *friend*?" he echoed. "Does she know what you are?"

"Shut up, Dad!"

Taylor was afraid he'd strike her right then, but he grabbed hold of her arm instead and started dragging her over to the kitchen sink, saying, "You think you can talk to your father that way? Huh? Maybe you'll learn your lesson if I wash your mouth out with soap."

"Sierra…" Taylor said, but Sierra shoved her as she passed and yelled, "Go!" and Taylor ran out the door.

What did that private investigator want?

Mary sat in her car, which she'd parked in the small lot behind the bookstore, running her thumb over the embossed letters on Mr. Owens's card. She needed to go inside and close up. Laurie was gone. When she pulled in and didn't see her best friend's car, she'd texted Laurie and learned that she was at the dentist— an appointment she might've mentioned but Mary forgot. Autumn had to be running the store on her own at the moment. But the sudden intrusion of her past—especially in such an up close and physical way—left Mary too stunned. She couldn't bring herself to get out of the car.

It'd been so long since she'd been held captive in the multi-million-dollar Atlanta mansion of Jeff and Nora Skinner. Even the press seemed to have forgotten the sad story that had once generated such morbid interest. If word got out that she'd been located, Mary had no doubt a bevy of reporters would be banging on her door again, or reaching out to her in other ways, requesting a follow-up story. After all, they'd hounded her for months after she escaped, which was partly why she'd changed her name from Bailey to Mary.

But she couldn't imagine a reporter had gone to the trouble and expense of hiring a private investigator thirty-five years after the fact. That would be far too speculative an endeavor, especially for the sake of a story that wouldn't be nearly as sensational as when it was fresh. Only someone who had more than a casual interest in her would go to such great lengths.

Was it her mother? After how sloppy and unconcerned Rae-Lynn had been with her care before the abduction, why would she suddenly be that desperate to reconnect? And would Rae-Lynn be able to afford an investigator? If so, how? Her mother had never had a lot of money—at least she hadn't when they were still in touch.

Maybe it wasn't RaeLynn. Maybe it was some other relative. But who and why? And why *now*?

She opened a web browser on her phone and typed the names of Jeff and Nora Skinner into the search bar. Jeff had received such a long sentence he'd most likely die in prison. Nora, on the other hand, had received only thirty-eight years for her part in what'd happened. She could be out by now. Most inmates didn't serve their full sentence, what with early parole and time off for good behavior. Could *she* be the one who was looking for Bailey?

That made Mary's skin crawl. Nora would be sixty-eight years old—no longer the young woman she'd been when she'd assisted her husband in kidnapping a child. But the thought that Nora was out in the world, free to do as she would, frightened Mary all the same. The memories she had of Nora were too terrible.

Surely, Nora wasn't the one who'd hired Drake D. Owens…

Or did she have some purpose in doing so? Did she blame Mary for her long incarceration and plan to get even? Was she still angry, after all of this time, that Mary had dared defy them after "being part of the family" for seven years—which was the twisted way she claimed to have looked at Mary's imprisonment? Jeff came from a very wealthy family; that was what had enabled them to do a lot of the things they did. Maybe they hadn't used all their money on their defense.

Mary wiped the sweat that was beading on her upper lip—despite the fact that she'd left the air-conditioning running—and scrolled through the links that popped up.

She couldn't find anything that mentioned Jeff or Nora, not recently. Because most people assumed Jeff was the mastermind behind it all, and he'd had a child with Mary when Mary was only sixteen, he'd received far more attention. Considering that, it was possible Nora had been released without anyone noticing.

Closing her eyes, Mary leaned her head back on the headrest as she remembered the cold stare Nora had given her upon being sentenced. Nora had remained unrepentant and defiant to the end—in some ways, more of a monster than Jeff, who'd at least pretended to feel some remorse.

Her phone dinged with a text. Taking a deep breath in an attempt to slow her breathing and her heartbeat, she glanced down.

Autumn. Again. Mary had been too rattled to respond to her daughter's previous calls and texts. She felt pressure to do so now, but she couldn't say she was sitting outside in the parking lot without going right in, and she still hadn't decided what to do about Drake Owens.

Lenore had never heard of Bailey North. She was too young. But if Owens continued to poke around Sable Beach, he'd eventually find someone who would. Even when he did, just remembering the story wouldn't necessarily reveal that Bailey North had become Mary Langford, but if Mr. Owens got everyone's curiosity up, and they began to look at each other more critically and piece together the past, she could find herself on a short list of possibilities. And once that happened, she couldn't imagine it would take long to arrive at the truth.

After turning the closest air-conditioning vent so that it hit her more directly, she blocked her number and called him. Now that he was here, she had to stop him from digging.

And the only way she could figure to do that would be to see what he wanted.

8

Acid churned in Mary's stomach as she waited to see if the private investigator would answer. Was she making a mistake to tackle this head-on?

Maybe. It was possible that he wouldn't get anywhere and he'd move on, assuming whatever had brought him to this small town had been a false lead. She could get that lucky. But it could just as easily go the other way. She couldn't have him out there asking about the girl who was held hostage thirty-five years ago, stirring up interest in her old case—especially with her daughter and grandchildren in town.

"'Lo?"

Just when she'd begun to hope he wouldn't answer, he did. "Mr. Owens?"

"Yes?"

"This is— This is Bailey North." Those were difficult words to get out. She hadn't said them in almost three and a half decades.

The resulting silence suggested she'd taken him by surprise. Then he said, "How do I know it's you?"

"Do you have a lot of people calling, trying to imperson-ate me?"

"If there's something to be gained, people will do almost anything," he replied.

She gripped the phone that much tighter. "And what is there to be gained in this situation?"

"I'd like to tell you. Can we meet?"

Panic welled up. "No."

"Are you here in Sable Beach?"

She'd called him right after he'd given his card to someone in the local drugstore, which had to suggest a cause-and-effect relationship. But she wasn't going to give him any information—not until she knew what he wanted. "I'd rather not answer that question."

"So you do live here. Do you also work here?"

He was direct. So she was going to be just as direct. "I'd rather not answer that question, either."

"I'm not the press, Bailey."

She winced at the sound of her given name. She'd hoped never to hear it on anyone else's lips again. She didn't want to be the person she used to be; to her, that person was dead. Along with everything else Jeff and Nora had taken from her, they'd murdered the young woman she'd once been. "I guessed as much. But knowing you're not the press doesn't tell me who you are—or why you're here."

"I'd be happy to explain it to you, but I can't do it over the phone."

She rubbed her forehead as she stared out the front windshield of her car. "Does this have to do with my mother?"

"No."

She didn't know whether to be hurt or relieved. That her mother had never tried to rectify, or even apologize, for what she'd done cut deeply. She'd endured rejection in its cruelest form. But having no contact with RaeLynn also made it easier to hide, so she supposed she should be grateful that her mother had been willing to let her go. "The people who kidnapped me?"

"Yes."

She tensed. Her feelings toward them were much less complicated. She never wanted to hear from them again. Period. "Don't tell me they're out of prison."

"We'll go over that. Just give me a few minutes of your time, will you?"

"Where?"

"You pick the location."

She was trying to decide where they could meet when she saw Laurie pull into the parking lot. "I've got to go," she said. "I'll call you tomorrow, and maybe we can arrange something."

He started to speak, but she hung up.

Laurie waved, and she forced herself to smile as she got out. She wished she would've told Owens to quit flashing his card around town, that she'd only meet with him if he'd be discreet.

But that would only confirm that he was, indeed, close to where she was—close to finding her.

Taylor milled around her grandmother's cottage, too agitated to sit down. She couldn't decide what to do—or if she should do anything. Should she wait and hope what was going on at Sierra's house would just blow over? Go to her mother for help? Call the police? *What?*

She doubted it was illegal for a parent to wash a teenager's mouth out with soap—not so long as the teen wasn't truly harmed. Even if it was crossing the line, Sierra had talked back. Taylor wasn't confident she could get others to step in, given what Sierra had said.

But what if Mr. Lambert's punishment didn't end there? The look on his face—the anger flashing in his eyes—had truly frightened her.

Relief rushed over her when she heard the door.

"There you are," Caden said as he strode into the house. "How was *A Handmaid's Tale*?"

"Okay, I guess." Taylor was too distracted and upset to talk about the TV show.

He stopped as soon as he got a good look at her. "What's wrong?"

She crossed to the window and craned her neck to be able to see the driveway. She didn't want her mother or grandmother to walk in and hear what she had to say. "It's Sierra."

"What about her?"

"Her father came home drunk and started a fight—and...and I don't know if she's going to be okay."

A scowl darkened his face. "What do you mean? He didn't hit her, did he?"

"Not in front of me. But who knows what happened after I left. Do you think I should call Mom?"

"Not unless you know for sure."

She started biting at the cuticles on her fingers, something she often did when she was nervous. "It looked like it was moving in that direction."

"But if you're wrong, Mom might stick her nose into their business for no reason and start a feud here in Sable Beach. If that happens, she'll probably take us back to Florida, and I'm having fun. I want to stay for the whole summer, don't you?"

She *did* want to stay. She would hate to be taken away from her new friends, especially Sierra. "But I can't just...abandon her to whatever's happening."

He shoved his hands in his pockets as he leaned up against the wall. "Did she cry out for help?"

"No. She just told me to leave. But a good friend would get help anyway, wouldn't she?"

He rubbed his chin as he considered the question. "Not if it would only make things worse."

Exactly her dilemma. "What about the police?" she asked. "If I call them, Mom won't have to get involved."

"But you'll feel pretty silly if you send the police over there and it was just an argument. Has he ever hit her before?"

She quickly sifted through the comments she could remember Sierra making about her father. Sierra had called him a jerk and an angry drunk, but she'd never indicated he physically abused her. "Not that she's told me about."

"She's almost eighteen, Tay."

"Which means…what?" Hearing the irritation in her own voice, she feared it would start a fight with her brother but, fortunately, he didn't snap at her in return.

"She's made it this long living with him. She must know how to get by. And she has only one more year of school. I wouldn't want to screw anything up for her. What if she gets kicked out of the house or something? Where will she go? How will she earn her diploma?"

Taylor twisted her hair into a knot. "I have no idea. But Mr. Jamison in English class said that so many bad things could be avoided if only someone would speak up or step in." She dropped her hair. "I can't ignore what I saw."

He shoved off the wall as he pulled out his phone and came closer to her. "I've got an idea. I'll block my number. Then we can call the police and ask them to check on things."

She looked down at her own phone, hoping to see a text or a missed call from Sierra—anything that might reassure her.

Unfortunately, it wasn't there. "But blocking your number won't help," Taylor said. "Sierra and her father will both know it was me. Who else could it be?"

"So what if they know it's you? It's a reasonable response, after what you saw. I'd still do it."

Taylor wanted to talk to her mother about it, but she didn't want to drag Autumn into something they might all regret. She wouldn't be any happier than Caden if they had to leave Sable Beach before the end of summer. And she certainly didn't want to make things worse for Sierra. In trying to help her friend, she could lose her instead.

In the end, she couldn't bear the thought of what might be going on at Sierra's house.

"Okay," she said. "Let's call."

Laurie was watching her closely. Mary could tell. No matter how hard she tried to pretend that everything was fine, her friend could always sense when it wasn't.

"What is it?" she asked, a worried expression on her face.

Autumn, who'd grabbed her purse and was digging out her keys to go home and start dinner, looked up in surprise, and Mary nearly groaned aloud. Couldn't Laurie have waited just five minutes, until Autumn was gone, to ask that question?

To avoid looking at either one of them, she remained focused on closing out the register. "What's what?"

"You've been quiet since you got back from the drugstore," Laurie replied. "Is something wrong?"

Mary spent so much time with her best friend. She should've expected Laurie to notice that she wasn't quite herself, should've alerted Laurie while they were in the parking lot that something had come up and not to say anything in front of Autumn. But she was still mulling it over, hadn't decided how, exactly, to handle this latest development. And she didn't want Laurie to start pressing her again to tell Autumn. "Nothing," she insisted.

"Did you have another nightmare last night?" Autumn sounded concerned, too.

Mary lifted one hand. "No, I've been sleeping great. I just have a little headache, that's all."

"Maybe it'll help to eat," Laurie suggested. "Go home with Autumn. I'll close up."

"That's not necessary."

"I don't mind," Laurie said. "Why not go take care of yourself?"

Mary wanted to give her a pointed look to let her know to

drop the subject, but Autumn was now watching her closely, too. "Because it's not a big deal, like I said. I can finish up." She caught a glimpse of the sack Autumn had just picked up and noticed the logo. "When did you go back to The Daily Catch?" She was eager to deflect attention from herself but she was honestly curious, too.

"I didn't. I—" Autumn's cheeks turned pink, a reaction that distracted Laurie, too. It wasn't often that Mary saw her daughter blush anymore.

"You what?" Laurie prodded when Autumn's words fell off.

"Quinn dropped it by," she admitted.

"He did, did he?" Laurie jumped on that, a self-satisfied smile curving her lips. "What do you think that means?"

Autumn waved her off. "It doesn't mean anything."

"It has to mean *something*," Laurie argued. "I love that cake, too, but he didn't bring me a piece."

"Or me," Mary pointed out. She felt bad ganging up on Autumn, but she was grateful Laurie was no longer questioning *her*.

"We went to high school together," Autumn said dismissively.

Laurie arched one eyebrow to show her skepticism. "So you're saying he'd do it for any old friend who came to town?"

Autumn seemed stumped. In exasperation, she said, "It's probably because he thinks I'm interested in him—after you called him over to the table when we went there to eat a couple of weeks ago!"

"Would that be so bad?" Laurie challenged.

"No," Autumn said. Then, "Yes, of course! I'm not open to a relationship."

Mary noticed that she hadn't said, "I'm married," and wondered if that meant her daughter was coming to terms with the loss of her marriage as well as her husband.

A penitent expression claimed Laurie's face the minute Autumn hurried out the back. "Do you think I upset her? I shouldn't have teased her, I guess."

"If I know Autumn, she's not upset—she's embarrassed."

"If that's true, she must like him. Otherwise, what would she have to be embarrassed about?"

"Don't let her know I told you this, but I think she does like him. She used to have a terrible crush on him when she was in high school, remember?"

"I remember. That's why I thought I was doing her a favor by calling him over. I wanted him to know she was in town and to see how gorgeous she is."

Mary finished putting the day's receipts in the bank bag and closed the register. "That was nice of you."

"But perhaps it was a tad too insensitive considering what's happened to Nick."

"It's been almost nineteen months since Nick went missing. If he's not coming back, maybe having someone else in her life will make that reality easier to take."

"I hope so."

"So do I." Mary put the money in her purse. "I'll make the deposit on my way home."

"Wait a second." Laurie stopped her before she could walk out. "You're not getting away that easily. Do you really have a headache? Or is it something else?"

Mary sighed. "There's a private investigator in town, looking for Bailey North. And I don't know why."

"Who told you that?"

"I saw him at the drugstore," she replied and explained the encounter and her phone call with him.

"Could it be your mother who hired him?"

"He said it wasn't."

"He could be lying. But...is your mother even still alive?"

"She'd only be seventy-four."

"But you told me she wasn't one to take care of herself."

"I don't know. I try not to look back."

"Are you going to meet him? The PI?"

"Do you think I should?"

Laurie leaned against the counter and crossed her arms. "Now that he's this close, he wouldn't have to look too hard to find you. You might as well try to put a stop to his questions before he brings others into it."

"That's what I was thinking."

"You won't want to be seen with him around here, though. Where will you go?"

Mary had been trying to decide. "Richmond, I guess. But it's a bit of a drive."

"Give him a call right now. See what you can arrange. Whenever you need to be there, I'll cover the store."

"I'll try to meet him first thing in the morning. But what will I say to Autumn if I'm not back when she comes in?"

"I'll tell her you're visiting a bookstore owner in Richmond who has a coffee shop and agreed to talk to us about how she sources her supplies."

"That should work." She was relieved to have a plan of action, was reasonably assured that the course of action she'd chosen was the best of her options, too. But she was still terribly nervous about what Drake D. Owens might have to say—and whether it would change the world as she knew it.

9

When Autumn went online that night, she didn't see any messages from Nick. There was no word from Yana or Mr. Olynyk, either, and nothing from the FBI or anyone she'd contacted in her search. But after so long, none of that came as any surprise. Neither did it pack the same kind of stomach-sickening punch. She wasn't crying, arguing with strangers about what might've happened or pressing those who could possibly help her to do more.

She'd done all of that. There was no one left to appeal to. All she could do was adjust to her new circumstances. While that came as a welcome reprieve, it also caused a tsunami of guilt. Nick could be in a desperate situation, and yet here she was enjoying carrot cake from The Daily Catch—just eating it felt like a betrayal—and eyeing the friend request she'd received from the man to whom she'd given her virginity.

"How disloyal can I be?" she muttered, disgusted with herself for being so tempted to accept Quinn's request. "What if Nick's still alive?"

But she couldn't hang on forever, could she? Not when there was literally no evidence that he was still breathing.

Closing her eyes, she shook her head. She wasn't hoping for Nick's death—far from it—but if he had died, and she could find proof of it, at least she'd have answers. Someone who passed away could be mourned and memorialized and then, with time, let go. But not knowing made the pain, doubt and anxiety interminable, open-ended.

A text came in. Hearing the signal, she reached over to retrieve her phone from the nightstand.

What are you doing?

It was from Taylor, who'd eaten dinner and then gone directly to her room, saying she wasn't feeling well.

How do you know I'm doing anything?

Autumn added a funny face emoji. Sometimes she and her daughter exchanged emoji after emoji, just being silly and having fun, but Taylor didn't react that way this time.

I can see the light above the garage from the dining room, she said.

Are you feeling better? Why aren't you in bed?

I wasn't really sick. Just worried about my friend.

She'd lied? Why?

Which friend?

Sierra. She smart-mouthed her father, and he got **really** angry.

Wasn't her mother there?

Her mother must've taken off when she was a baby. She won't talk about her. It's just her and her father, and it's been that way since she was eight.

You think he might've hurt her?

I don't know. Caden and I called the police and
asked them to check on her, but they haven't
called back. I don't think they're going to. And I
haven't heard from Sierra.

Surprised by what Taylor had just texted her, Autumn sat up straighter and called her daughter. "You sent the police over there?" she said as soon as Taylor answered.

"I had to make sure she was okay."

"Why didn't you tell me about it?"

"I was afraid I was wrong. I didn't want you to get involved if it was nothing."

"I see." Autumn decided to forgo her usual lecture on transparency. She could tell her daughter had only been trying to help. "Well, if it frightened you that badly, maybe we should drive over there."

"I just did."

Autumn got out of bed and walked to the window where she could see the house. "You left this late without telling me?"

"I'm sorry. I had to check on her."

"I see. Well, we'll discuss that later. What'd you find?"

"I couldn't tell anything. The house was dark, and I didn't dare go to the door."

"Who's Sierra's father? Do I know him?"

"I doubt it. They just moved here this year. His name's Dennis Lambert."

"What does he do for a living?"

"Something for an insurance company, I think."

Autumn leaned her forehead against the cool glass. It was nearly midnight. She couldn't imagine going over and banging on Mr. Lambert's door, was afraid that would only get his daughter in more trouble. "If you called the police, I'm sure they've looked into it. I'm afraid that's all we can do—at least until morning. I don't need to go anywhere until I head into the store after lunch. So you can use the car and take her a coffee first thing, after he's left for work, and make sure she's okay."

"So I should forget about it and go to bed?"

"That's all we can do, honey," she reiterated. "I know it's hard. But try to get some sleep."

"I will." Taylor sounded resigned but not happy.

"Want to come out and sleep with me?" Autumn asked.

Her daughter hesitated long enough that Autumn thought she'd accept. Autumn liked these moments when Taylor felt she still needed her mom. But in the end, she said, "No, I'll just assume everything is fine and see what happens in the morning."

She was growing up. "Good idea. I love you."

Taylor said the same and disconnected, and Autumn returned to bed. But when she set her phone aside and pulled her computer back into her lap, Quinn's friend request was still there, and once again, it caught her eye.

"Oh, what the hell," she said and clicked Accept. She assumed Quinn would be asleep, which was why she felt fairly safe messaging him.

The cake was great. Thank you.

She wasn't quite ready to go to sleep so she navigated away from Facebook and read a few click-bait news articles. When she grew frustrated with how slowly they moved the story along and constantly held out the most important detail, she returned to Facebook to see if she could find a profile for Sierra Lambert. Maybe the girl had posted about the argument with her father or the police showing up. It was a long shot, and Taylor had probably already checked Instagram, but Autumn figured she had the time. Worst case, she found nothing. Best case, she could text some reassurance to Taylor.

She couldn't find a Sierra Lambert, though, not one close to Sierra's age who revealed that she was from Sable Beach.

She was just about to close her computer when an instant message landed in her box.

You're up late.

It was Quinn! For some inexplicable reason, her heart started to pound, and her fingers hovered over the keyboard for a moment before she started typing. Nights can get long, she finally wrote.

Most people think they're too short.

Those are people who can sleep.

You can't?

Not until three or four in the morning.

It wasn't until then that she could finally get her mind to shut down.

What do you do during that time?

For the past nineteen months, I've been searching for my husband.

I heard he went missing. I'm sorry about that.

Autumn wasn't surprised that he knew. Most people in Sable Beach had probably been told about Nick, but she hated that Quinn was one of them. She was afraid he'd assume, like so many others, that Nick had walked out on her.

He could come back one day, she wrote, although she wasn't sure why she'd felt the need to say that. She'd given up on the idea, hadn't she? Wasn't that why she'd come to Sable Beach? To start the difficult task of putting it all behind her?

You have no clue what happened to him?

None, she wrote. He left to go on a business trip, supposedly to New York, and never came back. Then she added, and please don't suggest he ran off with another woman. I've heard that one before. Lots of times. I understand that could be a possibility—I'm not naive. But there are quite a few reasons I find it unbelievable.

Like…

He adored his kids, for one. And I can't imagine he wouldn't want half our assets. But he didn't take a dime. Everything he owned—his most prized possessions—are still where they always were. No one has emerged to say he had gambling debts or anything else that might make him want to bug out. I could go on.

Your mother speaks highly of him.

She blinked when she read his response.

What does that mean?

She seems like a good judge of character. I doubt she would've liked him if he was the kind of guy to run out on you.

If Autumn had learned anything in life, she'd learned that almost anyone could be "that kind of guy—or girl" given the right set of circumstances and temptations. In Tampa, her best friend's husband had gotten involved with his dental assistant, which tore their family apart, and he'd been nice, too. But she didn't believe those kinds of circumstances existed in Nick's life, not at the time he disappeared. Their marriage had been solid, and he'd seemed fulfilled in his work.

He had been hiding things from her, though. She'd assumed that was all related to what he was doing for the government. But maybe there was more.

He seemed to be sincere.

I have no doubt he was. You've heard what happened to me...

Should she lie? Let him think that his own scandal had died down? She was tempted to cut him a break, but he knew what the residents of Sable Beach were like, so she doubted he'd be-lieve her, anyway.

Yes.

I wasn't cheating, Autumn. I never went out on
Sarah once. It was her own insecurities and fears
that led to what happened.

She felt her eyebrows go up.

I didn't ask. That's none of my business.

I was hoping it might become your business.

"In what way?" she mumbled to herself but typed a question mark to keep it simple.

I'd like to ask you out, so I thought you should
know.

Sliding her computer onto the bed, she jumped up and began pacing in front of the window. Did he really just come right out and say that? She couldn't date him. She couldn't date any-one—but especially him. She'd wanted him too badly before,

was afraid all of that desire and admiration would come rushing back and catch her up in something she couldn't control.

Besides, she wasn't ready to start seeing other men. Nick's
rain boots were still in the corner of the room!

She took several deep breaths in an attempt to calm down.
By the time she'd managed to do so and returned to her computer, he'd written her again.

Was I too direct? Did I scare you away?

Yes! She was terrified of him. Well, not of him, exactly. Of
her. Just seeing him in the bookstore had reminded her of that day
in the tree house. All these years later, she could still remember
the incredible smell of him, the way he kissed, the warmth of his
hand as he touched her breast, the feel of his body against hers.

Of course she would remember those things. That was the
first time she'd ever made love, and instead of being the terrible, painful experience she'd heard it would be, it'd been wonderful. Not pleasurable in the way sex was pleasurable for her as
an adult, of course. But it had definitely been satisfying, if only
because she was *finally* able to touch the object of her desire, the
boy she'd craved for months.

The weird thing was that she was beginning to want him
again. Obviously, it had been too long since she'd been with a
man. But she didn't need an old crush, someone she'd been sexually attracted to from day 1, getting in the way of her recovery,
especially because she was no longer a teenager. She couldn't
imagine what Tay and Caden would think if she was to start seeing someone. She hadn't even considered dating, but if she was
going to start, the least she could do was wait until they were
both in college.

I'm not available. But thank you for the offer.

I'm sorry if I ever hurt you, Autumn. I feel bad

that you felt the need to apologize to me when I
shouldn't have let it go that far in the first place.

That's a generous thing to say, but I don't remember giving
you much choice, she wrote back and added a laughing emoji.

I could've stopped if I'd wanted to. I knew your
first time should be different, better. But that's
just it. I didn't want to stop. It was selfish of me.

She didn't blame him—she never had.

We were kids. I say we agree to forgive and forget. We both have a lot more to worry about
than what happened that day.

True, but…

What?

What if I can't forget?

Although her heart jumped into her throat, Autumn immediately started talking herself down. He had to be lonely. That
was the only reason he'd said what he did. Being stabbed by his
wife and then dealing with his mother's diagnosis and treatment
would be tough for anyone.

He was probably looking for a way out, something he could
do to make himself feel better, even if it was only temporary,
and thought she'd go right back to bed with him.

The thought crossed her mind that they could use each other.
She was certainly missing sexual contact. But getting involved
with Quinn, especially in that way, would only lead to trouble.
Getting over Nick was going to be hard enough. Why allow
herself to fall into a rebound relationship?

You've been through a lot, but it'll get easier,
with time. Did you know that Melissa Cunningham is back in town?

Yes. She's opened a nail salon here. I've seen her
around.

Well? Did he like what he saw? Autumn wasn't quite sure how
to state what she was thinking, so she was still trying to work
it out when he wrote What does that have to do with anything?

I hear she's divorced. I'm just letting you know
that there are other options.

You think I wanted to ask you out because I didn't
know there are other women out there?

She'd offended him, but she hadn't intended to. She'd been
trying to offer him a good substitute so that he'd move on and
she would no longer be tempted.

I didn't mean to be rude. Surely you know how
good-looking you are. A guy like you could have
almost anyone. It doesn't have to be me.

You said it's been nineteen months since your
husband went missing.

And...?

A year and a half is a long time, Autumn.

He could still come back, she insisted once again, even though
she'd pretty much decided that wasn't going to happen.

In the meantime, there's nothing wrong with us

being friends, is there? Why don't we go to dinner, just to have a night out and forget about our
problems? Nothing more serious has to come of it.

I can't. I don't think I'm ready—even for that.

I see. No problem. Have a good night.

A lump rose in her throat when the green dot signifying that
he was online disappeared. She told herself that she'd done the
right thing and should feel satisfied, even proud. She'd resisted
the boy she'd once made a fool of herself for—the boy who'd
been irresistible to her.

But she didn't feel good in any way. She had to get off her
computer before she wrote him back to demand that they meet
this very minute so they could fall into bed and get so caught up
in each other that nothing else could register. She was so tired
of the heartache and the loneliness she'd carried around like a
ball and chain for the past year and a half that she was looking
for any kind of release.

"Don't even think about it," she mumbled and put her computer away before climbing into bed, pulling the covers high
and praying for sleep to overtake her.

Taylor couldn't sleep for most of the night. She tossed and
turned and dreamed about the fight she'd witnessed between
Sierra and her father. So she was relieved when she finally saw
the first rays of sunlight glowing around the blinds in her room.
Thank God it was morning.

She made herself stay in bed until she heard Mimi putting
on a pot of coffee in the kitchen. Then she went into the bathroom to shower. Because Mimi would soon need to get ready
for work, she'd have to be quick, but the alternative was waiting
until her grandmother was finished, and she knew she'd never
have the patience for that.

"You're up early," Mimi said, understandably surprised when they passed in the hallway as Taylor, wrapped in a towel, relinquished the bathroom.

"I promised my friend I'd come over as soon as her father left for work."

Steam from Taylor's shower curled around Mimi as she paused outside the door. "Which friend?"

"Sierra Lambert."

"You should bring her by the bookstore sometime. I'd love to meet her."

"I will," she said, but she didn't have any real intention of doing that. She was afraid for her mother and grandmother to see Sierra's piercings and tattoos. She wasn't sure how they'd react. Her mother was cooler than most parents, but Autumn was still a stickler on making good decisions and hanging out with the right people, and Taylor didn't want Autumn or Mimi to jump to conclusions based on Sierra's appearance.

Although she could've poured some coffee into a thermos and taken it over to Sierra's from the pot Mimi had put on, she stopped by The Coffee Bean on her way over and purchased two soymilk lattes instead. She'd earned a little money helping at the store last Saturday and wanted to get something she knew Sierra would really like.

She'd texted Sierra several times and received no response, so she had no idea what she might find when she approached the house.

Fortunately, Sierra's father seemed to be gone—she didn't see his car in the drive. Although they had a garage, it was filled with a motorcycle, various car pieces and parts, tools and boxes of storage—so much stuff that no one could park in it.

She rang the doorbell, but no one answered.

Her stomach in knots, she was just backing up to take a look at the house to determine which window might be Sierra's when the door finally cracked open and a sleepy-eyed Sierra squinted out at her. "Hey, what's up?"

She seemed to be wearing a spaghetti strap top and a pair of panties, but she was mostly hidden by the door so Taylor couldn't tell if she'd been hurt. "Are you okay? I've been so worried about you."

She shrugged as though what Taylor had seen was nothing, which came as a relief, except that Taylor got the impression Sierra was embarrassed by what'd happened. "I'm fine."

"But last night—"

"Was just another day of living with my dad."

Taylor grimaced. "He's always like that?"

"Only when he drinks."

But he drank a lot. Taylor already knew that because Sierra had mentioned it before. Holding out one of the lattes, Taylor said, "I brought you this."

"Thanks." She swung the door wide as she took the proffered cup. "Come on in."

Once inside, Taylor had the chance to look her friend over and was relieved not to see any cuts or bruises. "So...he didn't hit you or anything?"

"No. Just tried to wash my mouth out with soap, but I wriggled away before he could, ran to my room and locked myself in. I swear, sometimes he still thinks I'm ten."

Taylor remembered how mad he'd been. "Didn't running away from him just make everything worse?" There was a glass pitcher lying broken on the floor. She pointed at it. "Please tell me he didn't throw that at you."

"No. We knocked it off when we were at the sink. Once I clean it up, chances are good he won't even remember we had a pitcher like that."

"I'm surprised he didn't clean it up. Someone could get cut."

"I'm the only one who cleans up around here, and I wasn't

about to come out of my room when he was in such a foul mood."

Taylor sipped the foam from her latte, scarcely tasting it. "What'd he do when you locked yourself in?"

She pulled up one of the straps on her tank top that had fallen off her shoulder. "What could he do? He couldn't reach me so he stomped around, yelling about what a lazy, no good, ungrateful daughter I am and took my phone, which I had to leave behind when I made a dash for my room."

That explained why Sierra hadn't answered any of her texts. "Where is it now?"

"My phone?" She ran her fingers through her short hair, making it stand up even more. "I'll have to check the recliner. I think that's where he slept last night. If it's not there, he might've remembered to take it with him, which would suck, because then it might be a while before I can get it back."

Taylor hated the idea of not being able to reach her. She walked over to look in the recliner herself. "I don't see it," she said, using her free hand to dig down the sides.

"Damn. Well, when he goes to sleep tonight, I'll search for it. It might be in his car."

Taylor didn't think she should make him mad again. "I wouldn't do anything to piss him off."

"He's mostly talk," Sierra said. "It's best to just ignore him when he gets like that. I have one year left at home—that's it. Then I'm gone."

Taylor couldn't imagine living with someone like Mr. Lambert for another three hundred and sixty-five days and suddenly felt like a big baby for feeling sorry for herself over her dad's disappearance. She missed him. It sucked to have him gone. But she still had her mother, who was good to her. At least she wasn't living with someone who got drunk and flew into a rage. "I drove by last night," she said. "But the house was dark, so I didn't dare come to the door."

She fixed the lid on her latte, which was coming off. "Are you the one who called the police?"

Taylor hated to admit it. She didn't want Sierra to be mad if she shouldn't have done that. But the thing she admired most about Sierra was her honesty and courage. She wanted to be just as honest and courageous. "Yes. Did they talk to you—or just your dad?"

"They insisted on seeing me, so my dad had me come out."

"What'd you say to them?"

"That I was okay."

"You didn't tell them what happened?"

"No. Why would I? There's nothing they can do, except take me away, and that would be even worse. Do you think I want to go into foster care?" She rolled her eyes. "No! It's not like my dad *beats* me."

"I thought he was going to."

"He's just lonely and miserable, which is why he drinks. And when he drinks, he becomes the worst version of himself. He's not always that bad."

"But…what if he *does* hit you one day?"

"He won't. For the most part, I know how to stay out of the way." She finally managed to get her lid on straight. "I've been doing it long enough, right?"

Taylor wasn't so sure Sierra should be that unconcerned, but she had no choice except to believe what she was told. "So how'd he react after you said what you did to the police?"

"He calmed down. I think he realized I could've said some shit that would've caused us both a lot of problems, but I'm not that stupid. After I went back to my room, he was quiet, and pretty soon I heard the TV go on. That's when I knew it was over."

Taylor couldn't believe that had been the extent of it. "I was… I was *really* afraid you were being hurt." Tears sprang to her eyes. Sierra was fine—she'd said so herself—but Taylor had genuinely believed she was in danger and still felt rattled by what she'd seen. It didn't help that she'd spent a long, sleepless night imagining the worst.

Embarrassed by her reaction, she turned away and was trying to think of something to say when Sierra set her coffee aside and took her hand.

"I'm okay. Really. Come here." She put Taylor's coffee on the side table, too, and pulled her in for a hug.

Taylor liked the way this strange, new, compelling person smelled. She liked the feeling of Sierra's hand running reassuringly up and down her back, too.

Taylor didn't let go right away, like she'd done with every other friend she'd ever had. She didn't want to let go. It surprised her that Sierra didn't break the hug, either. They stood in each other's arms for probably a minute or longer.

Taylor was feeling odd by the time Sierra did step back. Out of breath. Flushed even though it wasn't very hot. And her heart was racing.

"Thank you for caring," Sierra said.

That would've sounded totally lame coming from anyone else, but Sierra somehow made it sincere. Even better, Taylor could tell that Sierra's embarrassment was going away.

Relieved to think everything was okay and last night hadn't changed anything, after all, Taylor smiled. "Of course. We're friends, aren't we?"

Sierra peered into her face as though she was looking for something. "If that's what you want to be."

It wasn't until that moment that Taylor recalled something Mr. Lambert had said last night—a snippet that had been lost in all the anger and upset. When Sierra called her a friend, he'd scoffed and said, *Does she know what you are?*

Taylor hadn't known, but she was pretty sure she did now.

10

Mary showed up an hour early. She wanted to be the first one to reach the Starbucks she'd selected, didn't want Drake D. Owens to see what she drove or to get her license plate number. She'd even parked down the street and walked the rest of the way, just in case. She doubted it was worth the extra effort, was pretty sure he'd be able to find her, regardless. She was just so used to being cautious she couldn't help holding back when and where she could.

She shifted on the stool at the window and checked the time on her phone while keeping watch on the parking lot and making note of every car that came or went. At least she knew what Mr. Owens looked like, since she'd seen him in the drugstore.

He arrived early, too. At a quarter to ten, he walked in wearing chinos and a light blue button-down shirt, with the sleeves rolled up to his elbows, and got in line. He turned while he waited, scanning the small lobby filled with millennials tapping away on their computers. His expression was businesslike, neutral—until his gaze connected with hers and he froze.

He could tell that he'd found her, if not by the expectation he read on her face then by her age. Everyone else was younger, except a couple of men in the corner.

He tipped his head in acknowledgment, and she did the same.

Clasping her hands in her lap to stop them from shaking, she waited for him to put in his order. This was the first interaction she'd had with her past in almost thirty-five years. Autumn had been only three when she'd changed her name and moved to Sable Beach.

He didn't approach until he had his drink. Although he tried to act as if this was just another day for him, there was no mistaking the curiosity and interest in his eyes. "Hello, Bailey."

She chafed at the sound of her old name but didn't correct him by providing her new one. She was here to *get* information, not give it. "Hello, Mr. Owens."

He adjusted his glasses. "You can call me Drake, if you like."

She didn't plan to become familiar enough to call him by his first name, but she didn't say so.

"You look good," he told her. "Really good."

She supposed he was trying to make her feel comfortable, but that was impossible. "Thank you."

He set his drink on the wooden ledge running the length of the wall and straddled the stool next to hers. "I appreciate you taking the time to meet me."

"How did you find me—after so long?"

"*You* called *me*."

She didn't laugh, even though he was trying to be funny. "What brought you to Sable Beach?"

"The receptionist for the psychologist you used to see right after you escaped said you talked about this place, even showed her a picture of it once in a magazine. She said she'd always imagined you living here, finally happy."

"That's it?"

"That's it. It wasn't a lot, but it took a great deal of effort to find her, and it was the only lead I had. I guessed you wouldn't stick around Nashville, where you were born, because that was also where you'd been kidnapped. I believed you'd be eager to escape the memories, and that the beach would probably sound nice."

That was why he hadn't known her new name and had still been looking for a Bailey.

He jerked his head toward the cashier. "Can I get you something?"

The coffee she'd drunk this morning was already burning a hole in her stomach. "No. I don't mean to be rude, Mr. Owens, but I don't want to be here very long. Please, tell me what you've come to say so I can go."

He lowered his voice, which added more gravity to his words. "It's a bit unusual..."

Curling her nails into her palms, she said, "I'm listening..."

"Nora Skinner is out of prison."

Rubbing her temple, she stared at the floor as she processed this information. She'd expected as much, and yet it still came as a blow to hear that the woman who'd helped victimize her for seven long years was walking around free. So many times after she'd awakened from one of her nightmares, she'd soothed herself with the reminder that both Jeff and Nora were in prison—that they could never reach her again.

Now she knew for certain that was no longer true, which wouldn't make those nights any easier.

She lifted her gaze. "And her husband?"

"Still in."

She let her breath go, hadn't even realized she'd been holding it. "He deserves to rot there."

"I agree. And I don't doubt that he will."

A blast of hot, humid air rolled over Mary as a large group held the door open until they could all get in. "How long has it been since she was released?"

"It was November so...about seven months?"

"Where is she now?"

"I couldn't tell you. But just so you know, she goes by Lynette Workman these days."

Was he giving her this information in case Nora were ever to try and contact her? "After getting busted for what she did, she didn't want to stick with her real name, huh? So she switched to her middle name and her maiden name?"

"I'm surprised you remember such small details."

It had been three and a half decades since she'd been a prisoner of the Skinners. But certain memories refused to fade. A particular sight or smell, even a specific sound, could bring various details back to her—many of them terrible. "You have to remember, I lived with them for one-third of my childhood. I knew them *well*. There are so many things I can't forget—and I've tried," she said flatly.

He took off his glasses and used his shirttail to clean them. "I'm sorry for what they put you through. Truly."

"Then why are you here?" she asked earnestly. "Why are you working for Nora?"

"I was reluctant to take the job, at first," he admitted as he put his glasses back on. "I felt you should be left in peace. But I work for Tammy, not Nora."

Mary jerked up straighter, as if someone had just kicked her in the back. *Tammy...* That was another name Mary tried never to think about, although for very different reasons. Remembering Jeff and Nora's daughter affected her worse than remembering Jeff and Nora, because it took her back to that locked basement and how hard it had been to take care of Autumn in those circumstances, especially once Autumn grew old enough to understand that the door at the top of the stairs led to freedom. Autumn would stand there and bang on the panel, hoping someone would either let them out or Tammy would come play.

But sometimes it wasn't Tammy who opened it; it was Nora. And Nora was so intensely jealous of both Autumn and Bailey, even though her selfish husband mostly ignored them when she was home, that she'd try to kick Autumn down the stairs or scream at them that they'd be punished if they didn't pipe down—then slam the door whether Autumn's hand was in the way or not.

Trying to get Autumn to stop climbing those stairs and to be quiet so that she didn't anger Nora took up most of Mary's day, when she wasn't upstairs cooking, cleaning or babysitting Tammy. It, more than anything else, even the rapes, frazzled her nerves, because she was afraid Nora would do something to seriously harm the child.

Mary was so grateful she'd been able to escape before Autumn was old enough to form permanent memories, and that her daughter didn't seem to recall anything of their time in the Skinners' home.

"I don't want to talk about Tammy."

She got up, grabbed her purse and was about to walk out when he said, "I'll tell her I couldn't find you, if you want. But you should at least hear me out."

She came to a stop. She didn't believe he'd really do her that favor. She feared he was merely trying to earn her trust. She'd had reporters employ all sorts of cheap tactics. But as much as she didn't want to hear what he had to say, she wondered if Tammy needed her, and she couldn't let Tammy down again. It was hard enough to live with walking away from her the first time.

Summoning strength from somewhere deep inside, she pivoted to face him. "It's Tammy who's looking for me?"

"Yes."

"Why?"

"She controls her parents' money."

"They still have money?" she asked skeptically. The Skinners had been wealthy when she'd known them. Their standing in the community and the facade of normalcy their money allowed them—which came from Jeff's family, not from any work he'd done—was part of the reason it took so long for her to be able to get away from them. But once she escaped, they'd both had to mount very expensive defenses. She'd figured that must've taken a lot of the money.

She could've filed a civil suit and tried to take the rest—several attorneys had approached her with an offer to help her do that—but she'd chosen not to pursue it. She'd preferred to leave it for their daughter, who'd been only thirteen at the time of their trial. Tammy hadn't done anything wrong; she deserved to receive *something* from her no-good parents.

"Yes. Quite a bit," he replied. "She wants you to have a portion of it."

She could tell he expected her to change her mind, but Mary shook her head. "No."

"You deserve it," he insisted. "Money can't fix what you went through, but it might make life easier for you as you get older."

"I don't want it," she said, even though she didn't have much in savings and needed to start thinking about what would sustain her in her golden years, just as he'd suggested. "I won't have anything to do with the Skinners, even Tammy. Tell her...tell her I'm sorry. That I always wanted her to have a good, happy life, and that...and that I hope she understands why I couldn't be part of it."

Eager to get away from him as soon as possible, so that she could once again start the arduous process of trying to forget that whole era of her life, she started to go, but he caught her arm. "Here, then. She told me to give you this," he said and thrust a letter into her hands.

"Mom went where?" Autumn said when she arrived at the bookstore shortly after lunch to find Mary gone.

Laurie sat at the computer they kept on a small desk in the back room. "Richmond."

This came as a complete surprise. "But…she doesn't like to travel. I can't even get her to come to Tampa."

"She'll go to Richmond now and then. It's relatively close, and she can drive there. Only takes two hours."

"But she doesn't do it unless she has to—to get something she can't get here or whatever. What's she after?"

"She had the chance to meet with another bookstore owner who has a coffee shop and wanted to pick her brain," she replied. "You know how worried she is about taking out this loan. She's just doing her homework."

Autumn put her purse on one of the empty shelves where they kept the special orders. "I'm glad she's being cautious. I'm just shocked she didn't tell me she had to go to Richmond. I would've come in earlier so that the two of you could go together."

Laurie didn't look up. If it made any sense at all, Autumn would've thought she was purposely avoiding eye contact. "I had too much to do here."

So much that Laurie couldn't have taken the morning off? "Then *I* could've driven her."

After a slight pause, Laurie said, "She probably didn't want to put you out."

Autumn scratched her head. She wasn't a friend or associate, she was Mary's *daughter.* Could that polite turn of phrase—putting her out—even apply to her?

Or maybe she was the one who was out of sync. After all, she hadn't slept well. She woke up every couple of hours, at which point she'd remember her exchange on Messenger with Quinn and wrestle with the old memories—the feel of the sagging couch they'd used in that tree house, the terrible heartbreak of seeing him with Sarah not long after, how he'd avert his gaze whenever he saw her from that point on.

He'd swum out into the ocean to save her a year later, when she'd faked drowning, but he'd treated her distantly, politely—

as if they'd never had sex. Those humiliating memories meandered through her mind but also something else—fresh desire, which, when she did go to sleep, caused such odd dreams. In one, she was making love to Nick only to look again and find that it was actually Quinn.

Those dreams had been as disturbing and unsettling as they were disjointed. And then, when morning finally came and she'd gotten up, she'd had to worry about whether Taylor's friend had been hurt by her own father.

Fortunately, that bit of drama resolved itself quickly. Although Taylor hadn't immediately responded to her texts, she had indicated when she brought the car back that Sierra was all right.

Still, Autumn would've made arrangements to drive her mother, if only she'd been asked. It was unlike Mary not to mention that she planned to leave town, simply because doing so was such a big deal to her. "I wouldn't have minded."

The bell went off in the store. Since Laurie was busy, Autumn went to see who'd come in, but she returned after Devlin Riggs, the pharmacist in town, purchased the latest legal thriller and left.

"Laurie?" she said when Laurie didn't look up as she leaned against the doorjamb.

"Yes?" Laurie replied, but not with any of her usual enthusiasm. For some reason, she seemed oddly subdued. Maybe she and Mary had had one of their rare arguments, and that was why Mary had left for Richmond alone, without saying anything about it.

"Is something wrong?"

Her aunt suddenly flashed her usual smile. "No, honey. Nothing's wrong. Why?"

"You're quiet today."

"Just…busy. The website needs to be updated, so I'm trying to send the changes over to Caden."

Caden had volunteered to update the website for them. He

was so savvy on a computer, could do almost anything. But Autumn didn't remember Laurie or her mother arranging a specific time with him. He'd already left for the day to be with his friends and probably wouldn't get to the updates until later this evening, so Autumn didn't see why Laurie would've stayed behind for that. "Did you tell him you needed him to do it right away?"

"No. I just thought I'd send them over while I had the chance," she said as she continued to type.

Updating the website wasn't an emergency, not if Caden wasn't even going to get to it right away. But...whatever. "Aunt Laurie?" she said again.

"Yes?"

"Would you mind taking a minute to answer a few questions?"

She seemed almost...wary when she said, "About what?"

"About my father."

Her fingers froze on the keys. "I'm afraid I don't know anything about him. I don't think I ever met him."

Autumn had been tempted to ask Laurie about her father before, many times. But she knew Mary wouldn't like her digging around in the past. Autumn didn't want to dredge up anything her mother preferred to forget, but she had a right to know *something* about the other half of her DNA, didn't she? Maybe her aunt could provide a detail or two. "But surely, as close as you and my mother have always been, she's mentioned him."

"Not very often," she insisted. "I'm so much older than your mother that...that I was married and raising Jacob when she got pregnant. We definitely weren't as close then as we are now. I do know that you have his hair and eye color, though. She's said that before."

She offered that last bit by way of consolation, but Autumn wasn't necessarily interested in what features she'd inherited from her father. She wanted to know who he was, if, perhaps, he'd changed, how he felt about her—if she had half siblings. "That's it?"

She cleared her throat. "There isn't much more I can tell you."

"Was it a…a married man? A school teacher who took advantage of her? A cousin or uncle? It has to be something terrible like that, doesn't it?"

"She doesn't like to talk about it, so I don't bring it up."

Autumn couldn't help noticing that Laurie didn't answer the overarching question. "I get the impression that *you* don't want to talk about it, either," she said, disappointed.

"It's not that," Laurie argued. "It's just…like I told you, I don't know a lot. All I know is that your mother was glad to have you and has always loved you more than life itself. That's what matters."

As nice as that was, Autumn had trouble letting the rest go. There were a lot of other things that should've mattered, too. "I'm surprised you're not angrier at whoever my father was for not contributing anything, financially or otherwise."

"Oh, trust me," she said, her voice suddenly bitter, "I hate him. But like I said, *you* came out of it, and we're grateful to have you."

Hate was a strong word. Laurie obviously had an opinion, which meant there was more she could say, and Autumn was tempted to keep pushing. She might have, except the door opened and her mother walked in.

"Hello," Mary said, splitting her gaze between them.

Autumn felt instantly guilty, as if she'd been caught doing something wrong. Maybe she should leave well enough alone. It hadn't been easy for her mother to raise her. Autumn owed her so much. And if her father wanted to be part of her life, he would've made some attempt to look her up, wouldn't he? That was her mother's position on the matter.

But what if he'd tried, and he couldn't find her?

She was so torn when it came to him, and had been since she

was a child. She kept shoving the curiosity away, but the older
she got, the more it plagued her—and it seemed to be worse
now that she was back home without Nick. She didn't know
where her husband was, and she couldn't find him. But maybe
it would be different with her father. She couldn't tolerate having two big question marks in her life.

"What are you two doing?" Mary asked.

No doubt she was wondering why one of them wasn't in the
front, watching over the store. "Nothing." Laurie went right
back to her work on the computer. "Just trying to get the website updates over to Caden."

Autumn checked out front to make sure they weren't neglecting any customers. She hadn't heard anyone come in, but she'd
been so caught up in the conversation she hadn't been paying
attention. "How was Richmond?" she asked once she was re-
assured the store was empty.

Her mother put her purse on the shelf next to Autumn's.
"Fine."

"Just fine?" Autumn said. "What'd you learn there?"

"I think adding the coffee shop is going to be a good thing."

"That's vague," she said, once again feeling there must be
something she was missing.

"It's a risk," her mother said. "Any investment is a risk."

But Mary didn't have to drive all the way to Richmond,
when she didn't like to leave town, just to learn that taking a
loan out to add a coffee shop to the store would be a risk. She
was already well aware of that.

"I ran into Chris when I stopped to get gas," her mother told
Laurie.

"What's he up to?" Laurie asked.

"Said he was going to pick up a special painting from the
framer. He spoke to Mike about the possibility of doing a community fundraiser for Beth—and got him to agree—so he plans
to auction it off."

Autumn's ears perked up at the mention of Quinn's parents.

"He talked Mike into a fundraiser?" Laurie swiveled around to face her. "He hasn't even told me."

"Sounded like he'd just come from The Daily Catch. I'm sure he'll tell you tonight."

"Did he say who's going to chair this fundraiser?" she asked.

Mary gave her a sheepish look. "My guess is he's hoping you will."

"Well, he's going to need more help than I can give him," she exclaimed. "We'll need a place to hold it. Someone to gather other items to put up for auction. Someone to set up and break down the room. Someone to be in charge of the food and drink. Someone to act as MC and auctioneer. Someone to promote and sell tickets. In other words, we'll need an army to pull this off. These things don't come together overnight."

"Most everyone here knows Beth," her mother said. "I doubt we'll have a hard time finding people to step up."

"Did he and Mike set a date?"

"I got the impression it needed to be sooner rather than later, that the Vanderbilts are struggling more than they care to admit. He mentioned a week from tomorrow."

"That's crazy!" Laurie cried. "We'll never make it." She consulted a calendar. "Besides, that's July third! Won't too many people be out of town for the holiday weekend?"

"He said he considered that but felt as though plenty of people would be *in* town to celebrate on the beach. And they might be feeling more festive and willing to help."

"I can help." Autumn almost couldn't believe it when those words came out of her mouth. She'd vowed to stay as far away from Quinn as possible. But this wasn't for him. It was for his mother, who was dying of cancer. How could she not step up when she had the time and, after running several school fundraisers over the years, the experience, too?

Mary reached out to touch her arm. "That's nice of you, honey. I'm sure the Vanderbilts will appreciate it."

"Helping someone else will be good for me." What would it hurt? She already spent her afternoons working for her mother and her aunt for no pay. She could organize this fundraiser before she came in or at night. "It'll be a lot of work," she added. "But we can manage a nice event if we pull together."

"So it'll be the three of us?" Laurie still looked a little shell-shocked and uncertain.

"And whoever else we can get to help," Mary said.

"Even if no one else will lend a hand, we'll make it happen," Autumn said, feeling more committed as she thought about it. Part of her was even eager for the challenge. It would be good to get back to doing something productive again.

"Okay. I'll start looking for a venue right now." Laurie clicked away from the list of website changes she'd been making to open a browser.

Autumn heard the bell again and went out to serve their new customer. The store was busy for the rest of the afternoon, but whenever there was a break in traffic, she spent a few minutes making a list of what had to be done for the event.

"I booked the Rotary Club building," Laurie announced a couple of hours later. "They normally charge two hundred dollars, but they've agreed to waive the fee for this."

Mary, who seemed even more distracted and reserved than Laurie had earlier, murmured, "That's wonderful. See? It's a start. We can do it."

Autumn hoped her mother was right.

She also hoped that throwing all of her time and energy into this event would keep her from obsessing about things that were better off forgotten.

11

Mary had been too afraid of what was in Tammy's letter to read it. She'd shoved it in her purse when she left Mr. Owens at Starbucks, then drove back to Sable Beach and worked the rest of the day like an automaton while trying to come to terms with the news that Nora was out of prison and that Tammy had something important enough to say to her that she'd hired a private investigator all these years later.

Don't let Nora's release throw you, Mary had admonished herself again and again. She'd expected Nora to get out one day; she could cope with that.

She hoped.

But this letter…

She sat on the lid of the toilet in the bathroom after everyone else went to bed and turned it over in her hands, staring at her name in what was presumably Tammy's handwriting. Depending on what the Skinners' daughter had to say, this letter could cut her more deeply than almost anything else, and Mary knew it.

Tammy had been only six when Mary was held captive in the Skinners' house, so Jeff and Nora would put Tammy in the locked basement where they kept Mary whenever they needed a babysitter. They couldn't give anyone else free rein of their home, considering what they were hiding, which meant Mary spent a lot of time with Tammy. And it was the love Tammy had given her as an innocent child that had sustained her through the darkest chapter of her life, which was why Mary felt so guilty for having left Tammy behind.

She winced as her mind carried her back to that first year she'd been kidnapped when she'd been chained to the toilet in the Skinner mansion—what Jeff and Nora did to her whenever she displeased them. One time she hadn't been allowed any food for two days, and if she wanted water, she had to drink it out of the toilet. Without question, it was one of the lowest points of her life—so low that she'd wanted to die.

But every so often, Tammy would sneak down and slip a piece of paper under the door—a crayon drawing of stars or hearts or flowers with the words "I love you" written in jagged, imperfect letters along the bottom—and those small gifts had made all the difference. Tammy even shoved a piece of bread under the door so that Mary could have something to eat. To this day, nothing had ever tasted so good.

A tear dropped onto her arm. Mary hadn't realized she was crying, but she didn't bother trying to hold back. She *couldn't* stop, even if she wanted to. Yes, Tammy belonged to Jeff and Nora, and Mary didn't want anything to do with them. But Tammy hadn't been treated much better than Mary. And then, at only thirteen, Tammy had lost both parents when Jeff and Nora went to prison.

Mary had known that would most likely mean Tammy would be put into foster care, which was why she beat herself up so often for not taking the girl with her. But she'd been only nineteen when she'd been faced with that decision, and she hadn't been allowed to go to school since she was kidnapped, so she had no education. She couldn't imagine how she was going to care for one child, let alone two.

Besides, she knew the Skinners would never truly be out of her life as long as Tammy was in it. They'd write to Tammy, or Tammy might want to write to them, and as soon as they got out, they'd try to contact her.

That was something Mary simply couldn't take on, so she'd left Tammy, changed her name, moved away and never looked back. She'd believed that was the only way she could recover and provide a decent life for her own daughter.

But what had her leaving cost Tammy?

She wasn't sure she could bear to find out.

Intending to flush the letter down the toilet—whatever she'd done, it was too late to change anything—she stood and lifted the lid. But she'd only torn it four times when she stopped. She should at least be brave enough to read what Tammy had gone to so much trouble to tell her, shouldn't she?

"Damn it," she whispered. "*Why?* Why did you have to write me?"

Maybe the letter was just to warn her that Nora was out and had changed her name. Or maybe it was about that offer of money Mr. Owens had mentioned.

It could be that innocuous.

Or it could be something else entirely. After so much time, Mary had no idea how Tammy had turned out. She could be as bad as her parents. Or maybe Nora was using Tammy to get in touch with her. Nora was *that* crazy. She'd always claimed she "loved" Mary.

Still, Mary couldn't bring herself to destroy the letter, couldn't hide it for fear someone else would come across it, especially while Taylor and Caden were living in the house, and she couldn't turn her back on Tammy again—not if Tammy needed her. This could be her only opportunity to right an old wrong.

Steeling herself for whatever the letter might say, she pulled the pieces of it out of the bits of envelope and arranged them like a jigsaw puzzle on the vanity.

Dear Bailey,

I've often wondered what I would say to you if I ever had the chance.

Well, this is my attempt to figure that out.

First of all, I'm sorry for what my parents did. I know those may feel like empty words, far too easy to say when nothing can change what you went through. But they're sincere. I've spent most of my life, to this point, anyway, trying to come to grips with the question that has burned uppermost in my mind—why. Why were my parents so evil when almost everyone else's parents are loving and kind? And why did such a mind-warping thing happen to you and me and not someone else?

Sadly, I don't have any answers. My therapist has helped me to understand that sometimes people simply make bad choices—or are inherently bad—and bring others pain. I was born to people who don't have a conscience, and that's just something I have to learn to live with. But I'll be honest—some days I manage better than others.

What I remember from when you lived at the house (which seemed normal to me at the time—shows you what a child can be conditioned to accept) is now a heartbreaking and recurring nightmare. I try to avoid thinking about it whenever possible, and yet, there are times when it comes back to me, and there's nothing I can do to stop it.

My life hasn't been easy. But I'm sure it hasn't been as hard as yours, which is why I've never felt quite right thinking that you and your daughter might be out there somewhere, struggling to get by, while I had the financial means—once I turned eighteen—to help.

I should've tried to find you years ago and would have, except I've never been confident that you'd want to hear from me. I hope this letter isn't too much of an unwelcome intrusion.

Regardless, I will always consider you my sister.

Love—Tammy King

Mary closed her eyes and let her breath go in a long exhale. Tammy didn't seem to blame her. And she sounded okay, as though she'd weathered the rest of her childhood in spite of its difficulty.

Opening her eyes, she read the letter several more times until she could look for what wasn't there, as well as what was. Was Tammy married? "King" would suggest she was, or had been. Or she'd changed her name to escape the stain of her parents' behavior and to duck the media, as Mary had done. And what about children? Did she have any? What kind of a relationship did she have with her parents? Had she stayed in touch? Had she seen Nora since Nora had been released?

Mary couldn't help wondering all of that and more. But now she was faced with the same decision she'd had to make back then. Did she defend the clean break she'd made from the Skinners? Or did she allow the past back into her life?

She didn't have an answer, couldn't possibly decide right now—not with Autumn and Caden and Taylor in town for the summer.

So she tore off the part of the letter where Tammy had written her phone number and flushed the rest down the toilet.

"You will always be a sister to me, too," she murmured. They were sisters of the heart, but Autumn and Tammy were half sisters by blood. That was another facet to the confusing and painful ordeal she'd endured—one that raised two very important questions: Did Tammy and Autumn deserve to know each other? Was she wrong to keep them apart?

She didn't know. But just reading the letter had opened the door to a relationship, which was why she'd been so reluctant to do it.

Having fun?

Taylor's heart jumped into her throat when Oliver's text came in. He'd interacted with her a bit on social media, liking the posts she'd put up on Instagram, many of which showed the beach, as well as the one she'd just added of her and Sierra looking badass in front of Sierra's father's motorcycle. But Oliver hadn't called or texted her directly in a couple of weeks. She got the impression he'd tried standing in the wings, waiting for word, but had run out of patience. He was eager to know if he could relax.

She couldn't blame him. She'd been on edge, too, ever since she left Tampa. But she didn't have anything to tell him. She hadn't started her period. As much as she'd prayed for an end to the worrying and waiting, she still didn't know if she was pregnant.

Or maybe she just didn't want to accept what the absence of her period meant. She wasn't as regular as most girls, so she'd been holding out hope that this was one of "those" months and there was still a chance life as she knew it would not be over.

Sierra, who'd heard the phone ding, had lifted the arm she'd been using to block the sun from her eyes and was watching Taylor curiously. "Who's that?"

"Oliver."

They'd been swimming in nothing but their bras and panties,

since they hadn't thought to bring swimsuits when they took off on the motorcycle, and were now lying in a hidden alcove where a lot of teenagers came on weekends to build a bonfire and party. They were drying off and enjoying the sun, surrounded only by their discarded clothes, random pieces of driftwood, seaweed and the occasional bird that hopped over to take a closer look. But just because they were alone right now didn't mean others wouldn't or couldn't come upon them, which was why Taylor kept checking the path that led to where they were.

Fortunately, they'd had no surprises so far.

"Oliver's that boy from back home?" Sierra asked. "The one you said wasn't your boyfriend?"

Taylor put her phone back inside the pocket of the cutoffs she'd kicked off earlier. She needed to figure out some way to buy a pregnancy test. She would've tried to get one by now, so she could at least *know*, but she was afraid the attempt alone would somehow lead to her mother or grandmother catching on. Where would she go to get one? And would she borrow her mother's car to get there? What if she was seen at the store when she'd said she was going to a friend's house? "He's *not* my boyfriend."

"Must want to be," Sierra said. "He keeps contacting you."

Could the jealousy in her voice mean Sierra didn't want her to be with anyone else? "He might. But it doesn't matter. I'm not into him."

Sierra leaned up on one elbow, completely unconcerned about being out in the open in nothing but her bra and thong. She was absolutely fearless—and that was one of the things Taylor found so intoxicating about her. Sierra was willing to take risks. She'd insisted they bring the motorcycle here, saying they could take the back roads and not be seen by more than a handful of people. And even though Taylor had tried to talk her out of it, she had to admit it had been exhilarating.

"Then what is it?" Sierra asked.

Taylor was afraid to say. There was no way to predict how Sierra would react. She was as passionate and intense as she was unique, and they'd been getting along so well, were having so much fun. Taylor didn't want to do anything that might bring it all to an end, not when she was finally starting to care about life again. "Nothing."

"It's obviously *something*," Sierra argued. "You look like you're about to throw up. What did he say?"

Taylor needed a few seconds to grapple with the lump rising in her throat.

"Tay?" Sierra pressed. "If he said something to upset you, I'll tell him to fuck off. Give me your phone."

Still trying to fight back tears, Taylor shook her head. She couldn't have Sierra yelling at Oliver. The pregnancy wasn't his fault—at least not entirely.

"Hey." Sierra softened her voice and shaded her eyes as Taylor got up and started putting on her clothes. "What is it? I've never seen you like this."

"I don't want to tell you," she said.

"Why not?"

"Because you won't like it."

For the first time, Sierra looked worried. "What's going on?"

Taylor pulled her tank top on over her head. "I can't say."

"Of course you can. You can tell me anything."

"Is that true?" she challenged. "*Really* true? You won't turn your back on me no matter what?"

Sierra got to her feet and started dusting the sand from her legs. Her movements were routine, casual, but the look in her eyes was not. "Isn't that what love is all about?"

Love. Taylor wasn't yet fully dressed, but she was too upset to be self-conscious anymore. As she sank back down onto the sand, part of her wanted to ask Sierra what kind of love she was talking about. The love of a good friend? Or the love of…

She didn't dare put a name to the other kind. "I think I'm pregnant," she blurted out.

With a gasp, Sierra dropped down beside her. *"What'd you say?"*

Nibbling nervously at her bottom lip, she stared out to sea. "You heard me."

Sierra didn't speak—just pulled one knee into her chest and locked her arms around it as she followed Taylor's gaze.

"Well?" Tay said at length, finally braving a glance over at her. "Aren't you going to tell me how stupid I am to have gotten myself into this mess?"

"Sounds like you're already being pretty hard on yourself. I don't need to pile on."

"I can't believe I did this," she said with a groan, letting her head fall back and talking to the sky.

"This Oliver—he's the father?" Sierra asked.

Grateful that she didn't sound mad, Taylor nodded.

"How old is he?"

"He's Caden's age."

She began smoothing the sand on either side of her. "How far along are you?"

"Maybe a month?"

"When are you going to tell your mother?"

Taylor winced at the thought of how badly the news would disappoint Autumn. Her mother had such high expectations for her, wanted both her and Caden to go to college and make something of themselves. "Not until I have to."

"Will she be angry? What will she say?"

"I have no idea. My grandmother got pregnant at sixteen and wasn't able to finish high school. She got her GED in her twenties, but she and my mom always point to that as an example of what *not* to do."

"You can still build a good life," Sierra insisted. "Your grandmother has. She owns the bookstore in town, doesn't she?"

"Only because she ran it for years as an employee, and when the previous owner retired, he worked out a special deal so that my grandma and my aunt could take over. Without his kindness and trust, it may never have happened. It's not like it was easy."

"Nothing worth having is ever easy."

Taylor didn't know how to respond to that. Sometimes Sierra said stuff that sounded like a much older person—like a parent.

"How'd it happen?" Sierra asked at length. "Didn't you use any protection?"

Taylor hung her head. "No."

"Why not, for God's sake?"

That was the question she'd asked herself most often. "I don't have a good answer."

"Then tell me whatever answer is the truth."

"I've never been interested in Oliver. I was just trying to hurt Caden."

"How would that hurt Caden?"

"Oliver's an ex-friend of his. He'd hate knowing I've been with him…like that."

"So you did it to spite your brother?"

"Not exactly. That's probably why I chose Oliver, but I had sex with him because I wanted to feel something, to care about something, to find the girl I used to be. After my father went missing, everything went on pause. And then, when day after day passed and nothing happened, it's almost like I was getting numb from the constant disappointment, like I didn't care about anything. My mother was working around the clock, trying to bring him home. She didn't see me anymore. It felt like no one did, like I'd become a ghost. I believed *I* could disappear, and no one would notice. I mean, it happened to my father."

"*You* noticed," Sierra pointed out.

"But me and my mom are about the only ones. The rest of the world—including Caden—has gone on as if nothing happened. The night I had sex with Oliver, I think I was trying to shock myself awake, to force myself back into the high school scene and my former life, to see if it would make me care about what every other girl our age cares about—boys."

Sierra didn't comment right away, and when she did, it wasn't to say she didn't care about boys, as Taylor had come to suspect. "I've seen how you are with your brother."

The call of a seagull sounded overhead as Taylor dug her toes deeper into the sand. "What do you mean by that?"

"You seem...angry with him."

She started to say she wasn't angry but decided not to bother trying to deny it. "Like I said, he was able to go on as if nothing happened, as if we never had a father to begin with."

"What other choice did he have?" Sierra asked.

Stating it that way made Taylor feel childish. She would never really want to hurt her brother, anyway, so what she'd done was just stupid all around. "None, I guess. Maybe I'm jealous because I couldn't handle it the same way. And now here I am without my period."

Sierra picked up a stick, which she used to poke at a piece of seaweed. "What will Caden say when he learns you're pregnant?"

Taylor breathed deeply, filling her lungs with the salty air. "I don't know, but I'm terrified he'll never be able to look at me the same way."

"Was Oliver your first?" Sierra tossed that strand of seaweed farther away from them using her stick.

There was no judgment in her voice. Taylor could tell she was only curious. "No. I had a boyfriend for a year and a half. He was my first." She nudged Sierra's bare foot with hers. "What about you?"

"I've never been with anyone."

"Really?" Taylor couldn't hide her surprise. It was Sierra who was old for her age. Sierra who was always pushing boundaries. How was she still a virgin? "What have you been waiting for?"

"The right person, I guess." She flung another strand of sea-weed toward the hill behind them. "So…"

"So what?" Taylor asked, leery of her change in tone.

"Do you want to keep the baby?"

Taylor wished she knew. "Do you think I should give it up?"

"Only you can answer that question." With a sigh, Sierra dropped the stick, stood and held out her hand. "Come on. Let's get dressed so we can go."

"Home?"

"To get a pregnancy test. From what you've said, it sounds like you haven't actually taken one."

"I haven't."

"Well, there's no need to go through this—making the de-cisions that will need to be made—until we know for sure."

Taylor accepted her hand. "You hate me now, don't you."

"Hate you?" Sierra made a sound that suggested Taylor didn't know anything. "I'm pretty sure what I feel is as far as you can get from that."

12

Uncle Chris had gotten permission from his pastor to hold a planning meeting at the local Baptist church, so Autumn had created flyers that she and Caden—Taylor was with her friend—handed out to local businesses all morning in an attempt to alert as many people as possible to both the fundraiser and the meeting this afternoon. She also stopped in to talk to John Karpinski at the newspaper to ask him to help spread the word. He said he and Monica would be sure to run a notice, but the next issue wouldn't come out for four days. He put both the meeting and the fundraiser on the paper's website right away, but Autumn doubted many people would see it, at least in time to come to the meeting. So her mother called the president of the Chamber of Commerce and asked her to email all the members, and Laurie contacted the other churches in the area and asked them to notify their parishioners.

At a quarter to four on Saturday afternoon, when she and Laurie left Mary to mind the store and headed over to the Baptist Church at Seabreeze and Main, she could only hope they'd find enough support there. Her mother, aunt and uncle—none of whom had ever done anything like this before—were going to need more help than what she could offer them.

"Thank God," she said to Laurie when she pulled into the parking lot and found it so full she had trouble locating a space.

Although Autumn had expected to work mostly behind the scenes and let Laurie take the lead—after all, it was Uncle Chris who'd started this whole thing—as soon as Laurie made sure the microphone was working, she announced that Autumn would be in charge and went to sit in the front row with her husband, who was already there.

Shoot, Autumn thought as she felt the responsibility settle on her shoulders. While it was both hopeful and comforting that there were so many people in attendance—it showed how quickly the citizens of Sable Beach could come together when necessary—she wasn't ready to chair the whole thing, especially because she didn't have very long to pull off such a big undertaking.

As soon as she opened her mouth to protest, however, she closed it again. *What the heck.* It would be easier to do the talking than to try to prompt Aunt Laurie. So she took a deep breath, got up and walked to the pulpit.

As she called the room to order and went over the details of what she intended to do, she began to grow more comfortable and more confident. She recognized many of the faces she saw. These were people she'd grown up with, and they'd come to help. Together they could certainly pull off a fabulous fundraiser for the Vanderbilts.

Michele Salls, who ran the PTA for the local elementary school, was one of the first to approach after Autumn finished her speech. Michele said she and Mrs. Vanderbilt were in the same church choir and that she wanted to do all she could, so she volunteered to handle ticket sales and offered up her husband, who was waiting politely behind her, as auctioneer.

"But I don't know how to talk that fast!" he said, perking up as soon as he heard his name.

"Then talk slow," she told him. "It doesn't matter—as long as you get people to raise their paddles."

His eyes widened. "And how am I supposed to do that?"

"You'll figure it out," she said confidently.

His jaw was slack when he turned to Autumn. "I've never done anything like that before in my life," he said, obviously expecting her to bring his wife to her senses. But until Autumn had someone to replace him, she wasn't going to let him off the hook. That was the job she was most afraid of having to take on herself.

"I'm sure you'll do fine," she said with an encouraging pat and felt slightly guilty for ignoring his distress as she moved on through the crowd.

She lined up Lisa and Anthony Hamill, who owned an Italian restaurant at the edge of town, to chair the food committee. Lynn Hill, a travel agent, volunteered to put together a small group of people to gather auction items. And Barbara Stamper, a widow who prepared almost everyone's taxes in town, agreed to handle the paperwork and bookkeeping. Past experience had taught Autumn that almost all fundraisers encountered a bottleneck at the end of the evening, when it came time for everyone to check out and pay, so she wanted to focus on streamlining that process.

But she couldn't talk to Barbara about it right now. There was a line in front of Lynn, so she went over to help while Laurie and Chris met with the Hamills about the menu.

Autumn was so busy she didn't notice that Quinn had entered the building until the meeting was over and almost everyone was gone. Laurie had left to grab dinner with Chris, and Autumn was talking to a few stragglers, who were offering additional help if she needed it, when she saw him standing at the back of the room.

The moment their eyes met, he shoved off the wall and came toward her but waited patiently until the others realized he was there. At that point, they greeted him and gave their condolences—"I'm so sorry about your mother... She'll get through this... She's a fighter..."—before the last one patted him on the back as they left.

"Thanks for doing this," he said, once they were alone. "I was surprised it was you, but after hearing you speak, I can tell you have some experience and we're in good hands."

She refused to acknowledge how wonderful he smelled—or how nicely the crab on The Daily Catch T-shirt he was wearing stretched across his chest. "No problem," she said. "You should've spoken up sooner. I would've let you say something."

"I didn't want to say anything. I only came so my father wouldn't feel as though he had to. He's grateful—don't get me wrong—but asking everyone to donate on our behalf..." He shoved his hands into the pockets of his well-worn jeans and hung his head. "Well, I'll be honest—it's a little humiliating."

"To him or to you?"

"To both of us," he admitted. "I wish we didn't need the help. But if one of us has to eat humble pie, I would rather it be me."

He obviously loved and respected his father very much. "I admire you for trying to make things easier on him—on both your parents. I know that's the reason you moved home. It might be the only reason you're staying. But the fundraiser will be over before you know it, and it'll be painless. You'll see. You and your father don't even have to come to the event, if you don't want to. I can make up some excuse—say you're both busy at the restaurant or something."

"You're suggesting I take the coward's way out?" he said, looking up with a crooked smile.

"Just giving you the option."

The levity left his face. "We would never skip it. We'll leave the restaurant to our employees that night so we can both be there. Mom will come, too, if she's feeling strong enough. We owe that much to those who are sacrificing for us. It's an awkward thing, that's all—taking money from others. I hate it."

In an attempt to make her words more convincing, she gripped his forearm. "It's okay to accept help once in a while, Quinn."

When his gaze lowered to her hand, she felt foolish for touching him. His skin was so warm and smooth. She'd been in love with her husband—*still* loved her husband, she corrected—but she'd never experienced the kind of sexual awareness she'd felt in high school whenever Quinn was around. And that hadn't changed, even after all the intervening years, which was why she needed to keep her distance.

Clearing her throat, she let go of him. "Sorry."

"For…"

She wasn't sure why she'd apologized. "I didn't mean to… you know…"

"No, I don't know," he said, watching her closely. "What?"

She was sorry for what she'd felt a second ago—sorry to Nick more than Quinn. But she couldn't say that. She was pretty sure Quinn already knew he had a strange effect on her, which was why he was pressing her to admit it. "Nothing. Never mind." She whirled around and started gathering up the notepads she'd used to collect information during the meeting.

He watched her for several seconds before he said, "You really won't go out with me?"

The nave suddenly seemed small and confining, as though the walls had started closing in on them. Eager to escape, she pulled her purse strap over her shoulder and grabbed her phone as well as the notepads. "I'm married, Quinn."

He lowered his voice. "I don't mean any disrespect, Autumn, but your husband has been missing for nineteen months. Surely… I mean…that's quite a while, isn't it?"

"That doesn't make it okay," she insisted.

"How long does he have to be gone before it *is* okay?" he asked.

That was a good question. Unfortunately, there was no instruction manual for what she was going through, no one to tell her when she was released from the obligation of waiting and could still feel good about herself if she started seeing other men. "I don't know."

He studied her so closely she felt herself flush under his scrutiny. "What?" she said.

"If I was someone else, would you go out with me?"

"Maybe."

"So it's not Nick."

"What difference does the reason make? You've never been interested in me, anyway."

"It's been twenty years since we were in high school. A lot has changed."

"I don't think attraction changes. You're either attracted to someone or you're not." She tried to go around him, but he cut her off.

"I don't believe that. I was already involved with someone else. That's all."

She glanced around. She hadn't seen Chris's pastor—Pastor Todd—since he'd told her he had a conference call in his office, but he had to be around somewhere. "Considering that this is such a small town, where everyone knows everyone else, it can be difficult to find a—" she whispered the next two words "—*sexual outlet* without a lot of complications. Considering how I acted before, I can understand why you might think I'd be a good candidate, especially because I'll only be here a couple more months. But as tempting as that arrangement might be, I'm not ready for that sort of thing."

"Sounds like you've put a lot of thought into it."

She didn't know how to respond to that.

"But I don't remember hitting you up for sex."

She should've been embarrassed. He was essentially saying she was presuming too much. But she laughed instead. "So you *still* don't want to have sex with me. Good to know that I was worried for nothing."

He caught her arm as she tried to go around him. "I didn't say that. If it happens, it happens. I admit I wouldn't be unhappy if it did, but that's not the only thing I'm after. Truth is, I can't help wondering if I missed out on something special—some*one* special. I haven't been able to quit thinking about you since your aunt called me out of the kitchen at the restaurant and you acted like you wanted to slip under the table rather than face me."

"I didn't want to bother you at work."

"You didn't want to see me at all," he said with a laugh.

"Because it would be easier on both of us if we avoided each other whenever possible."

He dipped his head to hold her gaze. "Or we could just start over—as friends."

Pastor Todd came out. He wasn't close enough to speak, but he was making his way toward them, and with how briskly he was tidying up as he went along, Autumn got the impression he was eager to say goodbye to her and get on with the rest of his night.

"Autumn?" Quinn prompted as she deliberated on what to do. "We can be friends, can't we?"

How could she say no to friendship? Feeling some pressure to wrap this up, out of courtesy to Pastor Todd, she put out her hand. "Here, give me your phone. I'll type in my number and… and maybe we can grab a drink sometime."

He grinned as he took the files from her. "How about I walk you out and we go tonight instead?"

"This can't be happening," Taylor said, sinking down onto the closed lid of the toilet. "My mother's going to kill me."

Sierra didn't speak right away. She studied the receptacle with the pink line that indicated Taylor was pregnant as if something might change. Then she spread out the instructions on the vanity and read them again.

"Well?" Taylor said, still awaiting her reaction. "Tell me we did something wrong—that the result isn't what it appears to be. *Please.*"

Sierra cast her a sympathetic glance. "We didn't do anything wrong. And the line's pretty clear. I'm sorry."

Could this be real? Why did I do this to myself? Taylor hunched over. She needed to get more blood to her brain so that she wouldn't pass out.

Sierra put a reassuring hand on her back. "Tay? You okay?"

"No. I want to kill myself," she mumbled.

Kneeling in front of her, Sierra insisted Taylor look at her. "That isn't funny, Tay. Don't *ever* say that again."

Considering what she'd just learned about her future, Taylor was shocked by Sierra's reaction. It was just an expression. But Sierra was especially sensitive to suicide—wouldn't watch any TV show or movie that dealt with it. "Okay. Forget I said it. I—I didn't mean it literally."

"It might be just a saying to you, but it's not to me." Sierra paused, as if considering whether she should say something else. Finally, she added, "My mother committed suicide, and I'm the one who found her."

Taylor let her forehead fall against Sierra's. "That's terrible," she whispered. "You know…you know I'm not really myself right now."

Sierra stood, as stoic as always. "It's fine," she said brusquely. "I was eight so it's not like it just happened. Just…don't say that. I know you're upset, but I can't hear you say that."

"I get it. Do you want to tell me what happened?"

"No. Definitely not. I don't like to think about it."

"Okay." They stared at each other for several seconds. Then

Taylor, her arms and legs weak and tingly, lifted the tester. "So what am I going to do about *this*?"

After picking it up to take one last look, Sierra tossed it in the trash.

"Wait," Taylor said, but didn't dare get up for fear she'd fall down. "Shouldn't we take that outside so your father won't see it?"

"He won't see it," she replied. "He rarely comes into my bathroom—unless I'm in trouble and he wants to yell at me. And I'm the one who takes out the trash."

It seemed as though Sierra did *all* the housework. But Taylor couldn't worry about that right now, either.

She was *pregnant*. P–R–E–G–N–A–N–T—as in, she was going to have a real, live baby in eight months or so, one that would be part of the rest of her life. "This must be a nightmare," she said. "I'm going to wake up and everything will be fine. And then I'll be so much more careful in the future."

Sierra slid down the wall until she was sitting cross-legged on the floor. "It's real, Tay. We have to face it and find some way to deal with it."

"How?" she cried.

"Are you going to keep it? Let's start there."

"I think I might have to. I don't know that I can live with any other choice."

"Even though you might not be the best person to raise this baby? Have you thought of that?"

"Yes, I've thought of that," Taylor spat. "But I'm the baby's mother, so of course I'm the best person to raise it. I'm almost eighteen. I'll be an adult by the time the baby's born. It's not like I'm fourteen or fifteen."

Sierra looked up. "But what about college? Where will you work? How will you support a child?"

"Once my mother gets over being mad, I think she'll help me so that I can graduate—maybe she'll even help a little longer, until I can get a job."

"When are you going to tell her?"

Tears began to streak down Taylor's face at the prospect of Autumn's disappointment. "Not until I'm starting to show."

"Why wait that long?" Sierra asked in apparent surprise.

"Because I might as well enjoy my last summer, right? As long as no one knows, life can go on as it's been so far."

Sierra nodded. "What about Oliver?"

Taylor picked up her phone and scrolled down to the last text Oliver had sent her. He'd been waiting and worrying, too. He deserved an answer.

But what if he told his parents? And what if his parents contacted her mother? Oliver had been over at the house plenty of times. His mom and her mom knew each other.

"I can't tell him," she said, setting her phone back on the vanity.

"You told him you would," she pointed out.

"That was when I still had some hope that the answer was no. He doesn't want to hear that he's going to be a father at seventeen. Why ruin *his* summer?"

"What's your other option?" Sierra hugged her knees to her chest. "Let him think you're not pregnant and then shock him with the truth when you go back to school?"

That didn't sound very fair. But wouldn't he rather have two more months to believe he had a bright future? "I don't know," she said. "I need to give myself a few days to figure it all out." She dropped her head into her hands. "God, I'm such an idiot— and now I am *so* screwed."

Sierra slid closer to her. "Hey, it's going to be okay."

"For you!" she snapped. "You're not the one who's going to have a baby."

"I'm sorry you're so upset. But…"

"What?" Taylor demanded.

"I'll be there for moral support during the pregnancy, even if we don't live near each other."

"Oh, thanks for that," she said sarcastically. "And once I have the baby and the real work begins?"

"We'll both be out of school."

"So?"

"I'll help."

"How? You live here, and I live in Florida."

"Like I said, we'll both be out of school. I could move there."

At this, Taylor sat up straight. "You'd move to Tampa?"

"Sure. Why not?"

"Because that's a big deal."

"Nothing will be holding me here, so I plan to go *somewhere*. Might as well be there."

Taylor dried her eyes. "But…where would you live?"

"We could get an apartment together and share the rent. Then I can help with the baby."

"I can't believe you'd even consider that." Taylor wiped her nose with the back of her hand. "What about college?"

"You have a community college where you live, don't you?"

"There's one that's not too far."

"Then we could both take some classes while we work and care for the baby. We could manage. Other women have done it, haven't they? And some have had to do it alone. At least we'd have each other."

Sierra was willing to stand by her despite the pregnancy? To help her with a child? "But…why would you do that?"

"Because I care about you," she said simply.

Taylor was so relieved she could've kissed Sierra. It felt wonderful to have someone say what she'd just said. Taylor realized then just how much she was coming to love Sierra.

But in what way?

"This place okay?" Quinn asked.

Autumn had insisted they drive all the way to Richmond for dinner. Even then she wasn't completely confident that no one would recognize them. As they waited to be seated, she kept looking around, searching the shadows as though she might see someone she knew—and cringed at the thought of her children learning she'd gone out with another man.

Quinn had done nothing to make her uncomfortable on the drive over. They'd chatted about his college years, his job as an engineer, the fact that he hoped to go back to that line of work eventually, the details of his mother's treatment and prognosis, the fundraiser, The Daily Catch, Autumn's kids and what she'd done over the years—all innocuous subjects she might discuss with any friend.

They avoided any mention of Nick. She didn't want to think of her husband while she was with Quinn, and she knew Quinn didn't want to remind her of him. But her attraction to Quinn made it difficult to feel as though she wasn't cheating.

"It's fine," she said. "Looks great."

He'd chosen a steakhouse, a small mom-and-pop establishment that had almost five hundred positive reviews on Yelp. But she wasn't overly concerned with the quality of the food— probably wouldn't even be able to taste it. She was just glad it was dim inside, lit almost exclusively by a candle on each table. The darkness helped her feel less conspicuous. The only thing she had to worry about now was what she was going to tell her mother when she got home late because they'd driven so far.

She was still mulling that over—she certainly wasn't going to tell anyone she'd been with Quinn—as the hostess led them to a little round table in the corner.

Quinn ordered a bottle of wine. The one he chose wasn't very expensive, but she guessed it would taste good. With his experience in the restaurant business, he knew a lot about that sort of thing.

"Oh, this is nice," she said as soon as she took her first sip, thinking she'd been right to trust him.

"So you're okay hanging out with me?" he asked, a teasing glint in his eyes.

Determined to play along until the night was over and then to ignore him if he ever tried to call her, she smiled. "I'm fine."

"Then why do you keep looking over your shoulder as if we're doing something wrong?"

Since he could see through her, anyway, she quit pretending she wasn't nervous. "You know why."

"I'm sure Nick wouldn't begrudge you having dinner with a friend."

"I doubt he would. But it might be a little hard to explain how that *friend* was the guy we always laughed about."

He reared back in surprise. "You laughed about me?"

"Actually, not you. *Me*," she clarified. "That day I shocked you in the tree house by stripping off my clothes is kind of a standing joke between us. My husband thinks…or thought… or *thinks*—"

"That…" he prompted.

"It's funny I would be so naive and stupid."

A muscle moved in his cheek. "It was never funny to me."

"Oh, come on. You and Sarah must've laughed about it, too."

"No. I never told her."

"Because she'd be upset? You two were broken up at the time, weren't you?"

"We were, but she was always insanely jealous. My being with you would've caused an epic fight, whether we were broken up or not."

"Then I can see why you wouldn't tell her."

He turned his wineglass by the stem. "That wasn't the reason."

Curious, she shifted in her seat. "Really? What was?"

He took another drink before meeting her gaze. "I'm not going to say."

"Because…"

"You wouldn't believe me even if I did."

He sounded serious. How could he have stopped himself from making fun of the dumb girl who'd followed him around like a lost puppy and then cornered him for sex in his tree house? "Well, I always knew it was too much to hope that you'd forget about it." She tipped her glass against his. "Here's to some of the ridiculous things we do when we're young."

He didn't drink to her toast. "Can I ask you a favor?"

She swallowed. "Maybe. What is it?"

"Can we not talk about that day anymore? Somehow I always end up feeling shitty when we do."

"You didn't do anything wrong," she said. "You were surprisingly patient and kind. *I* was the idiot. But we can forget it. Believe me, I hate it, too."

"There you go again," he said. "Is that the only way you can be my friend—by making sure I understand how much you regret that encounter?"

Fortunately, the waitress came to take their order, saving her from having to answer. She was glad for the reprieve, at first— was going to let it go. She told herself she didn't understand his reaction. But the longer she thought about it, the more she realized she *did* understand and he was right. She'd purposely been trying to cheapen the memory—to turn it into a joke—so that she wouldn't have to be so embarrassed.

After the waitress walked away, she took another sip of her wine while gathering the courage to be more honest. Then she said, "You're right. It was a big deal to me. It was my first time, and you were all I wanted in the world." She took an even bigger gulp of wine than before. "Is that better?"

A boyish grin curved his lips. "You didn't have to be quite *that* generous, but thank you. That day actually means a lot to me. It's the last simple, sweet thing I remember before everything went bad in my life."

He had to be referring to his relationship with Sarah, which must not have been as wonderful as Autumn had always assumed, even in the beginning. Was the stabbing merely the climax to many painful years? "I'm sorry to hear it was rough, especially for so long."

"Not your problem. I just don't want you to ruin that day."

"Okay," she said simply. "I won't."

The table was so small that his hand was already resting close enough to hers that with only a little movement he was able to slide his fingers between hers, disengage them and rethread them—over and over. He was barely touching her, and yet her whole body tingled from the contact.

"I've got to use the ladies' room," she said and scooted back so she could stand.

She forced herself to walk at a normal pace until she could get inside the bathroom and lock the door. Then she went to the sink and stared at herself in the mirror. "What are you doing?" she whispered.

But the only answer seemed to be Sarah's mother's churlish words, which swirled around in her head: *Fishing lures look awfully attractive to the poor fish they hook.*

Was he already reeling her in?

And, if so, what about Nick?

13

After making small talk throughout dinner and meticulously adding that day in the tree house to the subjects that were off-limits, there didn't seem to be much more to say on the drive home. To Autumn, it seemed as though they'd said all the inconsequential things they could think of to say, and now they were left with all the things they wouldn't or couldn't say.

And left with the attraction, of course, threatening to pull them together whether she wanted it or not.

"You tired?" he asked as they finally reached the outskirts of town.

Autumn wasn't remotely tired. She was completely wired and struggling against a natural inclination to drop her defenses and accept him as a real friend. He'd been nothing but nice. He'd never been anything else, even if he did choose another woman. But she was afraid their relationship would quickly escalate into something more if she did. She was too vulnerable right now—too lonely, too hungry for love, and sex was sometimes a good substitute. Even now she could feel the warmth of Quinn's body, which was weird since he sat a foot or more away. She'd been with plenty of other people in a car and had never noticed such a phenomenon before.

What was it about him?

She wished she knew—and she wished she could kill it. But that seemed impossible. "Not too bad," she said. "What about you?"

"I was up at dawn this morning, but I'm okay."

"What got you up so early?"

"I run at six. I like it when the beach is deserted and I can watch the sun come up all by myself. It feels like I'm standing on the edge of the world."

"It's beautiful to be out at that time of day."

"It is. With what's going on with my mother, having to witness my father's worry and grief and helping with the restaurant—even though I never wanted to work there again—running gives me an escape."

"It's what's carrying you through this difficult time."

"I guess you could say that."

"My daughter and I like to do yoga on the beach in the mornings," she volunteered. "But we're probably there after you're gone."

"What time do you go?"

"Not until eight-thirty. That's early to Taylor," she added with a grin.

He chuckled. "Of course. She's a teenager. I've usually had breakfast and am jumping in the shower by then."

Autumn had tried to pay for half of dinner, but Quinn had refused to let her. He'd said he owed her for all the work she was doing on the fundraiser, that even though he couldn't pay hundreds of thousands of dollars in medical bills for his mother, he could manage to buy her a meal—and she'd let him because she could tell it was important to him not to come off like a charity case.

But now she regretted giving in. That he'd asked her out,

driven and paid, made it so much harder to pretend that this hadn't been a date.

She checked her phone to see if Mr. Olynyk had sent her anything. This time of night was usually when they communicated. She hadn't heard from him since she'd agreed to continue his services for another month, but their contact had been dwindling as time marched on, and she didn't see an email from him tonight, either.

Maybe Nick wasn't coming back. She had to accept that. As Caden had said in the car, if he was coming back, he would've done it by now.

"Is that your mother or your kids, wondering where you are?" he asked when he noticed her looking at her phone.

"No."

"Will they be waiting up for you?"

She put her phone back in her purse. "Caden will probably be awake. But he won't be waiting for me. He'll be playing video games. And Taylor will be watching Netflix on her laptop in her room. My mother will be in bed, though. It's after eleven, and, like you, she's an early riser."

"How many bedrooms does that cottage have?"

She could tell he was surprised they could all fit. It didn't look very big, and it wasn't. "Only two. My mom has her room, Taylor takes my old room and Caden sleeps on the couch."

"Where do you sleep?"

"There's an apartment above the garage. I stay there."

"So you won't have to go into the house tonight."

"No."

He turned down the music playing on the radio. "You sound relieved."

"I am. If I go into the house, they'll ask me where I've been, and I'm not quite sure what I'm going to say."

He brought the car to a stop at the only light in town, which wasn't far from his family's restaurant, before turning toward the church where she'd left her car. "Will your mother and children be upset to find out you were with me?"

"I think they'll be…surprised."

"We're just friends, remember?" His grin suggested he was hoping he could sell her that again. It had neutralized her resistance before. But after having dinner with him, she knew better. She could never be *just friends* with Quinn. Even now, despite eighteen years of being married to someone else, she wanted him as badly as she had back then.

"I remember," she said wryly.

"You could say we were working on the fundraiser."

"Yeah. I think I'll go with that." Since her car was still at the church, it made sense. Both her mother and her children had texted her earlier in the evening, and Mary had tried to call, but Autumn had ignored them all. She felt as though putting some time between now and when she talked to them would be a good idea.

The church was dark and so was its parking lot, save one lone streetlamp.

"Thanks for dinner," she said as he pulled up next to her car.

"No problem." Her hand moved for the handle, but he caught her other arm.

"I'd like to see you again," he said.

She'd been planning to avoid him in the future, hadn't expected him to be so direct. It forced her to be direct, too. "I'm sorry. I don't think that's a good idea. I wish you well, though. I really do."

"I know that," he said.

She opened the door but he still hadn't let go of her. "Can I at least get your number? An occasional text or call wouldn't be too bad, would it?"

Except that it would invariably lead to more. "It wouldn't be *bad*. There's just no reason to start anything."

His eyebrows came together. "So…we live in the same town

again, and we both feel something. But instead of exploring that spark, instead of seeing if it might turn into something bigger, this is it? One dinner?"

"This is it," she confirmed, because cutting it off right now, at this very moment, was the only way she could justify doing what she'd been dying to do all evening. Leaving her door ajar so that she could make a quick escape, she turned in her seat, took his face in her hands and brought his mouth to hers.

The move seemed to startle him, and she could understand why. She'd been skittish, especially since they'd touched at the restaurant—careful not to even brush against him, if she could avoid it. But all of that effort had only made her fantasize about this—just one kiss before the night was through.

He quickly adapted, even bringing up his hand to gently touch her cheek before curling his fingers around her neck so that he could pull her in closer.

When he parted his lips to deepen the kiss, Autumn told herself to stop. She'd already gone further than she should have. She was a married woman! But she hadn't felt anything like this in so long. Her heart was nearly pounding out of her chest, and she wanted to taste him so badly she couldn't help meeting his tongue with her own.

He was obviously being careful not to overwhelm her, and she was trying to block out everything except the satisfaction she was feeling in this moment. But the kiss started to spiral out of control almost immediately, making her want even more of him, so she pulled away.

"Thanks again," she said, breathlessly, and got out.

"Mom's home. I just saw headlights in the drive," Taylor said to Caden.

He was seated on the couch playing an online game with some friends back home. He made friends wherever he went and had a ton of them. Taylor envied him his flexibility.

"She coming in?" he asked without taking his eyes off the screen.

Taylor switched to a different window, trying to get a better vantage point. "Doesn't look like it."

"She never texted me back tonight."

"She didn't text me, either—which is weird."

"Must've been busy," he said.

"Doing what?" she asked.

"Working on the fundraiser for that lady who's got cancer. I helped her hand out flyers this morning—when *you* were off with Sierra."

She heard the sour note in his voice. "Why'd you say it like that? You're mad because you had to do it and I didn't?"

"I'm not *mad*. It's just...you're *always* with Sierra."

"So? What's it to you?" she snapped, instantly defensive.

He set his controller aside—something he typically didn't do if he could avoid it. "Everyone's starting to talk about the two of you," he said.

A chill ran down her spine. "What are they saying?"

"They're wondering what you could be doing—spending so much time alone together."

"We go to the beach sometimes," she said. "We've seen you there. We even played volleyball with you two days ago."

"That was an hour out of the day. You played a couple of games and then you left. I texted you later to see if you wanted to get some pizza with us. You said no. I texted you the next night to see if you wanted to join us for a movie. We put up a sheet as a screen in Shawn and Adrienne's backyard, and his father used a projector to make it like a drive-in. It was cool. But you weren't interested. Heck, today we decided to build ice cream sundaes, and when I texted you, you said no to that, too. What could you be doing all the time with Sierra that's so great you don't care about missing everything else?"

She'd just learned she was pregnant when she received his

text about the sundaes and hadn't wanted anyone to see her red, blotchy face. She still hadn't come to terms with the fact that her body was no longer entirely her own, felt queasy whenever she thought of all the ramifications—like how she was going to tell Caden and Oliver and her mother and Mimi. "We've just been hanging out," she said, feeling too guilty to put up her usual fight.

He peered closer at her. "You don't like Sierra as more than a friend, do you?"

She caught her breath. "What do you mean? What made you ask me that?"

"Penn says he's pretty sure Sierra's into girls."

This was hitting Taylor at the worst possible time, especially because she didn't know how she would answer him—if she was even willing to. She'd never been attracted to another girl before, but Sierra was different.

What would she do if Sierra tried to kiss her?

She didn't think she'd mind. Did that make her a lesbian? She wasn't sure. She only knew that she loved who Sierra was, how Sierra handled life and how Sierra treated her. Not only was Sierra tough and smart and nice, she was also so much fun—a free spirit.

But Taylor couldn't explain all of that to Caden. That left it too open-ended, revealed how conflicted she was. In the split second she had to decide, she felt she had no choice except to deny it. Otherwise, she'd be labeled a lesbian whether she really was one or not. "I'm *not* gay," she said.

He seemed even more skeptical. "That didn't sound very convincing."

She hadn't been able to sell it, because *she* wasn't convinced. So the only thing she could do was deflect his questions until she could figure it out herself. In any case, whoever she loved was nobody else's business but her own. She didn't want him and his friends speculating on it. "If you must know what's going on…"

Her face or manner must've signaled that she was about to reveal something important, because he got up and came toward her. "What?"

"I'm pregnant," she whispered.

His jaw fell open. *"No..."*

Tears sprang to her eyes, and a fresh lump formed in her throat, making it impossible for her to squeeze out even a one-word response. She had to nod instead.

"Oh, my God," he whispered. "But...you haven't even been with anyone. Who's the father?"

She tried to speak and, again, couldn't.

"You haven't had a boyfriend since you broke up with Trevor last Christmas." He leaned down to catch her eye. "Is it Trevor's baby? Were you two still hooking up?"

Swallowing hard, she dashed a hand across both cheeks. "No," she managed to say.

"Who, then?"

She didn't want to tell him. She knew he'd be upset with her, which would only make the world feel more hostile. "I can't say."

"Why not?"

"Because you'll hate me."

"You're my sister. I hate you already," he joked.

When she didn't laugh, he sobered, too. "Come on. You can tell me. Of course I won't hate you."

"It was just a one-time thing, Caden. I—I don't even know why I did it."

"So..."

"You have to swear you won't tell anyone. I don't know what I'm going to do yet. Sierra's the only other person I've told."

"I won't tell anyone," he promised.

She wrung her hands. "Do I *have* to say who the father is? Or can you give me a few days to...to deal with my shit?"

"You're trembling," he said, shocked. "I've never seen you like this."

She was relieved by the compassion in his eyes. "Because I don't want to tell you."

"Come here." He pulled her into the first hug they'd shared—probably since they were little. "I'm your brother. We may fight, but I'm the one who will always be there for you."

"No matter what?" The warmth of his body felt good. Somehow, she was freezing in spite of the heat and humidity.

"No matter what," he confirmed.

Grateful she had a brother like him, she rested her forehead on his shoulder as she tried to stop shaking. "Does that mean you'll give me a few days to tell you the rest?"

"If that's what you need. Just…take a deep breath and calm down. You're scaring me."

Thank God he had a sensitive heart. Although she was jealous of how easily he seemed to sail through life, she could see why so many people loved him. She began to warm up and calm down—until he said, "We'll get through this. At least you're not a lesbian, right?"

She was pretty sure he was joking, that he was just trying to cheer her up. But it was comments like that one that told her what she'd face if she was.

14

She'd just kissed a man who wasn't Nick. And it had been surprisingly easy. The hard part was stopping.

Autumn stared at the family photograph that included her husband on her dresser. When he was around, she'd been so certain of who she was—Mrs. Nick Divac—what she wanted and where she was going in life.

At least…she'd been resigned to her current situation, had remained fully committed to the relationship even if their marriage had lost the sizzle that'd made it so much easier in the beginning. They'd had far too much going, what with the kids and the comfortable life they'd lived, to walk away from each other.

And now…everything had been turned on its head. The future she'd envisioned had changed without warning. But until she knew one way or the other, she still owed Nick her full loyalty, didn't she? So why couldn't she quit thinking of Quinn?

Shaking her head at her own behavior, she got undressed for bed. But just before she plugged in her phone to charge for the night, she noticed a text from an unknown number.

Just wanted you to know—that had to be the most incredible kiss I've ever had.

Who is this?

It had to be Quinn, but she hadn't provided her number. How had he reached her?

She received a selfie, proving it was indeed him.

Have you kissed anyone else tonight?
[[laughing emoji]]

She stretched the screen to make the image bigger, just because she liked looking at him—and couldn't help saving that picture to her photos. *That grin*, she thought with a chuckle. It looked rather boyish, which was endearing. How'd you get my number? she wrote.

You put it on the flyers you handed out this morning. ☺

She groaned. Of course. The whole town had her number now, because she was hoping they'd use it to contribute to the fundraiser.

If you had a flyer, why did you ask for my number?

I would rather you had given it to me. But since you didn't... I'm not too proud to get it where I can.

Nick seemed to be glaring at her from that picture across the room—and glancing over there wiped the smile from her face.

Quinn, I can't see you again.

You can't wait for Nick forever, Autumn.

I can at least hold off from dating until my kids
are out of the house.

That's two more years.

I know.

I'm good with kids. Give me a chance. I bet they'd
like me. ☺

I don't want them to think I'm trying to replace
their father.

It doesn't have to be like that, he wrote. We can take it slow.
As slow as you want.

After all these years, she had Quinn Vanderbilt wanting to
go out with her—but she couldn't.

Let's meet at the beach in the morning, he wrote.

At 6:00 a.m.? You're crazy!

We can be alone then—go running, swimming
or walking. Whatever you want. Then we'll grab
a bagel. If someone sees us, we'll say we're going
over the fundraiser. And you can be back before
Taylor and Caden even roll out of bed.

She looked at the time at the top of the screen.

It's midnight—six hours will be enough sleep for
you?

I won't be able to sleep tonight, anyway.

Because…

I can't stop thinking about you.

Autumn's pulse sped up. She'd been having a difficult time resisting him *before* he was this charming.

You never wanted me when we were in high school. What's changed?

I told you. I think I missed out on someone special. You'll be there in the morning, right?

She twisted her wedding ring around and around on her finger. Say yes, Autumn, he wrote when she didn't respond for several minutes.
"What do I do?" she muttered.

Where do you want to meet?

The lifeguard chair where I was sitting the day you almost drowned. I think it was when I was back for the summer my first year of college.

You know I faked that, right?

Yeah. [[laughing emoji]]

God, I loved you, she wrote. And I certainly didn't make a secret of it. [[rolling eyes emoji]]

I'm just hoping there's enough of that left. Good night.

Autumn read over their exchange four times before she finally set her phone aside. She hated the thought that by opening herself up to a relationship with Quinn, she'd be betraying Nick. Or that it might upset her children. They'd already been through so much. But just texting with Quinn made her feel good—young and attractive with prospects, instead of a tired mom weighed down for far too long with grief.

If she had the chance to find happiness again, shouldn't she take it?

At six, Autumn got up and put on her swimsuit—although she changed twice before she found the most flattering one. It had been a long time since she'd even considered how she might look in a bikini and was glad that, as rough as the past nineteen months had been, she hadn't gained any weight. If anything, she was thinner than she'd been before Nick went missing. But she hadn't worked out much and didn't think she'd be able to keep up with a man as fit as Quinn looked if they ended up going jogging.

She thought she might be able to swim with him, though. She was a much stronger swimmer than she'd let on that day she'd made him come into the water to haul her back to shore. She'd grown up playing in the ocean, had never been afraid of the sea.

Or they could walk. He'd made it sound as though he'd be satisfied with any one of the three.

She put on her shorts and pulled a sports tank on over her bikini, tied her hair up in a messy bun and washed her face and brushed her teeth before slipping her feet into her newest pair of sneakers.

Dawn was breaking. Streaks of bronze, yellow and orange bled across the sky in a watercolor-like haze. It was a beautiful sight, but it wasn't the reason she was excited to get out of the house. She'd slept only in fits and starts and had awakened before her alarm, at which point she'd simply looked at the picture Quinn had sent last night.

She was acting like the infatuated teenage girl who'd followed him around twenty years ago, she realized. She would've thought she'd have matured more than that. But those years felt like they'd passed in the blink of an eye, and she was still that young girl whose heart skipped a beat every time she encountered him.

She checked out her window to see if anyone was stirring in the house. Her mother would be up at six-thirty—seven at the latest—but didn't seem to be moving around quite yet.

Autumn breathed a sigh of relief. She didn't want her mother to see her go, even though she could say she went for a swim in the ocean, if Mary asked, and doubted it would seem strange.

Leaving her apartment unlocked, she headed down the stairs, moving as quietly as possible, and stepped out into the warm morning air. She'd be back before her kids were up. They wouldn't even miss her. And they certainly couldn't hear her leave, so she didn't know why she was being so careful. It wasn't as if she had to worry about the sound of the car. With the beach only a block away, there was no point in driving.

The humidity was already high, and her shirt was sticking to her by the time she stepped onto the sand. A dip in the ocean would feel nice, she thought, and smiled, feeling a burst of excitement as she made her way to the guard's station.

She could see Quinn leaning against the wooden frame, waiting for her. He was shirtless—wearing only a pair of swim trunks, which sat low on his lean hips, and some running shoes.

He spotted her before she could reach him and strode over to meet her. "You came. I was afraid you'd decide it was too early."

Without being obvious, she looked for the scars where Sarah had stabbed him. She'd expected them to be somewhere on his abdomen. But she didn't see anything—except a slightly more muscular chest than she remembered. "It *is* early. But you're right, it's nice out."

"Want to walk?"

"For a bit. Then we should get in the water."

They ambled down the beach for probably half a mile, chatting about the town they'd both grown up in, and old friends and other people they'd known in high school and where those people were now. Autumn eventually found the scars where Sarah had stabbed him on his back, which seemed weird. Had his wife attacked him when he was walking away? Or maybe when he was sleeping?

Autumn wanted to ask. But they were still being careful to avoid talking about Sarah and Nick, and for that Autumn was glad. They'd carved out this magical hour just for themselves; it was too precious to inject anything that might bring guilt or regret.

Quinn stopped near an alcove where they couldn't be seen from the parking area or main part of the beach. "You ready to get in?"

She pulled off her tank and shorts and dropped them on top of her shoes. Then she ran down the beach, trying to beat him into the water. Once he realized it was a race, he got rid of his own shoes and caught up with her easily enough, and they dove under the waves together so that they could get beyond the churning.

She set out for a rock outcropping she used to swim to when she was younger, where she would get out and soak up the sun away from all the tourists on the beach, and he followed, keeping pace with her. But that rock was much farther than she remembered, and she tired before she could get there.

"I didn't realize I was this out of shape," she complained as she stopped and started treading water so she could catch her breath.

"We can take a break," he said. "We're not in any hurry."

Putting her head back, she floated on the water, riding the swells.

"You're a good swimmer," he said.

"Better than I let on nineteen years ago," she responded with a laugh and, catching hold of his arm, tried to dunk him.

She managed to get him under water, but he just pulled her down with him. Then they started wrestling, trying to get the best of each other, and before long, Autumn was so exhausted she couldn't continue. That they were laughing didn't help.

"Stop. You're going to drown me," she joked.

Catching hold of her, he pulled her up against his chest to give her some support. "Don't worry, I'm a lifeguard, remember? I'll save you."

They both sobered as their gazes locked, and she got the feeling that somehow they'd save each other—that she'd needed this hour with Quinn and hadn't even known it.

"You're beautiful," he said. "You know that, right?"

Not as beautiful as he was, she thought, but she didn't say it. She just smiled and relaxed, letting him pull her with him toward the shore, until he could stand.

The coldness of the water contrasted sharply with the heat of his body. She wrapped her legs around his hips to battle the current, which threatened to tear them apart, and felt him grow hard—which created such an immediate and poignant desire to suddenly flare up she couldn't bring herself to stop him when he kissed her.

"I love the way you taste, the way you feel," he said, closing his eyes.

She broke off the kiss and told herself to stop right there. She'd already kissed him in the car as one last hurrah. But she didn't pull away. The next thing she knew, she was moving her mouth hungrily down his neck, licking the salt water off his skin, and what she felt—what she'd unleashed of her emotions—gained so much momentum so fast she feared this would soon get out of control.

"I haven't felt anything like this in so long." He lifted his hand to untie her top—and even though he looked at her to make sure she wouldn't mind, giving her the chance to stop him, she didn't. She wanted to lower his trunks and pull her bikini bottoms to the side so they could join their bodies, knew how wonderful that would feel. When he lifted her slightly and bent his head so he could take her nipple in his mouth, she felt so much pleasure she almost did it.

But then she thought of her kids—and that was like throwing a bucket of water on a fire. Drawing a deep breath, she stiffened. Then she slipped away from him so that she could retie her top before wading back to shore.

He followed, but more slowly. "I'm sorry if I spooked you," he said, coming out of the water while she was putting on her clothes. "I told myself I wouldn't do that. Things just seem to move a little faster at this age."

"It wasn't only you," she said. "It's been a long time since I've… Anyway, it's fine. Nothing to worry about." She'd caught herself. That was what mattered. "I have to get back. I'm afraid my kids will be getting up soon."

He flung his wet hair out of his face. "Can I come by the house later? Meet them?"

She tried to imagine what that would be like and couldn't. Taylor and Caden were too smart. They'd see right through her if she claimed he was just a friend. "Not yet."

"Maybe you could bring them to the restaurant then, and I could meet them that way. That wouldn't be too weird, would it? We did know each other growing up."

She couldn't imagine having Quinn around her children. What about Nick? Wouldn't that be disrespectful to what they'd established as a family?

In her mind, if she was going to see Quinn, she had to keep their relationship separate from her regular life, protect her children by preserving the chance to go back to the way things were, if she ever found her husband. "Maybe I can meet you here tomorrow morning. Text me if you want to do that, okay?" she said and grabbed her shoes before running barefoot down the beach.

Quinn was in the restaurant doing some food prep when Fiona Gable, who'd worked for his father since Quinn was a child, came into the kitchen.

"I have two cute kids out there who I'm pretty sure belong to Mary's daughter," she said. "What's her name? Autumn?"

Fiona was talking to his father, who was busy readying the prime rib they served only on Sundays for roasting so it would be ready for the dinner rush, but Quinn couldn't help overhearing—especially because anything to do with Autumn caught his attention.

"What are they doing here?" his father asked. "Do they want to see me?"

"Nope. They're just here to eat."

"By themselves? Or are they meeting their mother or grandmother?"

"I shouldn't have said *kids*, I guess. They're teenagers, plenty old enough to be at a restaurant on their own. I get the impression the boy is trying to take his sister out. He's being really sweet with her. But I heard him tell her he could only afford to get them each a bowl of soup and thought, with everything their mother is doing to raise money for us, you wouldn't mind if I gave them a little something extra to eat."

Raise money for us. Fiona had worked for his father for so long she was part of the family—like an aunt to him.

"Of course," Mike said. "Our crab sandwich is good. Maybe they'd like one of those."

"Maybe for the boy, but his sister doesn't care for seafood. She said something about it when she ordered the potato soup. I'll take her the pecan and blue cheese chopped salad, along with the soup."

"Sounds good to me," Mike said. "They might like the artichoke dip with corn chips, too."

"Good idea," she said.

"Here, I'll get it all ready and take it out," Quinn volunteered.

Fiona's eyebrows, which she painted on to match the stark black color she dyed her shoulder-length hair, slid up as she looked over at him. "*You're* going to wait on my table?"

"If you don't mind. Autumn and I were friends in high school," he explained. "I'd like to meet her kids."

His father watched as Quinn filled a plate with the chopped salad he'd made and put in the fridge not twenty minutes earlier. "They say the quickest way to a man's heart is through his stomach," Mike said. "For a woman, I'd have to say it's through her children, if she already has some. Smart move."

Folding her arms across her ample bosom, Fiona fluttered her fake eyelashes at him. "So our boy has finally found someone he'd like to date? This is a romantic interest we're talking about?"

He shouldn't have admitted to his father that he'd taken Autumn out last night, but when he got in, Mike had asked him where he'd been and he'd felt too old to lie to his dad about that sort of thing. He'd also been frustrated by the fact that Autumn felt she couldn't tell anyone they'd been together, so he'd done the exact opposite and been up-front. "I don't know yet," he said. "It's new—too new to call. I just want to meet her kids."

Fiona, who'd been a smoker as far back as Quinn could remember, gave a throaty laugh. "It might be new, but I haven't seen you get excited about anyone else."

He didn't say anything.

"No salacious info?" she said. "Then you can have the table for twenty dollars."

"Twenty dollars!" he echoed. "You think they'd tip you that much?"

"It's not about what they'd tip. It's about how badly you want the table," she said with a wink.

He rolled his eyes—then jumped when she slapped his ass as he walked by. He would've made a joke about sexual harassment in the workplace—they teased each other constantly—but he knew she wasn't making any sort of move on him. She was older than his father and a little eccentric, all part of her charm.

She told him which table it was and heated the dip while he

made Caden's sandwich. After they arranged everything on a tray, she let him carry it out.

The restaurant wasn't full quite yet—it always did a bigger dinner business than lunch business—so he spotted Autumn's kids easily enough. Autumn's daughter was a beautiful young girl with brown eyes and thick, dark hair that tumbled around her shoulders. Her son had the same color of eyes and hair and looked more like a man than a boy—with the beard growth he was starting to get. Caden was probably taller than Quinn was. "Hello," he said. "I'm Quinn. Your mother and I went to high school together."

The girl smiled politely but put up a hand when he started to unload the tray. "I'm sorry—this isn't our food," she said. "I just got the potato soup."

"And I got the clam chowder," Caden said.

"I know," Quinn told them. "This is on me."

"On you?" Taylor echoed uncertainly.

"My treat. There will be no bill to pay today."

"But we can't eat for free," Taylor said. "Our mother wouldn't want us to take advantage. She—she doesn't even know we're here. We just thought...well, Caden was craving some clam chowder, so we decided to come in and try yours."

"I'm glad you did," he said. "You're not taking advantage. We're grateful for your mother's help with the fundraiser, and this is our way of showing it."

"Oh!" Caden perked up at the idea that he might be able to accept, after all. "Thank you. This looks great. But...are you sure?"

Quinn couldn't help smiling. He'd always wanted to have children. Autumn was lucky to have these two. "I'm positive. If I took this back now that it's been out of the kitchen, I'd just have to throw it away. You might as well eat it."

"If you say so," Caden said, suddenly eager to oblige, and

pointed at the appetizer Quinn had just put in the middle of the table. "Is that the artichoke dip I saw on the menu?"

"It is."

"That looks so good. I'm excited to try it."

"Enjoy," he said and started to walk away, but Caden spoke again.

"What'd you say your name was?"

"Quinn. My father owns this place."

"He does?" He lowered his voice. "I'm sorry about your mother."

"Thank you."

"I helped pass out flyers," he said proudly. "That's how I know."

"I appreciate your help. Where's your mother right now? She won't be joining you today?"

"No, she's helping at the bookstore my grandma owns. I'll be going over there after this to work on their website."

"I see. Well, I'm glad you both came in. Are you missing Tampa?"

"Not really," Caden said. "I like it better here."

"What about you?" Quinn directed the same question to Autumn's daughter.

"I like it better here, too," she said, but she seemed self-conscious and more subdued than her brother.

"Good. Enjoy your lunch. And before you go, I have something I'd like to send to your mother, since you're going over to the bookstore, anyway. Would that be okay?"

"Sure," Caden said, and Quinn made himself leave them alone even though he wanted to talk longer. He was curious about what their father had been like, for one.

"So? What do you think?" his father asked as soon as he returned to the kitchen.

"They seem like good kids, definitely well behaved."

"Do you think Autumn will go out with you again?"

Quinn looked around to make sure Fiona wasn't close enough to hear, but she wasn't even in the kitchen. "Maybe, maybe not. It's a complicated situation."

"Because of her missing husband."

Quinn recalled holding Autumn in his arms while they were in the ocean this morning and how she allowed him to remove her bikini top. Just remembering sent a jolt of testosterone through him. But he hadn't mentioned that he'd met her earlier, and didn't plan to. "Yes. You can imagine how hard it must be for her. She doesn't even know if he's dead or alive."

"That would be rough, but she must be lonely by now."

Quinn guessed she was—lonely and confused. "I haven't wanted to consider this, but do you think it's creepy of me to move in on another man's family?"

"Not at all. Her husband's been gone a long time, hasn't he? If he isn't coming back, there's no point in waiting for him."

Problem was…after what'd happened this morning in the ocean, Quinn wasn't sure he'd be able to stop himself from trying to win Autumn over even if Nick hadn't been gone quite so long. "Yeah. That's what I keep telling myself."

"No doubt she can still use the love of a good man, a good life partner. This could be the best thing for both of you."

Quinn gave his father's arm a squeeze. "Thanks for telling me what I want to hear, Dad. You're always looking out for me," he said with a laugh.

"You deserve to be happy, too," he called out as Quinn went back to his workstation. "Lord knows you deserve a much better woman than the one you got the first time."

"Amen," Fiona said, hearing just the tail end of the conversation as she walked into the kitchen. "What'd I miss?"

15

"Hey, Mom, guess what?"

Autumn looked up from her laptop, startled when her son, a sack in one hand and his backpack slung over his shoulder, charged into the store. She was manning the register since Laurie had taken the day off to go with Chris to visit their son, who worked as an accountant in Norfolk and was happily married with three kids. Her mother was in the back going over the budget for the coffee shop, something Mary tinkered with constantly—added proof that she was worried about spending the money. "What is it?" she asked Caden.

"Taylor and I just ate at The Daily Catch, and the owner's son wouldn't let us pay for any of it! Not only that, he sent this to you."

As soon as Caden set the sack on the counter and she saw the familiar logo, she knew what it was—another piece of delicious carrot cake. "What were you doing at The Daily Catch?"

"I was craving some clam chowder, so I told Taylor I'd take her to lunch before I had to work on the website. But as soon as we sat down and ordered, this guy came out of the kitchen with a tray *full* of food. A crab sandwich. Chopped salad. Soups.

Some cheesy artichoke dip. It was awesome! He even brought us free sodas."

Autumn couldn't help cringing inside. "He didn't think I sent you in there expecting a free meal, did he?"

"No. He's just really grateful for what you're doing for his mother."

"He said that?"

"He did. Taylor told him we couldn't accept his offer, that you wouldn't like it, and he said he *wanted* to do it, that he was grateful for all the work you're putting in on the fundraiser. Isn't that cool?"

"Very nice," she agreed and peeked inside the sack. Sure enough, it was another piece of carrot cake. How was she going to refuse a guy who kept feeding her the best dessert in the world, especially when she wanted him even without the enticement?

She had to admit that she was weakening. What she'd done this morning proved that. What kind of a fair-weather wife was she? Since she'd gone into the ocean with Quinn this morning, she'd thought of little besides his mouth on her breast. She had so much to do on the fundraiser. And yet, just while she'd been sitting there, exchanging emails with her various committee members, she'd caught herself several times staring off into space. "So...you liked him?" she asked, hoping to sound far less invested than she really felt.

"Quinn Vanderbilt? Yeah." He poked the sack with his index finger. "That's cake. He brought Taylor and me each a big piece. Wait till you taste the frosting. Oh, my God—it's amazing."

She laughed. "I've had it before. Where's Taylor?"

"She was going to stop by and say hello, but Sierra called, so she went over there instead. She said to tell you she'll be home for dinner."

"Is she bringing Sierra with her?"

"I don't know," he said with a shrug. "Was she supposed to?"

"Not necessarily, but we've been here since school let out, and I have yet to meet her. I'll text Taylor to suggest it."

"I'd like to meet Sierra, too," Mary said, coming out from the back. "Maybe I'll make lasagna. Taylor loves my lasagna."

Autumn loved it, too. "That would be wonderful—" she started to respond but Caden cut her off.

"Oh, Mimi! That reminds me. I have something for you, too." He reached into his pocket and pulled out what looked like a business card. "The woman who was waiting on our table before Quinn took over said that this guy came into the restaurant recently and was asking about someone named Bailey North. She thought, with as long as you've lived in town, that you or Aunt Laurie might know who she is and how to find her."

Autumn took the card from him. She was going to pass it off to her mother but hesitated once she got a look at it. "Drake D. Owens," she read aloud. "It's a private investigator from Atlanta. Wonder what he wants with this Bailey person. Do you know her?" she asked, looking up.

Mary took the card and threw it away. "No. Unfortunately, I won't be able to help him."

"Shouldn't we check with Laurie before we get rid of that?" Autumn asked, surprised by her mother's quick dismissal of something that was a rather strange occurrence for Sable Beach. How many PIs did they get coming through town, trying to locate someone?

"If I don't know her, Laurie won't," Mary replied.

"You don't know *all* the same people, do you?"

"Most of them." She gestured toward the trash. "But here, give it back to me. I'll ask her."

Autumn dug the card out of the garbage. "Even if Laurie doesn't know her, maybe Chris does—or someone else." She looked back at Caden. "Did the waitress tell you what Mr. Owens wanted with this Bailey North?"

"Someone left her some money or something. It would be

a bummer to miss out on that, right?" Caden hefted his backpack higher. "But I'd better get started on the website. Shawn
and Adrienne want to go surfing later."

"Except it's Sunday, and you're going to be home for dinner, right?"

He made a face. "Of course."

"Laurie emailed you the list of changes. Did you get it?"
Mary asked.

"I did, but it'll be easier to show you as I get various things
done—to be sure I get it the way you want it. That's why I
came in."

"You're such a good kid," Mary said and smiled, but Autumn
got the impression that she was upset about something.

"Are you okay?" she asked, catching her mother by the elbow
before she could walk away.

"Me?" Mary pressed a hand to her chest. "Of course. What
makes you ask?"

"Nothing, I guess." She couldn't point to anything specific,
so she decided she must've imagined it.

Mary nodded and smiled in all the right places while talking about the website with her grandson but felt extremely distracted the whole time. She hated that another business card of
Drake D. Owens's had surfaced in town. How many others had
he left behind? And how determined would the citizens of Sable
Beach become in their attempts to help an unknown individual
get their inheritance?

She wanted to believe that most people would toss his card and
forget about him and his questions. But all it would take was one
Good Samaritan to try to do more. A simple Google search on
the name Bailey North would get people talking, wondering if
the woman he was searching for was the same girl who'd been
kidnapped by a wealthy young couple and used as a babysitter
and housekeeper, when the husband wasn't using her for more.

And once people realized he might be looking for *that* Bailey North, it could lead to someone remembering that Mary came to town shortly after Bailey escaped from her captors, would've been close to the same age and had been secretive and skittish for the first few years—until she started to trust that, with the Skinners behind bars, she was finally safe.

Mary didn't want anyone to even see Owens's card. Just having a private investigator poking around would raise curiosity in this sleepy beach town.

"How does that look for the events page?" Caden asked.

She focused on the screen. "I like it."

"Good. Laurie also wanted me to set up a better system for the news page. We can do that next."

"We want to be able to update it ourselves."

"I've been looking at other bookstores to see how they handle that sort of thing and found this site. What do you think of doing the announcements on a slide, the way they do?"

"That's attractive." Mary was grateful for Caden's help, but she was struggling to take in anything new. She was too worried about Mr. Owens and the number of cards he might've spread around town. Not to mention the letter he'd given her. Tammy wanted to reach her, to talk to her.

Maybe she should call. What the Skinners did wasn't Tammy's fault...

"Are you listening, Mimi?"

She jumped when he touched her arm. "What, dear?"

"You have to pay attention if you're going to learn how to update this page on your own. When I go back to school, I'll be busy. You won't want to wait for me to do it."

"You're right. I'm listening," she said, but she knew, even as he was going over it, that she'd probably forget immediately after. She tried to write down a few tips that would jog her memory. But once Caden left and Autumn went to a pedicure appointment, she went online to see how much information was still out there about Bailey North, what others would find if they tried the same thing.

A Wikipedia link came up first. It was difficult to read her own story—and even more difficult to look at the pictures that were posted of Jeff and Nora at their trials. They were beautiful and impeccably dressed, as always, but their youthful faces hid such diabolical and cruel minds. And the article glossed over so much.

For seven years she hadn't been allowed to go to a doctor or a dentist, hadn't been allowed to go to school, hadn't been allowed to leave the house—until the end, when they started trusting her. For the first six years, they locked her up in the basement, so that no one would know she was there, and they punished her if she ever did anything to displease them.

As she studied a picture of herself at twelve years old—the school picture that had been on all the flyers her maternal grandmother had circulated, trying to find her after she was taken—she felt a profound sense of loss. She'd been a mere child when Jeff had first raped her. And once she got pregnant and Nora could no longer pretend to believe Jeff wasn't having sex with her, Nora's jealousy had burned so bright. She'd been the crueler of the two, and that was saying a lot.

Closing her eyes, she leaned her head back, remembering how hard she'd tried to please the Skinners while she was with them, to find love even in that setting. That she could behave with anything other than contempt and loathing toward people who'd done what they'd done to her was the worst part of what she'd been through, because she felt as though she'd betrayed herself.

After she was rescued, the police and the media had grilled her, demanding to know why she hadn't tried to escape when she'd had the opportunity. They cited various instances toward the end when she was allowed to go to the grocery store or answer the door and yet hadn't tried to alert anyone.

But they didn't understand, *couldn't* understand, the toll those years had taken on her. How the Skinners had groomed and shaped her and how frightened she'd been that a failed escape would only make matters worse. Jeff had threatened to sell Autumn to a man who ran a sex-trafficking ring, said she'd never see her daughter again, and she'd believed him.

Psychologists talked about Stockholm Syndrome. She supposed that was a real thing, but for her it came down to survival and the old cliché, "The devil you know is better than the devil you don't." When she was finally rescued because of something Tammy said to a neighbor, Mary had been afraid to be set free. The grandmother who'd done so much for her had died while she was held captive, which left her with a mother who was on drugs and hadn't been capable of caring for her in the first place. Although she was nineteen at the time, old enough to be on her own, she'd had no idea how she'd get by and be able to provide for Autumn.

Of course the Wikipedia article mentioned that she could've gotten away, citing the various examples and making her feel, once again, as if she owned some responsibility in her own victimization.

Victim shaming. She'd experienced it, even though she'd been only twelve when she was taken. That was largely why she didn't want to be reminded of anything to do with those years. They were bad enough without making her feel she was to blame for any of it. Why didn't she run? they'd asked—over and over. That was all they'd wanted to discuss, other than the dirty details of the abuse she'd suffered.

She checked several other links, enough to learn that there was still plenty of information out there about her kidnapping. Some of the more in-depth news stories even mentioned her drug-addicted mother and the various men who'd temporarily served as her stepfather—sometimes for only a handful of months, if that long. Like the man who'd sired her, they'd been addicts, too. Who else would be able to put up with a mother like hers? She'd called so many men "Daddy" in her young life that she couldn't even remember the names that went with some of the faces.

A wave of sadness rolled over her as she read one article that reported her beloved grandmother's death. Grandma Lillian had provided what little stability Mary had known in those early years only to die not knowing where her granddaughter was.

Mary desperately wished Lillian had lived long enough to meet Autumn. Autumn was worth every sacrifice. The love she'd felt for her daughter had somehow carried her through.

But she could say that about Tammy, too.

Pulling her phone out of her pocket, she went down her list of contacts until she located the record she'd created for the Skinners' daughter. No last name. Just Tammy.

She stared at the number for several minutes. Then she checked the time: 6:00. Finally. She could close the store.

She went out and turned the sign, locked the door and lowered the blinds on the front windows. Then she locked the back door, just in case Laurie or Autumn came back, and stood, because she was far too nervous to sit, as she sent the call.

The phone rang three times. "Hello?"

A female voice had answered. Was it Tammy? It'd been so long that Mary couldn't say she recognized the voice. But Tammy was an adult now; she wouldn't sound remotely the same.

"Hello?" the woman said again. "Is anyone there?"

Mary had blocked her number. She told herself to answer and identify herself. Tammy couldn't call back; she was safe.

But she didn't feel safe. She gripped the phone so tightly the edges were cutting into the palm of her hand.

"Hello? Please answer."

Telling herself she was just having a reaction to the trauma she'd been through, she opened her mouth to force the words that were jammed up in her throat. But before she could, Tammy lowered her voice. "Bailey? Is it you?" she asked, and the panic became so palpable that Mary hung up.

Taylor wasn't sure how to approach the subject she wanted to talk about. She and Sierra could discuss most things, and it all came naturally—flowed as if they'd known each other their whole lives.

But this subject seemed entirely off-limits. She was afraid just bringing it up could ruin the special bond that was forming between them. She was beginning to care about life again, to get over the loss of her father and reclaim her relationships with her brother and mother and Mimi. Even the pregnancy didn't seem as terrible as she'd initially thought it would be.

Because of Sierra.

"I like the name Leila for a girl. What do you think?" Sierra asked.

They both had their laptops and were in Sierra's room, sitting on her bed. *Bread* was playing on a phonograph, the shiny vinyl spinning under the needle on the nightstand next to her, so she could change albums once it ended. It could be a pain to do that—it was so easy to stream music instead—but Sierra didn't mind, and Taylor enjoyed the throwback.

While they listened and Sierra tossed out baby names she found on various websites, Taylor was looking at baby clothes and accessories, something that got her excited about the baby and took away some of the worry she felt—mostly when she contemplated telling her mother and Mimi.

"That's pretty," Taylor said. "I like L names. Lacy would be good, too." She turned her computer to show Sierra a pretty quilt. "If it's a girl, I'd love to have this. Isn't it awesome?"

Sierra peered closer at it. "It's expensive."

"Maybe Mimi will get it for my baby shower."

"Maybe. It's silver and pink? Are those the colors you'd like for the nursery?"

"I haven't decided. I just think it's cute."

"It is cute."

Taylor slanted her a look. "You're okay with pink?"

"Why wouldn't I be?" Sierra asked.

Taylor leaned against the headboard. "You don't seem like a pink kind of person." She was sort of hoping Sierra would use the comment as an opportunity to declare her sexuality. She didn't typically like feminine things, always chose darker colors, bolder and higher-risk activities. Taylor was driving herself mad, looking for clues, wondering, trying to guess.

"I'm not into pink, but you are," Sierra said. "And I like you."

As usual, there was nothing definite there. Taylor almost pressed the issue by asking, "How much do you like me—and in what way?" Sierra had made that comment at the beach, where she'd said that what she felt was as far as she could get from hate. But Taylor was afraid to take that too seriously. Sierra hadn't mentioned anything like that since.

Her phone buzzed with a text.

"That Oliver again?" Sierra asked.

"No. Thank goodness. I feel guilty not telling him about the baby."

"Since you've got to go through the pregnancy, labor and delivery, you deserve some time to get used to the idea and make certain decisions before you talk to him."

"You don't think that's too selfish?"

"Nope. It won't change anything on his end if you tell him later, will it?"

"I guess not." Her phone still in her hand, Taylor read the text again. "It's my mother. She wants me to invite you over for dinner. My grandmother is going to make lasagna."

Taylor had been hesitant to let her family meet Sierra. But the more Taylor got to know Sierra, the more she wanted Sierra to meet the people she loved, and the more she trusted the people she loved to see the goodness she saw.

Ironically, as she became more open to it, Sierra seemed to become almost...reluctant. She always suggested they go to her house or the beach or somewhere else—anywhere else. She hadn't even been willing to stop in at the bookstore.

Was it because she didn't want to meet Taylor's mother and grandmother?

"Probably not," Sierra said. "I can't eat lasagna. It's got meat and cheese."

"My grandma could use substitutes. You told me there's a great sausage substitute that you get when you're really craving meat."

"There is, but I should make dinner for my dad. Nights generally go better if there's a hot meal waiting for him when he gets home."

It was Sunday, so Taylor knew he wasn't at work. Sierra had said he was out with a friend, looking at motorcycles in Richmond. "You don't mind cooking for him?"

"Not really. He doesn't have a lot of good things in his life. If I cook, he's less likely to go out drinking."

"But he's in Richmond. How do you know he'll even come home for supper?"

Sierra studied her for a moment. The skeptical expression on her face suggested she was about to offer up another excuse—but suddenly that expression cleared. "I guess I don't. Okay. If you think it's a good idea, I'll come."

"Why wouldn't it be a good idea?"

"I'm not sure your family will like me."

"Of course they'll like you. Caden already does."

Sierra shook her head. "Not anymore. He'll hardly speak to me."

"He's just jealous that I'm spending so much time with you and not hanging out with him anymore."

"Is that why he took you to lunch today?"

Taylor hadn't mentioned to Sierra that she'd told her brother about the baby. Maybe this was the perfect lead-in to what she wanted to talk about. She could say her brother had asked about the nature of their relationship, and she wasn't sure how to answer. Maybe Sierra would clarify how she felt, and deny the suggestion that she was gay.

But once again, Taylor chickened out. As much as she wanted to discuss it, wanted to *know*, she was afraid to find out. "Yeah."

"What did you two talk about?"

"I told him about the baby."

Sierra got off the bed. "Are you kidding? Why didn't you say anything about that when you first got here? How'd he react? He won't narc on you to your mother, will he?"

"No, he would never do that. He took it well, so it was okay, especially because I haven't told him everything."

"What do you mean?"

"I haven't told him that Oliver is the father."

"How'd you avoid that?"

"I asked him for some time to deal with the news before I get into the details. Right now he's so blown away that he's respecting my wishes and just trying to be supportive."

"That's nice."

"He's a good brother," she admitted. But she wasn't sure they'd be able to maintain their current peace. She'd let him believe she wasn't gay, allowed him to make that assumption. And she wasn't totally convinced it was true. She'd never felt this way about anyone before, was afraid she was falling in love for the first time—and it was with a girl. "So will you come tonight?"

Sierra closed her laptop and put it on her desk. "If you really want me to."

16

Taylor watched her mother's face as she introduced Sierra, searching for clues to her reaction. She wasn't afraid Autumn would be rude. She knew her mother would be nice no matter what. But she didn't want her to be polite for politeness's sake. She wanted her to be open to getting to know Sierra, to truly like her.

"I've heard so much about you," her mother said. "Taylor has really enjoyed finding such a good friend."

Was she put off by Sierra's piercings? Judging Sierra, or her father, assuming he let her get the tattoo? Taylor wished Sierra had worn long sleeves. But it was so hot and humid that would've looked ridiculous. The air conditioner could barely keep up.

"I've enjoyed getting to know her, too," Sierra said.

Mimi stepped out of the kitchen, where she'd been making her lasagna with sausage and cheese substitutes, and a little bit of eggplant, so that Sierra could eat it. Taylor could tell it was almost done by the smell, which permeated the whole house. "So this is Sierra! It's really nice to meet you. Taylor talks about you all the time. How do you do?"

"I'm great." Sierra held out her hand, and Mimi smiled as she clasped it between hers instead of shaking it.

"I hope you're hungry because I've made a lot of food."

"It smells delicious."

Sierra acted uncomfortable, which took Taylor by surprise. She always seemed so cool in any situation. If someone didn't like her, she'd just as soon flip them off and walk away as try to change their mind. But she didn't have that attitude tonight.

"Hey, Sierra." Caden turned off the gaming console and got up from the couch. "Penn said he saw you driving a motorcycle the other day. I didn't know you had a bike."

Sierra hesitated as though she knew this probably wasn't a good subject to bring up in front of parents. Caden could be sort of clueless sometimes.

"It's my dad's," Sierra explained. "He forgot his lunch and said I could bring it over to him on the bike."

Caden whistled in apparent envy. "Man, I'd *love* to have a bike."

"No way," Mimi said. "Don't even think about it."

Taylor sent him a warning glance, trying to get him to change the subject, but he was looking at Sierra.

"Do you have a motorcycle license?"

"I have a Class M designation on my license, so I went through the training," Sierra said, obviously trying to make it sound better. "And I don't ride very far. Usually, I just take the back roads."

Although Taylor had been on the bike with Sierra several times, Sierra didn't mention it. Taylor had known at the time that her mother and grandmother wouldn't approve. But that was part of the thrill of doing it.

"It's still dangerous," Mimi insisted.

"I'm sure she's a good driver or her father wouldn't allow it," Autumn said, the slight edge to her voice stopping Mimi, who was scared of everything, from going on and on about it. "What can I get you to drink, Sierra?"

Sierra accepted a Coke and, as they got dinner on the table

and sat down to eat, answered about a zillion questions—about where she was born, where she'd lived in the past, what brought her and her father to Sable Beach, what her father did for a living. Taylor was relieved that no one asked about Sierra's mother. Taylor had already told them that Sierra's mother wasn't part of her life, so she was grateful they didn't put her on the spot.

"Where do you plan to go to college?" Autumn asked as they finished eating.

"I'm not sure yet." Sierra nudged Taylor under the table with her foot—a reassurance, Taylor supposed, about moving in together and going to a community college in Tampa.

Mimi began to collect the dirty plates. "What are your favorite subjects in school?"

"I like art, so I'm thinking about graphic design. Something I can do from my home. You know, run my own business."

"It's always nice to be your own boss," Autumn said. "But won't it be hard to find customers?"

"Not necessarily," Sierra said. "There's a lot of demand for that type of work, and I could get jobs online. Places like Upworks. That sort of thing."

Autumn smiled. "Sounds like you're savvy enough to get it all figured out."

"I hope so."

Taylor watched her mother carefully. Had that comment been sincere? Did she like Sierra?

They ate vegan brownies for dessert, and the conversation finally veered away from Sierra. Caden talked about how cool it was of Quinn Vanderbilt to give them a free lunch at The Daily Catch, Sierra asked about the coffee shop Mimi was adding to her bookstore—something Taylor had tipped her off would be a good subject—and Autumn talked about the fundraiser.

After dinner, Sierra stayed to watch a movie. Caden joined them, but Autumn and Mimi were busy working on the fundraiser at the kitchen table. They didn't seem to be paying them any attention, but as soon as the movie ended, Taylor could tell Sierra was eager to go. "I'm pretty tired," she said. "I'd better head home."

"Okay."

Everyone said goodbye and told her they were glad she'd come. She said she was grateful for the invite and the food was delicious, and Taylor walked her out.

"Are you okay?" Taylor asked as they reached Sierra's father's car, parked in front of the house. He'd let her take it, saying that if he needed to go out tonight he could use the bike. Taylor was beginning to see that Mr. Lambert wasn't *all* bad. He had his shortcomings, but as Sierra had once said, at least he'd stuck by her and taken care of the basics—like making sure she had a roof over her head, food to eat and clothes to wear.

"I'm fine," she replied, but Taylor got the impression that she hadn't truly enjoyed herself.

"You didn't like meeting my family?"

She got into the driver's seat and started the engine so she could roll down the window before closing the door. "I think your family's awesome."

Taylor bent down, resting her elbows on the window ledge. "Then what's wrong?"

"Nothing."

"I can tell there is," Taylor insisted. "Why won't you just tell me?"

Sierra nibbled on her bottom lip as she stared through the windshield, in the direction of the beach.

"We can tell each other anything, remember?" Taylor said.

"You're very lucky. Your family loves you so much."

"I know. I love them, too. Why is that a problem?"

She sighed. "Because I think I've been fooling myself all along."

Taylor toed a rock in the gravel. "In what way?"

"I'll never fit in with you, with them. I might as well face it."

"What are you talking about? You don't have to fit in. People need to accept you as you are, and that includes my family."

"That's a nice thing to say, but that isn't always how it works—not when…not when you care."

"I'm confused. Care about what?"

Sierra put the car in Reverse. "If I care about you, I have to care about them—whether they like me or feel I'm good enough for you or whatever."

Taylor straightened and let go of the window ledge. "You're good enough for anyone, the best person I've ever met. Where's this coming from?"

"You honestly don't understand what I'm saying? I'm different, Taylor. Whether you want to acknowledge it or not, they can already see it. And they won't want you to be different like me," she said and drove off.

The sun was just lifting its sleepy head over the Atlantic as Quinn waited at the lifeguard station.

Would Autumn show up this morning?

He'd tried talking himself out of texting her last night. After wrestling with the temptation for a couple of hours, he'd decided to back off and leave her alone. She wasn't in a good position to start a relationship. She'd said as much. And although he wanted to be with her, and had already pursued her, the truth was, neither was he.

As terrible as it was to watch his mother suffer and to know that he could lose her in the next few months, at least he was free of the intense and emotionally draining outbursts that had characterized his twenty something years with Sarah. He didn't have to deal with any more screaming matches, no one throwing objects into a TV screen or window, no one showing up and embarrassing him at his office, no one demanding more than he could give.

But he was closing in on forty, he'd always wanted a family

and there was something about Autumn he found hard to resist. It wasn't her beauty, although he thought she was even prettier now than she'd been in high school. It was her steadiness, her normalcy. She'd lost her husband in the past couple of years, and while the mystery of it had no doubt been difficult, it hadn't broken her. She seemed strong yet vulnerable and open in spite of it all, and that was an intoxicating combination, especially for someone who'd dealt with an unstable spouse. His ex would go from laughing one second to screaming obscenities at him in the next. And the fact that he couldn't make her happy no matter how hard he tried had left him feeling frustrated and helpless. The more she accused him of not loving her, the more difficult it became to convince her that he did—until they were locked in a terrible cycle, one in which her words eventually became a self-fulfilling prophecy.

In the end, Quinn had grown so weary of her unceasing demands for more and more proof of his love and loyalty—to the point that she demanded he give up his friends, family and other interests and remain devoted solely to her—he could no longer stay in the marriage. So although it was true that he hadn't had an affair, he'd been planning to leave Sarah, had been looking for a way out. And she could sense him slipping away. *That* was the "betrayal" that had precipitated the stabbing.

A figure appeared, walking toward him from the direction he'd been looking for Autumn.

She'd come.

A spike of excitement and pure happiness—emotions he hadn't felt in a long while—shattered his misgivings. He had only an hour to spend with her; he wasn't going to let anything ruin it.

He walked out to meet her and felt his smile widen as she looked up at him. When she smiled back, he could tell she was feeling at least some of the same things he was.

He held out his hand.

She bit her lip, and he caught his breath while he waited for her to decide whether to accept it. He understood why she hesitated. He was forcing her to make a difficult decision. Holding his hand as they walked down the beach was different than a hormone-fueled kiss in the car or the ocean. It was even different than having sex, if they were only in it for the physical pleasure and release. He was asking her to be open to the possibility of letting him become more than just a friend, and they both knew it.

"Autumn," he said finally. "If Nick *truly* loved you, and I have no doubt he did, he wouldn't want you to be alone—not if there was someone who would be good to you."

As he watched a tear roll down her cheek, his stomach sank. He thought she was going to refuse him. But she wiped that tear away and slipped her fingers through his.

He lifted her hand to kiss her knuckles. "I won't rush you," he said. "We'll take it day by day, see where it goes. There's no pressure."

"I'm not ready for my mother or my kids to know that...that I'm seeing someone," she said.

"I understand. It'll be the best-kept secret in Sable Beach."

"It's not easy to keep a secret in this town. If we manage, it'll be the *only* secret in Sable Beach," she joked.

Quinn laughed, but then they walked in silence until they reached the place where they'd stopped to go swimming yesterday.

"Thanks for feeding Caden and Taylor lunch at the restaurant," she said. "I wasn't even aware that they were there. I certainly didn't send them to The Daily Catch expecting—"

"I know you'd never do that," he broke in and sat down, facing the sunrise. When she sat beside him, he offered her his hand again and felt gratified when she took it more readily and scooted closer to him. "I was happy that they were there. I understand that you'd like to keep them separate from me—in case this thing between us doesn't work out or whatever. Then our relationship doesn't impact their lives, too. But I was happy I had the chance to at least meet them."

She watched as he moved his thumb over hers. "They were shocked that you would cover their lunch—and bring out all that extra food."

"They have no clue I have a thing for their mom."

Autumn glanced up. "Are we crazy for trying this?"

He knew what she was talking about. "I think we'd be crazy not to."

She nodded and faced the sunrise. "So? What did you think? Did you like Caden and Taylor?"

"I did. They were exactly what I thought they'd be—great kids. You're lucky to have them."

Letting go, she began building up a pile of sand in front of her. "You never wanted children?"

"I did, but—" he nudged a crab, causing it to burrow deeper into the sand "—we couldn't."

Quinn could tell she didn't want to be rude enough to ask, so he volunteered the answer to what she had to be wondering. "Sarah had infertility issues."

"Oh, I had no idea—of course. I'm sorry."

"I haven't told anyone except my parents. I didn't want her to be embarrassed or feel...less than."

"That's thoughtful of you."

"It was also a little selfish," he admitted. "I didn't want to make my own situation any worse. I think not being able to conceive was a big part of her unhappiness." He'd been disappointed, too. But he'd been so busy trying to convince her he didn't mind that he could never admit it.

"That would be hard for someone who wants a family. Did you ever consider adoption?"

"*I* wanted to adopt. I tried talking to her about it several times. But she refused, said it was too much of a gamble—that we could end up with a demon child. And if I tried to push the issue, she'd assume that I wasn't happy the way we were—that she wasn't enough for me—and it would start a fight."

"I know things went bad at the end. But…were you *ever* happy in your marriage?"

He thought back to the beginning. It hadn't been so terrible then. "Our marriage was going along pretty good until we started trying to have a family."

"I see." She lifted a fresh handful of sand and let it run through her fingers, building her pile that much higher. "So…would you like to have a child at this stage of life? I mean, if you find the right woman?"

He nudged her. "Are you checking to see what you might be getting into?"

Her eyebrows slid up. "My youngest is sixteen, Quinn. That would be a big decision."

"Stop thinking so far down the road. You wouldn't have to have my baby. That isn't a prerequisite to what I hope will happen between us." Unable to resist any longer, he pressed her back onto the sand, pinning her beneath him. "But I wouldn't complain if you wanted to."

He expected her to say that she couldn't make any promises. He'd said he'd take things slow. Talking about having a baby together was *not* taking it slow. Wanting to peel her clothes off right now wasn't taking it slow, either. Even if she couldn't feel the pounding of his heart, he had no doubt she could feel his erection. But she didn't shove him off. Their gazes locked for several seconds. Then she said, "It feels like I've been in love with you my whole life. How am I supposed to resist that?"

The relief and excitement that poured through him made him both weak and strong at the same time. He'd never experienced such a strange but heady sensation. "I hope you won't even try," he said and lowered his head to kiss her.

Autumn was making love with a man who wasn't her husband on the beach. Her top was pushed up, her shorts and swimsuit bottoms had been kicked aside, and Quinn's lower body was between her legs.

She'd never done anything like this in a public place. There was no one else around, but still. Nick had been far too proper for public displays of emotion, let alone touching her in a more sexual way outside their bedroom. As a matter of fact, toward the end he'd become so preoccupied with his work that they'd often go a week or longer without any intimacy at all. She needed this. She wanted this. But part of her was horrified that she could be reckless enough to ignore propriety. She wasn't a teenager anymore.

Briefly, she thought of stopping, but it was far too late for that. She was completely carried away, drunk on desire, and she already knew she'd never forget this experience—Quinn's soft T-shirt beneath her serving as their only scrap of blanket, the briny scent of the sea filling her nostrils with every breath, the waves rushing up to curl around their ankles.

And Quinn, of course, who was no longer a boy.

As much as she'd allowed Nick to make fun of what she'd done that day in Quinn's tree house, it was still one of her all-time favorite memories. But this second experience was on an entirely new level. This time Quinn was fully engaged and making it clear how badly he wanted her. Since he'd been only half-interested before, she felt a small sense of victory. But at the same time, she knew she'd lost the battle she'd been waging against herself, that she'd severed one of the last ties that bound her to Nick: her fidelity.

As she tilted her head to give Quinn better access to the sensitive skin below her ear, she wondered if she'd regret what she was doing. Was she destroying something precious? She'd always considered her marriage to be sacrosanct, had never imagined it coming to an end via an act of desire for another man, especially on a beach in her hometown. On some level, she still loved her husband.

But Nick was becoming part of the past—a memory that was fading—and Quinn was alive and well and capable of touching her, laughing with her, sharing the here and now.

She closed her eyes as he pressed more deeply inside her, reveling in the satisfaction it gave her while letting her hands move over him, feeling the contours of the muscles that contracted beneath the smooth skin of his arms and shoulders and back. She wanted to memorize every detail, just in case this was the only time they'd be together like this before regular life intervened and tore them apart. She didn't trust what was happening; it was too good to last.

"Are you okay?" he asked, his breath hoarse.

Their lovemaking had escalated so quickly that she could understand why he'd be uncertain. It had only been a few minutes since he first kissed her. But the second she'd tasted him, she'd known she didn't stand a chance against the rush of desire that overwhelmed her. She'd slid her arms around his neck, fisted her hands in his hair and deepened the kiss herself, allowing it to turn hungry and demanding, and the clothes had come off from there.

The last thing she wanted him to do was stop.

"I'm good," she gasped. "This is…good."

The white of his teeth flashed in a grin. "Thank God," he muttered.

She tried to laugh but didn't have the breath for it.

"We'll go slow after this," he joked, referring to what he'd said earlier, and again she tried to laugh.

"Just make me forget," she said as the tension began to build, promising an incredible release. "Make me forget *everything.*"

When she said that, he surprised her by pausing to smooth the hair out of her eyes. "There's nothing to forget, Autumn," he said. "You're not doing anything wrong, and I'm not out to take anything away from you, to ruin what you had with Nick.

I just want you to trust that what we could have together might
be just as good."

    After that, he became singularly intent on proving to her that
she certainly wouldn't be missing out on anything in the bedroom. And when he was done, she had to admit—he'd turned
her into a believer.

17

The first thing Autumn saw when she got home was Nick's rain boots in the corner of the apartment. She stared at them for a long time, battling a sudden upwelling of guilt, despair and uncertainty. What had she done? She'd had a wonderful, intimate experience with another man, after which they'd both dressed and sat side by side on the beach to watch the rest of a gorgeous sunrise. She'd felt so close to Quinn. There'd been nothing cheap or tawdry about what they'd done. Their love-making had been moving and intense and hopeful—promising. It had made her feel as though there was new life and happiness ahead, in spite of everything.

But had she just been unfaithful to her husband?

As other evidences of Nick's existence and his rightful place in her life began to jump out at her—his business books and legal tomes next to her novels on the shelves, the picture of their family on the dresser and the knowledge that the drawers in that same dresser held his shorts, T-shirts, socks and underwear, which she'd washed and folded countless times—she wondered what she was going to do.

She couldn't stop seeing Quinn. It felt as though they belonged together.

Grabbing her cell phone, which she'd put on the nightstand when she left because she was afraid her children might randomly check on "Where's my iPhone" and know she wasn't home, she called Mr. Olynyk using WhatsApp.

"Alo."

"This is…this is Autumn Divac."

He switched to English. "Of course."

WhatsApp had, no doubt, already announced her identity. "I haven't heard from you in a few weeks, and I… I thought I'd check in, see how things are going."

"I am afraid I do not have much to report, Mrs. Divac. I am sorry."

After making love with Quinn on the beach she didn't know whether to be disappointed, as usual, or relieved. That was how torn she felt between the man with whom she'd had two children and the boy she seemed to be falling in love with all over again. "That friend you mentioned before, the one you said might've seen my husband several months ago. Did you ever speak with him?"

"I did. He led me to another man who is part of the Azov battalion near Travneve, a small town along the eastern border. This other man believes he spoke with your husband almost eighteen months ago—in the fall, so not long after Nick arrived in this part of the world."

Her stomach tightened into knots. What did she hope to learn? Did she want evidence that would indicate Nick was alive and might still be coming back? Or did she want proof that he wouldn't?

That she could even consider the second question made her feel terrible—intensely disloyal—not only to Nick but also to her children, both of whom wanted and needed their father back.

She stretched her neck, trying to cope with the stress. "And?"

"He said your husband was asking about weapons he believed might have come from Rostov."

Rostov was a military base in Russia. She knew that much from the research she'd already done. Only thirty miles from the Russian border, it had been in the news before. "That's where the Russians used to train separatist fighters."

"I believe they are still doing that. But they are so focused on getting the European Union to ease the sanctions that are crippling their economy they must be very careful."

"Does either of the men you spoke to have any idea where Nick might have gone after he visited Travneve?"

"No. And I cannot find anyone who does. My associate has been circulating Nick's picture along the border towns, since that was where he was last seen, but so far no one has come forward with any new information."

There'd been over 13,000 killed since the conflict began. *So many people. Was Nick one of them?*

"It's almost July," she said.

"Yes. What would you like me to do?"

When he'd called her before, she'd told him June would be her final month.

Closing her eyes, she let her head drop back—and heard the door open downstairs. Someone was coming.

"Just through June," she reiterated quickly, and hung up as her daughter came into the room.

"You're awake already?" Taylor asked, obviously surprised to see her up and fully dressed.

Autumn hadn't stripped off her swimsuit since returning from the beach. It was dry because she and Quinn hadn't gone in the water—they'd been more intent on remaining joined, if only by their hands, while watching the sunrise. She was pretty sure they'd both been surprised by the intensity of their lovemaking and how close they felt afterward. They'd hardly spoken a word when it was over—just enjoyed the companionship they'd both been missing lately. "I was thinking about going for a swim. But since you're up, we could go to the beach and do yoga instead, if you'd like."

A frown tugged at Taylor's lips and creased her forehead. "I don't think so. Not this morning. I didn't sleep well."

With her own words to Mr. Olynyk still echoing in her ears— *only through June*—Autumn sat on the bed and patted the spot next to her. She'd effectively cut off the search for Nick, and Taylor and Caden didn't know it. Maybe she should've discussed it with them first. Asked for their input. They were all part of the same family and had a stake in Nick's coming home, too. "Come here. Is there something wrong?"

Taylor looked troubled when she said, "Did you like Sierra?"

"I did," Autumn replied and meant it. "She seems smart, savvy, nice. And she looks out for you. I saw her take the last bit of lasagna on her own plate and then slide it over to you. She said she was too full when she gave it to you, but I was watching her. I think she was protecting it to be sure you got enough, since it's your favorite meal. That was pretty special, proof of how devoted she is to you."

"Yeah, I noticed that, too."

"That had to have felt pretty nice. We could all use someone looking out for us, right?"

"It is nice," she admitted. Autumn finally saw a small smile appear on her daughter's face—but it slipped away as she sobered again and said, "Have you ever had a friend like that?"

"A best friend? Sure. I still keep in touch with some of the girls I knew in high school and college, but I married young and had you right away, and when my focus changed, we drifted apart. It's hard to keep up with long-distance relationships, especially once everyone gets on with their life and everything gets so busy." She bent her head to catch her daughter's eye. "Why? What's going on? Don't tell me you and Sierra had a fight."

"No. We aren't fighting. She just said something that's sort of bothering me."

"Last night at dinner? What was it?"

"It was after dinner, when I walked her out. She said that she was different, and that you could tell."

"Well, I noticed the tattoo and the piercings right away."

"So you didn't like them."

"I'd want you to wait until you were older to make those kinds of decisions, but I've never believed that sort of self-expression means a person's *bad* in any way."

Taylor stared down at her hands while digging at her cuticles. "What if it's not just the piercings and the tattoo?"

She'd lowered her voice, but fortunately, Autumn was still able to hear. "What do you mean?"

"I think she might be…you know…not like most other girls."

"You're saying she's different in more than the way she looks?"

She nodded. "I—I think she might be…into girls."

"A lesbian."

"I can't say for sure," she said quickly. "She hasn't come right out and said that. I just… I think maybe that's the case and wonder what you'd think if she was."

"Well, let me ask you—do you believe people choose their sexuality?"

"No. But even if some do, I don't think it's anyone else's business."

"Neither do I."

"So you wouldn't care if Sierra was a lesbian."

Autumn struggled to choose the right words. This obviously meant a great deal to her daughter. "I'll tell you what's important to me."

Taylor pulled back the curtain of her hair, tucking it behind her ears so that she could see. "What's that?"

"Is Sierra a good person?"

Taylor began to blink quickly, which led Autumn to believe
she was fighting tears. "She's the best person I've ever known."

"Then she must be a great friend."

Taylor nodded. After a sniff, the sheen of tears in her eyes
disappeared, and she seemed much happier. "What if *I* get a tattoo?" she asked.

"Before you're eighteen, you mean?"

"This summer."

Autumn put an arm around her daughter and gave her a
squeeze. "*That* I might have a problem with," she said, and they
both laughed.

Mary was manning the register when the phone rang at the
store. Autumn hadn't arrived yet, but Laurie was rearranging
the back room to make space for a large shipment they were
expecting this afternoon.

"Beach Front Books," Mary answered.

"Is this…is this Mary Langford?"

Her heart skipped a beat. It was a woman, and she was fairly
certain she recognized the voice. But she couldn't believe what
her brain was telling her. She thought she was just being para-
noid. So she answered. "Yes…"

"This is Tammy."

Mary almost dropped the phone. She'd blocked her number
when she called the Skinners' daughter, but Tammy wasn't calling her cell. She was calling the store, which meant Drake D.
Owens had lied when he'd said he'd protect her identity. Not
only had he given Tammy her assumed name, he'd told Tammy
where she worked, and it made sense—after all, Tammy had
paid him to find her.

"Please…don't hang up," Tammy said when Mary hesitated.

Mary glanced over her shoulder. She didn't want to have this
conversation, not with Laurie around. She told Laurie almost
everything, and she would probably tell her about this, too, but

later, once she'd had a chance to process it herself—not when she was filled with panic that everything she'd worked so hard to protect was now compromised.

"I—I don't mean you any harm," Tammy said. "I'd like to talk. I miss you. I've missed you so much."

Mary's chest and throat tightened.

"I can't even imagine what you must be feeling right now," Tammy rushed on. "What my parents did to you was…unthinkable, unforgiveable. I can completely understand why you might not want to hear from me. But no one else could ever even begin to understand what my childhood was like. And I loved Autumn so much. She's my half sister, the only flesh and blood I've got, really, and yet I haven't seen her since she was three. I would be so grateful if we could change that—if I could see you both again. I feel as though you're my only real family."

Laurie came out from the back and froze the moment she saw Mary. "What is it? You look like you've seen a ghost."

The three patrons they had in the store looked up, causing Mary to force a smile. "Nothing. Everything's fine. It's just… I have someone on the phone who wants an old, collectible book and…and we don't carry that type of thing."

"Did you tell him about that company online? They might have it. What's the title of the book he's looking for?"

"I told him to try Abe's," she said, purposefully using the wrong pronoun since Laurie had already assumed it was a man. "I'll do some checking on this end, too," she said into the phone, "and get back to you if…if anything changes."

"I'm sorry if I called at a bad time," Tammy said. "I didn't want to frighten or upset you—"

"I'll see what I can find," Mary interrupted and hung up.

Laurie was watching as Heather Mannefort brought a stack of romance novels to the counter.

"Did you find everything you need?" Mary asked, trying to keep her voice even.

"I hope so," Heather replied. "Even if I didn't, I'd better play it safe and stop here. My husband bought me one of those e-readers so that he won't have to build any more bookshelves—he says we're swimming in books as it is—but I love the feel and smell of a real book, don't you? I can't seem to make the switch."

"I've always been partial to print books." Mary's smile was probably a bit *too* bright as she rang up Heather's purchases, proof that she was trying hard to compensate for something. Laurie knew her so well; no doubt she could tell. But right after Heather checked out, two other customers approached the register, and rather than continue waiting, Laurie went back to work, which gave Mary a chance to recover before having to explain what was going on.

As soon as they were alone, it didn't take Laurie long to re-appear at the register. "That was the private investigator, wasn't it?" she said.

Mary shook her head.

"Who, then?"

"It was Tammy."

Laurie's jaw dropped. "And you hung up on her?"

Mary burst into tears. She hadn't even felt them coming, had thought she'd managed to subdue the emotions that'd slammed into her the moment she realized she had Tammy on the line. But the memory of Tammy's words, the supplication in her voice, left Mary shaken and upset. "I didn't know what else to do," she admitted.

Laurie brought her in for a hug. "Are you going to be okay?"

Mary nodded as she pulled away. "I want to call her back." She had no idea where it might lead. But she couldn't reject her.

Tammy was as innocent in what had happened as she was.

18

Taylor finally found Sierra in her father's garage, working on the motorcycle, which she had up on a stand. It was as hot and humid as Sable Beach ever got, and yet she was wearing a pair of tattered Converse sneakers, distressed jeans with holes in both knees and a loose-fitting Whitey's Garage T-shirt, all of which were smeared with motor oil. "What are you doing?"

Sierra grabbed a rag to wipe her hands, which were covered with grease. There was even a smudge on her cheek. "Told my dad I'd change the oil in the bike today."

"You know how to do that?"

She shrugged. "It's not hard. I've been doing it since I was twelve."

"I rang the bell at the house twice."

She removed the funnel, careful not to let any oil drip across the floor as she laid it on a piece of cardboard. "Didn't hear it."

"What about your phone? I've been trying to call you, too. And I sent a text."

She wiped the sweat rolling down from her temple. "Sorry. Don't have my phone out here."

From what Taylor could see, that was true. The question was,

why not? They typically saw each other every day. Other than
what Sierra had said before she'd left last night, Taylor had no
reason to believe this morning would be any different. "Are
you upset?"

"With you? No."

Taylor wasn't sure she could believe that. She dragged over a
stool and perched on it while Sierra went back to work on the
bike. "Then what's going on?"

"I always lead with my heart. Can't seem to stop doing that.
But like my dad says, it's fucking stupid. I need to use my head
once in a while."

Taylor was beginning to figure out that Sierra actually admired her father in many ways. They were close in spite of his
drinking and their epic fights. In some ways, they acted more
like friends than father and daughter. "What does that mean?"

"It means I need to be smart enough not to walk off an emotional cliff if I can avoid it. That's what it means."

Taylor shook her head in confusion. "I don't understand." She
couldn't help noticing how Sierra's T-shirt clung to her torso as
she finished tightening a cap on the bike.

"It's what I said last night, okay? I'm different, and you should
be aware of that."

"In what way?"

She sighed audibly. "Really? You haven't figured it out?"

"I think I can guess. But…how do you know I'm not different, too?"

"Because you seem to have a choice." She removed the pan
she'd used to catch the old oil. "You're pregnant, aren't you?"

"You're saying you'd never sleep with a boy."

"I have no desire to. That's what I'm saying."

Taylor lifted her hair off her neck to help with the heat. "How
do you know, if you've never been with one?"

Sierra laughed but Taylor could tell she didn't find this funny.
"See what I mean? If you were like me, you'd understand."

"Not everyone can be as sure as you are, Sierra. Maybe for you, guys aren't appealing *at all*. Maybe for me, some of them are. It's also possible I just never realized there was something more appealing out there."

She put the pan away and turned around. "So are you interested in me or not?"

"I'm not sure I'm gay, but… I know I care about you. That I enjoy being with you. That I've never met anyone like you. So I'm open to finding out if…if whatever is happening between us goes anywhere."

"That's just it," she said. "If you have a choice, you don't want to choose me."

Taylor blinked in surprise. "Why not?"

"You know why not."

"Then I'll be different, too," Taylor guessed.

"Yes. Everyone says love is love. But trust me. You'll be judged by people who feel they have a right to tell you how to live. Some will look down on you and believe, even if they don't say it out loud, that God hates you or that you're going to hell. You can feel that negative shit washing over you and threatening to carry you away into self-loathing. It's hard no matter how many times you think, 'Fuck 'em.' And even if none of that happens—at least to your face—people will gawk at you for something as simple as holding my hand in public. Do you really want to live like that?"

"I understand," she said. "But if I don't explore what I feel with you, I could be missing out on the greatest thing to ever happen to me. You're different. Special." In so many ways. It wasn't just that Sierra had stepped up to help her with the baby; that was only part of what revealed the kind of person she was.

For the first time since Taylor met her, Sierra seemed unsure of herself, vulnerable. "So…what are you saying?" she asked, narrowing her eyes.

"I'm saying we can't decide anything too soon. We're still

getting to know each other. But I'm willing to see what happens—if you are."

The tension around her eyes disappeared. "It's a risk," she said, but matter-of-factly.

"For both of us," Taylor agreed.

Sierra pursed her lips as she thought it over but, finally, cracked a smile. "Oh, what the hell. I've always been a risk-taker." She picked up the rag so she could wipe her hands again. "Let me get showered, and we'll take the bike to the beach for a picnic."

Taylor never felt freer than when she was riding on the back of the motorcycle, her head in the bubble of her helmet, the roar of the engine drowning out everything else and the wind whipping at her clothes.

Relieved to have Sierra back, she smiled in return. "Okay."

Laurie had promised she'd watch for Autumn, so that Mary could go in the back, lock the door and have the privacy she needed to talk to Tammy. She could hear Laurie speaking to a customer through the curtained doorway that separated them, but she was too busy trying to gather the nerve she needed to bother listening to what they were saying.

As she searched for Tammy's number on her cell phone, she wondered what would come of this. As loath as she was to pick up the terrible burden of her past, she no longer felt she had a choice.

Taking a deep breath, she placed the call and closed her eyes as it began to ring. She hadn't blocked her number. What was the point, if Tammy could just reach her through the store? Or come to Sable Beach in person?

"Hello?"

Mary opened her eyes and stared, without seeing, at the thin carpet in the storeroom. "I'm sorry I hung up on you. I—I panicked."

"Bailey."

The emotion in Tammy's voice when she said Mary's real name brought Mary to her feet. "That's who I used to be."

There was a slight pause. "And who are you now?"

Mary hadn't expected that question. "You already know my name," she said as she started to pace.

"That's not what I'm talking about."

Mary began to knead her forehead. "I'm a mother, a grandmother, a bookstore owner."

"*Are you happy*? That's what I'm most interested in."

"Yes." Despite it all, she was happy. And maybe everything had turned out okay because she'd put up a firewall between her and that era of her life. As hard as that wall was to build, it had done its job; it had protected her.

"Then that's really saying something, considering…everything."

Mary dropped her head into her hands. She could hear the hope in Tammy's voice and simply couldn't crush her. "I… I want to tell you how sorry I am."

"For…"

Although Mary had never spoken the words out loud, guilt over Tammy had weighed her down for thirty-five years, especially in the dead of night when nightmares left her unable to sleep and she could no longer hide behind her daily distractions. "Leaving you behind."

There. She'd said it. She gripped the phone tighter while she waited for Tammy's response. Did Tammy harbor resentment? How had she fared on her own?

"I won't lie. It hurt," she admitted. "I thought of you *all* the time and wanted to be with you so badly. But as an adult, can I blame you? No. You were only nineteen when you were set free, after being held against your will for seven long years. My parents had stolen your childhood. I can see why you wouldn't want to take their kid with you."

"If I'd felt capable, I would've taken you. Or at least tried. But… I didn't know how I was going to make it."

"I understand. Autumn needed to come first. How is she?"

"Gorgeous. Healthy. Strong. And completely oblivious to who I really am—and who her father is."

After a long silence, Tammy said, "You've never told her?"

"No. After the trial, I was determined to leave it all behind and start over. I didn't want to live with the stigma. I didn't want her to have to live with it, either. And I stopped associating with my real mother, who kept bugging me to write a book or do another interview so that she could cash in on the lurid interest of strangers. Talking about it was like walking over broken glass. I had to disappear in order to save what was left of me, which is what I did. I couldn't handle the way she behaved on top of everything else."

"I see. So…you've had your privacy for thirty-five years."

"Yes."

"And you seem to have overcome what happened."

Mary heard someone at the back door. It had to be her daughter. Autumn would go around to the front of the store; Mary knew she didn't have much longer to be on the phone. "As much as possible, I guess. And now I need some time to decide how to handle this."

"You don't want me even now."

The heartbreak in those words felt like a punch in the stomach. "That isn't it. I just…it's been a long time, Tammy. And with you comes the truth, the memories, all of it."

"I know," she said sadly.

"But it isn't as though I haven't thought of you—thousands of times. Are you married? Do you have kids?"

"I'm divorced. The man I married had five children—three girls and two boys. He used me to finish raising them, then he ran off with a younger, skinnier woman who has less emotional baggage, I'm sure."

Mary sighed. "I'm sorry. When did that happen?"

"It's been eight years since he moved out. I don't have any family. That's why I decided to find you. I told myself you might need me, probably so that I wouldn't have to admit that *I* need *you*."

Mary's throat began to burn, and it felt like she had an elephant sitting on her chest. "Tammy, what your parents did was so cruel—to both of us."

"We were just children. And I loved you so much."

Mary wasn't sure if Tammy was agreeing with her or accusing her, but she couldn't stop the tears that were beginning to slide down her cheeks. Yes, they'd been children, but Mary had been older than Tammy. Could she have done more to protect her? "I loved you, too. Let me get through the summer, okay? Then…then maybe we can pick a place to meet. And who knows where it might go from there."

"Are you sure? I'm not trying to force my way into your life. I just…want to be wanted by someone, I guess."

"You deserve that."

Laurie pulled back the curtain, one eyebrow cocked in warning. "Autumn just came through the front."

"I've got to go," she said into the phone. "I'll call you later."

"Would you mind sending me a picture of Autumn?" Tammy asked before she could hang up.

Although Tammy's request wasn't a big one—a photograph of her half sister—Mary was reluctant to provide it. She preferred to maintain a barrier until she knew more about Tammy and gained some confidence that she could let down her guard.

But how could she say no? Risk hurting Tammy again? Besides, Autumn was an adult. It was possible she'd want to know her half sister—if only she knew of her. "Sure," she said.

"I'd be grateful to get one of you, too."

"Drake D. Owens didn't provide one?" She hoped she'd managed to keep the bitterness out of her voice—evidence that she wasn't happy to be rousted out of her hiding place.

"There were quite a few in the file he gave me," she admitted. "He caught you from behind, as you were walking out the door of Starbucks. Then there were several as he followed you back to Sable Beach and to the bookstore—but mainly of the back of your car and then the business."

Bastard, Mary thought. She'd been so shaken she hadn't even noticed him.

"About the only one that shows you from the front shows you sitting on a stool in the same Starbucks," Tammy went on. "You look so worried. I was hoping to get one that shows you a bit…happier."

"Right. Of course." No doubt Tammy interpreted that worried expression as more rejection. "I'll text them to you later."

"Mom?"

At the sound of Autumn's voice, Mary said goodbye, clicked the end button and parted the drape. "Yes, dear?"

"Didn't you hear me at the door?"

She blinked, feigning shock. "No. Did you try to come in this way?"

"I did, but it's locked."

"I lock it when I'm here alone. I must've done it after I came in this morning without realizing it," she lied.

Autumn seemed perturbed, but she waved it away. "I brought you some lunch." She lifted a small brown bag. "It's an Italian sub from Huckabee's deli. Are you hungry?"

"Starving," she said, but nothing could be further from the truth. She was sick to her stomach.

19

Autumn didn't know what to expect when she arrived at The Daily Catch. Quinn had texted her earlier and asked her to meet him at the restaurant, and he'd said to come hungry. But the time he gave her was after the restaurant was closed, so no one else was around.

What did he have planned? She was excited to find out. But she would've been excited to see him, regardless. The sting of having to cut off the search for Nick and the reality of what her life might look like without her husband didn't seem quite as terrible since she'd come to Sable Beach.

The human spirit was more resilient than most people thought, she told herself, but she knew Quinn had a lot to do with how optimistic she was feeling about her future.

How could she still care about Nick and yet be so selfish? she wondered as she knocked on the front door.

While she waited, she looked back at her car. She should have parked down the street and walked over. Quinn's Audi and her Volvo were the only two vehicles in the lot, and it was getting late. If someone noticed, it could stir up gossip.

But sneaking around seemed so juvenile. She was too old for

that. Besides, she wanted to feel as though she wasn't doing anything wrong, that it'd been long enough since Nick went missing that no one would fault her for seeing Quinn. Since there was no roadmap for what she was going through—and very few other people had ever gone through it—she was tempted to rely on public opinion even though that was probably the last thing she should do. Why would it be up to anyone else to decide when she was in the clear?

She heard the door and turned as Quinn poked his head out, gave her a sexy smile and stepped aside to let her past him.

The aroma that hit her as she walked in tempted her to stop and just stand there, breathing it in. "Wow, smells incredible in here," she said. "What are you making?"

"Dinner," he replied.

"What's on the menu?"

Dressed in a pair of jeans that fit him far too well not to be a distraction and a red polo, he flourished the hand towel he'd thrown over his shoulder, settled it on his forearm and bent toward her like a waiter. "Butternut squash soup along with a balsamic roasted beet salad and fresh sourdough bread for starters. Plank wood grilled salmon topped with avocado salsa, garlic-roasted broccoli and almond asparagus spears for the main course."

"Sounds fancy."

"And I've got whatever you want for dessert," he added.

She told herself he was referring to the carrot cake she liked so well, but it was a testament to what he did to her that her mind would venture elsewhere.

"I never planned on becoming a chef," he said. "But after being raised by parents who own a restaurant—" he tossed the towel back over his shoulder "—I've learned a few things. I hope you're hungry."

She was, but for all the wrong things. "I don't think I realized just how hungry until I walked through that door."

Quinn led her to a table in the middle of the restaurant set with a white tablecloth and a bouquet of matching hydrangeas.

"This looks like something out of a magazine," she said.

He pulled out her chair. "It's a special occasion, so I decided to break out the good stuff."

"What's the special occasion?"

"You," he replied without hesitation.

Had there been the slightest insincerity in that statement, it would've sounded ridiculous. Instead, she felt the same powerful magnetism she had on the beach.

"White okay?" he asked, holding out a bottle of wine.

"Definitely."

He poured them each a glass of chardonnay but didn't sit down with her. "You look beautiful."

Autumn had worn a simple black sheath dress, black sandals and gold hoop earrings, and she'd pulled her hair into a low ponytail. She'd gotten some sun since coming to town, and with the dark circles now gone beneath her eyes, she hadn't bothered to put on a lot of makeup.

She opened her mouth to thank him, but the words were lost as she met his gaze. They were going to make love again. She could see it in his face, feel it in the rapid beat of her heart. But she'd been hoping for that, hadn't she?

"I'll go get the first course." He went to the kitchen and returned with the soups, the salads and the bread, so she put the linen napkin that had been folded next to her silverware in her lap.

"Your parents don't mind that you're using the restaurant tonight?"

"Not at all."

"What'd you tell them you were going to do?" she asked while he arranged the plates.

"I said I was going to make a meal for someone."

She gazed at the little swirl of sour cream and sprig of cilantro he'd used to garnish the soup. "They didn't ask who?"

He left the empty tray on another table and sat across from her. "They didn't have to."

She felt her eyebrows slide up. "They knew it would be me? How?"

A sheepish expression claimed his face. "I'm not sure I should tell you."

She'd been about to taste the soup, but at this she held her spoon in midair. "Are people already gossiping about us? Is Mrs. Vizii trying to stir things up?"

"If so, not with my parents. She knows better than to bother them. They never liked Sarah to begin with."

"Why not?"

"Let's just say my ex wasn't very supportive of our relationship."

"How does a wife not support her husband's relationship with his own parents?"

He motioned at the food. "Go ahead and eat before it gets cold."

She tasted the soup and nodded appreciatively. "This is good. Really good."

"Thanks." His boyish smile was endearing.

"So…are you going to answer my question?" she asked.

He grimaced. "Sarah got jealous every time I spoke to my folks, insisted we stay with her family whenever we came back, got angry when I would fly home to see my mother once she got cancer the first time and would punish me when I got back in whatever small ways she could—withhold sex, disappear overnight so I'd worry or think she was with another man, leave me scathing messages on my voice mail or charge into my office, screaming at me. That sort of thing."

"I'm beginning to wonder how you stayed in that marriage as long as you did."

"I didn't want to fail," he explained, starting on his salad first. "I hated the idea of being divorced. That's what it came down to. That and my own stubbornness, I guess. I felt sorry for Sarah, fully believed if only I could fulfill her, she'd calm down and be happy—at last."

"That's not so unusual, I guess. Most people like to feel needed."

"I was being naive. There was no fulfilling her. Her behavior only got worse and worse." He picked up his spoon to switch to his soup. "But I don't want to talk about her. Not tonight."

Autumn held her wineglass loosely in one hand while she watched him eat. "Okay. Back to the other subject. You still haven't told me how your parents knew it was me you were cooking for tonight."

"On second thought, maybe we should keep talking about Sarah," he joked.

She chuckled. "Come on."

"It's no big deal. My parents know you're back in town. They know I already took you out once. I hope you don't mind that I didn't keep it a secret from them."

She didn't want anyone to know, but he was living with them. She could see how silly it would seem for him to lie about where he was going. "Are they aware of how I felt about you in high school?"

His smile grew lopsided. "Yes. My father saw us when we were in the tree house all those years ago."

"He *what*?" she cried. "I don't remember that!"

"He didn't want to embarrass you, so he waited until you were gone. But then he sat me down, gave me a stern lecture and grounded me for two weeks."

She squeezed her forehead with one hand. "I'm mortified. What did he say? That if you weren't careful you'd get some girl pregnant and ruin your future?"

"No. We'd already been over the whole birth control issue—many times. If you'll remember, I was prepared."

She felt her face grow even hotter. "Yes, I remember." She also remembered how careful Quinn had been when he pushed inside her. Knowing it was her first time he'd been trying not to hurt her. The way he'd behaved, his basic kindness, was probably why she didn't end up hating him after he went back to Sarah.

He leaned forward, a nostalgic expression on his face. "He was trying to teach me to be careful with a woman's heart. He explained that it was wrong of me to take advantage of your feelings."

"Your father's a good man. But he should've had a talk with me, too, and explained that stalking isn't right, either. I must've driven past your house three or four times a night."

Quinn laughed with her. "I remember."

"You *knew?*"

"Of course. You came by so often I couldn't miss it."

"Ugh!" she groaned. "What was I thinking?"

"You're making too big a deal out of it. We were just kids. Isn't that what you said to me in the bookstore?"

"Yes. But I'll never be able to look your father in the eye again."

"Oh, come on. He really likes you." He frowned as he finished his soup. "I shouldn't have told you. I thought you'd think it was funny."

"Hilarious," she said drily but that only made him laugh harder. "You're terrible."

He reached out to touch her arm. "I'll quit teasing you."

"Does your mother know about the tree house, too?" she asked with a sulky glance.

"I have no idea. But even if she did, I wouldn't be stupid enough to tell you now."

"Good. Forget I asked, because I don't really want to know." She tore off a piece of her roll and shoved it into her mouth.

"What would you do if you caught Caden having sex with a girl in your backyard?" he asked.

She finished her salad as she tried to decide. "I'm not sure. That's definitely something I would want his father to talk to him about. But since Nick is no longer around... I guess I'm lucky that Caden hasn't had a steady girlfriend."

"You realize there's not necessarily a correlation between those two things," he pointed out.

She admired the laugh lines around his mouth and eyes as he buttered his roll. "True, but I don't think he's sexually active quite yet. Taylor, on the other hand, got a boyfriend right before Nick disappeared, and they were together for over a year. I'm guessing they did some experimenting, even if they didn't go all the way. I warned her about using birth control, of course, just in case. But I was going through so much myself—was up all hours of the night trying to find Nick, and then I struggled through most of the day taking care of my kids and the rest of my life. I couldn't watch over her as closely as I should have."

"Well, it all worked out. Even if they did go all the way, at least she didn't get pregnant."

"Thank God." She put her empty bowl on top of her salad plate. "Everything has been delicious so far, Quinn."

"One of the benefits of dating the son of a restaurateur," he joked.

"Is that what we're doing? Dating?" That word sounded so odd to her ears. She'd never imagined herself having to go back on the singles market, hadn't even reconciled herself to the fact that she was now available. Her husband was gone, but what did one do to make it official in a situation like this?

There was some protocol for divorced and widowed people. But she wasn't divorced and wasn't certain she'd been widowed.

Once he finished with his soup and salad, Quinn folded his arms and leaned back. "I would hope whatever we're doing isn't only about sex. As good as it was this morning, I'm looking for more than hooking up now and then."

"You want a wife, a family."

He said nothing. He'd already admitted as much at the beach.

"But I don't really know where I stand with my marriage, my life. What I can do and feel good about. What to tell you to expect."

"We don't have to make those decisions right now," he said.

He'd indicated that they'd take it slow, and she'd tried to accept that. But what she was feeling didn't reflect slow. When she looked at him, she felt completely swallowed up by desire, almost as if nothing had changed in twenty years. "And yet we'd be reckless—with your heart and mine—to ignore what we might face in the future."

He studied her for several seconds. "Are you still in love with Nick, Autumn?"

"I love him. I don't know if I'm 'in love' with him anymore. Would I want you as badly as I did this morning if I was in love with someone else? That's what I can't figure out. I'm hurt, confused, angry—and lonely. And as much as I can't believe my husband left me for another woman, there's always that possibility. So I don't even know if I owe him my fidelity, which of course I broke this morning." She gazed into the liquid in her glass. "I'm going back to Tampa in less than two months, Quinn, and long-distance relationships rarely work out. If I were you, I'd probably play it safe and stay away from me."

"If I could, I would, but..."

She looked up.

"I'm not sure I've ever felt the way I felt on the beach this morning. That alive. That engaged. Certainly not for a long time."

"That's just because you're lonely, too," she said, but he shook his head.

"That isn't all of it. Given our history, maybe it's poetic justice for me to want you and for you not to want me in return. But this time, I wasn't in it just for the sex. Whatever was happening, it felt right—like it was meant to be."

She toyed with the edge of her napkin. "There's so much to consider. I can't promise you anything. And you've been through so much already, with Sarah."

"You and I could have something special, Autumn," he said. "I suspect you think that's true, too. That's why you're spooked."

"This morning was the first time I've had sex with anyone except Nick since I met him. And instead of being appalled and regretful, I want more. That's terrible, isn't it?"

His nostrils flared slightly. "I can hardly be objective here, so I think I'm the wrong person to ask."

"What I'm saying is that I'm sitting here, enjoying your food and your company and hoping we make love again. I can feel myself falling away from Nick. My memories of him are growing dimmer by the second. It's such a strange sensation."

"It's natural for you to be scared of letting go of what you had."

"I'm too wound up, too unpredictable, too confused. It would be better—for you—if we didn't keep this going."

"I don't believe it would be better for either one of us."

She said nothing. He seemed so confident, and she wanted to believe him.

"What if I was willing to take my chances?" he asked. "Would you quit worrying about me, at least?"

She felt as though she was standing in a doorway, hanging on to Nick with one hand while reaching out to Quinn with the other. In order to take Quinn's hand, however, she first had to let go of Nick's. "If I continue seeing you, my kids are bound to find out. Heck, my car's in the lot right now, next to yours. I'm sure that won't go unnoticed."

"Then tell Taylor and Caden that we're seeing each other," he said. "Be completely up-front."

She was trying to imagine how that might go over when he got up and came around to kneel by her.

"Autumn, it's me."

She closed her eyes. "I know. That's the problem."

"I'd rather not be a secret. I don't want to have to sneak around. And I don't want you to feel as though we're doing something wrong."

She opened her eyes to find him watching her intently and couldn't help admiring the thick black eyelashes that framed his blue eyes. How many times had she dreamed of him? "You're not making this easy."

One hand went around her neck and pulled her forward so he could peck her lips. "Give me a real shot."

"I want to." She rested her forehead against his. "I just don't know how to make it work. I can't bring a new man into my life. I don't want to rush my kids, not after what they've been through."

"My being part of your life—and theirs—doesn't have to be a negative thing. You want them to be happy, right?"

"Of course."

He kissed her again, this time softly, gently, but with more intent. "Then why not assume they want you to be happy, too?" he murmured.

"I'll think about it. But right now, all I can think about is you."

Mary was wide awake and sitting on Autumn's bed, waiting for her to come home, when she heard the engine of a car and got up to see Autumn pull into the drive. It was nearly two. Where had she been? Nothing was open after midnight in Sable Beach.

"Autumn?" she called as soon as her daughter entered the garage and started climbing the stairs to the apartment. She didn't want to scare her.

The footsteps stopped. "It's just me," she added to let her know Taylor and Caden weren't with her.

The footsteps started again, this time moving more quickly, and Autumn appeared in the doorway. "Has something happened to the kids?" she asked, sounding worried.

"No, they're fine."

"And you?"

"I'm fine, too," Mary replied, even though she'd just had a vivid nightmare in which she'd gone to meet Tammy, and as soon as she got there, Tammy had locked her into the basement of a strange house and disappeared, and Jeff and Nora had emerged from some dark corner. No matter what they did to her, no matter how many times she cried out for help, Tammy would not come to her rescue. In the weird way of dreams, Tammy had been there in the beginning, and then she wasn't, and she didn't seem to care that she'd put Mary right back into the terrifying situation she'd escaped so long ago.

When Mary had finally jerked awake, she'd been drenched in sweat. Fortunately, if she'd made any noise, it was late enough that Caden and Taylor were sleeping so soundly she hadn't disturbed anyone. "The question is…are *you* okay? I was worried when I looked out and noticed that your car was gone. I tried calling and texting you. When I got no response, I came up here and found you'd left your cell phone." She pointed to where it was charging on the nightstand.

Mary had thought that maybe Autumn had gone somewhere because she was upset and couldn't sleep—possibly to the beach. But she had clearly never been in bed and didn't even seem tired. On the contrary. She looked lovely—tan and slender in a flattering black dress that fell to just above her knees.

Autumn's chest lifted as she took a deep breath and released it in a relieved sigh. "I'm sorry if I scared you."

"It's okay. Are you upset, or—"

"I'm not upset. I was—" she shot Mary a look "—with Quinn."

"At his parents' house?" she asked in surprise.

"At the restaurant." She walked over, took off her sandals and sat on the bed, too. "He made me dinner after they closed. That's why I was out so late."

Mary couldn't help grinning. "The cake he keeps sending you is paying off?"

"Sadly, that's only a small part of it."

"I know. You're seeing him, then?"

"Yes." She hung her head. "Does that make me a terrible person—that I can move on so quickly even though I was happily married to Nick not long ago?"

"You've always been attracted to Quinn."

"I'm not sure that justifies it."

"I think it does. You haven't moved on *that* quickly, anyway. Nick's been gone for almost two years." Mary had always cared about her son-in-law. He'd been a fabulous provider and treated his wife and children well. He'd also been busy and preoccupied and didn't have a lot of time for anyone beyond his immediate family, but he indulged Autumn by letting her bring the children to Sable Beach each summer. Mary supposed there were a lot of partners who wouldn't have been so amenable to that. She was grateful for the many things he did right. But she wanted nothing more than to see her daughter happy again, and she believed Autumn could only be happy if she let go and moved on.

"What do you think the kids will say?" Autumn asked.

"Taylor has only one year of high school left. Then she'll go off to college and what you do won't affect her too much."

"Still. She doesn't need me dumping something like this on her right now. And Caden has two years."

"Maybe you can keep your relationship with Quinn a secret for a while. Make sure it's going to work out before you take the risk of upsetting them."

"I would be tempted, but sneaking around feels ridiculous, and I don't see how it will work. Maybe it would be more viable in a big city, but here in Sable Beach, someone is bound to figure it out. Quinn doesn't even have his own house right now, is still planning to move somewhere else when his mother...well, depending on what happens with his mother."

"He's going through a lot, too. Like you, he could use a friend."

"I know."

"Then tell your children you're helping him through a difficult time. Downplay the romantic element of the relationship until it's safe to be more open."

Autumn pulled the tie out of her hair and scratched her head. "Apparently, you don't fully understand the constraints of living in a small town. There's no way to downplay anything."

She lifted her daughter's chin. "Your happiness is important, too."

"I'm not being a martyr. It's just that it's...too soon."

"We don't get to plan when certain people come into our lives. The timing isn't always perfect. But when it's right, it's right. So...maybe you should give it a chance. You could maintain a long-distance relationship with Quinn that doesn't involve your children until after they go to college."

She fell back onto the bed. "Since I doubt I'll be able to give him up, that's what I'll have to do."

Mary hesitated. "You're already in love?"

"There's just something about him. That's all. I don't know how to explain it."

"You'll certainly never find a more handsome man."

"That isn't the reason." She pushed up onto her elbows. "But it doesn't hurt."

"I bet. I'll let you get some sleep." Mary started to go but Autumn called her back.

"Mom?"

She turned at the stairs. "Yes?"

Autumn sat up again.

"What is it?" Mary asked when her daughter seemed reluctant to speak.

"Are you ever going to tell me about my father?"

Mary caught her breath. Here it was, at last. The question she'd been expecting for some time now. At least it didn't sound as though Autumn had already taken a DNA test and was actively engaged in finding him. Mary was grateful for that small mercy. "Honey, we've been over this—"

"No, we haven't," she broke in. "Not really. I've just known better than to ask. I understand that whatever happened—it's difficult for you. But it's natural for me to want to know who I am, where I come from. And I've waited all my life. How long will it take? Will I *ever* learn? I'm afraid my father will be dead before you feel comfortable enough to tell me, and then I'll never get the chance to meet him."

Mary gripped the stair rail to steady herself. "That's what you want? To meet him?" That was exactly what she'd been afraid of...

Autumn's eyebrows snapped together. "Sometimes. I guess. All the question marks in my life are hard. Think about it. I don't know who my father is, not even what he looks like. I don't know anyone from his side of the family. I don't know why you won't tell me more about him. I don't know where my husband went. I don't know why he left. I don't know if I can allow myself to fall in love with someone else." She threw up her hands. "I just want some fucking answers!"

Mary threw her shoulders back. "You love your children so much you'd do almost anything to protect them, right? Isn't that what we were just talking about?"

"Of course!"

"Well, take it from me—sometimes it's better not to know," Mary told her and let herself out.

She couldn't tell Autumn about the Skinners right now, not so soon after coming into contact with Tammy. First, she had to determine if Autumn's half sister was as trustworthy as she pretended to be—or if she'd turned out more like her parents than she'd ever willingly admit.

20

Taylor was startled awake by Caden pounding on her bedroom door.

"Hey, you up?" he called out.

"I wasn't," she grumbled, rolling away from the noise and dragging most of the blankets to the far side of the bed.

"We need to talk."

She squinted at the light coming in around the edge of the blinds. "What time is it? Why are you bothering me?"

Instead of answering, he came in and plopped on the bed.

"Caden!" she cried, irritated that he'd jiggled the mattress. "Stop it. Go away."

He easily resisted her attempt to shove him off with her foot. "It's eight-thirty, so not *that* early. Mimi just left for work, and Mom will be in soon to make breakfast. She won't sleep in because she has that fundraiser this weekend and has a lot to do. We might only have a few minutes."

"A few minutes for what?" she asked, although she was afraid she already knew the answer to that question.

"To talk."

She felt her heart sink. She could guess where this was going, all right. "There's always later," she suggested weakly.

"Except I want to know now," he said. "I've waited long enough."

A fissure of alarm brought Taylor fully awake. She'd known she wouldn't have much time before Caden started pressing her for the name of her baby's father. He'd given her a couple of days, and he'd been patient and kind during that time—probably more patient and kind than she would've been had their roles been reversed.

And now the moment she'd been dreading had arrived.

"Tay?" he prodded when she kept her eyes closed, anyway.

She buried her head beneath her pillow. "Not now, Caden. I couldn't sleep last night. I'm tired." She doubted she'd be able to stall any longer. The news she'd given him was too big. But she was desperate enough to try.

"I can understand why you're freaked out. I'm freaked out, too. God, Tay, a baby! But you can sleep all you want after I leave. Right now I want to know what's going on, and I want you to tell me it has nothing to do with Oliver."

Her heart started to pound against her ribs. "Oliver who?" she asked, stalling.

"Oliver Hancock. The only Oliver we know. I got a weird text from him last night."

A knot formed in the pit of Taylor's stomach as she sat up. She should've responded to Oliver. Maybe then he wouldn't have contacted Caden.

Oliver had texted her several times the past few days. It'd been over a month since they'd had sex. He knew she should've had her period by now. But she'd been ignoring him. She didn't want to lie to him, but she didn't want to tell him about the baby yet, either. That would make the pregnancy too real and start the avalanche of repercussions she was trying to put off until the summer was over.

"Weird in what way?" she asked, feeling as though she was marching toward the death chamber.

"He was acting like we're still friends, as if he didn't ask Miranda to the prom even though he knew *I* was going to ask her."

Oliver had been a jerk to do that to Caden. Taylor felt terrible that she hadn't stood behind her brother, especially because he'd been so good when she told him about the baby. "It was just a stupid dance. Maybe he doesn't think that should've been enough to ruin your friendship," she said, hoping that when she told Caden she'd slept with Oliver she could claim she hadn't thought the whole Miranda thing was a big deal.

"You're kidding, right? I had it all planned out, and he purposely went over there and asked her before I could. You'd be royally pissed if one of your friends did that to you."

It was true. She couldn't deny it. So she didn't try. Curving her fingernails into her palms, she dove into the inevitable instead. "What'd he say?"

"He asked how I liked being back in Sable Beach and when we'd be coming home."

"That's nice…"

"Because it was only the lead-in. Then he asked about you." She couldn't quite meet her brother's eyes. "What about me?"

"He said you two have been talking. That isn't true, is it?"

"Not really," she mumbled.

His chin jutted forward as he searched for the truth on her face. "That was a yes or no question."

"Oliver and I are not talking." At least she could say that with some certainty.

"But…"

Tears welled up. As soon as she felt them coming, she pressed her fingertips over her eyelids to try to stop them.

"No way," Caden said and climbed off the bed. "Don't tell me it's Oliver, Tay. You'd never sleep with that prick, would you? He's a junior, for crying out loud. Almost any guy in school would count himself lucky to get in your pants. You should hear how they talk about you. And…and I hate him! You know that! You know what he did to me!"

She wished she could reassure him, tell him she wasn't that kind of sister. But she *had* been that kind of sister. She'd been angry and vengeful and out to hurt him because she was hurting so badly herself.

"Tay?" he cried.

She couldn't hold back the tears any longer. They trickled down her cheeks as she peered up at him. "I'm sorry."

"No!" He backed away from the bed as though she held a gun.

"I told you you'd hate me," she whispered.

He stood there for a few seconds, looking as though she not only held a gun but had also just shot him. Then he shook his head in disgust and bewilderment. "You know what?" he said. "You're right."

And with that, he turned on his heel, stomped out and slammed the door.

When Autumn came out of the garage, she nearly stumbled over a vase filled with wildflowers. Then she glanced around, trying to figure out who'd left it—and if anyone was watching her now.

Her mother's car was gone. Autumn had expected that. She'd heard the engine earlier, right before she stepped into the shower. She supposed Mary had left them for her as a sort of apology for all she refused to tell Autumn about her father—until she saw the card.

She heard the door of the house open and shoved it in her back pocket before Caden came striding toward her.

"Morning, honey," she said and couldn't help smiling because she was once again enjoying life, especially the time she spent with her children. Now that she was sleeping at night instead of spending hours upon hours on the internet searching for Nick, they were living like normal people—like they had before Nick went missing.

Dressed in swim trunks, flip-flops and an old T-shirt, Caden had a volleyball tucked under one arm, and he was moving toward the back gate. For a moment she thought he wasn't going to respond to her, that he hadn't heard her even though she'd spoken loudly enough. But when he spotted the flowers, he came to an abrupt halt. "Where'd those come from?"

Her face grew hot. "I don't know. I just walked out and… and nearly knocked them over."

"They'd better not be from Oliver," he grumbled. "I won't have anything to do with him, no matter what."

"Oliver?" she repeated in surprise. "Oliver who?"

"Why does everyone say that?" he asked in exasperation. "Oliver Hancock! Who else?"

"Why would your friend send me flowers?" she asked in confusion.

"Not you, *Tay*," he clarified.

They'd been left on *her* doorstep, but she could see why he still wouldn't assume they were for her. She'd been absolutely devoted to her husband their entire marriage. And not that long ago, she'd been proving that devotion was alive, even if he wasn't, by searching tirelessly for him. Caden would have no clue that her heart and mind had started to wander.

"Why would Oliver be sending Tay flowers?" she asked. "He's your friend, not hers. Isn't he?"

"He was. Maybe you should tell *her* that," he said and started to leave again.

"Caden!"

"What?" A dark scowl rumpled his forehead when he whipped around.

"Where are you going?"

"Anywhere but here," he replied.

"What's the matter?"

He gestured at the house. "Why don't you ask Tay?"

She sighed. They must've had an argument. "What are you two fighting about now?" she asked wearily.

"I want to tell you. Believe me, I'm *dying* to tell you. But I can't be that big an asshole, even if she deserves it."

Since Nick had gone missing and her two children had started to argue like never before, Caden was usually eager to get Taylor in trouble, if he could. So why was he holding back? "Why not?"

"If I could tell you that, I could tell you everything. Now, can I go? Please? I have to get out of here before I explode."

She wanted to get to the bottom of this, but she was hesitant to tackle it while standing there with flowers that were from a man other than his father. If Caden stayed to talk, the subject of the flowers would come up again. She figured she'd let him go to the beach where he could blow off some steam. She could approach him later. Or Taylor would tell her what was wrong, and she'd call him if she felt the need to. "Okay, fine. Go."

She watched him stride through the gate, which he let slam behind him. Only once he was out of sight did she pull the card out of her pocket and read it again.

It wasn't signed, but she knew who the flowers were from:

Thinking of you.

Remembering how Quinn had slid her dress up last night—and everything that'd happened afterward—she nearly groaned aloud. She was in trouble, and she knew it.

Dropping her head back, she stared up at the wide blue sky. "What am I going to do?" she whispered.

As happy as she'd been feeling, maybe it'd been a mistake to come home, after all.

Molly, Quinn's mother's golden retriever, loved nothing more than chasing a Frisbee on the beach. Quinn would've brought her out with him when he went running earlier, but his parents generally walked her themselves. They said it was good for them to get outdoors and spend a little time together, and he agreed. He hoped it was an hour during which they could forget about the cancer.

But this morning, when he'd returned home to find them getting ready to leave the house, he'd realized he'd forgotten that his mother had a doctor's appointment, and since his father always drove her to her chemo and radiation treatments, he'd have to walk Molly.

Fortunately, he didn't mind returning to the beach. As difficult as it was to watch what his mother was going through, *he* was doing better than he'd done in years, and he felt the sun, the sand and the sea were part of the reason. He was finding himself again, recovering.

He checked one of the scars on his lower back while waiting for Molly to return the Frisbee he'd just thrown. Sarah had stabbed him three times before he'd been able to wake up and gather his senses enough to understand what was happening to him. The first wound wasn't very deep because she'd hit a rib. The second had missed his kidney by less than a centimeter, and it'd gotten infected, which meant it had taken forever to heal. The third had just sliced the skin. But he was finally there. Despite the presence of Sarah's parents, who cast a dark cloud over him whenever he ran into them, he'd been able to heal physically and emotionally.

"Here you go, girl." He took the Frisbee from the dog and threw it again, but this time Molly didn't bring it back. She'd found some poor sucker who was sitting on the beach to pet and scratch her, which was the only thing she loved better than chasing a Frisbee.

"Hey, you little hedonist. Back to your exercise," Quinn called, but then he recognized the person she'd discovered. Caden sat alone, a volleyball in the sand beside him.

"This your dog?" he asked as Quinn reached them.

"My mother's."

He ducked a lick from Molly. "She's friendly."

"She doesn't like other dogs, but she loves humans. And she's not above begging," he joked and gestured at the volleyball. "You waiting for some friends?"

Caden looked at the ball as if he'd only just remembered he had it with him. "Not really. Not until later."

Something was off. Caden didn't seem to be the same happy boy who'd come into the restaurant. "You okay?"

"As okay as anyone would be, I guess," he replied.

Quinn hesitated. He didn't want to invade Caden's privacy, but he could tell something was wrong. "That didn't sound too convincing. You want to talk about it?"

"Naw."

"You sure?" Quinn sat down beside him. "This isn't about your father, is it?"

"It probably wouldn't have happened if my father was still around but…not really."

Quinn remembered Autumn telling him that her daughter had taken Nick's disappearance much harder than her son and figured that maybe Caden was having a delayed reaction. "Sometimes we don't have any control over the stuff that knocks us down. We just have to figure out how to deal with it and do our best to get back up."

Caden flipped his bangs out of his eyes and looked over. "Your mom's fighting cancer, right?"

"She is."

"I'm sorry about that." He squinted against the glint of the sun as he stared out to sea. "Do you think she's going to make it?"

Everyone in town was being so careful to insist his mother would win the battle that Quinn sort of appreciated someone who was willing to confront the reality of the situation. "I want to believe she will. She beat it last time. But now it's back."

"I hope she can beat it again."

"So do I. I don't want her to die, but if she's going to die, I'd rather she die quickly and not have to suffer."

"I get that." He gave Molly, who kept nudging his hand and sidling up next to him, another scratch. "It might be that you've had too much warning—had to watch it coming for a long time—and I had none."

"You're right," Quinn said, surprised by the maturity of that insight. "Neither is easy."

Caden picked up his ball and began to spin it in his hands as Molly finally wandered off to smell a piece of seaweed. "I get so mad at him sometimes, you know?"

"Mad at him?"

"For leaving. At least you know your mother has no choice. Why'd my father have to get involved in whatever he got involved in? Why'd he have to go to Ukraine? We were doing fine! We were happy!"

"What do you think the answer is?"

"My mom said he was trying to serve our country. She said that's an honorable thing to do, and I should be proud of him. But what did he really accomplish?"

"Maybe that's something you'll learn later. Or maybe it's something you'll never learn. Either way, I get why you're mad. His sacrifice turned out to be your sacrifice, and you didn't get a choice in the matter."

"Yes," Caden said, looking relieved to at least be understood. "That's it."

"But dying while trying to do something courageous is just as admirable as getting it done, Caden. Maybe more so. He made the ultimate sacrifice, even though he had so much to live for—his work and, more important, his wife, his daughter and his son."

"I guess I'm letting him down by being a big baby, huh?"

"Not at all. You have the right to grieve. And anger is part of that. But he wouldn't want you to let what happened to him destroy *your* life, you know?"

"Yeah."

"So you need to remember how much he loved you. Hang on to that always—and keep your chin up."

When he started blinking quickly, Quinn decided they'd dealt with enough emotion and stood. "Want to serve me a few? It might be good practice for you."

"You play?" Caden asked in surprise.

"I grew up here," Quinn said. "Course I play."

Molly ran around while they took the closest court until it got too crowded on the beach to allow her that much freedom, at which point Quinn tied her up so they could play a little longer. Caden was better than he'd expected, and the longer they practiced digs and dives and other hard returns, the happier Autumn's son seemed to get. He was working through his anger and pain physically, and Quinn knew how good that felt, so he kept going as long as he could.

It was almost noon by the time he told Caden he had to get over to the restaurant.

"Thanks," Caden said. "I really appreciate you hanging out with me this morning."

"No problem. Come in and have another crab sandwich later. You've got to be getting hungry. You can bring Taylor again, too, if you want."

"No way," he said with a grimace. "I'm not even talking to her."

"Why not?"

He seemed uncertain for a second, then he said, "Can I trust you?"

Quinn didn't know how to answer that question. He didn't want Caden to tell him something he'd feel obligated to relay to Autumn. "You know how adults are," he said. "Depending on the secret, you probably shouldn't tell me."

"I don't think this is one of those kinds of secrets. My mom's going to find out about it eventually, regardless."

Intrigued, Quinn couldn't help saying, "Okay, then. What is it?"

"Taylor's pregnant," he replied.

Quinn felt his jaw drop. "What did you say?"

"Yeah, man. Can you believe it?"

A snippet of conversation from last night went through Quinn's mind: *Even if they did go all the way, at least she didn't get pregnant.* "No, I can't."

21

Autumn couldn't get much out of Taylor. She sat on her daughter's bed and tried talking to her, but Taylor insisted her latest argument with Caden wasn't a big deal—even though Autumn could tell it was much worse than usual.

"What does this have to do with Oliver Hancock?" she asked, trying a different tack.

She could feel her daughter stiffen under the covers. "Nothing. Why do you ask about him?"

"Caden said to tell you that Oliver was *his* friend."

"I know that."

"He's a year younger than you, anyway."

"I know that, too. But so what? I'm friends with all kinds of kids—seniors, juniors, even sophomores. What does age have to do with anything? Besides, just because Caden doesn't like Oliver doesn't mean *I* have to hate him, too."

"Your brother was pretty hurt when Oliver asked Miranda to the prom," Autumn pointed out. "Caden had made it clear he was going to ask her."

"So? Maybe Oliver had planned on asking her even before that. Regardless, it was just a stupid dance. No big deal. Miranda isn't a nice girl, anyway. She's catty and selfish—no one he should be interested in."

Autumn wasn't happy with her daughter's response, and she made sure it showed in her face. "That may be true from your vantage point, but he should be allowed to decide for himself, shouldn't he?"

"Then he can decide. I'm just saying he took someone else to the dance so he didn't miss out on anything. And if he can decide for himself about Miranda, I can decide for myself about Oliver."

Autumn sighed. Taylor was stubbornly missing the point, but she figured it might help to back off and give her daughter some time to think things over. Pushing Taylor never seemed to work. She'd only dig in deeper. She was like her father that way, Autumn thought. "Okay. I'm going to chalk this one up to the usual teenage squabbles. But I hope you understand that this is more about Oliver's betrayal of Caden's friendship than whether or not he got to go to the dance or Miranda is the girl of Caden's dreams."

"Mom, it's over, okay? Do we have to keep going on and on about it?" She broke into tears. "I'm a terrible sister *and* a terrible daughter! Is that what you want to hear?"

"I didn't say you were a terrible sister *or* daughter. I think you could be kinder to Caden, though, and I think he could be kinder to you. That's all."

She buried her head beneath the pillow, but confused by this sudden display of emotion, Autumn kept talking. "Taylor? Will you at least try?"

"Okay." Her capitulation was muffled by the pillow, but figuring she'd gotten all she was going to get, Autumn stood and gave her daughter's arm a comforting squeeze. "I'm sorry your day started off so badly. Do you want to get up and have breakfast with me?"

"Where's Caden?" she asked, her head still under the pillow.

"He went to the beach."

Autumn assumed that meant she would come to breakfast, since Caden wouldn't be around. But Taylor didn't move. "No, I just want to go back to sleep."

"Okay. You do that. Maybe when you wake up, you'll be in a better mood," she joked. "How are you feeling about Sierra, by the way?"

Taylor threw the pillow onto the floor and lifted her head. "Why do you ask?"

Autumn hadn't expected her simple question to elicit such a defensive response. "Because after she was here for dinner on Sunday, you were worried about your friendship, remember? I'm just curious if everything is okay between you."

"Oh." Her hair was flying around from static electricity. She smoothed it down as her expression softened. "I'm feeling fine about her."

"Good. What about the rest of your new friends?" Hoping to see a smile before she left the room, she said, "Is there any boy in particular you might be interested in?"

"No!" she snapped. "And why would it have to be a boy?"

Autumn blinked in surprise. "You had a boyfriend for over a year and a half in Tampa. I thought—"

"Well, I don't know, okay?" she broke in. "It could be that I'm more into girls. Does that disappoint you, too?"

Suddenly, all the things that Taylor had said and done recently made more sense—the fact that she was hanging out with Sierra almost exclusively, the fact that she'd mentioned Sierra was "different" to sort of test the waters, the fact that Caden was so upset. Maybe she'd told her brother she had romantic feelings for Sierra, or he'd guessed, and he hadn't taken the news well.

I want to tell you. Believe me, I'm dying to tell you. But I can't be that big an asshole, even if she deserves it.

If Autumn's guess was correct, that would certainly explain Caden's statement before he charged out of the gate toward the beach. Maybe the fight had erupted because Taylor was texting with Oliver, and it had gone from there to Taylor claiming she wasn't interested in Caden's friend because she was interested in Sierra. "Are you confused about your sexuality?" she asked.

Fresh tears welled up. "Yes! I've never met anyone like Sierra. I like her more than a friend. But she's…she's not a guy."

Autumn sank back onto the bed. "No, she's not."

"So…that's bad, right? That's something to be sad about."

Autumn didn't want to say anything that would make what her daughter was going through any worse. Taylor had to be free to be herself in order to be happy. That was the one thing Autumn felt she had to remember as she dealt with this. "It's definitely the harder path."

"Why does it have to be harder?" Taylor asked. "It's so unfair! Why do people have to care about something that's none of their business?"

"It goes back to what people have been taught for generations and generations, I suppose. And different has never been an easy thing to be. I see the world moving toward greater acceptance—at least in the bigger cities. I'm sure you do, too. But it's going to be a while before the stigma of same-sex relationships disappears for good." If it ever did. Racism remained regardless of greater education. Although advances had definitely been made when it came to racial discrimination, persecution was still a problem, especially in some areas, and acceptance of sexual preference lagged behind that.

"You don't want me to be gay," she guessed.

Autumn could tell Taylor was watching her closely. She did feel a strange sense of loss—for the sudden disappearance of the traditional life Autumn had expected for her daughter, which included a husband and kids, she supposed. "I want you to be happy. Period."

"Which means…"

"You can't try to be something you're not. And I'll accept you no matter who you love."

"Do you really mean that?" she asked, her tone relieved and beseeching at the same time.

Autumn pulled her in for a hug. "One hundred percent."

Taylor sat in bed long after her mother left the house. She felt a lot better. She hadn't told Autumn the whole truth, but she'd told her some of it, and sharing even part of her secret somehow made it easier to breathe.

She was still sad about Caden, though. And she was a little surprised that, as angry as he'd been, he hadn't ratted her out. That made her feel even worse about what she'd done to him.

Grabbing her phone, she texted Sierra.

Caden found out Oliver is the father of my baby.

You told him? Sierra texted back.

No, Oliver messaged him. What an idiot!

Except you never answered him. What did you expect him to do?

I know, but I can't talk to him—not without telling him about the baby.

Maybe if you ask him not to tell anyone until you get back, he'd keep his mouth shut.

I'm afraid to take that risk.

Taylor's phone rang. "How'd Caden take the news?" Sierra asked without saying hello.

"He's pissed—just like I knew he would be."

"I'm sorry."

Taylor slumped against the headboard. "I am, too. I feel so bad. I wish I'd never done what I did—but especially with Oliver."

"Have you told Caden that?"

"I've tried."

"How hard?"

That was a good question. Not very hard. She'd been too panicked over the pregnancy. "Maybe I need to try again."

"I would. From what I've seen, he's a pretty cool brother. And you're going to need him and your mother more than ever before once the baby comes."

That was an ominous statement; it was also true. Even if Sierra moved to Tampa, she wouldn't be able to get there until after she graduated, and the baby would be born by then. "I'll talk to him."

"When?"

"Later. He's at the beach right now. I don't want to make a big scene in front of his friends."

"Better to avoid that," Sierra agreed.

Taylor frowned at her swollen eyes in the mirror over the dresser. "What are you doing today?"

"Job applications."

"This late in the summer? All the jobs are taken."

"I've got to find something. My dad and I had another blowout last night, and he told me that it was time for me to start helping with the bills."

"But you've got school in...what? Only six weeks?" She knew Sierra had had a job at the Tastee Burger until the owner's daughter got a divorce and moved home in March. They'd talked about it. She also knew Sierra had put in a few applications since then, but with so many college kids returning for the summer, she didn't get any callbacks.

"I was planning to try again once everyone left to go back to school, but my father says I'm costing him a fortune, and he doesn't want to wait that long."

Douchebag, Taylor thought. But she didn't say that. "So where will you apply?"

"I'll try the ice cream store again and hit up the tourist shops."

"And if that doesn't work?"

"I'll go online, see if there's a nanny position available. I'll find something."

"Are you upset?" she asked, feeling a little guilty for how good she had it. Her father had gone missing, but they'd never had to stress about how to cover their basic needs.

"Not really. This had to happen eventually, right? Besides, it'll be good to have my own money. I don't like asking him when I need something."

"Isn't that sort of his job? To take care of you until you graduate? I mean, he is your father."

"Yeah, well, I once had a mother, too. Just having the title doesn't mean you do the job."

Taylor winced at that response. Not only had she had the benefit of what money could buy, she'd also had good parents. The best. "My grandma is putting a coffee shop in her bookstore. If it takes off, she might be able to hire some part-time help. I'll talk to her about you. The only problem is…the contractor won't even start until fall. My grandma didn't want the place torn apart during tourist season. That's when she makes most of her money."

"That would be cool," Sierra said. "I'd love working at the bookstore. Thanks for putting in a good word for me."

"Sure thing. What are you doing later?"

"Cleaning and getting groceries. There's nothing to eat in this house."

Sierra already did so much for her father. Taylor wondered how he was going to get by without her, once she moved to Tampa. Maybe then he'd realize how much easier life was when she was around. "Wait for me. I'll go with you."

"Okay. Come over whenever you can."

Sierra obviously thought that was the end of the conversation, but Taylor caught her before she could hang up. "Sierra?"

"Yes?"

Taylor wanted to tell her about the discussion she'd had with her mother a few minutes ago. She'd cleared a huge hurdle just by letting Autumn know she *might* be gay. But if she still wasn't sure, there wasn't a lot for Sierra to get excited about. "Never mind."

"Say it," Sierra insisted.

Taylor drew a deep breath and said something else—something that was equally true—instead. "You mean more to me than any of my other friends ever have. I just want you to know that."

There was a long silence. Then Sierra said, "You already know how I feel about you," and hung up.

"Autumn brought up her father last night," Mary said while she and Laurie were preparing to have a sandwich in the back room. "She wants to know more about him."

Laurie had just parted the drape to check the front of the store. Since Autumn hadn't come in yet, she wanted to be sure they weren't neglecting a customer while they had lunch. But hearing this, she let the drape fall back into place with only a cursory glance. "See? I told you she did. It's on her mind or she wouldn't have hit me up. What'd you tell her?"

"Nothing."

Her eyes went wide. "She let you get away with that?"

"I told her there were reasons I couldn't say more, that sometimes mothers have to make difficult decisions to protect their children."

Laurie unwrapped the sandwich Mary had brought her from the deli. "But she's not a child anymore. And that was the perfect opportunity. You should've told her everything."

Mary shook her head. "I have to meet Tammy first, get some

sort of feel for who she turned out to be. The timing of her search for me makes me nervous. Why now? After all these years? I mean, Nora just got out of prison. Did *she* trigger the search?"

Laurie sent her a disgruntled look as she opened a bag of barbecue potato chips. "That's pretty cynical."

"*Cautious* is the word I prefer to use." Sometimes Laurie didn't understand—because she'd never been through what Mary had.

"So how did she react when you wouldn't tell her anything?"

Mary took the onions off her Italian sub. She'd forgotten to order it without them. "Resigned, I guess."

"Don't let that fool you. She's spent months and months searching for her husband. She'll start searching for her father next—you wait and see."

"She might. But it'll take six weeks before she can get the results of a DNA test. That's all I'm really looking for—enough time to meet Tammy, get to know her a little bit and figure out where Nora is."

"A sister could be a wonderful addition to Autumn's life, especially now that she's lost Nick."

"Tammy could also turn out to be the bane of her existence," Mary pointed out, frustrated that Laurie could advocate so tirelessly for the truth without realizing what was at stake.

"I can't help feeling sorry for her."

"You're not the only one. I loved her. I still love the child I knew back then. And I owe her. That's what makes this so hard."

"When are you two going to meet?" Laurie sipped her kombucha. "And don't tell me you're going to wait until Autumn and the kids go home. I'm tired of lying to Autumn," Laurie went on. "She thinks I'm her real aunt. That my son is her cousin and my mother her grandmother."

Mary poured some of Laurie's chips out on her own plate. "You've never minded that before," she said as she popped one into her mouth. As a matter of fact, Laurie was the one who'd initially suggested it. She'd offered to give context to Mary's life so that it would be easier to hide from her past, and the closer they grew the more Mary *did* become part of the family.

"It's not that I *mind*. I was happy to step into the gap and play that role. I knew you needed it. But Autumn was so little when I met her. Being her aunt meant something a little different then. It didn't seem like it had to be taken so literally. Now she's thirty-eight and will feel betrayed by me when she learns the truth. So I panic every time she corners me, like she did not long ago, right here—" she gestured around the room "—asking about her father."

"I can understand that. And I appreciate you supporting me in spite of it, especially for so long." She drew a deep breath. All roads led to the same destination. As much as Mary wanted to forget for good, the Skinners were going to have the last laugh— and, because of Tammy, might derail her life all over again. "I was going to wait until after they left. But maybe I should do it sooner, just in case. We're closed on Mondays. I'll do it then."

"*This* Monday?"

"No. The fundraiser is this weekend. Let's get through that first and give ourselves a chance to recover. But soon."

"It doesn't have to be on a Monday. I can always watch the store if you need me to."

Mary remembered how hard it had been to hear Tammy's voice on the phone and knew it would probably be much harder to see her in person—harder not to trust, and trust was the very thing that could get her into trouble. "We'll see how it goes."

22

Taylor was surprised when she showed up at Sierra's to find her brother there. She'd thought he was off playing volleyball with his friends—kids that'd been her friends, too, until she and Sierra had broken away from the group and started hanging out alone.

"Caden. What are you doing here?" she asked, closing the door behind her. She hadn't knocked. Sierra had texted her to say she could let herself in.

He was sitting stiffly on the couch. "Sierra sent me a message," he said, his words clipped with anger. "Asked me to come."

"And you did?" Taylor glanced at her friend for an explanation.

"This is probably the only place you two could have any privacy. You wouldn't want to talk in front of the twins and everyone else—or at home, where your mother or grandmother could walk in."

Sierra was always looking out for her. Taylor had never known anyone like her. She just understood and tried to help.

Relieved she had the chance to make things right with Caden, that she wouldn't have to stew about it all day, she offered her friend a grateful smile. "Thanks."

"No problem," she said. "I'm going to take the bike to the store and leave you two alone."

Sierra grabbed her wallet and went out through the garage, after which they heard the roar of her father's motorcycle. As she drove away and the sound of the engine dimmed, Taylor wished she was on the back of that bike. But she had to clean up her mess. Caden was obviously still mad. He was glaring at the coffee table and jiggling his leg.

"Caden, I feel terrible about what I've done."

He didn't even look at her.

"I want you to know that I'm really sorry."

His leg kept moving, something he did when he was anxious, impatient or angry. She knew which it was today.

"You knew how I felt about Oliver," he said.

"I did," she admitted. "I was… I was mad at you or I wouldn't have done it."

He scowled as he looked over. "Mad at *me*? For what?"

"For being okay. For still being able to function normally when I felt like I'd dropped into some alternate reality. It was hard watching you having fun and being normal when I couldn't get back to the world I'd known."

"Really? You're going to use Dad as an excuse?"

She stiffened her spine. "It's not an excuse. Maybe you've been able to continue on just fine since Dad left but, in case you haven't noticed, I've been drowning over here."

"So you went out and got yourself knocked up—by a dude I hate?"

She sank onto the closest chair. "I was just trying to feel something, Caden. I know that sounds lame, but it's the truth."

"You realize that every time I see my little niece or nephew I'll think of Oliver."

"I hope that isn't the case. What he did to you with Miranda was a dick move, but what I did was even worse. I wish I could take it back—for both our sakes—but I can't. All I can do is tell you how sorry I am."

He set his jaw. "I'm going to kick his ass as soon as we get home."

"Caden, no." She scooted to the edge of her chair. "If this was his fault, I'd let you. But it was *my* fault. It never would've happened if I hadn't gone to that party and…and gotten so messed up. I was out of it. He was out of it. And now my life is pretty much over—at least the life I had planned before."

"You could get an abortion," he suggested.

She hadn't even let herself contemplate that option. She didn't want to have to wrestle with such a big decision, one she might wind up regretting for the rest of her life. But maybe an abortion would be the best thing. "I'm thinking about it."

"Will you tell Mom if you do?"

"Are you kidding? No. Not if I go that route."

"When will you tell her you're pregnant?"

"I was hoping to wait until after the summer was over. These last few weeks—they're all I've got left of my life before it changes forever."

"Shit, Tay. Why didn't Oliver use protection?"

"He didn't have any," she said with a mirthless chuckle. "Most sixteen-year-old boys don't walk around with condoms in their pocket. Do you?"

He blushed.

"See what I mean? He didn't expect what happened."

"Yeah, well, I'm going to kick his ass, anyway," he said matter-of-factly. "I should've done it when he asked Miranda to prom."

"What's happening is bad enough. The last thing you need to do is get expelled from school or picked up by the cops. Think about Mom."

"I wish *you* would've thought about Mom at that party," he grumbled, but there was no longer such a harsh edge to his voice, and that gave her hope she could at least be on speaking terms with her only sibling again.

"So do I," she said softly.

He shot her a dirty look. "You really fucked up."

Normally, she would've pointed out that she'd already admitted that and apologized. But she deserved his anger. "I know."

He dropped his head in his hands.

"I'm sorry," she repeated. "If it makes you feel any better, I got the worst of it. I mean, think about it. You'll be okay. You can finish school and still go off to college and play water polo or whatever. It's Oliver who will have to help support a kid for the next eighteen years."

"That's true," he muttered. "He fucked up, too."

"Does that make you happy?"

He scratched his head. "Nothing about this makes me happy. So when are you going to tell him?"

"If I don't say something soon, he'll figure it out for himself."

"He's already suspicious or he wouldn't have texted me."

"I'll have to call him."

Caden, head bowed as though he was still thinking it all over, sat there for several seconds before looking up again. "So...are you and Sierra getting together now or what?"

Oh, God. Were they going to tackle that topic, too? He must've figured out that he'd been right before, when he'd approached her about Sierra liking girls. "How'd you guess that might be a possibility?"

"Before you got here, she was giving me every reason there could be for why I should understand and cut you some slack. You were going through a hard time. Everyone reacts to circumstances in a different way. Yada, yada."

"So?"

"She loves you," he said simply. "That's obvious in the way she talks about you, how quickly she comes to your defense. The question is—do you love her back?"

"I don't know that I'm gay, Caden. But I could be. Would it be so terrible if I am?"

He stood. "Of course not. I can see why you'd be attracted to Sierra. Even I can tell she's pretty cool."

Taylor smiled at his unexpected response, especially because he didn't add anything derogatory like, "For a lesbian."

"Thanks."

"Everybody's waiting for me. I've got to go."

She followed him to the door. "I'm glad you came over."

"So am I."

"Caden?" she said as he stepped out.

He turned back.

"You're a good brother."

"Not good enough to let you ride shotgun for the rest of the summer," he joked. "Now you owe me that."

She leaned against the door she was holding. "You'd make a pregnant girl sit in the backseat?"

"You're not even showing yet!"

"Fine," she said with a laugh. "Take it."

Autumn wasn't sure whether to mention to her mother what Taylor had revealed on Tuesday. She didn't believe Mary would think any less of Taylor, and she wanted to discuss what she'd learned—and how she should react to it—with someone she could trust to have Taylor's best interest at heart. But she caught herself every time she was about to bring it up.

Ordinarily, she would've turned to Nick. That she couldn't made her miss him more than she had in a long time. Mary loved Taylor, too. Autumn knew that. But sexuality was such a private matter. It didn't feel right to say anything to anyone other than Taylor's father.

In the end, she decided to leave whether or not Mary found out up to Taylor. If Taylor got together with Sierra and they made it obvious around town, it was possible Mary would hear about them. Or Caden would hear and say something. But Autumn decided to take that risk in favor of minding her own business and being a trustworthy confidante to her daughter.

The only downside to keeping her mouth shut? If Taylor was gay, Autumn would have to come to grips with it on her own.

She felt guilty even thinking that way, as if she now had something else to mourn. Love was love. She honestly believed it. But it wasn't easy to accept that her daughter would at some point be reviled or possibly harmed by narrow-minded bigots.

Her only escape from worrying about Taylor was the upcoming fundraiser. She even used that as an excuse not to see Quinn. Her children still needed her; she had to put them first.

She was sitting up in bed Friday night with her laptop, going over the many lists she'd made of everything that had to be done in time for the event tomorrow night, checking and double-checking that she hadn't missed anything, when her phone dinged. She picked it up to see who'd sent her a text—and froze when she saw Quinn's name.

She almost ignored it. It was late enough that she should be asleep. But then she read it: I miss you, he'd said, and she couldn't resist responding.

I miss you, too. As hard as she'd tried not to allow herself to daydream about him, or dwell on the time they'd spent together, it was impossible. The second she lowered her guard, like right before she fell asleep at night, he invaded her thoughts and dreams. She'd even packed up Nick's belongings yesterday and moved the boxes into the garage, because it felt too dishonest to be living among the daily reminders of the fact that she might still have a husband out there somewhere.

When can I see you?

She bit her lip as she contemplated how she should answer that question.

I don't know. Maybe after the fundraiser. I have
a lot to do before tomorrow night.

Let me help you. I've offered—many times. It's my
mother who's sick. I want to be a bigger part of it.

She felt bad that she hadn't responded to his offers. But she'd
been trying to avoid getting even deeper into a relationship with
him, needed to slow everything down and reevaluate.

If I see you, I doubt I'll want to work.

We can work afterward, he wrote back with a winking emoji.
Pinching the bridge of her nose, she battled the temptation
to tell him to come over right now. She wanted to feel his arms
around her, to tell him about Taylor and see what he thought,
which was weird, since she hadn't even told her mother.

I'm too tired tonight, she said and forced herself to power
down her phone.

Mike and Beth Vanderbilt were the first to arrive at the Rotary Clubhouse for the start of the fundraiser. Autumn had told
them they didn't need to be there until seven. That was when
it officially began. But they walked through the doors at six, as
dressed up and polished as though they were going to church.

Autumn couldn't help noticing how uncomfortable they both
looked—not only because he was wearing a suit and tie and she
a dress and heels—but because they were unable to hide the fact
that they were dreading the rest of the evening.

She tried to put them at ease with a bright smile and gave
them each a hug, being careful not to disturb the wig Beth sometimes wore since losing her hair. "This won't be as bad as you
think," she whispered to Mike before letting him go, and realized afterward that she probably shouldn't have said anything,

because tears welled up, at which point he pretended to pick a piece of lint off his jacket.

"Please," Autumn said. "These are your friends. They love you and are grateful for all you have done for this community."

"I haven't done anything—" he started, but she cut him off.

"You employ people who can support their families because of your business, and you've pitched in and donated every time anyone else has had a need. Beth is one of us. You're not the only one who has a responsibility to care for her."

Mike nodded grudgingly, and Beth, her face pale, her dress hanging on what was now a bony frame, seemed too sick and weary to bother with being quite as embarrassed as her husband. With a faint smile, she gripped Autumn's hand and thanked her for all the hard work she'd put into the fundraiser.

"It's my pleasure," Autumn assured her. "But should you really stay for the event when you'd be more comfortable resting at home?"

"I'd rather thank everyone in person," she said softly.

The Vanderbilts were stubborn people. *Good* people, as Laurie had proclaimed when Autumn first arrived in town. "Okay. I've got a seat for you both right up front." She pointed to the table closest to the podium. "Mike, why don't you get Beth settled? Then I have a few things you could do to help out, if you don't mind," she said, knowing he would feel far less self-conscious if he could stay busy and contribute.

"You got it," he responded and led his wife to the table marked Reserved.

Autumn was still trying to swallow the lump in her throat, put there by Mike's emotion and the fact that she was beginning to believe Beth wasn't going to make it, regardless of what they did, when she spotted Quinn, who must've come in on the heels of his parents. Freshly shaven, his thick hair still damp, he was dressed up, too, but he hadn't yet tied his tie. It dangled around his neck while he carried his jacket over one arm.

"I'm sorry that this event is so hard for you and your parents," she said.

"We'll get through it." After casting a quick glance at the table where Mike was helping Beth sit down, he indicated all the decorations and the tables she and her committee members had set up. They'd been at the clubhouse since early this morning. Even Taylor and Caden had helped, although they were home now, getting ready. "Thanks for doing this. I would've been here earlier, but I was busy with the food prep at the restaurant, trying to make sure the staff we left to cover it doesn't run into a problem. With most people here, I don't expect them to have a large crowd, but you never know."

"I'm glad you took care of it. We had this."

He looked as though he wanted to say something more personal, but Lynn Hill walked up. "Will you come take a look at the silent auction? Make sure I have the items arranged the way you want?"

"Sure."

"And I can't find enough pens for the bid sheets," Lynn said. "I bought a pack but can't remember where I put them."

"I saw them over by my bag," Autumn told her and tossed Quinn an apologetic smile as she walked away. She told herself to forget about what she was feeling and do the job she'd committed to doing, but whenever she looked up and saw him, she felt the longing she'd been trying to deny. The way he watched her, she could tell he knew something had changed, that she'd shut him out again. She felt bad about that, because she could tell he was disappointed. But he didn't know what it was like to have children, the sacrifices that being a parent sometimes required.

It wasn't until after her speech and the silent auction were over, and poor Mr. Salls was bumbling his way through the live auction—which was turning out to be a success in spite of the fact that he was every bit as terrible at auctioneering as he'd tried to tell them he would be—that Autumn began to relax.

The bulk of the fundraiser was over and had gone surprisingly well, given how little time she'd had to plan it.

She was standing at the back, watching various people raise their paddles for a seven-day vacation in Hawaii, when Caden, Sierra and Taylor approached.

"Can we go home and change?" Caden asked. "It'll be a lot easier to help clean up if we can throw on some comfortable clothes."

Relieved to see that her son and daughter were friends again, she nodded, and they hurried for the door.

"We're raising even more than we anticipated."

Autumn turned to find Mary standing slightly behind her. Her mother and Laurie had been busy working in the kitchen all night, helping with the spaghetti, garlic bread and green salad dinner, so she was a little startled to hear her mother's voice. "It seems like it, doesn't it? I can't wait to see how much."

"It'll be at least fifty thousand."

"That's five months of medicine."

"Doesn't sound like a lot when you put it that way. But it's better than leaving the Vanderbilts fifty thousand deeper in debt."

"True."

Mary seemed distracted for a brief moment. Then she said, "Don't look now, but Quinn can't take his eyes off you."

Autumn had been having a hard time not staring at him, too. "He's grateful for all the work I've put into this," she mumbled.

Her mother wasn't that easily fooled. "That isn't all," she said with a chuckle. "Things must be going well between you two."

"No, they're not going well. There's nothing between us."

Mary sobered. "Seriously? Why not?"

"Because my children come first." The auction had just ended, and Mr. Salls, drenched in flop sweat, was looking at her with a "Hallelujah!" expression. She started toward the staff table so she could get the tally from Barbara Stamper, who'd agreed to keep track of the money so she could announce the total raised before the end of the evening.

Autumn didn't want to talk about Quinn. Her emotions were too jumbled. But her mother caught her wrist before she could get more than a few steps away.

"Your happiness and their happiness don't have to be mutually exclusive," she said and returned to the kitchen.

Quinn sat on the beach in his suit pants and white cotton shirt, which he'd unbuttoned at the neck when he removed his tie and jacket in the car. He'd taken off his shoes and tossed them on the sand beside him when he chose this spot. He seemed to be alone and he was glad. That was the whole idea of coming here.

In the pale moonlight, he couldn't see much more than the white crests of the waves as they rushed toward him. They came to within a few inches before falling back into the sea. The tide was coming in. If he didn't move, he'd soon get wet, suit and all, but he didn't care.

As he drank the beer he'd grabbed when he'd returned the stuff they'd borrowed from the restaurant, he told himself that he should be celebrating. They'd raised $56,493 to help pay for his mother's cancer treatments. That was a significant amount and would bring him and his father some much-needed relief. He'd already given his parents every dime of his savings and couldn't earn more now that he was working for them, so having the community rally behind them was a beautiful thing.

And yet, here he sat, feeling like shit. Money wouldn't necessarily ensure his mother's survival. He told himself that was the reason. But the money gave him hope. The real problem was Autumn. She'd pulled away from him just when he'd begun to believe he'd finally found someone he could love *and* admire.

After wedging the bottle into the sand, he fell back onto his elbows and stared up at the velvety sky. His father had always been a strong man. Quinn had never seen Mike cry in public before, and yet he'd stood up at the end of the fundraiser, his voice breaking as he thanked everyone who contributed. Quinn understood how helpless his father felt in the face of Beth's cancer; he felt helpless, too. But he was beginning to worry about his father almost as much as his mother. Every day that Beth grew weaker, Mike changed, too. Quinn was afraid he wouldn't be the same man if they lost her.

"Fuck love," he muttered. He wasn't sure anything else caused quite as much suffering. His marriage had been a nightmare— the night Sarah had stabbed him surreal—and he'd hated every difficult decision he'd had to make after, when it came time for her trial. He was stupid to sign up for another relationship, anyway.

His phone went off in his pocket, but he let it ring. He didn't want to talk to anybody, even if it was Autumn. He was sincerely grateful for all she'd done to help his family, but they seemed to be at the end of what he'd expected to be a new beginning, and he didn't have the reserves to deal with more disappointment right now.

Had she backed away because she'd found out that Taylor was pregnant? All week, he'd been going back and forth on whether he should tell her what he'd learned from Caden. But she'd never given him the chance. She'd refused to see him, had been brief and in a hurry to get off the phone if he called and had barely texted him back.

Now he could safely say Taylor's pregnancy was none of his business. He'd just stay away from Autumn and her kids, let them go on with their lives. That was what she obviously wanted.

His phone started to ring again. Afraid that maybe he'd been wrong to ignore it the first time, that maybe his mother had taken a turn for the worse, he pulled it out of his pocket.

It wasn't either of his parents—thank God. It was, in fact, Autumn.

Hitting the ignore button, he put it back in his pocket and

finished his beer. He was about to grab his shoes so he could leave, when it rang a third time.

With a sigh, he checked: Autumn.

Again, he silenced it—and this time he turned on the do not disturb feature.

"Really?" a voice said, coming from close by. "You're not going to take my call?"

Leaving his shoes where they were, he came quickly to his feet.

He squinted in the direction from which he'd heard Autumn's voice, but he couldn't see her until she emerged from the darkness only a few feet away. "Sorry," he said. "Didn't mean to be rude. I just needed some time, and figured, as late as it is, you'd think I was asleep, anyway."

"I would have, except that your car's here in the lot, and the ring of your phone led me right to you."

It was also the spot where he'd brought her. "Did you walk over?" She was wearing yoga pants and a T-shirt with flip-flops, so he knew she'd been home.

"No. I have my car. I've been all over town—"

"The fundraiser was a lot of work," he interrupted. "I'm sorry about that."

"It wasn't because of the fundraiser. I was looking for you."

He bit back a groan. "Autumn, I'm not in the mood to talk. I know what you're going to say, and you don't need to bother. I understand that you've been through a lot with the loss of your husband. And I appreciate all you've done for my mother. Truly. I meant it when I thanked you at the fundraiser. But the past few years haven't been that kind to me, either, and…if you're not ready to give me a real shot, I understand. I was wrong to push you."

"You've written me off that easily?"

He felt his eyebrows come together. "You've made it clear that's what you want me to do."

"What if I've changed my mind?"

He was excited by the thought that she might've done just that but leery at the same time. He didn't want to get his hopes up again. He needed peace and calm, not to step onto another emotional hand grenade. "I'd ask if you were sure," he said. "Because my heart's already been put through a meat grinder. I can't sign up for more of the same—not with my mother dying. And..."

"And?" she echoed.

"And not with someone I want as badly as you," he admitted.

Stepping closer, she rose up on tiptoe and pecked his lips. "I just...panicked, Quinn. It frightened me that I could care for you so quickly and so easily when, as happy as I was with Nick, it should've been hard. And I don't want to do anything that might hurt my kids. But my mother made a good point in the car tonight."

He resisted the urge to pull her into his arms, was still afraid to trust her sudden reversal. "What was it?"

"She said you're a good man. And the love of a good man is hard to come by."

He allowed himself to reach up and trace the side of her face with his finger. "How do I know you won't bail out on me again?"

"I guess there are no guarantees, for either one of us, but it might be reassuring to know I've already told my kids about you."

Shocked, he stepped back. He'd liked everything she'd said so far, but this is what really gave him hope. "You did? When?"

"On the way home from the fundraiser. Caden was telling me how you played volleyball with him all morning the other day. And Taylor said she liked you, too, and that she felt bad for what was happening to your mother. So I took the opportunity to tell them that you'd asked me out."

He felt a smile coming on. "What'd they say?"

"It was a little awkward, I'm not going to lie," she replied with a nervous laugh. "They aren't used to thinking about their mother dating, especially when there's no closure with their dad. But my mother was in the car with us, which helped. She said that I'd done all I could do to find Nick, that they'd be leaving home soon and there wasn't any reason for me to be alone."

"In other words, she used guilt to get them to agree," he said wryly.

"A little, I guess. This kind of transition is never easy, so I don't think it's fair to expect it to be. But I'm hoping it'll be worth it, for all of us. They said they want me to go out with you if that's what I want to do."

He thought of what Caden had told him about Taylor. Autumn hadn't mentioned the pregnancy. But he wasn't about to bring it up right now. "Do you think they were being sincere?"

"I hope so. Either way, seeing you won't stop me from continuing to be a good mother. I'm just going to remember that and take them at their word."

Pulling her against him, he kissed her before tucking her head under his chin and simply holding her. His mother was still dying of cancer. Continuing to watch her suffer was one of the most difficult things he'd ever experienced. But having Autumn in his arms somehow made everything easier. "I'll treat them right," he said. "I promise."

23

Taylor had promised she'd spend the Fourth of July with her family. Mimi and Aunt Laurie had closed the store early, and her mother was making homemade salsa, guacamole, enchiladas and rice and beans for dinner. It was another one of Taylor's favorite meals, but she couldn't get excited about food when all she could think about was her mother hitting the dating scene.

She'd known something like this might happen eventually. She didn't expect her mother to stay single forever. But so soon?

And wouldn't you know it, Sierra wasn't even available so they could talk about it. Dennis had insisted she go with him to visit his brother, who lived two hours away. She probably had her phone, but Taylor didn't want to interrupt when her mean father was around.

A knock sounded at her bedroom door. "Come in." She needed to set the table, so she was expecting her mother to roust her out.

But Caden poked his head in. "Hey, what're you doing?"

She'd been writing in her journal, trying to decide what to do about the baby, which was proving much more difficult than she'd at first thought. She'd also been trying to come up with some way to tell Oliver. She hadn't been able to make herself call or text him. She was afraid, even if he promised he wouldn't tell anyone, that he'd confide in a friend, if not a family member, and word would get out before she even returned home.

She shuddered at the thought of showing up at school, could almost hear people whispering about her: *Did you hear? Taylor's pregnant! She's having Oliver Hancock's baby!*

She winced at the humiliation and embarrassment that would cause. It didn't help that Oliver was only a junior. Everyone would be surprised and wonder why she'd ever slept with him.

Caden was going to struggle when word got out, too. She imagined he'd be torn between defending her and wanting, once again, to beat Oliver up.

"Nothing, really," she said and shut her journal.

He came in and closed the door behind him. "You okay?"

"Feeling kind of weird."

"You have that thing pregnant women get—morning sickness?"

"No. I haven't felt any of that yet. Hopefully, I won't. It's Mom going out with Quinn Vanderbilt that feels weird."

"Yeah. Having Dad go missing was bad enough."

"Exactly. And now Mom's starting to date? What if it gets serious and they wind up married? That would make him our stepdad. Eww!"

He sat on the edge of the bed. "You don't like him? I think he's cool."

She put her journal in the top drawer of her nightstand. She planned to shove it under the mattress later, but she didn't want her brother to see her do it. "Because he gave us a free lunch at his restaurant? I don't want anyone else in my life trying to tell me what to do, let alone a stranger."

"Maybe it wouldn't be like that."

"It would definitely be like that. That's what stepdads do."

"We're almost adults. And Mimi is right. It wouldn't be fair of us to expect Mom to be alone. It's not her fault Dad left."

She rolled her eyes. "You always take everything in stride."

"What else can I do? Getting upset doesn't bring Dad back. Letting Mom know how we really feel might cause her to turn Quinn away. But she'd start dating someone else eventually. And maybe it would be someone we don't like at all. Have you thought about that?"

"I've been busy thinking about my own problems," she grumbled.

He shot her a sheepish glance. "Speaking of the baby, I need to tell you something."

"What?"

"Remember when I said in the car that Quinn played volleyball with me for a few hours on Tuesday?"

"Yes…"

"Well, that was the morning that I found out Oliver was the father of your baby."

"And?" she asked, narrowing her eyes.

"I was pretty upset and—"

"And?"

"I told him about the baby."

She jumped off the bed. "No! Please say you didn't!"

He stood, too. "I didn't know he had any interest in Mom, let alone hoped to date her. I just thought he was someone I could talk to. It's not like I can tell anyone else."

Taylor started to fan herself and pace up and down beside the bed. "Oh shit, oh shit, oh shit."

"Don't freak out," he said. "He hasn't told Mom, or you'd know about it."

"But he *will* tell her! That's the thing!"

"No. He's cool, like I said. This proves it."

Taylor pressed a hand to her chest as if she could slow the pounding of her heart. Her mother was starting to date, even though she was sort of still married, and she was seeing someone Caden had confided in about the baby. "Could my luck get any worse?" she asked with a groan.

"Yes," he insisted, and that made her realize he was right. It could definitely get worse. She needed to work on damage control.

"Quinn's taking us all to the fireworks show tonight," he said. "You should try to get a moment with him and ask him to let you be the one to tell Mom. I bet he'd go for that. He might even have some advice on *how* to tell her."

She stopped pacing, dropped her head back and stared up at the ceiling. "That's going to be so awkward! He doesn't really know me. He'll think I'm a…a slut or something."

"No, he won't, Tay. I promise. He's not like that."

Wishing she could just go back in time and never go to the party where she'd been with Oliver, she rubbed her forehead. "I can't believe you told him."

"I know," Caden said. "I'm sorry! I had no clue it would come to this."

"That was probably why he was interested in playing volleyball with you to begin with—he likes Mom." She was tempted to say he should've known that, but how would he? She was just upset and looking for a target.

"Maybe that was part of it," he allowed. "But I had a lot of fun that day. It would be great to do it again. I'm telling you, I like him."

"You would," she grumbled. "Everything's always easier for you."

"Only because you make life harder than it has to be," he snapped back.

She scowled at him as though she was still mad, but deep inside, she was actually a little relieved to have an adult she could talk to. It wouldn't be easy to start the conversation she needed to have with Quinn. But maybe he'd be able to help her in some way.

★ ★ ★

Autumn kept wringing her hands. It was one thing to spend time with Quinn herself. As long as she didn't allow him around her kids, she could sort of compartmentalize that she was falling in love with a man who wasn't her husband. But letting him take her and her children to the fireworks celebration on the beach made him seem like part of the family already.

Maybe that decision had been a mistake. She'd been tempted to put off something like this and probably would have, to give her children some time to adjust, except she was afraid Quinn would feel like she'd never really let him in.

Besides, they wouldn't be in Sable Beach long enough for Taylor and Caden to get to know him if they didn't start soon. They had to go back to Tampa next month. She didn't know what her relationship with Quinn would look like at that point, but she knew she wanted to explore what she felt—and that he did, too. So until they could figure out the future, she might as well accept his invitation and see how it went.

Both Caden and Taylor had been quiet all day. She could tell they were leery of this new change. She couldn't blame them; it would affect their lives, too. And because she'd mentioned dating, they'd suddenly noticed that she'd packed up Nick's belongings and put them in the garage. That realization had probably been more traumatic than saying she wanted to go out with Quinn. She'd had to reassure Taylor that she still loved Nick and always would. He'd given her two beautiful children, and they'd had eighteen wonderful years together.

Autumn felt her mother's arm go around her as she stood at the front window, looking out at the street. She hadn't heard Mary approach; she'd been too lost in her own thoughts. But she knew her mother's smell, her mother's touch.

"Stop worrying," her mother said. "Everything's going to be fine."

The blow-dryer went on in the bathroom, where Taylor was

getting ready. Since she had the bathroom, Caden was in Taylor's room, changing into a clean pair of shorts. "This is just… such a big step," she confided.

"Caden and Taylor both know how much we love them. As soon as they get to know Quinn, they'll be happy to have him in their lives, too."

Autumn drew a deep breath as she nodded. "I hope so."

Mary checked her watch. "What time is he supposed to be here?"

"Not until eight." She lowered her voice. "He invited us to go out to dinner beforehand, but I didn't want to go that far. A Fourth of July celebration seems less… I don't know…in their face, especially because you're going with us. It'll be just like we celebrate every year—except Quinn will be with us instead of Nick." She heard herself and frowned. "Actually, on second thought, that isn't such a small change. What was I thinking?"

Mary kissed her temple. "Like I said, stop worrying. Caden and Taylor are nearly adults. They'll understand."

"They understand too well," she muttered. "This would be much easier if they were little."

"That's true, I suppose. Little children are so flexible."

Although Autumn would rather have had them meet Quinn at the celebration, which would make it even less like a date, parking was going to be a nightmare, so she'd suggested he leave his car in her mother's driveway and they all walk.

"There he is," Mary said, spotting Quinn's Audi at the same time Autumn did.

He parked and got out, wearing a pair of golf shorts, a polo shirt and some topsiders, and the excitement that lanced through Autumn—at just the sight of him—made her feel maybe she *was* doing the right thing. At least for her.

She prayed it would be okay for her kids, too.

"Is everybody ready?" she called.

Caden came out. Taylor was still blow-drying her hair, but

Autumn didn't rush her. She shot her son a smile and waited for him to return it before she answered the door.

"Hi," Quinn said good-naturedly, but she could tell he was a little nervous, too.

It was always warm and humid in the middle of the summer, even at night, but there was a breeze coming in off the ocean as everyone gathered for the fireworks that helped compensate. Quinn knew Autumn and her family had already eaten dinner, but he'd asked Darby, one of the cooks at the restaurant, to add a few hot dogs to what he was grilling for his own family just in case.

They found Darby exactly where he'd said he'd be, but Caden was the only one who'd accept a dog. Quinn showed him how he liked to make it—with grilled onions and green peppers piled high, a few jalapeños and plenty of Dijon mustard and ketchup. After they'd both finished their first, they lamented the fact that they were too stuffed to have another.

"How about a slice of grilled pineapple for dessert?" Quinn asked.

Not surprisingly, Caden accepted despite complaining about his stomach being full only seconds before. Quinn chuckled; he'd been able to eat a tremendous amount at that age, too. "What about you?" he asked Taylor. "Have you ever tried grilled pineapple?"

She shook her head.

He couldn't tell if she wasn't interested in opening up to him, or she just didn't like him. Of the two kids, he got the impression she was going to be much harder to win over than Caden. "You should have a bite, at least. It's delicious."

"Okay," she said grudgingly.

"I'll definitely have some," Mary said. "Your father's given me a slice before, probably on another Fourth of July when we were out here to watch the show, and I loved it."

"Great." He turned to Autumn. "What about you?"

She grinned. "Of course. I'm not missing out."

They all exclaimed at how good the smoky, caramelized pine-apple was, thanked Darby and moved down toward the water, where Quinn's parents had two blankets stretched out on the sand.

"My folks were nice enough to come early and get us a spot," he said.

Although his father stood when they arrived, his mother remained seated. She looked so weak that he asked if she'd rather go home. "I'll drive you," he offered. "Dad can stay, since the show's about to start."

"No. I don't want to be home alone when you're all here," she said, and while everyone else was busy choosing one of the cookies and drinks Mike was passing out, she leaned over to add, "I want to see how you get on with Autumn. My dying wish is to see you happy."

He kissed the sharp angle of her cheek. Even her skin felt different since the cancer came back—papery thin. "Don't talk about dying. Just focus on getting well. You don't have to worry about me."

"I will, anyway. But if you're with a good woman, I'll worry less." She'd liked Sarah in the beginning, but once they got married and Sarah became so difficult, Beth had struggled to fully embrace her daughter-in-law, and he couldn't blame her. Sarah had been far more jealous of the love he had for his mother than his father. She wanted to be the only woman in his life.

He squeezed his mother's hand and moved to make room for the others as they settled in for the show.

Autumn sat next to him, but Quinn was careful not to even hold her hand. He wanted this to be a comfortable, friendly gathering, which was why he'd included his parents. He figured both families would enjoy it, and the atmosphere of the large group would be less threatening to Autumn's kids.

Because of the morning he'd spent with Caden on the beach, he felt as though he'd already connected with her son to a certain degree. Familiarity helped ease the awkwardness of their current situation, but he caught Taylor watching him every few minutes as though she didn't know what to make of him. Although he went out of his way to try to draw her out, she didn't seem to warm up to him.

After the fireworks were over, they visited with his folks for a few minutes longer. Then he walked Autumn and her family over to a vendor at the edge of the beach, where he bought them each a snow cone to help battle the heat. While they ate, he carried his folks' blanket and picnic basket to the car.

He was just weaving through the parking lot and the mass of people who were heading home, trying to get back to where he'd left his parents on the beach, so he could help his father get his mother to the car, when he spotted Taylor. She looked anxious as she searched the lot. He assumed she was looking for a friend. But as soon as she saw him, her face cleared, and she started toward him with purpose.

Surprised that she would seek him out, especially when she'd been so guarded all evening, he smiled as soon as she reached him. "Hi. Are you all done with your snow cone?"

"Not yet. I told everyone I had to go to the bathroom, but… really I just wanted to talk to you."

He tried not to reveal his shock. "Sure thing. About what?"

She folded her arms tightly. "It's about what Caden told you."

Now he understood why she'd wanted a moment alone. But it was still a bold move. Were they really going to talk about this?

He lowered his voice. "You mean…the baby."

She stared at her feet. "Yes."

"Since we're having this discussion out here, I'm guessing you haven't told your mother or your grandmother about the pregnancy."

She kicked a pebble across the blacktop. "No. I don't want

to ruin the rest of the summer. It's my last six weeks of…you know…of being who I've always been. Besides, why humiliate myself in Sable Beach *and* Tampa, especially if I have a choice?"

Everything was going to change in a big way, and she knew it. He couldn't blame her for trying to hang on to the life she had for a little longer. "I understand. So…are you here to ask me not to tell your mother?"

"Yes."

He scratched his neck. He wished Caden had never confided in him. He didn't want to be in the middle of this. But he couldn't see how allowing Taylor six weeks in which to break the news to her mother would make much of a difference. "Is it dangerous for you not to see a doctor right away?"

"No. I've looked it up online. I'll only be three months when we go back to Tampa. There's nothing a doctor can do for me at this stage, anyway—except tell me I'm pregnant, and I already know that."

Reluctant to keep this kind of secret from Autumn, he hesitated. He hated to see what would happen if she found out. But maybe he was making too big a deal out of it. After all, there was a risk involved in telling her, too. Alienating her children right from the start would also make their relationship more difficult—and might do irreparable damage to his relationships with Taylor and Caden. And if it was only for a few weeks, this probably wouldn't amount to anything. Besides, he didn't feel as though he had the right to get involved in something so private. "As long as waiting doesn't endanger you or the baby, I'd rather stay out of it."

She looked relieved. "You'll let me tell her?"

"Sure. It's not my place. I get that. But I need you to do *me* a favor, too."

Instantly suspicious, her expression darkened. "What's that?"

"Don't ever let her know I knew before she did," he said.

She perked up at his response. "I won't. I promise. And I'll tell Caden to keep his mouth shut, too."

"Deal."

Obviously relieved, she seemed ready to head back, but he had something else he wanted to say while he had the chance. "You know your mother and I went to school together, don't you?"

"Yeah, you told us that at the restaurant." Her expression said she understood this was leading somewhere.

"So we didn't just meet."

"What are you trying to say?" she asked, once again skeptical.

Despite the heat, Quinn suddenly felt as though he was walking on a pond covered with ice and had to move carefully or he'd fall through. "I like her, Taylor—I like her a lot. But I don't want the fact that I like her to make you feel threatened in any way. I'm not trying to take your father's place. Even if your mother and I end up getting into a serious relationship, you never have to accept me as a father if you don't want to. Whatever relationship we have, I'd rather it be genuine, so I'd settle for being your friend, if that's all you want me to be."

She seemed to relax again as she nodded.

"I'm sorry for what you've been through," he added. "But your mother loves you very much, and I'm not going to come between you. I'm not even going to try."

Her lip trembled slightly. A girl her age facing a pregnancy had to be terrified. But at least she had a good mother.

Standing taller, she cleared her throat. "Got it. Okay. Thanks."

"Come on. Everything's going to be fine. You'll see," he said and hoped to God it was true—not only for her sake but his own. Now that he'd agreed to keep her secret, if Autumn ever found out, he'd have something to lose, too.

24

The latest batch of pictures you sent is awesome.
Autumn is so beautiful. So are Taylor and Caden.
Wow. Thank you for sharing these.

Mary was alone at the bookstore when that message came in. She'd been communicating with Tammy almost every day since they'd spoken on the phone, usually by text, which was less threatening to her because she could take some time to consider her response before sending it.

Although she'd been reluctant at first, she was beginning to enjoy getting to know the adult Tammy, which came as a complete surprise. She'd had herself so convinced that she needed to stay away from anything to do with the Skinners that she would've missed this chance to reconnect had Tammy not paid Drake D. Owens to find her.

Does Taylor have a boyfriend? Tammy asked.

Mary thought she might have a girlfriend, but she didn't mention that.

Not right now. She did a while back, but they
broke up after Christmas.

What about Caden?

He's never had a girlfriend, as far as I know.

How's Autumn and Quinn getting along?

She'd told Tammy about the fireworks show and how ex-cited she was that her daughter was starting a new relationship.

Great. She's as giddy as a teenager.

I'm thrilled she's found someone. It must've been
difficult to lose Nick.

Mary was surprised that Tammy remembered so much of what she'd been told. Names, facts, what was going on with each in-dividual. She seemed to be genuinely interested in their lives.

He was a great guy in so many ways. But I think
she and Quinn were meant to be together from
the beginning.

Are you hoping she'll move back to Sable Beach?

I am. She only went to Tampa for Nick.

Sable Beach seems like such a great town. How
did you wind up there?

I saw it in a travel magazine your mother had—
Ten Best Beach Towns on the East Coast. I loved
it so much I tore out the page and kept it with
me for probably years. The wholesome look of
the town made me feel safe, and I decided I was
going to raise Autumn in such a place.

The bell rang over the door as Joann Hunter came in with

her granddaughter, Megan, who was maybe thirteen. As usual, they were carrying a sack of donuts and a drink they'd purchased from down the street. Mary was eager to get the coffee shop in and opened, so that she could sell pastries and fresh-squeezed juice and coffee, especially now that she'd committed to the loan and it was no longer just a pipe dream. "Morning."

"Morning," they said and then laughed at each other because they'd spoken in unison.

"You here alone today?" Joann asked as they came toward the cash register.

Mary set her phone aside. "For now. Laurie had a hair appointment, but she'll be in shortly."

"What about Autumn?"

"She doesn't usually come in until noon or one."

Joann waved at the racks of books. "Anything new we should be aware of?"

Mary led them to the science fiction section, which was Megan's favorite. "I ordered a dystopian novel by a woman named Tosca Lee I thought Megan would like." She pulled it off the shelf and handed it to Joann's granddaughter. "It's been getting some great reviews."

Joann sipped her coffee while Megan read the back cover and began to flip through the beginning of the story. "I saw your family with Quinn and his folks at the fireworks show on Sunday night. Are Autumn and Quinn getting together? Because Bev Vizii is running around telling everyone that Autumn and Quinn were probably having an online affair the whole time, that maybe she was the one he was cheating with."

"That's crazy. He wasn't cheating. He's said as much. And Nick was still around back then."

"You know Bev. She insists that her daughter was justified."

"It's time someone told Bev to shut her trap. She's been bad-mouthing Quinn ever since he came home. We're all tired of it. Her daughter *stabbed* him, for crying out loud. How can she blame *him*?"

"Someone stabbed Quinn?" Megan asked, eyes wide. "The guy who owns that restaurant?"

"Never you mind. It was a long time ago," Joann replied, quickly smoothing over it. "Do you want that book or not?"

"It looks good to me."

"Then get it. We've got to meet your grandpa at the post office."

Megan handed Mary the novel, and Mary returned to the register to ring it up. "Thanks for coming in," she said as she put it in a bag with the Beach Front Books logo and handed it over the counter.

"Of course," Joann said as her granddaughter accepted it. "We love books, but I'll have to come back and find something for myself later."

Mary told them goodbye and then picked up her phone again. She was expecting to continue her conversation with Tammy, and sure enough, there was another message waiting for her.

I'd like to see your place someday. And your store. Beach Front Books. It sounds so quaint and fabulous.

She was tempted to write, *You're welcome to come out whenever you can.* But first she needed to know that Tammy no longer had a relationship with Nora.

Where's your mother? she finally asked. Do you know?

No clue.

You don't have any contact with her?

None. She knows how I feel about her.

That was comforting. But it still felt too risky—given how terrible the past had been—to bring anything that had to do with the Skinners into the careful life she'd built here.

Does she know where you live?

Who can say?

What would you do if she ever contacted you?

At this point, I'm not sure. It's been so long.

This answer was less comforting. It gave Mary the impression that Tammy was softening toward her mother. Nora had proved herself to be such a psychopath that Mary had decided she'd have to be a fool to feel any empathy for her. But she wasn't related to Nora like Tammy was, so maybe she could be more objective.

"Who are you texting?"

Mary jumped. She'd been so engrossed in her exchange with Tammy that she hadn't heard Laurie come in. There was no bell on the back door. "Oh, it's you," she said. "You scared me."

"It's not like I snuck in," Laurie said with a laugh. "Is that Tammy?"

"Yeah."

"I should've guessed. You've been texting her nonstop since you two first spoke."

"More and more as the days go by. It was never Tammy I had a problem with," she mumbled, but Tammy's response had made her uneasy. She read the words two or three more times before she could convince herself that Tammy didn't necessarily mean she'd allow her mother back into her life.

Or did she?

What difference does the length of time make? she asked.

She could be a completely different person these days.

You think prison might have improved her?

She certainly had plenty of time to think while
she was behind bars. Wouldn't you say? It's also
possible she would never have done what she did
without my father's influence.

                        And that might only be what you want to
                                              believe.

"What's she saying?" Laurie looked concerned, probably because of Mary's own expression.

"Nothing." She put her phone away and got busy doing all
the stuff she'd neglected while she was caught up with Tammy.
She didn't want to argue with the Skinners' daughter or try to
convince her. That was exactly the type of thing she'd been trying to avoid by staying away.

But when she checked her phone to see if she'd heard from
Autumn just before leaving to pick up lunch, she saw that
Tammy had written her again.

I hope I didn't scare you away. I'm not in touch
with my mother. You don't have to worry.

Okay, she wrote back. But the fact that Tammy would make
any excuses for Nora led Mary to believe future contact wasn't
out of the realm of possibilities.

And that wasn't a good sign.

Taylor and Sierra were lying on Sierra's bed, talking, while
Taylor was trying to gather the nerve to call Oliver. He'd been
blowing up her phone for the past several days and the last text
he'd sent her read, Really? You won't even respond? Uncool.

He was right, and she knew it. Although the pregnancy
wouldn't affect him nearly as much as it would affect her, he
had a stake in what was happening, too, and deserved to know
one way or the other.

"So…have you scrapped the tattoo idea?" Sierra asked as she tossed a small, spongy football into the air and caught it, over and over.

Taylor lifted her head to be able to gather all her hair into a knot before falling back onto the pillow. "For now. I think I've done enough to piss off my mom, don't you?"

"Yeah. Probably smarter to wait." She put the football on the nightstand and rolled off the bed. "You can get a tattoo later, if you're still interested," she said as she removed the Queen album they'd been listening to and put on the Beatles. "You'll be eighteen before you give birth."

Give birth. Those words freaked Taylor out. But turning eighteen was just as scary. A baby and adulthood. She wasn't prepared for either.

"Have you heard back on any of your job applications?" she asked, trying to steer the conversation away from those two subjects.

"Not yet. I won't be able to get anything until fall."

"Is that okay with your dad?"

"It'll have to be. There's nothing out there. Did you ask your grandma if I might be able to work at the store?"

"I did. She said it's a possibility. But like I told you, it'll be Christmastime before the coffee shop is finished."

"That's better than next summer."

"What about the nanny idea?"

"I don't have any experience, so I don't think anyone's going to hire me, especially because I'll be going back to school soon and won't be able to babysit until after three."

"I'd ask Quinn if you could maybe hostess at The Daily Catch, but with what his mother's going through, I don't think it would be fair to put him under any more pressure."

"Yeah. Don't worry about it. My dad gets pissed and starts harping on me to find work, but he forgets about it for long stretches. I'll tell him that I might have something at Christmas. It'll be fine."

"Are you sure?"

"Yeah. How're things going with Quinn, by the way? Have you seen him since Sunday?"

"No."

"Do you think your mother has?"

"I know she has."

"How do you feel about that?"

"I'll think about it later. For right now, I'm just glad she's distracted."

Sierra flopped back down on the bed. "So..."

"So what?" she said.

"Are you going to call Oliver or not?"

Taylor groaned. "Do I have to?"

Sierra leaned up on one elbow. "You've been dreading it long enough. You might as well get it over with."

"I know." Sighing, she sat up, leaned against the wall and scrolled through her contacts. "Maybe he won't answer," she said, holding out hope that she could procrastinate just a little longer.

But he picked up almost as soon as she sent the call. "Is it what I think?" he said without so much as a hello.

She squeezed her eyes shut, fighting the inevitable emotion that welled up whenever she talked about the pregnancy. "Yes."

"Shit. Are you kidding me? You're *pregnant*? What are we going to do? What am I going to tell my folks?"

So much for the way he'd behaved when there was still some hope. She swallowed hard. "The same thing I'm going to tell my mother."

"Which is..."

"That I'm going to have a baby."

"You're having it? You're keeping it?"

She could hear the panic in his voice. "I think so. I don't know what else to do."

"You have options," he insisted.

"But would *you* like to be responsible for making the decision to end this pregnancy or put our baby up for adoption?"

The phone went silent. She couldn't even hear him breathe. "Oliver? Are you there?"

"God, this is crazy," he muttered so softly she could barely make out the words. Then, louder, "So what are we going to do?"

"We're going to wait until I get back before we tell anyone. That's one thing. Can you do that?"

"What good does it do to wait? Why do you care about that?"

"Because *you* won't have to face the humiliation I'll have to face, that's why. How would you like to be me and know that everyone in school is talking about you?"

"They'll be talking about me, too."

"Not in the same way. I'm the one they'll call a slut or a whore."

More silence. Then he said, "Okay."

She gripped the phone tighter. "No. Promise me. You will tell no one, and I mean *no one*, until I get back."

"I promise. It's not like I'm eager for word to get out, either."

Neither one of them said anything after that until she asked, "What will your mother say?"

"She'll cry while my father kicks my ass," he said flatly.

Sierra scooted closer and took her hand. Grateful for the support, Taylor glanced up and smiled through her tears.

"You're shaking," Sierra whispered. "Relax. It's going to be okay."

"I don't want you to...to go through that," she said into the phone.

"You won't be able to stop it. Neither will I. My father will say I've screwed up my entire life and he won't help me because he warned me against something like this happening."

She closed her eyes as she tried to block out the mental picture of that. "He'll soften after…after he gets used to the idea, won't he?"

"No, he won't. He'll wish me good luck making minimum wage for the rest of my life and kick me out of the house."

"At sixteen?"

"He'll say if I'm man enough to have a baby, I'm man enough to make it on my own."

"You don't think he'll change his mind?"

"Maybe. Eventually. Or maybe not." She heard what she thought was a tremor in his voice. "I'm so dead."

Taylor hated that she felt responsible for the consequences he'd suffer. He'd participated, too! "I'm sorry," she mumbled.

"I can't breathe right now. Can I call you back?"

"Of course."

"Will you answer this time?"

She flinched at the sharp edge to his voice. "Yes."

He disconnected, and she dropped her phone in her lap. "As if things weren't bad enough, now I have to worry about him."

Sierra curled her fingers through Taylor's. "You've already got enough to deal with. Let Oliver worry about Oliver."

"I will," she said and rested her head on Sierra's shoulder. But his words were still echoing in her mind hours later: *My father will say I've screwed up my entire life and he won't help me because he warned me against something like this happening.*

Would Oliver get kicked out of the house?

When Melissa Cunningham asked Autumn if she and Quinn were now an item, Autumn looked up from the salad the waitress had just placed in front of her. She'd agreed to meet her old friend for lunch at a small restaurant next to the nail salon, and she'd known they'd probably dish. Thanks to Melissa's line of work, she was privy to most town gossip. But Autumn hadn't expected this to be almost the first thing out of her friend's mouth. "We're…seeing each other," she hedged.

Melissa used her long, fake nails to flip her hair, which had been short and blond a week ago but was now long, thanks to hair extensions. "And? Do you think it might get serious?"

It was already getting serious. Quinn had been over every night since the fireworks show. After her mother and kids went to bed, he'd park down the street and come to the garage. She'd thought sleeping with him for the first time in the apartment she'd shared with her husband would be difficult. But she was almost embarrassed by how easy it had been. She was falling in love so fast that propriety didn't seem to matter—nothing mattered except touching and tasting the object of her desire. She was deliriously happy. Eager to see him whenever she could. And she couldn't help grinning like a fool every time he texted.

It felt like they were having a torrid affair—mostly because they were sneaking around so her kids wouldn't realize how much time they were spending together. While he was at work, she couldn't wait for him to get off. And by the time he got to her place, she was so starved for his touch they came together immediately. It was crazy. She'd never had such great sex in her life. On Tuesday she'd driven all the way to Richmond just to buy lingerie. When was the last time she'd even thought of doing something like that?

"I have to go back to Tampa in a month," she said as if that meant they couldn't get *too* serious.

"Why do you have to go back?" she asked.

"I wouldn't move Taylor and Caden at this age. Starting at a brand-new high school would be hell for them. You know how it is. Kids already have their cliques well formed by then."

Her perfectly threaded eyebrows lifted. "Maybe he'll follow you to Tampa."

"He can't leave his folks. Not while his mother's sick. So…

we're keeping it casual." It was almost hard to say that with a straight face, because this was the most intense relationship she'd ever had.

"You should tell the town gossips that," she barked with a laugh.

"What do you mean?"

"You know how nail salons are. The talk that goes on. You and Quinn? That's all I've been hearing about lately."

"Because of the fundraiser? That was all it took?"

"The fundraiser, the fireworks show—and Bev Vizii."

Autumn rolled her eyes. "What's she saying now?"

"That you're a fool to get involved with a known cheater."

"She drives me crazy."

"She doesn't want to see Quinn happy—not when her daughter's sitting in prison."

Autumn lifted her water glass. "Well, as far as I'm concerned, he's been through enough. You should see the scars on his back."

"I heard she attacked him while he was sleeping. Does he ever talk about that?"

"Not much. I can't imagine it's something he enjoys remembering."

She stirred some sugar into her iced tea. "Does she ever write him?"

"They're divorced. Why would she?"

Melissa shrugged. "I'd be surprised if she doesn't. She was so fiercely possessive. My mother once told me she witnessed a huge argument between them at the beach, where Sarah went off because Quinn wanted to swing by and see his mother."

"How selfish can you be?" Autumn asked, shaking her head.

"I get the impression she destroyed what he felt for her, drove him away."

Autumn got the same impression, but she was careful about what she said, not wanting to add to the gossip about Quinn. "What's going on with you?" she asked, changing the subject.

Melissa told her about an online love interest, how her ex wanted to reconcile but she wasn't willing to move back to Maryland and all about what she was doing to grow her business, but when they finished eating, she circled back around to Quinn.

"Is Quinn any good in bed?" she asked, a wicked sparkle in her eye.

"I haven't slept with him yet," Autumn said.

"Sure you haven't," Melissa said, rolling her eyes.

The waitress brought their check. Autumn offered to pay for it, and Melissa let her but insisted on covering the tip. As she dug her wallet out of her purse, a business card fell onto the table— one that Autumn was surprised she recognized.

"You talked to this guy, too?"

Melissa found the five-dollar bill she'd been looking for and put it on the table. "What guy?"

"The private investigator—Drake D. Owens. This is his card."

"Oh, yeah. He came into the salon looking for someone named—" she took it and checked the back, where she'd written the name "—Bailey North. I said I'd ask around and get back to him. Apparently, she'll get some sort of inheritance if he can find her. But after I stuck his card in my purse, I forgot about it."

Autumn ran her thumb over the raised lettering. "Bailey North. Who do you think she is?"

"No clue."

"Whoever hired him must really want to find her. He spread his business cards all over town. What makes him think she might be here?"

"Didn't say."

Autumn remembered that her mother was going to ask Laurie about Bailey North but then she never heard any more about it. "Do you think he's still around? Or that he'll come back?"

"Who knows? I haven't seen him since he gave me his card."

"I wonder if anyone has gotten back to him..."

Melissa shrugged. "This might sound bad, but what does it matter to us?"

"I understand what it's like to search for someone you can't find. It's frustrating and exhausting and…" She let her words fall away as she held up his card. "Mind if I keep this?"

"Not if you'll tell me the truth," she said, her voice playful.

For the first time since the fireworks show, Autumn was caught up thinking about Nick. All those years with him felt like another lifetime. Even the months of fruitless searching seemed distant. "What truth?"

"About Quinn. Are you two sleeping together?"

Autumn slipped Mr. Owens's card into her pocket. "I'll tell you this—he was the first boy I ever slept with. We had sex in his tree house back in high school."

"Seriously?" she gasped. "When he was with Sarah?"

"They were broken up, and it happened only once." She shook her head as she remembered. "I cried so hard when he got back with her."

"Well, she should've taken better care of what she had because he's yours now," she said.

25

Mary purposely chose a time when Laurie and Autumn would both be in the store to start a conversation she hoped would pave the way for her to disappear for a day without Autumn knowing she was going so far from home. She'd told Tammy she'd send some old pictures, ones that weren't digitized from when Autumn was younger, and Tammy had readily provided her address. But Mary didn't plan to mail anything. If she could overcome her fear of travel, she was going to fly to Nashville and surprise the Skinners' daughter. She'd been enjoying getting to know Tammy so much via text—they'd also had two recent phone calls that had gone very well—that she had to put her final qualms to rest. She couldn't continue to invest in this person until she met the adult Tammy, face-to-face, and felt reasonably assured that it was safe to fully embrace her. At this point, that was the only thing holding her back, just that little bit of hesitation, and she was eager to let go of it and relax at last, to tell Autumn, Taylor and Caden the truth and introduce them.

"I heard from that woman who owns the bookstore in Richmond," she said to Laurie as she dusted near the register, where

Laurie was making a list so they could submit their latest orders to the various publishers.

Laurie had been primed beforehand and knew to play along. "The one you met with before?" she said. "Eve Dallas?"

Autumn, who was building a new display, peered around a tower of books. "The bookstore owner in Richmond has the same name as the protagonist in the J.D. Robb series? How funny."

Once Autumn had disappeared back behind her stack of books, Mary shot Laurie a look that said, "Why the heck did you throw out *that* name?" No doubt it had popped into her head because she was familiar with it—they sold a lot of those books—but it was a dumb mistake. Autumn read as much as they did; of course she'd recognized it. "Yeah, funny coincidence," she said in an attempt to cover for the gaffe. "Dallas is her married name."

Fortunately, Autumn didn't seem to think it was *too* odd, because she didn't follow up on that comment. "What'd she have to say?"

"She bought a new software system that helps her run everything. Wants me to come back and see it."

Getting to her feet, Autumn dusted off her knees. "When? I'll take you."

Mary's breath caught in her throat, but given her past reluctance to leave town, especially on her own, she'd been anticipating the offer. "That's nice, honey, but I was thinking, if I went on a Monday when the store's closed, Laurie could come with me. We should both take a look at it, don't you think?"

"That makes sense," she said at the same time Laurie indicated she'd like to see it. "Are you shooting for this Monday?"

"No, I've got too much going on. But the following Monday should work."

"Okay," Laurie said. "Let's do it."

Autumn didn't bother to comment—a sign that this conversation had come across as casually as Mary hoped it would. Relieved, she hurried to change the subject before Autumn could think too much about the bookstore owner in Richmond having the same name as a popular J.D. Robb character. "So…what are you thinking about Quinn these days?"

"I enjoy spending time with him," Autumn replied, suddenly fiddling with the display again, even though she'd finished it.

Mary hid a smile. She knew her daughter's attachment to Quinn was much stronger than she made it sound. He'd been spending most nights in the garage apartment—if not all. Mary had seen him come or go a time or two, not that she'd mentioned that to anyone except Laurie. "He was so sweet with me and the kids when he took us all to the fireworks show."

"Your mother told me he had the whole thing set up so that you'd have food and treats and a great view," Laurie chimed in.

Bless her heart, she was always there to help, Mary thought.

"What a sweetheart," Laurie added.

The smile that curved her daughter's lips made her look smitten indeed. "He seems to get along really well with Caden," Autumn said as she came toward the register.

"Caden likes him, too," Mary pointed out.

Laurie shifted on her stool. "How's Taylor taking you getting involved with another man?"

Autumn's smile disappeared. "She's a bit more…remote, a little harder for him to reach than Caden. I know he's worried about it."

Mary knew Autumn was worried about it, too.

"She'll warm up," Laurie predicted.

"She seemed to be friendlier toward him at the end of the evening, after the fireworks were over," Mary said. "Didn't you notice?"

Autumn shoved her hands in her pockets as she leaned up against the counter. "Sort of. Everything will be all right, I hope."

Mary touched her daughter's arm. "Of course it will. Who can resist him?"

"Certainly not her," Laurie said, indicating Autumn with a laugh.

Autumn made a face, but she laughed, too.

Seeing her daughter happy and excited about love again helped ease some of the nagging worry Mary had been wrestling with since Tammy came back into her life. She'd figure out this thing with her past, she told herself. She just had to get to Nashville and back without Autumn discovering she didn't really go to Richmond.

"You don't like me very much, do you?"

Taylor froze the second Sierra's father pinned her with that question. He'd come home early from work carrying a bag of groceries in one tattoo-covered arm, a six-pack of beer in the other, and said he was going to grill some burgers, including a veggie burger for Sierra.

Typically, Taylor tried to scoot out of the house if he appeared, but today he'd invited her to stay and eat with them, and Sierra had seemed so glad that her father was in a good mood that Taylor hadn't had the heart to leave.

"W-what do you mean?" she stammered.

His belly, which was as big and round as hers would be in several months, jiggled as he put down the groceries and laughed at her response. "Just what I said."

"Of course I like you," she argued, but she didn't sound convincing, even to herself, and that made him laugh even louder.

"You'd better get used to me. This old bastard could become your father-in-law one day." She could smell alcohol on his breath as he leaned closer. "Ever thought of that?"

"Dad!" Sierra said, obviously embarrassed.

He grabbed a can of beer from the six-pack and popped the top. "What? You telling me you two little lesbians aren't a couple?" This time he got right in Sierra's face. "Have you found the balls to kiss her yet?"

Sierra surprised Taylor by shoving her father away. "You just said we were going to have a barbecue. And now you're trying to ruin it?"

Afraid this was about to turn into another fight, Taylor edged toward the door. "Actually, I don't think I can stay," she said. "I just remembered that my mother asked me to…to help with something."

Instead of continuing to argue with Sierra, as Taylor expected him to, Dennis scowled at her. "Oh, stop. Don't be such a little pussy. I'm just messing with you."

Taylor didn't know what to do. She wanted to leave, but she'd already said she'd stay, and she hated to disappoint Sierra.

"He doesn't mean anything by it," Sierra said. "Stay."

Sierra had been so good to her throughout all *her* drama that Taylor decided she could hang out with Sierra's old man for one evening. "Okay," she said. "Why don't I start cutting the lettuce, tomatoes and onions?"

He downed several more beers while grilling the burgers, but they managed to eat with only a few uncomfortable moments. As Taylor helped Sierra carry everything inside from the screened-in porch so they could clean up the kitchen, she thought they were in the clear. But before they could finish the dishes, Dennis came in from where he'd been sitting and drinking on the patio, and just by the way he let the screen door slam, she knew they were in trouble.

"Wasn't that the best burger you ever ate?" he asked, his voice overloud.

"It was really good," Taylor said.

"Now what are you two going to do?"

Noting the slur in his words and the hurt and embarrassment in Sierra's eyes, Taylor jumped in to answer so that her friend wouldn't say anything that might anger him. "We thought we'd go play some pool with my brother and his friends." They hadn't actually been invited to play pool, but she wanted to make it sound as though they had something definite.

"Fine. You two get out of here," he said. "But don't stay out late."

"What's late?" Sierra asked.

"Be home at ten."

Assuming Sierra would resist such an early curfew on a Friday night, Taylor caught her breath.

Fortunately, Sierra didn't say anything. She just finished wiping the counter and tossed the rag in the sink.

But before she could get past him, he grabbed her by the arm. "I guess I don't have to warn you two to pick up some condoms. There's *one* benefit to having a gay daughter, huh?" he said and slapped his leg as he laughed uproariously.

"Dad, quit being a jerk," Sierra muttered, her voice low as she yanked away from him and started for the door.

The change in his pants pockets jingled he moved so fast to get in front of her. "You're going to talk to me that way?"

"I'm not going to talk to you at all. I'm leaving. Just get out of the way."

Taylor was beginning to sweat. She was sure this was about to explode—but then the doorbell rang.

Grateful for the interruption, she answered immediately— even though it wasn't her house—and there stood Quinn. "W- what are you doing here?" she asked.

"Your mother's been trying to reach you. We were hoping you'd like to watch a movie with us tonight, but you haven't been answering your phone, so I said I'd swing by on my way over."

Taylor pulled Sierra outside with her. "Sounds fun. Can my friend come, too?"

"Um, sure."

She could tell he was a little surprised that she'd ask him that.

It wasn't really up to him. But she didn't care. She surprised him again by looping her arm through his. She wasn't about to let him leave without her. She felt if she hung on to him, he'd get her and Sierra out of there.

"You don't mind, do you?" he said to Dennis.

Dennis glowered at his daughter as though he might refuse, but three sets of eyes staring back at him seemed to make him think twice. Ultimately, he shook his meaty head and closed the door.

"You all right?" Quinn asked, searching her face.

She couldn't let go of him quite yet, not until they were safely away, but she managed what she hoped was a believable smile. "Yeah. Thanks for coming."

"You bet." He returned her smile as though he was grateful to be accepted, which made her glad her mother was at least dating someone who was cool.

"I'm telling you, she slipped her arm through mine," Quinn said.

He'd returned to Autumn's—this time to the garage instead of her mother's house—only half an hour after the movie ended and he'd left, but they'd hardly spoken in that time. He'd kissed her as soon as she let him in, which led to the removal of her robe and the discovery that she was wearing some silky white and barely there lingerie.

As soon as he saw that, he wasn't interested in talking; he was interested in doing other things. He had a hunger for her he'd never experienced before. Since he'd been with one person essentially since high school, other than a few random encounters with other women during the short windows of time that he and Sarah were broken up, he'd never realized what a relationship like this could be. If he and Sarah had ever loved and wanted each other equally, they'd gotten out of balance and lived that way for so long he couldn't remember feeling the same rush of testosterone or that subtle possessiveness that made him want to commit to her—and have her commit to him.

Shoving her hair back, Autumn leaned up on one elbow. "You're talking about Taylor?"

"Yeah, Taylor. So she must like me, right?"

"People don't typically touch someone they hate," she said, sounding slightly surprised by her daughter's friendliness. "Taylor doesn't, anyway. When did she slip her arm through yours?"

He pulled her back down next to him so he could continue to feel her soft, warm body. "When I picked her up. I was so shocked I almost asked if we could take a selfie so I could show you," he joked.

She chuckled as she caressed his chest.

"She's definitely been more remote with me than Caden. I was worried she wouldn't accept me, and I know you were, too. But I think everything's going to be okay."

She pressed her lips to his throat. "I'm glad you care whether she likes you."

"Thank you for giving me a chance," he said, rolling her beneath him and resting the bulk of his weight on his elbows. "I honestly can't remember ever being so happy."

"You said you were happy with Sarah once."

"I was at times. Our marriage got so turbulent it's hard to remember. But this—what we have—it's different."

She stared up at him for several seconds before she said, "In what way?"

"In a lot of ways. It's healthier, for one." He kissed her lips. "More stable."

"You can say that after a week?" she joked.

"Yeah, I can." He remembered having a knock-down, drag-out with Sarah on their *honeymoon* and wished he'd bailed out then.

"I never dreamed we'd end up together," she said, reaching up to push his hair out of his eyes.

"I should've gotten with you way back in high school." Then he'd probably have children, too. So many things about his life would be different.

"What's going to happen when the summer ends?" she asked.

"I've been trying not to think about that."

"It's not so far away, you know. The kids start school at the end of August."

He rolled off her, and she settled against him. "We'll figure out something. Because I already know I don't want to lose you."

The next week passed quickly. Taylor was able to avoid encountering Mr. Lambert through those days by making sure she left Sierra's house well before dinnertime. She was relieved about that. But that didn't mean she'd been having an easy time. Oliver kept calling. He was trying to talk her into getting an abortion before she returned to Tampa so that no one would have to know and they could both go on with their lives as if the pregnancy never happened.

"I just…don't know if I can do it," she told Sierra on Saturday, while they were waiting at the beach for Caden and his friends to join them. They were planning to play volleyball and then start a bonfire, blast some music and roast s'mores. "I'm only seventeen. What if it's the wrong decision? I don't want to hate myself every time I see a baby, thinking about the one that… well, that I was once pregnant."

Sierra twisted around to check behind them as though she was afraid the others might already be approaching. Taylor turned, too, her face burning at the thought that she might've given herself away, but didn't see anyone she recognized.

"You don't have to listen to him," Sierra said.

"It's hard not to. He's so desperate. You should hear him. I don't want to be responsible for getting him kicked out of the house."

"I feel sorry for him, too, but that doesn't mean he's the only thing you have to worry about."

Taylor frowned as she studied her stomach, trying to determine whether she saw a slight bulge. According to what she'd found on the internet, a six-week-old fetus was only the size of a sweet pea, but she'd read that it would double in the next week. "I didn't anticipate this part of it." She groaned. "God, there's so much to think about."

"You have to be able to live with whatever you choose. I'd focus on figuring out what that is." A beach ball landed nearby. Sierra picked it up and tossed it back to two young boys. "How are you feeling about Quinn and your mom?"

"Better," she said. "But only because I like him."

"How often do you see him?"

"This week? It's been almost every day."

"So they're getting closer."

"Seems like it."

"Do you think they're sleeping together?"

She wrinkled her nose. "Eww. Don't ask. I don't want that mental picture in my mind."

"Oh, stop." She rolled her eyes. "Sex is just sex. It's perfectly natural, no big deal. Does your mom seem happy?"

Sometimes Sierra made her feel childish. She supposed her reaction had been childish. "A lot happier than before we got here."

"Then they're probably sleeping together," she joked.

The ball landed next to Taylor this time. She tossed it back. "It's nice that she's always in a good mood these days, at least."

"That might be something to be thankful for when you have to tell her…what you have to tell her."

"True."

"Does Caden like Quinn, too?"

"Definitely. They're always messing around, throwing almost any kind of ball they can get their hands on, wrestling for the best spot on the couch, talking about sports. He even played some video games with Caden last night while my mom made dinner, which is something even our dad wouldn't do. Our dad was too busy, would never take the time."

"That's nice of Quinn."

"I think Caden misses having a dad more than he ever let on and likes having Quinn around, even if he isn't our real father."

"I can understand that. There are times when I wish… Never mind."

"What?"

"Nothing. I'm just saying that as long as Quinn's a cool dude, what will it hurt to let him be part of the family? I believe any people who are willing to love each other can be a family, don't you?"

Once again Sierra had said something Taylor had never really considered but instantly felt was right. "I guess so."

"Besides, you told me he said he'd never try to replace your real father. Do you believe him?"

"I do. He's not pushy at all. He acts interested in us but he lets us decide how much to interact with him."

"Sounds nice to me." They heard Caden call out to them from a distance and got up to see him and the others walking toward them. "Is Quinn's mother going to die?" Sierra asked, her expression pained as though the question had been difficult to ask.

"I think so. I believe he knows it, too."

When Sierra said nothing, Taylor wondered if she was thinking about her mother and tried to take her hand, but Sierra resisted. "You don't want to hold my hand?" she asked in surprise. "You don't mind holding it when we're at home."

"We're not at home," she said. "It's better not to give anyone any reason to open their big mouths."

Taylor knew she wasn't worried about herself. Sierra didn't care what people thought. Her father already knew what she was and most others had guessed. So Taylor grabbed her hand, anyway.

"What are you doing?" she asked.

"I don't care what anyone says," Taylor replied. "Being with you makes me happy."

26

As Mary stood at the kitchen window, gazing out at the moon, she saw the light go on over the garage where her daughter was staying, even though it was late and the apartment had been dark for an hour or longer. Quinn snuck over so often Mary was afraid Caden and Taylor would catch him at some point, but she did her best to watch out for that, just in case she had to run interference.

"Mimi?"

At the sound of Taylor's voice, Mary whirled around. "Yes?" She kept her voice low, so as not to wake Caden on the couch.

"What are you looking at?"

"Nothing." Moving away from the window so that Taylor wouldn't come any closer, she crossed over to her granddaughter. "I just…couldn't sleep."

"Why not?"

Because she was nervous about flying to Nashville tomorrow. Not only was she afraid to leave her comfort zone after so many years, she'd also never been on a plane. And she was going to meet someone she'd left behind so long ago she had no idea if she could trust that Tammy was still the same sweet person. "I'm not sure," she said to Taylor, since she couldn't be totally honest. "It happens sometimes. What are you doing up?"

"I can't sleep, either."

Mary could guess why. According to Caden, Taylor had come out today, in front of him and all his friends. She'd also brought Sierra home for supper and made it clear by her behavior—holding Sierra's hand and curling up with her on the couch to watch a movie—that they were now a couple. "How are you feeling?"

"Relieved."

Her response surprised Mary. She'd thought Taylor might be torn about what she'd done, maybe even regretful. *"Relieved?"*

"Yeah. It felt good to quit worrying about what other people might think, and whether I'll be stuck with this decision for the rest of my life, and just…act on what I feel, you know? Be spontaneous. Be me. Sierra and I have never had more fun."

"How did the other kids treat you at the beach?"

"They were fine with it. I'm pretty sure they'd already guessed. They were just surprised that we weren't hiding it anymore."

Relieved herself, that her granddaughter wasn't experiencing a great deal of angst and turmoil, she pulled Taylor in for a hug. "I'm glad, honey. You have to live your own truth. That's what matters most. I'm proud of you."

Mary thought that would be that. Taylor would go back to bed, and she would be left to stew until it was time to leave for Richmond, so she could make her flight. But Taylor wasn't smiling once Mary released her. Tears were swimming in her eyes as she said, "Don't say you're proud of me."

"Why not? It's true."

"You don't know everything yet."

"What are you talking about?" she asked, instantly concerned.

"I have to tell you and Mom something. I wanted to wait until the end of the summer, but I can't keep it to myself any longer. It's getting to where I feel sick and worried and anxious all the time. I need help."

Mary glanced over her shoulder at the window she'd just been peering out. They couldn't barge in on Autumn right now. "What are you talking about? Your mother's fine with whomever you choose to love. So am I."

"This isn't about that. It—it's worse."

"Tay?" Caden lifted his head from where he was on the couch. "You're going to tell them *now*?"

"I have to," she said. "I have to decide what to do and can't manage that all by myself." She started toward the French doors that would let her out, so she could cross the yard to the garage, but Mary cut her off.

"Then let's call your mom and have her come in. There's no need for us to go traipsing out to the garage."

"I already tried to call her," Taylor said. "She's not answering."

Taylor obviously assumed her mother was asleep, but Mary knew better. "Why don't you make some hot chocolate while I go get her, then? We'll sit down as a family, since Caden already knows what's going on, anyway. We're here for you. Whatever it is, we'll work it out."

"I don't want any hot chocolate. I just want my mom," she said with a fresh downpour of tears, and slipped around Mary to go get Autumn herself.

Taylor was relieved to see that there was a light on in the apartment over the garage. Maybe her mother wasn't paying attention to her phone, but at least she wasn't asleep.

Although the door to the garage was locked, Taylor knew where to find the Hide-A-Key. It'd been under the glass frog in the planter ever since she could remember.

She sniffed as she opened the case and let herself in. She couldn't believe she was going to tell her mom about the baby. But she couldn't keep going as she was, even if the summer wasn't over. Oliver wouldn't leave her alone. He called and texted her over and over, begging her to have an abortion.

She couldn't take the constant pressure. Just before bed, she'd received a nasty text from his older brother, telling her she'd better not ruin Oliver's life, which proved he hadn't kept his word. He'd told one person, at a minimum. And if he'd told his brother, there could be others—or soon would be.

She had to talk to someone. Someone she trusted. Sierra made it possible for her to feel almost normal during the day. She could shove the pregnancy out of her mind and carry on as usual, pretend it didn't exist. But at night, it was an entirely different story. After Sierra was asleep and the house fell quiet, the walls seemed to close in on her. Tonight the panic had been so intense she'd been frozen in her bed for the past hour.

If revealing her sexuality today had taught her anything, it was that telling the truth brought relief. So she was going to face what she'd been dreading and get it over with. Maybe then she could have someone on her side, an adult like Oliver did, while she decided what to do about the baby.

Breathe, she told herself. Although she dreaded what she had to do, at the same time, she suddenly couldn't wait. She wanted to spill it all, drop the heavy burden she'd been carrying into her mother's capable arms.

The door to the apartment was closed, which was unusual. Taylor tried to walk in—but it wasn't only closed, it was locked.

"Mom?" she said with a knock.

There was a thump and then some movement.

"Mom?" Taylor called louder, trying to peer through the misted glass panels in the door. She thought she saw someone, but then the light went off.

"Hey, what's going on?" she asked.

"Coming!" her mother replied.

When the door opened, her mother was wearing a robe, from what Taylor could tell. Her hair seemed mussed, too, but Autumn left the light off so it was difficult to see very clearly. "It's after one, Taylor," she said. "What's going on?"

Taylor started to cry—not just cry but bawl like she hadn't since she was a little girl. She didn't care if she was being immature; she couldn't help it. "I'm pregnant," she sobbed, throwing herself into her mother's arms. "I'm sorry. I'm *so* sorry. I didn't mean to screw up my life. I don't know why I slept with Oliver Hancock. I don't even like him."

Just hearing her daughter's voice come through the door had almost given Autumn a heart attack. Quinn had barely had time to get up, grab his clothes and slip into the bathroom, where he was hopefully hiding in the shower, while she turned off the light so that Taylor couldn't see two naked bodies spring into action. Painfully aware of her nudity under her robe, she tried to calm herself.

Quinn had managed to get out of the room in time. But calming down proved futile when her daughter's words began to sink in. "*What'd* you say?" she asked.

Mary came hurrying up the stairs behind Taylor. "Why don't we all come back to the house and have a cup of hot chocolate?" She sounded slightly desperate, and breathless besides, giving Autumn the impression her mother knew Quinn was over and had been trying to chase down Taylor before she barged in on them.

Too bad she hadn't been successful. That was Autumn's first thought. But in her next thought, she realized how trivial that was in comparison to what her daughter had just revealed.

"I'm going to have a baby," Taylor repeated. She was clinging to Autumn so tightly that her words were muffled by Autumn's robe, but there could be no mistaking them. It was essentially the same thing Taylor had said only seconds before.

"Mom?" Caden called. "Mimi?"

Her son was now clomping up the stairs. Soon, her mother, daughter and son would be in the small apartment—while

Quinn was hiding in the bathroom. Autumn needed to get them all out, but she couldn't think straight, couldn't do anything except hold her sobbing daughter.

"Did she just say *pregnant*?" Mary asked, her mouth hanging open as though she hadn't been prepared for this news, either. "Can that be true?"

Caden shoved a hand through his hair, which was already sticking up. "Yeah, it's true," he said.

"How long have you known about this?" Autumn asked.

"A while."

"How long has *she* known?"

He shrugged. "A while longer."

"And you didn't tell me?"

"I *couldn't* tell you," he said. "I was pretty pissed off that it was Oliver who got her pregnant, but she begged me not to say anything."

The shock of this revelation had created a fog in Autumn's mind. "Oliver *Hancock* is only sixteen."

"Yeah. He used to be *my* friend, remember?"

The echo of that statement brought back the morning Caden had been so upset with Taylor. Now she knew *this* was why. At the time, she'd assumed their squabble was over Taylor's sexuality—or Taylor's general grumpiness because she was going through such a difficult time.

Holy shit. What were they going to do? She was just beginning to adjust to the fact that her daughter was gay. How could Taylor be both gay *and* pregnant? While Autumn understood how that was technically possible, the combination had to be unlikely—in a seventeen-year-old, at least.

"That's why I was so upset," Caden was saying.

Autumn could feel the pressure of Taylor's embrace but was otherwise numb, except for her hands and feet, which tingled. She'd just gotten over what'd happened to Nick, was finally happy again.

"I think she should get an abortion, don't you?" Caden blurted. "That would solve everything."

Autumn flinched. Just the word seemed to have sharp edges. "That's not a decision to be made lightly. How did this happen?" She was asking Taylor, but once again, Caden answered.

"How do you think it happened?"

Autumn lifted a hand to signal for him to stop talking. She was already upset, and his involvement was only making matters worse.

"Taylor?" She pulled back, catching her daughter's face between her hands. "I need *you* to answer. Talk to me."

Even in the darkness, she could see the shine of tears on Taylor's cheeks. Then Caden snapped on the light, making his sister's misery even more apparent. "We were…we were at a party," Taylor choked out, crying so hard she hiccoughed between some of the words.

As Autumn listened to how Taylor had bumped into Oliver, that they'd been drinking, that he kept coming on to her, that she was hurt and angry even though she didn't know why and that she finally went into the back bedroom with him, Autumn had to ask herself if she was partially responsible for this outcome. She'd been so preoccupied the past twenty months. Maybe if she'd been paying closer attention to what Taylor was doing this wouldn't have happened. They'd discussed birth control, but that was back when Taylor had a boyfriend. "And Oliver didn't use any protection?" she asked when the sad tale was over.

Taylor pressed her face back into Autumn's shoulder. "He didn't have any. It wasn't like…like we planned it."

Autumn was beginning to feel nauseated. What did this mean for her beautiful daughter? A pregnancy during her senior year. A baby before she graduated. What about college?

"I'm sorry, Mom."

"It's okay," she said, but she was too shocked to speak with any real conviction. "Anyone can make a mistake."

"What are we going to do?" Taylor asked. "Oliver keeps texting me, begging me to get an abortion."

"Why not do it?" Caden asked. "Neither one of them is ready for a baby," he added for Autumn's benefit. He sounded so much like his father. She knew Nick, forever practical, would probably have said the same. He wouldn't let anything get in the way of Taylor's success.

So did she follow what she knew he'd want? What *she* felt was right? Or what Taylor wanted?

Her gut said it should be up to her daughter, but she was the one who would have to help shoulder the load, if Taylor decided to keep the baby. Shouldn't she have a say, too?

"There are…there are other options," she said. "We'll talk about them." Despite her shock and upset, Autumn remembered Quinn, hiding in the bathroom, and wondered what he was making of all of this. "I—I think your Mimi was right. Let's go over to the house and make some hot chocolate."

"How's that going to help anything?" Caden asked.

Again, he sounded a great deal like his father. "It'll give me a moment to think—that's what it will do," she replied more candidly.

It would also give Quinn a chance to escape…

She was just looking for her slippers when she saw one of Quinn's flip-flops lying on the floor not far from where they stood. He must've dropped it when he scooped up his things; he'd been moving fast.

The sight of it caused her heart to jump into her throat. Fortunately, her mother must've spotted it at the same moment, because she slid over and nudged it under the bed.

"Let's go over while your mother gets dressed—er, finds her slippers," her mother said and started to herd them down the stairs.

Autumn didn't wait for Quinn to come out so that she could speak to him. It had been far too close a call to let down her guard that quickly. She just tightened the belt on her robe, shoved her feet into her slippers and murmured, "I'll call you tomorrow," before hurrying out after them.

27

The clock in the kitchen ticked loudly as Mary sat across from her daughter, their hot chocolate now cold while she waited to see what Autumn would say now that Caden and Taylor had gone back to bed. "What are you going to do?" she asked her daughter.

"I don't know," Autumn replied, her voice low. Although Caden was back on the couch, there was no way to tell whether he was sleeping or listening to what he could make out of their conversation. "I'm so worried. This is not what I ever wanted for her."

"Of course it isn't."

Autumn tapped her finger against the handle of her mug. "Taylor and Oliver are both minors. I'll have to contact Oliver's parents and get their input before we decide anything."

"I hope they won't be too difficult to deal with."

"So do I."

"What do you think about what Caden suggested?"

She looked up. "An abortion?"

"Might be the best thing for both of them."

"Abortion isn't our only choice. There's adoption, too."

"Only after she goes through nine months of pregnancy— her whole senior year—and the painful delivery."

"Yeah. I don't like the idea of that, either. But it's Taylor's baby. My grandbaby. Your great-grandbaby. Would we regret not raising this child?"

Mary sighed. "Hard to say. What do you think Nick would want you to do?"

"I believe he'd push for an abortion. But I'm less pragmatic and more sentimental than he ever was, and I don't know if I could live with that."

Mary carried their mugs to the sink so she could rinse them out. "It'll be easier to decide once you've had a chance to process everything. Why don't you try to get some rest, and we'll talk later, after I get back from Richmond."

"You're not still going tomorrow, are you?" she asked, her voice growing louder due to her surprise. "It's after two. You'll be exhausted before you even start."

Especially because she had to leave the house by six to make her flight. But she'd already paid for her plane ticket. And she felt a decision had to be made where Tammy was concerned. "I can rest in the car while Laurie drives."

"Aunt Laurie is awesome," she said, sounding relieved that she didn't need to offer to go along herself. "She's always there for us."

"Laurie's a wonderful person." Mary turned off the water. "Have you ever wished you had a sibling, Autumn?" she asked and held her breath as her daughter took a moment to consider the question.

"I used to, growing up," she admitted. "Being an only child gets lonely—especially an only child who doesn't have a father. But when Caden and Taylor are at each other's throats, I realize that I never had to compete for the front seat of the car, the last piece of cake, what movie we'll watch or what game we'll play." She smiled. "I'm fine, Mom. You did a great job."

That was what every mother longed to hear. But what would Autumn say when she learned that she could've had a sibling all along?

Sunlight, slanting through the blinds, woke Autumn the following morning. Still groggy, she smiled when she smelled Quinn's cologne on her bedding and wished he was beside her—until she grew alert enough to remember what had unfolded last night. Then her heart didn't feel quite so light.

With a groan, she shoved her head under the pillow. Her seventeen-year-old daughter was going to have a baby. "No!" she yelled, because no one was around and she could do it without being heard.

Throwing off the pillow, she rose up on her elbows to see the alarm clock on the nightstand. It was only eight; not too late. Had her mother left? Or after such a brutal night, had she and Laurie decided to postpone their trip to Richmond, after all?

Autumn climbed out of bed to go to the bathroom and lifted the blind so she could check the drive on the way back. Her mother's sensible Chevy was gone, suggesting she'd left as planned.

"If she feels half as bad as I do, she should've waited until next Monday," she mumbled. The coffee shop wouldn't be finished for months. What would it matter to wait another week to check out the Richmond store's new software when they'd been running the bookstore the same way for years?

Knowing her mother, Mary had kept the appointment just so she wouldn't have to cancel at the last moment. It was the courteous thing to do, so Autumn couldn't pinpoint why she was annoyed. She was just mad in general.

Her phone buzzed. It was Quinn.

She checked to make sure her door was locked before answering, just in case she said something she'd rather not have one of her children overhear. Had she not taken that small precaution last night, her kids would've walked in and found Quinn in her bed.

She was definitely going to be more careful in the future. These days, Taylor and Caden were so caught up in their own lives that she'd been lulled into a false sense of security, had taken her privacy out here in the garage too much for granted.

"Hello?"

"You okay?" he asked.

She dropped back onto the bed and pulled up the covers. The air-conditioning was already chumming along, trying to combat the oppressive humidity—a battle the humidity would win as the day progressed—but she was chilled to the bone. "I feel like crying," she admitted. "I'm shocked. I'm sad. I'm disappointed. I'm worried about how this will impact her life and how well it will go with Oliver and his parents."

"Relief has to be in there somewhere. That was a close call," he said with a chuckle. "Things could've been much worse."

She was too upset to find *anything* about last night funny, but she couldn't help agreeing on the close call. "That's true. Did you find your flip-flop? Or is it still hiding under my bed?"

"I found it. Thanks for leaving the light on when you left."

"No problem."

"What are you doing today?"

"Sulking." She didn't feel like leaving the house. Fortunately, the store was closed, so she didn't have to man it while Laurie and her mother were away.

He chuckled again, but this time more sympathetically. "I'm sorry."

"So am I."

There was a slight pause before he said, "You know, I don't really want to do this, especially right now, but with everything coming out, I feel like I should make a confession."

The somber tone of his voice put her on edge. "Oh, God. If

you're going to say you don't want to see me anymore, please save it for another time. I'm not up to any more heartbreak."

"It's nothing like that. I hope you won't write me off, either, when you hear. It's just… I want to be completely honest with you. I don't want you to find out later and be angry."

She sat up. "What are you talking about?"

He drew such a deep breath she could hear the intake of it. "I really hope this isn't a mistake…"

"Tell me," she said. "You're scaring me."

"I knew Taylor was pregnant, Autumn—before last night."

"How?"

He didn't seem eager to answer, but he did. "Caden told me the day I played volleyball with him on the beach."

"He did? But…why would he tell you? He didn't even tell me!"

"He was pretty upset. My guess is he needed someone to talk to."

Holding the phone tightly to her ear, she got up and crossed to the window. "So why didn't *you* tell me?"

"I was tempted, many times. But I knew Taylor would never forgive me."

Tears welled up. "You chose to keep it from me, even though I'm Taylor's mother and the only one who was in the dark among the four of us?" That just felt…wrong. She'd begun to trust Quinn, to believe he would look out for her.

"I only made that choice because I care so much about you," he said. "I didn't want your kids to reject me right from the start. That would only make it harder for you and me to be happy together."

She wiped away a tear that spilled over her eyelashes. "So when would you have told me?"

"Taylor asked me to give her a few weeks to break the news herself, and that sounded reasonable, given my newness to your life and theirs. So I agreed."

"We've been sleeping together almost every night since then," she said, feeling betrayed.

"I know. I'm sorry."

Autumn stared at the empty place in the driveway where her mother normally parked. "Well, thanks for letting me know."

"I can tell this is making you feel bad—"

"I'm fine," she interrupted. "But I have to go, okay?"

"Autumn, please try to understand."

"I understand, Quinn. I just can't help feeling hurt," she said and disconnected. She wasn't in the mood to continue the conversation. She wasn't in the mood to try to navigate their relationship while figuring out how to fix what had gone so wrong in her daughter's life. For that matter, she wasn't even sure she wanted to get out of bed today.

This was all Nick's fault, she decided as she climbed back in and pulled the covers high. If he hadn't left them, none of this would be happening.

Quinn dropped his head in his hand. Maybe it had been a mistake to tell Autumn that he'd already known about the baby, but he cared too much about her to let something like that hang out there. If she found out some other way, it would damage her trust even worse. And since Taylor's pregnancy was going to be top of mind for quite some time, he felt it could easily come out—maybe even today, before he could see her again, which was why he'd acted to prevent that.

A soft knock sounded at his door. "Quinn?"

His mother. He'd been out so late he'd just rolled out of bed. "Hey," he said as he opened his door wearing only the basketball shorts he'd changed into last night. "How are you feeling?"

"A bit stronger this morning. I was hoping you'd feel like going for a walk with me."

"Sure. Around here?"

"At the beach."

"Of course." He was happy to accompany her, but she was getting so fragile he was afraid that she might not be able to make it very far.

He threw on a Surf's Up T-shirt, grabbed his flip-flops and hurried out to take her while she had the energy.

"How are things going between you and Autumn?" she asked, once they'd parked and he'd helped her down to the water.

"Good," he said, watching the white foam of the waves as the surf crashed only a few feet away from them. He didn't want to mention Taylor's pregnancy. It wasn't anything his mother needed to worry about.

The scarf she'd wrapped around her head—something she wore whenever she left the house since losing her hair—flapped in the breeze. "You seem to really like her."

"I do," he admitted. "This might sound crazy, since we've been together such a short time, but I've never been so excited about anyone else."

A smile curved her pale lips, and they started to walk slowly toward the promontory. "That's *so* wonderful."

"You're such a romantic," he teased.

"So are you," she responded. "You may seem tough to everyone else, but I know how sensitive that heart of yours really is."

When he grinned at her, she gripped his arm. "Will you two have children?"

"*Children*? Don't you think we have a ways to go before we confront that question?"

She stopped and tilted her face up to the sun. "I like to imagine you with babies. I dream about it all the time."

She was fading, and she knew it. Now he did, too. He could sense the change. "Her kids are almost out of high school. I don't know how eager she'll be to have a baby, but she knows I'd like children."

She kept her eyes closed. "You told her so?"

"I did."

"What'd she say?"

"She didn't say it was out of the question."

She started them moving again. "How many kids would you like to have?"

"I'll take as many as I can get," he joked. "So I guess that would be up to her."

"I wish I could be around to see that."

His chest constricted. "You'll be here," he insisted, because he couldn't bear to hear the opposite.

"No, Quinn," she said softly. "You need to be prepared. I don't have long now."

"What makes you so sure? The treatments could work."

She stopped to avoid a runner who was jogging past. Then she said, "The doctor called this morning. He doesn't see any improvement."

Quinn felt as though a liquid coolant had suddenly replaced all the blood in his body. "Then we'll try something else."

She smiled sadly. "We're out of options, honey. But it's okay. Knowing you are happy makes this so much easier for me."

Quinn kept his head down as they continued to meander along the beach. What could he say? How could he express how grateful he was for the love and care she'd always given him?

"How long do you have?" he asked, stooping to pick up a shell, which he tossed back into the sea.

"Three to five months," she said as she retied her scarf.

He couldn't speak, so they just stood there, side by side, staring out at the vastness of the sea. "I'm sorry, Mom," he said when he could get the words out without breaking down. "I don't know what Dad and I will do without you."

"You will carry on and find joy in life because being sad doesn't help me. You and your father are what matter most to me. That's why I'm so excited about Autumn," she added, smiling again. "She's brought me such hope. I love thinking about the possibilities. The prospect of a fresh start for you, a new love, a new life."

His vision blurred with tears. "Have you told Dad what the doctor said?"

He heard the emotion in his own voice but couldn't do anything about it.

"Not yet," she replied.

Now he knew why she'd asked to get out of the house. This was not only a graceful goodbye, it was also a preparatory, private talk. "He'll be devastated."

She slipped her arm through his again. "I'm telling you this now, so you can tell him later..." Her words fell off as a bird strutted right up to them.

"What's that?" he asked.

The bird squawked and fluttered away.

"I can't bear the thought of your father being sad. I want him to find someone else and marry again. In six months or a year, when he's grieved long enough and it's time to move on, let him know that it's okay to do that. It's *more* than okay. It's what I want."

Tears rolled down Quinn's face and dripped off his chin as he took his mother's hand. He wanted to memorize everything about her, so that he could continue to carry her with him—the fragile bones in her once-capable fingers, the tenderness in her eyes, the gentleness of her voice.

"It's going to be so hard to lose you," he murmured, struggling to get those words past the lump in his throat.

She gave his hand a slight squeeze. "*I* might die, Quinn, but my love for you never will."

28

Mary had sworn she'd never go back to Tennessee. Maybe it was the place where she was born, but it was also the place where so many terrible things had happened. But here she was. And as if that wasn't bad enough, she'd never ridden on a plane. She'd driven everywhere she needed to go in the rattletrap Datsun that had belonged to her late grandmother, something her great-aunt had provided because it was just sitting in her garage.

Laurie had insisted that it wasn't a big deal to fly. Everyone did it. But once they were in the air, Mary could barely keep her panic at bay. Her fingers clutched the armrests so tightly as the plane took off that Laurie said she was going to leave permanent impressions.

The ride was a bumpy one, which didn't help. Fortunately, it didn't last long. When she'd decided to take this trip, she'd used Google Earth to look up Tammy's address. But she hadn't learned much. The house was out away from the city, where there were too many trees to see anything.

What would they find when they landed?

She hoped they'd find a person she could both love and trust.

Because they hadn't brought any luggage, they were able to

circumvent the other passengers waiting at baggage claim and be first in line to rent a car. Once Laurie climbed behind the wheel and Mary took the passenger seat, she couldn't help marveling at the fact that they'd made it this far.

"You okay?" Laurie asked.

Mary shoved the rental agreement in the glove box before snapping on her seat belt and putting Tammy's address into GPS. "I'm feeling a long way from home," she said. "The only thing stopping me from turning around and going straight back is that we have to wait for our flight, anyway."

"You've come all this way, you might as well get a feel for who Autumn's half sister has turned out to be. Hopefully, you'll be comfortable telling Autumn the truth and will no longer have anything to hide. This could bring an end to it all."

"God willing."

"You'll get through it," Laurie muttered as she tried to familiarize herself with the rental car, which was a model neither one of them had ever seen before.

After fiddling with several buttons and knobs, Laurie figured out how to start the engine—even though there was no place to put a key.

They escaped the rental car lot, but that only dumped them onto an unfamiliar freeway system. Mary was so tense that she sat stiffly the entire ride and only grew more anxious when it began to rain.

Fortunately, she wasn't tired despite her lack of sleep. She had that going for her, at least.

What she noticed of Tennessee was beautiful, just as she remembered it, but it wasn't Sable Beach, and she didn't want to be here. She believed she'd be glad she came in the end, but she was sweating through her simple white dress by the time Laurie turned down the narrow country lane that led to Tammy's house.

As the windshield wipers worked in a rhythmic *swish/swish* and the car bounced and swayed, thanks to several deep potholes, they began to wonder if GPS had led them astray. This could not be where Tammy lived. The homes they passed weren't exactly hovels, but they weren't much better.

"I wasn't expecting this," Laurie said.

Dogs ran along chain-link fences, barking viciously at them as they passed, rusty cars sat up on blocks, halfway torn apart, and other junk—toys, car parts, cinderblocks, motorcycles, a stroller here and there—filled carports and outbuildings that looked as though a stiff wind would blow them down. "If Tammy received a large inheritance, why would she live *here*?" Mary asked.

"Maybe we'll reach a better area soon," Laurie replied.

Assuming that would happen, they continued to follow the directions given by the mechanical voice coming through Mary's phone. But when that voice said, "Arrived," they'd just navigated a long, windy drive that had opened up on a small clearing with a wooden clapboard house that looked as though it hadn't been painted since the beginning of the twentieth century.

"This is it?" Laurie muttered as she put the car in Park.

Mary turned off her maps and peered out, trying to get a better look at Tammy's place. But she couldn't see the finer details. The rain painted only a watery, blurry picture of what looked like an old one-room schoolhouse with a beat-up car to one side.

"I must've put in the wrong address," Mary said.

But a quick check confirmed that they'd come to the right place.

"This is strange," Laurie said. "What do you think's going on?"

"Maybe Tammy's too frugal to find a nicer house?"

"Or she craves the anonymity that would go along with living in such a backwater area."

That was possible, Mary supposed. She hadn't come out of those years with the Skinners without a few personality quirks of her own. It was possible Tammy had fared no better.

"Should we go to the door together?"

"No, I'd rather go alone." Laurie had been great to come

along, but Mary felt safer having someone in the car, able to call the police if anything went wrong.

"Maybe you should text her first and double-check the address."

"I don't want her to have any warning that I'm here. I'll just go talk to her. The car's here, so it looks like she's home," she said and got out.

The rain that pelted her bare arms and face was warm. Since she didn't have a jacket, she was glad of that. She'd also neglected to bring an umbrella, so she kept her head down as she hurried to the stoop and tried to shake off what she could of the wet.

A blanket covered the front window, and there wasn't any lawn furniture or pots of flowers—not even a welcome mat. The house didn't look dangerous exactly. She had no reason to think it might be. But it didn't seem very welcoming, either.

She glanced back at Laurie, who was watching her with the engine running. They could go back to Sable Beach, forget about this. But after all the effort they'd put into coming here, she knew Laurie would insist on knocking even if she decided not to.

There had to be a good explanation for why Tammy lived in this house.

Throwing back her shoulders, Mary gathered the nerve to ring the bell.

The wait seemed interminable. Every second that dragged by felt like an hour. But after banging on the door when no one answered the bell, she heard movement inside the house.

Standing with her back to the window in case Tammy lifted the blanket to look out, she held her breath as she waited—and the door finally opened.

But it wasn't Tammy who answered; it was Nora.

Taylor was lying on the dusty old couch on Sierra's screened-in porch, her head resting in Sierra's lap as they gazed out at a yard that wavered and shimmered in the heat.

"Are you glad you did it?" Sierra asked, running her fingers through Taylor's hair. The repetitive action was so relaxing Taylor could hardly keep her eyes open.

"Told my mom? Definitely. It makes the pregnancy more real. I mean, I'll have to face it now. But it was getting pretty real, anyway."

"Thanks to Oliver and his brother," Sierra muttered with a scowl. "They're lucky they live far away from me. They've been such dicks lately."

Taylor knew Sierra was reacting to her swollen eyes and tear-streaked face. It upset Sierra to see her unhappy. But Taylor was actually feeling better. "I've cried a lot the last twenty-four hours," she admitted. "The reality of what I'm facing will hit me randomly, and tears just…well up, out of nowhere. But I think I'm finally all cried out."

"It's cool that your mom's taking the news so well."

The buzz of a wasp, dancing around the door leading outside, drew Taylor's attention, but it couldn't get in, so she watched it without any real interest. "My grandma took it pretty good, too. My Mimi is awesome. And now they'll both help me. I shouldn't have waited so long."

"Do you think there's any chance your mom will let you stay in Sable Beach for the winter?"

Her mother hadn't mentioned that as a possibility. But Taylor had certainly thought of it. "Doubt it."

Sierra scratched Taylor's scalp, then ran a finger over her face, both of which felt better than Taylor could ever have imagined. "Why not?" she asked. "Now that your senior year's screwed up, anyway, there's no reason to go back."

"Oliver wouldn't be able to see the baby."

"Oliver doesn't want to see the baby. He keeps asking you to get an abortion."

"As much as I'd like to stay here, I don't know if I could go through the pregnancy without my mom."

"You'll have your grandma. Or…maybe you'll all move here."

Taylor finally let her eyes close. "That would be hard on Caden," she murmured. "He has water polo."

"Water polo isn't everything. We're talking about a *baby*."

The heat was making her even sleepier. "Yeah, but my mom will try to keep things as normal for him as possible. He's not the one who screwed up."

"Maybe he would be better off here, too."

Taylor wasn't compelled enough to comment.

"So what are you going to tell Oliver?"

It took a lot of energy to respond, but she managed to summon it. "Nothing. My mom made me block him and his brother so that they can't bother me anymore, said she'd call them herself."

"When?"

"I don't know," she said and that was the last thing she remembered before drifting off to sleep.

Autumn needed to call Oliver and have him get his parents on the line, but every time she started to punch in the number Taylor had given her, she stopped. She wasn't ready to deal with that, was still too uncertain and upset about too many things.

For one, she knew she hadn't been completely fair with Quinn. He'd faced a no-win situation, and he'd navigated it the best way he could. But she couldn't reach out to him. She was too busy punishing herself for letting something else threaten the well-being of her family—essentially sabotaging the relationship because she felt guilty for being so happy.

But even acknowledging that didn't make her break down. She was too fatalistic at the moment.

As she moved around the house, tidying up while her mother was gone, she thought about so many things. What'd happened to Nick and why she'd never been able to find him. What was about to happen to Taylor and what they should do about the baby. Whether she could seriously allow herself to give her whole heart to Quinn.

And something else, too: her father. She wasn't sure why, but any crisis she went through somehow brought her back to what she used to obsess over as a child. Where did she come from? Who was she really? Was she related to other people out there that she didn't know?

She'd already decided to take a DNA test once she returned to Tampa. Her mother didn't have to know about it. She'd see what the results were before making up her mind whether to go any further. It was entirely possible that no one on her father's side had been tested, which meant the results wouldn't be definitive, anyway.

Maybe that was why, as she began to clean out her purse, she paused when she came across the card her friend had let her take home from their lunch together. The detective's card—Drake D. Owens.

Had he ever found the woman he'd been searching for?

Even if he hadn't, the fact that she'd heard about him more than once suggested he was conscientious and thorough. Given her own experience searching for Nick, she understood how valuable those traits were in a private investigator.

Perhaps he could help her find her father before it was too late and her father was dead. Putting it off any longer meant she might never get to meet him.

With a sigh, she slumped into a chair at the kitchen table and called the number on that card.

"This is Drake."

She cleared her throat. "Mr. Owens?"

"Yes?"

"My name is Autumn Divac."

"What can I do for you, Autumn?"

"I was wondering…did you ever find Bailey North?"

The atmosphere on the phone suddenly changed, grew tense in some indefinable way. "What'd you say your name was?"

"Autumn Divac. I live in Sable Beach?"

"Right. I see. Well, I've already found Bailey. But thanks so much for trying to help."

She hadn't told him she was trying to help. He had no idea why she was calling, and yet he was eager to get rid of her. Why? "Where'd you find her?" she asked before he could hang up.

He paused as though he couldn't decide whether to answer. Then he said, "In... Virginia Beach. She was living down there."

"So she got the money?"

"The *money*?" he repeated.

"I was told she'd receive an inheritance, if only you could find her."

"You *really* don't know who Bailey is?"

Autumn blinked in surprise. "Why would I?"

"I'm getting another call. I've got to go."

"Wait—can't you just answer the question?"

Silence.

"Mr. Owens?"

"If you really want to know, all you have to do is Google Bailey North," he said and hung up.

Autumn rocked back in her chair. What a strange conversation! It was as if he'd recognized her name, as if he'd thought she and this Bailey North should be acquainted in some way.

She rubbed her forehead as their conversation ran through her mind again. *All you have to do is Google Bailey North...*

Using her phone, she performed the search and was astonished by the number of links that came up.

Bailey North, kidnapped and held hostage for seven years...
Jeff and Nora Skinner to stand trial for the kidnapping of Bailey North...
Bailey North's daring escape...

Was Nora Skinner as culpable as her husband in the kidnapping
of twelve-year-old Bailey North?
Kept in chains—one girl's tragic story and how she survived…
Bailey North, mother at sixteen…
Jeff Skinner gets life; Nora Skinner gets thirty-eight years…

There was so much information about this old case. It must've been big news at the time, but according to the dates on these articles, she would've been only three years old.

She read article after article, growing more horrified by what this Bailey had been through with each one. She'd been taken by a woman asking for directions and held captive in a mansion by a man named Jeff Skinner, who'd raped her for years, getting her pregnant when she was sixteen. She had his baby in the basement of his home one night, alone and frightened, and she only escaped her captivity because of a neighbor who grew suspicious about the Skinners when their own daughter mentioned having a sister—someone *they* called a niece—yet the girl rarely came out of the house.

Concerned, especially when the Skinners' daughter started talking about her sister having a baby, the neighbor snuck over one night when the Skinners were gone and discovered the terrible secret they'd been hiding for years.

This had to be the Bailey North he'd been looking for. He'd said to Google it, and this was the only Bailey who came up in any significant way. But Autumn was confused why he'd think she'd recognize this woman's name or have any affiliation with her—until she read one article that mentioned the name of Bailey's child: Autumn.

29

"Where's Tammy?" Mary's legs felt so rubbery she had to grip the railing to keep from crumpling onto the porch. "How dare she lie to me the way she has! She's been associating with you the whole time?"

"No, Bailey—I mean, Mary." Nora lifted a placating hand. "It—it's not what you think. Tammy's not here. Tammy has never been here."

"She's the one who sent me this address. I—I spoke to her on the phone," Mary said, but even as the words came out, she realized that she'd been tricked. She hadn't recognized the voice she heard, but she hadn't expected to recognize it because it had been thirty-five years and Tammy had been only a child when they were separated. That voice had actually been Nora's, who, as an old woman, didn't sound remotely the same. She'd been talking and texting with Nora the whole time, and she'd never suspected a thing.

"I'm sorry. I had no idea you'd show up here out of the blue. You told me you haven't been able to travel since…well, that you haven't been anywhere farther than a hundred miles from Sable Beach since you moved there."

"Because of you!" she said, astounded that Nora could be so callous and oblivious. "Because of what you did to me!"

"I only gave you my address because you said you were going to send pictures. How could I resist that? I have nothing left. I'm trying to build a new life now and need some type of foundation, some way to fill in the missing years. I would've told you the truth eventually, I swear it."

"I can't believe it," Mary said. "I suppose I shouldn't be surprised. But how evil does a person have to be to contact their kidnap victim decades later to continue the abuse?"

"Not to continue the abuse, no. I'm not trying to hurt you," she said, her voice plaintive. "I swear it. I just thought…if—if only you could get to know the person I am now—which is completely different than the person I was before—maybe you could forgive me. Maybe I could make amends in some way, and it would be good for both of us. Then I could tell Tammy we were associating, that you were able to leave everything that happened in the past and move on, and maybe she could, too. I want my baby back!" she cried on a sob.

Mary heard Laurie get out of the car, but she didn't look in that direction. She couldn't tear her eyes from her old captor's face. Nora was only fourteen years older than she was—sixty-eight—and yet she looked eighty. She'd once been attractive, but all those years in prison had not been kind to her.

She was, however, just as narcissistic as she'd ever been. Only a narcissist could continue to try to manipulate the situation for her own benefit. This wasn't about Mary, about making amends, or any true regret. This was about trying to get her own daughter to associate with her again.

Mary couldn't help being proud of Tammy for refusing to do that.

"What's going on?" Laurie asked, her voice stern as she reached the porch. "Where's Tammy? Who the hell are you?"

"Laurie, meet the woman who kidnapped me, beat me,

chained me up, yelled and cursed at me constantly, used me like a slave and allowed her husband to rape me at will."

"I didn't know he was doing that!" Nora screamed. "Why won't anyone believe me?"

"You knew it once I got pregnant," Mary countered.

Nora looked between her and Laurie. "He said he was sorry, that it only happened once. And even if he was lying, what could I do? We couldn't let you go. We'd go to prison. I had no choice but to continue living with the terrible decision I made when I pulled over to ask you for directions. But we treated you better and better as time went on," she added as though she somehow deserved credit for that. "I saw to it myself."

The outrage that poured through Mary brought her strength back. Her hands curled into fists as she stepped closer to the woman who, along with Jeff, had given her nightmares for most of her life. "Because you'd abused me so badly you knew you had me cowed, that I wouldn't dare make a break for it. How can you expect any gratitude for that? After you starved me for days for the slightest thing? After you locked me up and forced me to work like a slave? After how you acted once you found out I was pregnant? Your jealousy was so out of control you left me alone in the basement to have your husband's baby without any help at all!"

She looked furtive, nervous, as she rubbed her hands on her sweatshirt. "I—I didn't realize you were in labor. How was I supposed to know?"

"Because I was banging on the door, pleading with you. I've never been so terrified in my whole life. Even Tammy woke up and tried to get you to come, and you yelled at her and put her back to bed."

"I don't remember it that way," she tried to say but Mary continued talking over her.

"I truly believe you were hoping my baby would die, so that you wouldn't have to live with the constant reminder of what your husband was doing to me the whole time, that you'd been stupid enough to fall for his lies when he claimed he wanted your help to kidnap a girl so you wouldn't have to be the one to scrub the toilets in the mansion his family's money provided you both."

Nora winced. "Look at me. I have nothing, no one. I've paid the price for what I've done," she said, falling back on that argument since Mary wasn't willing to accept her lies.

"As far as I'm concerned, you haven't paid nearly enough," Mary said and whirled around so fast she nearly bumped into Laurie. "Let's go."

"No, don't go," Nora said. "Please. Allow me to apologize. I'm sorry for what I did. Truly. You were more than a slave to me. I remember you fondly."

Mary could feel her fingernails cutting into her palms. "You're lying again, Nora," she said over her shoulder. "You just want your daughter to allow you into her life. But there's no way you're going to use me to accomplish that. Don't ever contact me again."

Mary expected Laurie to fall in step with her, but she didn't. She lingered behind, yelling at Nora, telling her that she'd have to answer to Laurie if she ever attempted to speak to Mary again. There was more. They were both screaming before it was over. But at some point, Mary quit listening. Her ears were ringing so loudly she couldn't hear, anyway.

Eventually, Laurie marched over, got behind the wheel and tore out of the drive, leaving Nora standing in her yard in the rain looking after them. "I can't believe that just happened," she said.

Mary didn't respond. She was still trying to process it herself. She was sweating and shaking and couldn't seem to stop.

"Mary?" Laurie said once they were well away. "Are you okay?"

Mary nodded. "Just keep driving. Get me out of this state. I want to go home."

★ ★ ★

Quinn checked his phone at every opportunity. He was hoping to hear from Autumn. They typically texted each other several times a day. Sometimes it was only a heart emoji, but he didn't care what she sent today as long as it indicated she'd be able to forgive him at some point.

When he didn't hear from her, he thought she might stop by instead. Occasionally, she'd bring him a treat from another restaurant or cookies she'd baked with her kids. Or he'd take a break and walk over to the bookstore to say hello. Sometimes he'd even buy a book, just so it wasn't quite so obvious how badly he wanted to see her.

The bookstore was closed on Mondays, but he was tempted to go over to her house. He wanted to plead his case, convince her that he was in a difficult position and couldn't betray her daughter's trust any more than he could betray hers, and that he'd only agreed because he knew she would be finding out in a matter of weeks. But after what he'd been through with Sarah, he needed a relationship in which his partner was capable, as Sarah never was, of flexibility and forgiveness.

Although he was determined not to recreate the situation he'd had with his ex-wife, it wasn't easy to hold back. It felt ominous not to hear from her. He knew it couldn't mean anything good. But…was it enough to break them up?

As the day turned into night and the restaurant got busy, he tried to focus on work, but Autumn was always on his mind—her and the fact that he hadn't received a single text or phone call from her all day.

"What's wrong?" his father asked once everyone else had left and they were getting ready to lock up.

Quinn hadn't realized his father was watching him. "Nothing," he said, immediately improving his expression. He didn't need to bring his father in on the fact that he and Autumn weren't getting along. Mike would only tell Beth, and Quinn didn't want her to hear about it.

"You going over to see your girl?"

Quinn pretended to be preoccupied with gathering up the towels and cleaning rags, which he took home and washed each night. "I don't think so. She's got something going with her kids," he said and figured that was probably true, although he didn't know for sure.

"So I'll see you at home?"

"I've got a pair of shorts in my car. I'm going to throw them on and go for a run on the beach, since I didn't get to go this morning."

His father paused before stepping outside. "You go to the beach whenever you're upset," he pointed out.

Because he had to go somewhere. He didn't have a lot of privacy now that he was living with his parents. "I also go there to work out," Quinn said, "so stop worrying."

His father gave him a tired smile, even though it was only ten o'clock. "Okay. I'm exhausted. If you won't be home until late, I won't see you until tomorrow."

"You'll probably beat me to the restaurant, like most days, but I'll be here."

With a nod, Mike left and, once the door closed, Quinn sighed and checked his phone one last time.

Nothing.

"Damn it." After wiping down the grill, he grabbed the laundry bag and went out and checked to make sure the door was locked before starting across the lot to his car.

He didn't see her until he was about ten feet away. Then he realized there was a tall girl leaning against his car.

As he got closer, he could tell it was Taylor. "Hey," he said.

She was wearing cutoffs and a tank top with sandals and had her hair pulled into a ponytail. "Hey."

"How'd you get here?" He looked around, hoping to see Autumn but didn't spot her car.

"Sierra brought me over on the motorcycle. I told her you'd give me a ride home, if that's okay. If not, I can call my mom. She's just over at the bookstore, taking care of something for my grandma."

He used the clicker on his key fob to unlock the doors. "I can give you a ride, no problem," he said as he tossed the laundry in his trunk.

She got into the passenger side while he climbed behind the wheel. "Everything okay?"

"I told my mom about the baby," she said.

He started the engine. "How'd that go?"

"She took it pretty well. She's not happy. What mother would be? But she wasn't mean about it or anything."

"Does your mother ever get mean?"

"Not really. But…this is a pretty big deal. I knew it would upset her."

"Fortunately, a baby isn't the end of the world."

"It seems like the end of mine," she grumbled.

"You'll get through it. I'm glad it's out in the open."

"So am I. I just thought you should know that it's not a secret anymore, in case Mom hasn't already told you about it."

He turned down the radio that had come on when he started the car. "Actually, she did tell me, Taylor. This morning on the phone. And I admitted to her that I already knew."

"You did?" she asked, her eyes round.

"I did. I kept my word to you, but I didn't want to lie to her. Pretending not to know felt too dishonest."

She tucked a few stray wisps of hair behind her ears. "How'd she react?"

"Not so well."

She wrinkled her nose. "She got mad?"

"I haven't heard from her all day, so… I don't know what to think."

"I haven't been at the house. I've been with Sierra, so I don't know how she's been feeling. I'm sorry if it's my fault."

"I'm not placing any blame," he said. "Just…wanted to be up-front with both of you."

She nibbled on her bottom lip while he finished navigating the last few blocks to Mary Langford's beach house. "You really care about my mom, don't you?" she said once he pulled into the driveway.

He gazed up at the window over the garage. "I'm in love with her," he said, and in that moment, he realized it was true. He didn't care if they'd been dating only a short time. He'd fallen hard.

Taylor's smile was sympathetic. "Don't worry. My mom's not the type to stay mad for long."

He grinned. "Glad to hear it. Put in a good word for me," he joked, and she surprised him by squeezing his arm before climbing out.

"I will."

30

Autumn paced the narrow aisles of the bookstore, too filled with anxiety to stand in one place. She would've made herself stop and get some work done while she was waiting, but there wasn't much to do. With three of them manning the store these days, they'd been able to keep up. She'd only come here because she was looking for some privacy. The conversation she was hoping to have with her mother couldn't be had at the house or even in the apartment over the garage, not without the risk of her children interrupting or overhearing. And she wasn't ready to include Caden and Taylor. There were too many things she needed to learn first.

Maybe she'd never tell them about the Skinners. Maybe her mother wouldn't want them to know. If that was the case, Autumn could certainly understand. It was hard for rape survivors to open up and talk about what they'd been through. She could only imagine what it must be like for her mother—to be that one in a million who'd been held hostage and victimized for years.

Not only had Mary been victimized, she'd also been impregnated by her abuser. At last, Autumn had the answers she'd been looking for where her father was concerned, but they weren't anything she could be happy about. That was why her mother hadn't told her. Jeff Skinner was a psychopath without empathy or regard for others, who was currently in prison. He couldn't add anything to her life or anyone else's.

Everything made sense now. Why her father had never tried to track her down. Why Mary had been so vague about him. Why Mary often had trouble sleeping, refused to venture farther than a couple of hours from Sable Beach and never married or even dated.

Mary had been a twelve-year-old girl lured into a car by a young mother—Nora Skinner—who had taken her prize home to her handsome, wealthy husband. Autumn could understand why a child would feel safe approaching a vehicle with a woman in it who was asking for directions, especially a woman like Nora Skinner. Nora hadn't been disheveled and unkempt, strung out on drugs or driving a rattletrap car. She'd been young, well-dressed and behind the wheel of a BMW with her own daughter in the backseat. Who wouldn't trust that?

Unbelievable. She'd spent the past several hours reading everything she could find on her mother's case. She'd also spent some time thinking about the various people named in those articles, and featured in the accompanying pictures, and how they fit in with what she knew—or had been told. Mary's mother, for instance, couldn't be Nana. Several of the articles named someone else. And yet, Laurie was most certainly connected to Nana. They looked just alike. Did that mean that Laurie wasn't really her aunt? Chris not her uncle? Jacob not her cousin? How much of her life was a lie?

The entire landscape of Autumn's past had changed in an instant. So where had Mary's real mother gone? Why hadn't she been around after Mary had escaped the Skinners? For that matter, where were Mary's other relatives?

Autumn recalled the conversation she'd had, not too long ago, with Laurie when she'd asked if Laurie could offer any information on who Autumn's father might be. What she'd learned today explained even that interaction. Laurie knew the truth, obviously. She knew but she'd kept Mary's secret, because she was Mary's best friend if not her true sister.

A rattle at the back door suggested her mother was back—finally—and had received her text to come to the store.

"There you are!" Autumn said, rushing into the back room to meet her. "What took you so long?"

"It's been...quite a day," she replied and slumped into the seat at the desk.

"Where's Laurie?" Autumn asked, expecting her "aunt" to walk in next.

"At home. My car was at her place, so I picked it up and drove over alone. What's going on? Did you get hold of Oliver's parents?"

Her mother assumed this was about the pregnancy. That Autumn was still upset about that. And she was. But for the time being, she'd shoved that problem into the back of her mind. She needed to deal with this first. "Not yet."

Mary's eyebrows slid up. "Then...what's wrong?"

Autumn knelt before her mother and took her hands. "I know, Mom," she said simply.

Mary stiffened. She even withdrew her hands. "You know what?"

"I know who you really are, what happened to you, who my father is."

Her mother's mouth fell open. "Who told you?" she asked, her voice hoarse from the shock.

"No one, really."

"Then how..."

Autumn took a few minutes to explain. She figured her mother could use the time to come to grips with the fact that the secret she'd carried for so long, and guarded so fiercely, was no longer a secret at all.

By the time she finished, Mary sat, silent, her head bowed.

"Mom? Aren't you going to say anything?"

"I'm sorry," she murmured without looking up. "Laurie has been after me to tell you the truth for years. I probably should have. I've been living a lie—my whole identity was…manufactured. But I chose protection over honesty. I didn't want you to know the truth, didn't want you to ever question my love for you or feel as though you might be less than what you are because of who your father is. I didn't want Taylor and Caden to be burdened with the knowledge of that, either." A tear dropped onto her lap as she added, "I wanted to stop the poison, to suck it all up and hold it within myself so that it could never touch you or your kids."

It was hard to learn her mother had been living a lie. Autumn had to ask herself—would she rather have known? There were so many ramifications that it was tough to say. Certainly not when she was a child. She wasn't sure she'd feel comfortable telling Taylor and Caden even now, and they were further removed from it than she'd been. "You know what?" she said softly.

Her mother looked pale and drawn—and seemed somewhat resigned—as she lifted her gaze. "What?"

"You did the right thing."

Mary blinked more quickly. "I did?"

"I would've done the same," she admitted and knew it was true. Learning who her father was hadn't changed her life in any positive way. Not knowing had driven her crazy at times, but was this any better? "Why did that private investigator come to town after so long? Who sent him?"

"He told me it was the Skinners' daughter."

"The child you had to watch whenever they went out." Autumn had read about that in one of the articles.

"Yes. Her name was Tammy. She was the only thing that made what I went through bearable. I loved her like a little sister, and she did what she could to help me, considering she was young and vulnerable, too."

Like a little sister. Those words stuck out. It hadn't escaped Autumn that Tammy would actually be *her* sister.

"But it wasn't Tammy," her mother continued. "It was Nora." Autumn rocked back. "She's out of prison?"

"You didn't find anything that mentioned her release?"

"None of the articles I came across were recent enough. They were all from back when it happened—or later, once you were free and the trial started."

"Doesn't surprise me," she said. "I've looked on the internet myself, periodically, and found no mention of her. But then Owens showed up in town, and I knew something had changed."

Autumn listened quietly as her mother told her about Owens claiming it was Tammy, the texts and phone calls she'd unknowingly had with Nora since then, and her trip to Nashville today with Laurie.

"If Nora is living in such a dump, how'd she have the money to hire Owens?" Autumn asked.

"I have no idea. Someone in her family must've helped her. That's all I can figure."

"And she wanted to contact you so she could apologize?" Autumn asked, trying to imagine the day as her mother had painted it.

"That was what she said."

"But that doesn't make any sense. Surely, even she would have realized it would only make you angry to pretend to be Tammy."

"Not in her twisted mind. If I know her, she thought that having the opportunity to talk to me, to try to convince me of her remorse, would get me to feel sorry for her and the high price *she's* paid."

"That's pretty ironic. That she would try to play on your empathy when she's never had any."

"That's what psychopaths do," Mary answered dully. "She's

hoping I'll forgive her so that she can hold me out as a carrot to get Tammy to forgive her, too."

"You're not going to—you're not going to have anything to do with any of them, are you?"

She sighed as she smoothed Autumn's hair off her forehead, like she used to do when Autumn was a little girl. "Not Nora, or Jeff, who's still in prison and will probably spend the rest of his life there. But now that you know the truth, maybe we should reach out to Tammy. She did nothing wrong. And since we know that she's not in contact with her mother, it might be nice to see who she turned out to be. What do you think? Would you be interested in meeting your half sister?"

Autumn blew out a lungful of air. This morning she hadn't even known she had a sibling. "I need some time to think about that," she said. "I'm still trying to figure everything out."

"I'm sorry, Autumn."

Autumn forced a smile. Her mother had been through enough. No matter how shocked or upset she was by the implications of what she'd learned, she would not put her mother through anything else. "It's okay. Really. Right now all I need is answers."

"Ask me anything."

Autumn could tell by the tone of her mother's voice that she was ready to be completely honest. She could also tell that Mary was bracing for probing questions about what she'd suffered at the hands of the Skinners. But Autumn couldn't bring herself to make her mother relive all of that. "Is Laurie really related to us?"

Her lips parted in surprise, but she shook her head.

"So Nana isn't my nana, either," Autumn said sadly.

"No. And Jacob isn't your cousin."

"How did you meet them? When I was a child, you told me that you and Laurie decided to come to Sable Beach because you once saw a picture in a magazine and fell in love with the idea of living in such an idyllic place. Does that mean you knew her in Nashville?"

"No. I don't remember saying that Laurie came with me. She was already here. Chris's father bought a vacation home on the beach when he was just a child. That's why they were familiar with it."

"You didn't meet her until you moved here."

"That's right. After I left Nashville, I rented a room from an old widow who lived two blocks away from here. She needed a little help keeping her house up and some company, and I needed a place to stay and someone to watch you during the day."

"I don't remember her," Autumn said. "I just remember going to the bookstore with you."

"You were too young. Her name was Lula Belle, and she was a wonderful person. But by the time she passed away, I'd been working at the bookstore for a year, and Laurie had been working there even longer. So I guess Laurie and I first bonded over our love of books, and we've been inseparable ever since."

"She's aware of your history?" Autumn knew this, but she was still reeling, trying to figure out what was true and what wasn't.

"Yes. That's why she became our family. She knew we didn't really have any and that it would help give me a history—some credibility and cover so that I could leave my past behind. Then, when the owner of the bookstore decided to retire so that he and his wife could move closer to their kids, he made it possible for us to buy the store with no money down, so we decided to do it together, and you know the rest."

"I'm glad you've had her," Autumn said sadly.

Mary must've been able to tell that Autumn felt a sense of loss, because she said, "You have her, too. Laurie, Chris, Jacob, Nana. They all love us, so does it really matter that we aren't genetically connected?"

Did it matter? They'd stuck by them so far, hadn't they? Autumn had no reason to believe those relationships would change. "I guess not. But…where's your real mother?"

"I don't know," she replied.

"You haven't had any contact with her over all these years?"

"None."

"Because…"

Mary smiled sadly. "She wasn't much of a mother."

Autumn got up and kissed her cheek. "Then she's nothing like you."

Quinn checked his phone as soon as he woke up.

He still hadn't heard from Autumn, which made him feel sick, so he rolled over and went back to sleep. He wasn't eager to get up two hours later, either, but he had no choice. His parents were counting on him.

After dragging himself into the shower, he threw on some clothes, got the laundry out of the dryer and stuffed it back into the bag he'd brought home and hurried downstairs to grab a cup of coffee. His father was expecting him so they could start the food prep for the day, which meant he'd have to wait to eat anything else until he arrived at the restaurant.

He hoped to find his mother puttering around the kitchen, something she did when she was feeling strong enough.

When he reached the landing, he heard her talking, but she wasn't alone. He also heard Autumn's voice.

Dropping the laundry, he rounded the corner to see both of them sitting on the sofa.

"Look who stopped by to say hello," Beth said.

Autumn was holding a cup of coffee, but when she saw him, she set it on the side table and stood up. "Sleep good?"

"I've slept better," he replied.

"Are you in a hurry to get to the restaurant, or do you have a moment to talk?"

He was late and feeling some pressure because of it, but he

wasn't going to forgo this opportunity. "I can talk. Why don't we go for a drive?"

"Sounds good."

She thanked his mother for the coffee, carried her cup over to the sink and, after he grabbed the laundry he needed to return to the restaurant, left with him through the side door.

"Is this good news or bad?" he asked as he put the bag in his car.

She shifted to her other foot. "What do you think?"

He came back to her as he fished his keys out of his pocket. "I don't want to hear it if it's going to be bad."

She held out a piece of paper.

"What's this?"

"I found it on my bed last night when I got home."

He unfolded it. It was a note from Taylor.

Mom, please don't be mad at Quinn. He really cares about you. And he hasn't done anything wrong. I asked him not to tell you, and he was nice enough to let me handle it. I know you would've done the same if you were him, because it was the right thing to do. I'm sorry—for everything. I love you! XOXO Tay

"Wow. How nice of her," he said.

"She must like you."

He was starting to feel better. "I like her, too."

Autumn took the letter, folded it up and shoved it into the pocket of her capri pants. "I'm sorry, Quinn," she said. "Yesterday was a rough day for me, but I know now that you had good reason to do what you did."

They were still in the garage, but they had the privacy they were after, so they didn't bother getting into his car. "I'm glad to hear that."

"Will you forgive me?"

Relief coursed through him. "Of course. It couldn't have been easy to hear about the pregnancy. And I understand why you felt betrayed. I just didn't have a good choice."

"I know, but it wasn't only Taylor's pregnancy. You won't believe what else happened."

What else could there be? "You want to tell me about it?"

"Not right now. I know you have to go to work. I just… I wanted you to know that…that I was miserable without you. I don't know how I'll survive when I have to leave for Florida."

He pressed her up against the wall and caught her chin in his hand. "Don't leave."

"I have to," she said. "Caden has water polo. It might be his ticket to college."

"So? We'll help him pay for school."

"That's an expensive solution," she said with a chuckle.

"You're worth it to me. And we have Taylor to think of, too. I believe she'd be better off here."

"You do," she said with a laugh.

"I do," he insisted, "because I've found the perfect couple to raise her baby."

All levity fled her face. "Who?"

He kissed her. *"Us."*

31

Autumn hummed the song she'd last heard on the radio as she puttered around the bookstore that afternoon. She still had the same problems she'd had before, but they seemed so much more manageable since she'd gone to visit Quinn. He insisted that they could face anything together, and she was beginning to believe him. Taylor's pregnancy wasn't anything she would have wished for. But Quinn's solution made her feel as though there *was* a solution—and it was one that wouldn't tear her heart out. He actually *wanted* a baby. And she was sort of excited, too, now that she was over the shock of it. Instead of being alone, her husband missing and presumed dead, her children gone to college, she'd be with Quinn, devoting her life to him and her first grandchild, which she knew he would consider his grandchild, as well. She was even open to the possibility of having a baby herself in a couple of years. She and Quinn could raise both children together, at least until Taylor got out of college and was in a position to take over with hers.

"How is it that you're smiling and singing today?" her mother asked, coming out of the back room where she and Laurie had been paying some bills and doing other business.

Autumn looked up from changing the receipt roll on the register. "I'm starting to view things from a different perspective."

"Oh, really," her mother said with a laugh. "Does this new perspective have anything to do with Quinn Vanderbilt?"

That wasn't a difficult guess. Just after lunch, he'd sent flowers to the store—a huge arrangement of peach roses, carnations and Asiatic lilies. "He wants me to stay here in Sable Beach," she said.

"How nice, especially because *I* want you to stay in Sable Beach, too." She leaned up against the counter. "Is that a possibility?"

Autumn got the roll of paper seated properly and closed the cover of the register. "He says it would probably be better for Taylor not to have to go back and face her old friends, pregnant with an underclassman's baby. And he has a point. She could homeschool this year and still graduate. When she leaves for college, he and I could care for the baby."

"He said that?" she asked, straightening in surprise.

Autumn couldn't have stopped smiling if she'd wanted to. "He did."

"That's quite an offer. I'm trying not to get my hopes up too high."

"You'd love to be around the baby yourself."

"Of course I would. And I'd make a great babysitter for when you and Quinn wanted to go out. Think of how handy that would be," she joked. "But—" her smile wilted a bit "—what about Caden?"

"He seems to like it here," she said, hopeful that he might be open to the idea, after all.

"So you won't wait for him to graduate?"

"I planned to stay in Tampa when I thought Nick might come back. I didn't feel I could uproot the family and move, make the kids go to a new high school when they were so close to graduating. But so much has changed."

"What about Caden's water polo?" her mother asked.

"There are water polo teams in Virginia. But I hate to make him leave his friends."

"He seems to have made plenty of new ones here," her mother pointed out. "Maybe they don't all live in Sable Beach year-round, but the twins do. So does Sierra. And she would be a great support to Taylor during the pregnancy."

"I have no doubt. She's completely devoted." Other than Caden, it seemed as though it would be better for everyone. Her mother had no other real family; Autumn knew that now. Mary had been through so much, and yet she'd found the strength and resolve to be able to give Autumn a good life. Autumn felt it was time to move back and be there for her for a change. Mary and Laurie would soon have a coffee shop to manage as well as the store; Sierra and Taylor would help out here and there, but Autumn would run it. Then she wouldn't have to be separated from Quinn, and Taylor wouldn't have to be separated from Sierra.

It would be wonderful to leave behind the life that had imploded when Nick disappeared and start over. Her son was the only thing holding her back. "I'll talk to Caden," she said. "See if he's even open to the idea."

"Am I hearing right?" Laurie asked as she joined them at the register. "Are you thinking about staying in Sable Beach?"

"We'll see," Autumn said.

She bent to get her purse. "You know Chris and I would love that."

"I would love it, too," she admitted.

Mary and Laurie had to meet with the architect to have something changed on the plans for the coffee shop. After they left, Autumn walked around the store, running her fingers over the shelves and spines of the books. This place had shaped her childhood. She felt such a sense of promise as she considered making it part of her future, too—like bookends, she thought with a chuckle.

For her, this town, this bookshop, was home and home was where her heart would always be.

That night, Taylor sat at the kitchen table with her mother, Caden and Mimi. They were about to call Oliver's parents; she was so nervous she had butterflies in her stomach. How mad would the Hancocks get? Would they blame the pregnancy entirely on her? Make her out to be some sort of slut? Oliver had said his father would kick him out of the house. Taylor couldn't help worrying about that. As upset as she was at Oliver for telling his brother about the baby, she wasn't out to ruin his life.

"You ready?" her mother asked.

She wasn't ready, but she couldn't put this off any longer. Now that she'd told her mother, she felt like she was halfway across a high and very shaky bridge, one that could break and let her fall through at any second. She wasn't eager to stay on it any longer than she had to.

"Tay?" her mother prompted.

She nodded. *Do it*, she thought. *Just do it*. Fortunately, Autumn had Oliver's mother's number from before, when Caden used to hang out with him.

Caden, Mimi and her mother looked at each other, drew a deep breath—and her mother dialed the call, which she had on speakerphone.

A woman answered right away. "Hello?"

"Mrs. Hancock?"

"Yes?"

"This is Autumn Divac."

"Caden's mom."

"Yes. I've got my mother, my daughter and Caden on the line with me."

"Oh, okay." She sounded taken aback. "How are you all?"

Jill Hancock seemed to be curious about this call but in a good mood.

She must not know, Taylor mouthed to Caden, and he agreed with a nod.

"We've been better," Autumn admitted.

"Have you learned anything about Nick?"

"No, I'm afraid not."

"I'm so sorry."

"Thank you for your condolences."

There was an awkward lull, during which Mrs. Hancock had to be wondering why they'd called her. Meanwhile, Taylor could tell that Autumn was looking for a way to start the *real* part of the conversation, and she felt sorry that she'd caused this whole thing.

"Listen, um, I'm afraid we have a problem," Autumn said, plunging in.

"We do?" Jill responded, sounding uncertain.

"Yes. You know Taylor, Caden's sister, don't you?"

"I believe so. She's older than Caden and Oliver, will be a senior this year."

"That's right."

"She's a pretty girl. Popular, too. I've seen her at school."

The lump in Taylor's throat swelled at the thought of the humiliation and embarrassment she would face when she returned to Tampa, and the fact that her life would take a dramatically different turn than the lives of her friends. But she hoped appealing to Oliver's mother would help, that they could convince the Hancocks not to be too hard on him, which was why she'd asked her mother to place this call.

"Well…my daughter and your son were…together at a party before the school year ended, and… I'm afraid there's no easy to way to say this, but… Taylor's pregnant."

Dead silence.

Taylor bit her bottom lip as she waited for Oliver's mother's reaction.

"You're not saying..." Jill started but couldn't bring herself to finish the sentence.

"Yes. I'm saying that," Autumn said.

"It's *Oliver's* baby?"

"I'm afraid so."

"That can't be. Oliver and your daughter haven't even been dating!"

Again, Taylor winced. That was true.

"It was a...a one-time thing," Taylor heard her mom say. "At a party."

"Oh, God," she groaned. "You can't be serious. Surely, it can't be Oliver's baby. His father will kill him!"

Taylor cringed as Mimi and her mother exchanged a worried look.

"I hope he won't be that upset," Autumn continued. "There's no need for things to get ugly. After all, what's done is done."

"That's not how his father will look at it."

"I know it's not good news, but we'd like to talk about this as calmly as possible and...and figure out the best path to take—together."

"One minute," she said, after which they could hear her calling for Oliver.

A few seconds later Mrs. Hancock put her phone on speaker, too. "Oliver, shut the door. The Divacs are on the line. They claim you and Caden's sister... That you're responsible for...for getting his older sister pregnant."

Jill had to put in the *older* part, as if one year made Taylor more to blame. Taylor knew there would be other people who'd make a big deal of that, too.

Oliver didn't answer. At least, he didn't say anything they could hear. After a stretch of nothing, his mother started crying, which made Taylor feel even worse. "What are we going to tell your father?" she asked him.

That part they *could* hear.

"Do we *have* to tell him?" Oliver's voice was tight with emotion. "There are...there are other options. I've been talking to Taylor about some of them."

"He's been trying to convince Taylor to get an abortion," Autumn explained. "Is that really what he wants? Is that what you all want?"

Jill didn't answer right away. She seemed to be thinking. Eventually, they could hear Oliver pleading with her, telling her that it was the only way, that he couldn't support a child at sixteen.

"Just think what Dad will do," he said. "We *can't* tell him."

When tears started to roll down Taylor's cheeks, her grandmother gave her a sympathetic look, but it was Caden, sitting next to her, who attempted to comfort her. Not wanting the Hancocks to hear her crying, she stifled a sniff as her brother's bigger hand enveloped hers.

"Is that an option?" his mother asked at length.

Autumn rubbed her forehead. "Would you be supportive of that?"

There was another brief pause, but then she said softly, "Yes. Yes, we would."

"You're *positive*. Would you like some time to talk it over and decide?"

"No," she replied immediately. "Can you think of a better way for this to end?"

Taylor pictured her mother driving her to an abortion clinic—and all that would happen there, if she agreed to it, and felt weak and shaky.

"Fortunately, I can," Autumn said.

Taylor, who'd been staring down at her lap while trying to hold herself together, looked up. Caden seemed surprised, too.

Jill's voice came through the phone again. "What is it?"

"That's something I need to discuss with my own family, so I'll have to call you back."

"Please text me before you call so I can...so I can find a private spot where we can talk."

They were going to try to keep the pregnancy from Oliver's father, if they could. Taylor didn't need her to say it. That was obvious.

"I will," Autumn said and hung up.

Caden let go of Taylor's hand. "So...what are we going to do?"

Their mother gave him a searching look. "That depends on you."

"On *me*?" he said. "I don't have anything to do with this."

"But I love you, too."

"What does that mean?"

Taylor was wondering the same thing.

"Quinn has asked us to stay here, where...where he and I can take care of the baby while Taylor goes off to college."

"He has?" Taylor wiped the tears from her face. "So we'd *keep* the baby?"

"I can't stand the thought of any other alternative," her mother said. "Can you?"

"No," Taylor admitted. "But if we stay in Sable Beach..." She turned to Caden. "You'd have to change schools, and it might mess up your chances for a scholarship."

His eyebrows knitted as he looked from her to their mother and then Mimi. "You all want this," he said.

"We can go back to Tampa and wait for you to graduate," their mother said. "Your goals and happiness matter, too."

"But then Taylor would have to face the humiliation of being pregnant, chances are good Oliver's father will find out and you'd have to take care of the baby alone for the next two years. Maybe you and Quinn wouldn't be able to outlast the separation."

"I feel like I owe you these two years, Caden," Autumn said, "so I'm willing to go back in spite of everything."

Caden's knee began to jiggle.

"You don't have to move," Taylor said. "It wouldn't be fair. This is my fault, not yours."

His leg stopped moving. "Oh, what the hell," he said, throwing up his hands. "I guess I can have just as much fun in Sable Beach as Tampa. I'm going to have to leave the friends I have there eventually, anyway."

"What about water polo?" Mimi asked.

"If I'm good enough, I should be able to get a scholarship while going to any high school. And if not, I'll try to walk on."

"Are you *sure*?" their mother asked. "I don't want you to regret this."

"I'm sure," he replied. "There's just one thing."

Taylor could tell their mother was trying not to get excited too soon. So was she.

"What's that?" Autumn asked tentatively.

"We have to get our own place before school starts, because I'm not going to spend the next two years sleeping on Mimi's couch."

They all started laughing. "What's wrong with my couch?" Mimi joked.

"Agreed," Autumn told Caden. "The two of you can even help me pick out the house."

Taylor felt *so* much better. But she had a question herself. "Will Quinn be moving in with us?"

"Would it be okay if he did?" Autumn asked.

Taylor missed her father. There was no way she could ever love Quinn as much. But she could tell he was a good person. He'd already done a lot for her, and she liked him. She figured that was a start. Besides, she didn't feel as though she could stand in the way of her mother's happiness when her mother was doing so much for her. "It's okay with me."

"I'm fine with it, too," Caden said. "I love you all—don't get me wrong—but it'll be nice to have a little more testosterone in the house."

Taylor got up and gave her brother a hug. "Thank you," she said. Then she went around the table to thank her mother and grandmother, and when she saw the relief and happiness on her mother's face, she loved her brother even more.

32

The next few weeks were some of the happiest of Mary's life. Although Autumn knew about the past, she was so caught up with Quinn that she never broached the subject. It felt wonderful to Mary to know she no longer had something terrible to hide, at least from the person she loved most. She'd also been afraid that, if the truth got out, word would spread quickly through town and she'd have to deal with the curiosity of all the people she knew in Sable Beach, and she didn't want to talk about the past. Didn't want to think about it, either. The only way to truly vanquish Jeff and Nora was to cut them out of her life completely.

So it came as a relief that Drake D. Owens's visit hadn't led to anyone else in Sable Beach figuring out that *she* was Bailey North. To her surprise, life continued much as it always had, except for the excitement surrounding Autumn's big move.

They spent the majority of their time, when they weren't at the bookstore, house hunting and had found a darling three-bedroom cottage Autumn hoped to buy. It wasn't in town; it was set off by itself on the beach about ten minutes away, and it had recently been remodeled with new cupboards and countertops, hardwood floors throughout and windows and doors that faced the sea and opened onto a large deck. Mary could easily imagine sitting on that deck with a glass of wine, enjoying the sunset with her daughter and Quinn, so she hoped Autumn would be able to come to an agreement with the owner. Autumn, the kids—even Quinn—thought it was perfect.

"Hey, Mimi!" Taylor called breezily as she strolled into the bookstore with Sierra at her side.

"Hi, honey. What are the two of you up to today?" Mary had been expecting Autumn, but she hadn't shown up yet.

"Nothing much."

"Where's your mother?" Laurie asked. "I'm excited to show her Chris's new painting."

"She's going to be late today. That's why we're here," Taylor explained. "She asked us to come by and see if you needed help with anything, because she's busy negotiating on the house."

Mary felt a surge of anticipation. "How's it going?"

"They didn't accept her first offer, but they seem open to working something out."

"I hope she can get it," Laurie said before trundling into the back.

Sierra asked if she could use the restroom and, as soon as she and Laurie were both gone, Mary lowered her voice. "Any word from Oliver and his family?" Autumn had been talking about getting back to them this morning.

"None. After breakfast, Mom texted them to say that I wasn't going to get an abortion, but that we would allow Oliver to walk away as if there had never been a baby. Once he turns eighteen, he can decide if he wants to sign over his parental rights or make up past child support and be part of the baby's life."

"And? How did they respond?"

"Mrs. Hancock wrote back, 'Okay,' and left it at that. I think they're relieved his life can go on as planned, and they won't have to tell his father."

"His father sounds like a real piece of work," Laurie said.

The unexpected intrusion of her voice startled Mary. She hadn't realized her best friend had come right back.

"Yeah," Taylor said with a sigh. "I'm glad he's not *my* father."

Laurie stuck a handful of new pens in the drawer. "Where's Caden today?"

"He went over to register for school."

"By himself?" Mary said. "I would've gone over with him."

"Mom offered, too, but he was with the twins. They wanted to do it on their own."

"I see."

Taylor glanced around the store. "I'm really glad we're staying here." Her grandmother and aunt Laurie had promised that both she and Sierra could help with the coffee shop when it opened, so they were looking forward to that.

"But… You sound a little hesitant. Why?"

"It feels strange that I won't be going to school with every-one else, I guess."

"I'm sorry that phase of your life is over a bit too soon," Mary said.

"It's my own fault, and this is the best way things could've worked out, so I'm grateful for that."

"Quinn played a big role in your moving here, you know," she pointed out.

"Yeah, but I feel weird where he's concerned, too." Taylor frowned as though she knew she should leave it there but needed to tell someone what she was feeling. "Part of me wants to hate him, Mimi."

"I'm glad you don't," Mary said. "That would make every-thing so much harder on your mother."

"I know. And he's a cool guy. It's not that. I just feel like a traitor to my dad."

It would be hard to see someone move in and take her father's place. "I suppose that's natural."

"It is?"

Sierra came out of the bathroom, and they let the conversation go. "Let's get some ice cream," Sierra said, and they left the shop as a customer came in.

While Laurie helped Ann Mathewson, who was looking for a regional cookbook she wanted to send as a gift, Mary took out her phone and read her latest text exchange with Nora. She'd written, asking for Tammy's phone number, and Nora had given it to her. No doubt she'd done so hoping to curry favor with them both, but after saving Tammy's number in her contacts, Mary had blocked Nora.

She'd been thinking about reaching out to Autumn's half sister ever since she'd visited Nashville. But with so much going on, she'd put it off. How was Tammy doing? Did she need friendship, support? Was it too late to offer her those things?

"What are you thinking about?"

Mary blinked and looked over at Laurie. Ann Mathewson was already gone? She'd been so lost in her own thoughts that what was going on around her hadn't even registered. "I'm considering reaching out to Tammy."

"Now?" Laurie squawked. "Just when everything is so nice for you? Why would you risk it?"

Mary considered that for several seconds. Then she said, "Because I'm finally at a point in my life where I can."

After letting herself and Quinn inside the empty house using the Realtor's lockbox, Autumn twirled around in the living room. "I can't believe I'm doing this," she said. "I'm buying this house and moving home—it's actually going to work out."

Quinn, who'd come to see the place with her for the third time—but the first since she'd gone into contract—caught her hand and pulled her up against him. "I can't believe it, either. But I can't tell you how glad I am that you are."

"It's scary to be this happy, isn't it?" she asked as she slipped

her arms around his neck and looked up into his eyes. "It terri-
fies me. I keep waiting for the other shoe to drop."

He pecked her lips. "Everything's going to be fine. Stop worrying."

"I don't have any right to worry. It's you that must be worried.
I'm so sorry about what's happening to your mother," she said,
sobering. Beth wasn't going to make it. Everyone knew that now.
They were already talking about hospice. "I'm sorry, Quinn."

"It'll be easier to get through what's coming with your support. I don't want her to suffer—I'd rather she pass. I guess it
helps a little that we expect to lose our parents at some point.
But I'm not sure my father will be able to bounce back."

"We'll be there for him as much as we can. Caden really likes
him. I was shocked by how quickly they hit it off."

He nuzzled her neck. "It was a good idea to have my folks
over for dinner last weekend. Very nice of you."

"It was cramped in my mother's little house, but it was fun.
For most of their lives, my kids have had only one grandpar-
ent. I think they like the idea of having an experience more
like other kids."

His smile broadened.

"What?" she prompted when the look on his face suggested
he was holding something back.

"Nothing."

"Say it."

"It'll sound too presumptuous."

"Come on. You can tell me anything."

He looked slightly abashed when he said, "Fine. I love thinking of my parents as Taylor and Caden's grandparents. I guess,
because your kids are almost adults, I haven't held out much
hope that they'd ever really accept me as a father. But when I
saw the way Caden interacted with my dad on Sunday, as if he
was so open to giving love and receiving love... I don't know.
It gave me hope."

She caught his face in her hands. "It's wonderful that my kids are important to you. Because you care so much, I know they'll accept you—if not right away, with time. Who wouldn't want a man like you as a father?"

"I hope you're right." He rested his forehead against hers. "Can you believe that we'll soon be taking care of a baby? That blows my mind." He lowered his voice. "Sometimes I'm so excited about it I can't sleep."

"I wasn't looking forward to it at first, but thanks to you, I am now," she admitted.

"I've waited a long time for this."

"You got a raw deal with your first marriage."

"That doesn't matter anymore." His hand moved to the buttons on her blouse. "Should we christen your new place?"

She closed her eyes as he unhooked her bra and his hand came around to cup her breast, but she still had the presence of mind to correct him. "*Our* place."

"Not yet. I feel terrible that I can't contribute."

"You will. It's fine."

"My dad's going to start paying me a salary, now that…now that there's nothing more we can do for my mother. You'll be putting up the down payment, so I'll pay the mortgage until I catch up to you."

"I'm not concerned about that. I'm just excited we'll be together—and that we'll be raising Taylor's baby."

He lifted her chin with one finger. "Autumn?"

"What?" she said, slightly breathless with anticipation.

"What do you think about…one day, and it doesn't have to be soon…having *my* baby?"

She ran her thumb over his bottom lip before kissing him tenderly. "I think yes," she said.

When Autumn took the kids over to The Daily Catch for dinner, she invited Mary to go along, but Mary declined. She was looking for some alone time. Ever since she'd decided to contact Tammy, she'd been waiting for the right moment—when she wasn't working, when she wasn't with Caden and Taylor, who had no idea of her background because she and Autumn had decided that it wouldn't serve any good purpose to tell them, and when she wasn't with Laurie, who was a loyal friend and great support but always had a strong opinion about everything.

Mary wanted to do this on her own, and tonight seemed like the perfect opportunity. She had the house to herself, could speak without fear of being overheard. And since everyone had just left, she knew it would be an hour or longer before they came back.

She carried Caden's bedding—he was getting lax about moving it himself—into Taylor's room. Then she sat on the couch and tried to calm her mind.

What had Tammy turned out like? Would she be happy to hear from Mary? Or would reaching out only bring back memories Tammy would rather forget?

Maybe Tammy wasn't ready for this; maybe she'd never be ready for this.

But Mary wouldn't know unless she tried…

Pulling out her phone, she scrolled through her contacts until she came to Tammy's name. She'd stared at that number so often in the past two weeks that she had it memorized.

"Here we go," she murmured and touched the link.

The phone rang five times before Tammy's voice mail came on. "This is Tamara King. Please leave a message at the beep, and I'll return your call as soon as I can."

Mary froze. Should she leave a message? Her first inclination was to hang up. But she decided speaking to Tammy's voice mail might actually be better than speaking to Tammy directly. A message would allow her the chance to decide if she wanted to return the call.

Perfect.

"Tammy, this is…this is Bailey North," Mary said, hurrying to speak before Tammy's phone could cut her off. "I go by Mary Langford now. I—I know this call has to come as a shock to you. It's been so long. I'm sorry if…if you'd rather not hear from me. But I feel as though I owe you an apology, and I would love the chance to give it to you, if it wouldn't be too unwelcome." After she left her number, she disconnected and sprang to her feet. She had to do something to ease the anxiety that was bringing on a terrible hot flash, so she began to pace around the living room.

"Whew!" When she could bring herself to stop moving, she set her phone on the side table and fanned her face. "I did it. Now it's up to her."

She didn't expect to hear back from Tammy right away, if ever, so once she managed to calm down, she made herself a cup of tea and picked up her latest book, a memoir by Jeanette Walls. She was just about to dive in when her phone went off.

Sliding her reading glasses higher on her nose, she leaned over to take a look at the screen and felt her stomach muscles tighten when she saw Tammy's name.

This is it. Taking off her glasses and setting her book aside, she drew a deep breath before she answered. "Hello?"

"Bailey?"

"Yes?"

"It's me. Tammy."

Mary let her head fall onto the back of the couch and stared up at the ceiling. "Thank you for returning my call."

"Of course. You said you owe me an apology, but I want you to know that you don't owe me anything. I owe *you* an apology for the despicable things my parents did to you. I still have nightmares about the night you had your baby—the terror in your voice as you begged for help. That's something I'll never forget. Neither will I *ever* forgive my parents for sending me back to cry myself to sleep when I tried to get them to help you."

"You were such a brave little girl," Mary said with a smile.

"You did all you could for me. If it wasn't for you, for how much I loved you, I would not have survived that dark time."

"That's just it," she said. "I can't believe you *could* love me. I'm connected to them. Not only did they put you through unspeakable horrors, they treated me so much better than they did you."

"You were their child, Tammy. I understood that and was never jealous. Just grateful to have you there with me—not to mention, if it wasn't for you saying what you did to the neighbor, I might never have escaped."

"I'm the child of not one but *two* complete psychopaths," she grumbled. "It's a wonder I'm functional at all."

"What happened to you after I was rescued?" Mary asked. "Where did you go?"

"My father's single aunt took me in."

"He had an aunt?" Neither one of them had ever mentioned that, and Mary felt she'd lived with them long enough to know of most of their family. "Where did she live?"

"In Memphis. I moved back to Nashville from there."

Which was, no doubt, why Nora had also returned to Nashville.

"She wasn't close to him," Tammy continued. "But when she heard what happened, she decided to step up and soon became my guardian."

"Had you ever met her?"

"Only once or twice, at my grandma's house."

"Going to live with a complete stranger must've been hard."

"Not as hard as what you endured," she said.

"Were you happy there with her?" Mary asked. "For the most part?"

A sigh came through the phone. "The transition wasn't easy, but if not for her, I would've been put into foster care. So I'm grateful my life wasn't worse. She was strict, but fair. Paid for my college. I can't complain."

"Then *I'm* grateful to her, too. Is she still alive?"

"Not anymore. She was in her fifties when she took me and had lupus. She had a stroke and passed three years ago."

"I'm sorry to hear that." Despite the sad news about Tammy's aunt, Mary was starting to relax. This wasn't turning out to be nearly as difficult as she'd anticipated. Tammy seemed to have turned out as normal as anyone could, and she was warm, understanding. That helped to alleviate Mary's fears.

"How'd you get my number?" she asked. "I never dreamed I'd hear from you."

"That's an interesting story," Mary replied and settled back to tell it.

She spent the next thirty minutes talking about Nora and Jeff and hearing about Tammy's marriage, the five children she raised and her divorce. Tammy's deceased great-aunt had left her with enough money that she was able to open a clothing boutique, which she loved, but she'd never inherited any money from her parents. Mary had been right when she'd assumed they'd spent every dime on their defense, which explained why Nora was living as she was. Tammy told her Nora had expected to pick up right where they'd left off once she was released from prison, but Tammy had told her to stay away.

They were still on the phone and Mary was explaining why she'd changed her name, and how she'd chosen Sable Beach as the place where she wanted to live, when there was a knock at the door.

Assuming that it was her family, that they were back from the restaurant already and Caden had beat everyone else to the door, she figured Autumn would let him in as soon as she could get out of the car. But that didn't happen. Whoever it was knocked again, this time more insistently.

"Just a sec," she told Tammy and got up to answer.

Eager to get back to her phone call, she jerked the door open without looking through the peephole. She knew everyone in Sable Beach, and although she locked her doors out of an abundance of caution, she was currently too preoccupied to be that careful. It was 6:30 p.m. on a Friday night, not too late or even dark outside.

But as soon as she saw who it was, she gasped and dropped the phone.

"Nick!"

33

Nick looked ten years older. He had much more gray in his hair, and he'd lost at least forty pounds. The man standing before Autumn seemed like a gaunt stranger—and yet, he was her husband and the father of her children.

"Dad!" Taylor cried as soon as she saw him and threw herself into his chest and burst into tears.

Caden, who'd come into the house last, stood in stunned surprise, apparently as shocked as Autumn was.

"I texted you," Mary said to Autumn. "I tried to tell you, but…"

But Autumn had been having too much fun at the restaurant. Quinn kept coming out to their table, even though he was supposed to be cooking in back, bringing dish after dish— far more than they could ever eat. She hadn't even bothered to check her phone.

"Where have you *been*?" Caden asked.

Autumn couldn't breathe as she awaited Nick's response. Where *had* he been? Why hadn't he contacted her instead of just showing up out of the blue?

"It's a long, complicated story." His eyes remained riveted on her face as he spoke. "Maybe…maybe your mother and I should go out to the apartment and talk for a bit before…before I go into everything with you."

Everyone turned to her, but Autumn didn't know what to say. It would feel odd to have Nick in her apartment again. Quinn's shoes were now the ones that were kicked into the corner of the room! Had he left any of his other things there? His sunglasses on the nightstand? His toothbrush in the bathroom? His razor in the medicine cabinet?

What was she going to say? What was she going to do?

"Mom?" Taylor prompted. She'd let go of her father so that Caden could hug him, and now Caden had stepped back so that she could reach him. But Autumn didn't rush toward him as they had. She couldn't move, couldn't find her voice, either. It felt as though someone had knocked the wind out of her.

"I think that would be a great idea," Mary said, speaking up on her behalf. "Why don't you two put on a movie or a game while your parents take a few minutes. I'm sure they'll be back in soon."

Taylor and Caden looked uncertain. They were probably afraid to let Nick out of their sight. Autumn could understand why. She wanted to reassure them, to soothe their fears, but the words were stuck in her throat.

Fortunately, Mary had more presence of mind than she did. Her mother grabbed her hand and led her to the French doors— and probably would've marched her across the yard, too. But once Mary got her moving, Autumn was able to continue, albeit on wooden legs.

"Aren't you even a little excited to see me?" Nick asked, obviously crestfallen. "When I got to Tampa and you weren't there, I knew you had to be here and wanted my arrival to be a bit more of a…pleasant surprise."

Her chest tightened until it was so painful that all she could do was cry. She didn't even know whether she was happy or sad. She'd prayed for Nick's return. She'd given everything she had to finding him. And she was relieved and happy for her kids. They had their father back. But what about Quinn? What about their plans?

"Of course," she managed to say. How else could she answer that question? But she wasn't sure how she felt. It was as if someone had taken an electric mixer to her emotions.

He got the key from behind the ceramic frog, as he had so many times over the years, and opened the door, stepping back to allow her to precede him.

She went in, but before she could climb the stairs, he caught her hand and pulled her against him for a hug. "God, I've missed you," he whispered, his nose in her hair as he held her tight.

Autumn had missed him, too. She'd grieved for almost two years. But now? She just felt numb, confused. This was not how things were supposed to go. "Nick, what happened to you?" she asked.

He leaned back and framed her face with his hands. "It was unreal," he said. "The stuff of spy novels, only much less glamorous."

"Were you...held captive?"

"Yes. But...give me a second before I go into that. I—I need to look at you."

Guilt caused Autumn to squirm inside. At what point was she going to have to tell him about Quinn? She was looking into Nick's face, but what she saw was Quinn laughing at the restaurant as he brought her the biggest piece of carrot cake she'd ever seen.

That had only been twenty minutes ago.

"I'm sorry," she said. "I—I can't wait. I have to know. What happened? I searched for you, night and day, for so long. Where were you?"

"I was captured by Russians and accused of being a spy."

"*Were* you a spy?"

"No, not really. The Kremlin pretends to support Ukraine's sovereignty over the Donetsk and Luhansk People's Republics, but it views their friendliness to Western interests as an attempt by the West to isolate Russia. It's a long story, but I was basically supposed to find out if a Russian spy had infiltrated the SBU. They were worried there'd been a security breach. Instead, when I was visiting Travneve and checking on some guns a certain member of the SBU had purchased from an unknown source, I was captured and taken to a military base—I don't even know where. I was blindfolded when they took me in and when they brought me back out."

"How'd you get away?"

"Eventually, they just let me go."

"*Why?*"

He spread out his hands. "I don't know. A guard I became somewhat friendly with thinks it's because people were still asking questions about me. If they killed me, word could possibly get out that they had no real proof I was a spy and yet they killed me, anyway—and no one wanted to take the heat for making such a permanent decision. Or maybe they finally believed I was only trying to find out where those guns had come from to be sure that there wasn't a Russian spy in the SBU."

"I—I hired a private investigator who lives in Ukraine," she said, wondering if Mr. Olynyk had been one of those who kept asking questions. Or was it someone or something bigger? The FBI?

"Thank you," he said. "That could be why I'm alive today."

She couldn't absorb all of this, needed to sit down. "Let's go upstairs," she said, but as soon as they climbed to the apartment, instead of sitting on the bed so they could talk, as she'd envisioned, he walked around the room as though he couldn't believe he was finally safe and in his old surroundings. But then he opened the closet and saw that his side was empty—that the drawers once filled with his clothes were, too. And, eventually, he came across Quinn's shoes.

"Please tell me these are Caden's," he said softly as he stared down at them.

Autumn wanted to tell him what he wanted to hear, to escape the accusation inherent in that question—or maybe it was just Nick's disappointment and her guilt that made her feel so reluctant. Her husband had obviously suffered trying to help Ukraine, and while he'd been doing that, she'd fallen in love with another man.

But what was the use of lying? She wouldn't be able to hide the truth for long. "No."

Taylor nibbled nervously on her bottom lip. Her parents had been talking for a while now. What were they saying? When would they finally come back in? Was her mother telling her father about the baby? That she was in a relationship with another girl? That Caden wouldn't finish high school in Tampa, because they were moving to Sable Beach?

Or would her father's reappearance change all that? Would they be going back to Tampa, after all? And what about Quinn? Her mother must feel terrible! What could Autumn possibly say about the man who'd been planning to move in with them after the house closed?

"Everything's going to be okay," Mimi said, but her words were far from convincing. She looked worried herself.

"What's going to happen?" Caden asked.

"I have no idea," she replied. "But both of your parents love you very much. They will do what's best for you."

"What if that's not what's best for them?" Taylor asked.

Mimi kept fidgeting and looking out the window. "They'll figure it all out," she mumbled.

"Do you think we'll go back to Tampa?" Caden asked.

"That's where Dad's job is—if he still has a job," Taylor replied. "But I don't want to live there. I don't want to leave Sierra, and I don't want to face Oliver and his friends—or my old friends, either." Fortunately, none of her friends had messaged her, shocked to hear that she was pregnant. Oliver and his family seemed to be able to keep a secret. Thank goodness keeping their mouths shut was in Oliver's best interest, too.

Caden didn't say whether he preferred to stay in Sable Beach or return to Tampa. He just jiggled his leg and stared at the TV, even though she could tell he wasn't really watching the movie Mimi had put on.

"This is terrible," Taylor said and began to rub her stomach. She'd been experiencing some morning sickness lately, and being this nervous was making it worse, especially after eating such a big meal.

"Are you okay?" Mimi asked.

"Yeah." She hoped that was true, but only a few minutes later, she had to bolt into the bathroom, where she lost her dinner.

Mimi came to hold her hair back as she leaned over the toilet. "You need to calm down," she said.

"I'm trying!" Taylor responded. "I don't know how."

She got up and rinsed out her mouth and then stared at herself in the mirror. Her world had once again been turned upside down. "What about Quinn?" she said to Mimi, whom she could see in the mirror, hovering behind her.

"What's his number? It's getting late, so I imagine he'll be off work soon. I'd better let him know not to swing by on his way home. I think we've had enough surprises for one night, don't you?"

Taylor wiped her face and hands. "I'll tell him," she said and slipped into her bedroom to make the call.

Quinn was wiping down the grill, the last thing he did each night before leaving the restaurant, when his phone went off. He would've ignored it in favor of finishing up. But assuming

Autumn was wondering what time he'd be over, he decided to answer.

The caller wasn't her, though—it was Taylor. He had her number because they'd been texting each other funny memes about pregnancy for a week or more. The last one he'd sent her was a picture of a glass of milk and some Oreo cookies with the words, "I'm pregnant. This morning I told my friend to put the Oreos somewhere I couldn't reach them... She put them on the floor." And she'd responded with a picture of a woman in the hospital, about to have a baby, and the words, "The pain of labor is so great a woman can almost imagine what a man feels when he has a fever."

"Is that your mom?" his father asked, seeing him pick up his phone.

"No, it's Taylor." Happy that Autumn's daughter would feel comfortable enough to call him, he clicked the accept button. "Hey, don't tell me you're getting a craving for ice cream or something after everything you ate at the restaurant tonight," he said into the phone.

She didn't come back at him with a joke of her own, like usual. He thought he heard her sniff. Was she crying?

"Taylor? Are you okay?" he asked, immediately concerned.

"I don't know," she replied. "I don't know if any of us will be okay."

His heart lurched into his throat. "What do you mean? Have you been in an accident or something? Nothing's wrong with the baby..."

"No, it's nothing like that," she said. "But you—you'd better not come over tonight."

Taken aback, he straightened. "Why not?"

"My dad's home."

Those three words hit Quinn like a strong right hook. *"What?"*

"When we got home from the restaurant, my dad was here waiting for us."

"How? I mean…where did he come from? Where's he been? And why was he gone for so long?"

"I don't know," she said. "I don't know anything except…he and my mom are out in the apartment, talking."

Suddenly weak in the knees, Quinn leaned on the counter for support. He knew Taylor was awaiting his response, but he had nothing. Maybe Nick's return was good news for her, but it definitely wasn't good news for him.

What was he going to do?

"Uh-oh, I hear them. They're coming in. I have to go."

"Thanks for letting me know," he said, mechanically, but he was pretty sure she was already gone by then.

Autumn felt like roadkill by the time she settled onto her mother's couch so that she and Nick could speak to their children. She couldn't remember ever being quite so emotionally exhausted, and that included all the crying she'd done after Nick went missing.

Her mother sat down beside her and took her hand. Grateful for Mary's constant support, Autumn squeezed, and somehow her mother managed a smile—but that only brought her back to tears.

"It's going to be okay," Mary murmured, but Autumn couldn't see how. How could she give up her marriage—break up her family—when they'd been so happy together?

On the other hand, how could she walk away from Quinn? Just the thought of that made her feel as though someone was tearing her heart from her chest.

"What's happening?" Caden was watching them both closely as Taylor came out of her bedroom to join the gathering and perched, as tentative as a bird ready to take flight, on a side chair.

Nick sighed but dug deep enough to produce a smile, albeit

a tired one. The two of them had spent the past hour talking, but they hadn't achieved much—just that whatever happened, they didn't want their children to take the brunt of it. "Wow, have I missed you," he said.

"We missed you, too," Caden said, but Taylor didn't comment. She just looked worried. Autumn felt sorry for her. She knew her daughter had to be wondering how Nick was going to react to her sexuality *and* her pregnancy. He'd sunk onto the bed and dropped his face in his hands when she'd told him about both, but then he'd said he'd love her just as she is.

He didn't mention either of those things now, thank goodness. Autumn supposed he was planning to speak to Taylor alone later. This wasn't the time or place for a heart-to-heart about those things, not when they were still reeling with shock to find that he was alive.

Autumn sat in silence as he allowed the children to drill him with question after question, many of them the same ones she'd asked in the apartment over the garage. And Nick patiently explained what'd happened to him—how he'd gone over to Ukraine at the request of the FBI to discover if the SBU had a Russian spy, how someone became suspicious of him and a group of armed men dragged him from his bed one night and took him to a prison cell at a military base, where they treated him poorly for almost two years.

"So…how'd you get home?" Caden asked.

"Once they released me, I contacted the American embassy and told them what happened. They must've verified my story because, the next thing I knew, they were putting me on a plane headed for home."

"Why didn't you call us?" Taylor asked.

"I guess I thought it would be too hard to explain everything over the phone. I just wanted to get here, where I could see you and be with you and tell you in person, so I rushed home as soon as I was released. I never expected…" He started again. "I never expected that to be a problem."

Caden's leg started to jiggle. "So you know."

"About Quinn? Yes."

"Then, are we staying here in Sable Beach or moving back to Tampa?" Caden asked.

"It's too soon to make any big decisions," Nick said. "I'm going to get a motel for tonight and…and I hope to get to know you all again over the next few days."

"Get a motel!" Caden sounded understandably shocked.

Autumn winced. It would seem strange that his father would need to stay somewhere else. That certainly wasn't the warm welcome anyone would want to give a father who'd been through what Nick had been through. But there was only one bed in the apartment over the garage, and Autumn couldn't bear to share it with him. Not yet. She needed time, and she needed space to figure out what she was going to do.

"I don't mind," he assured them. "It'll be far better than what I've become accustomed to. Besides, I'm not the only one who's been through a lot. I know the past two years haven't been easy on any of you."

Taylor jumped to her feet as soon as he came to his. "So you'll be back in the morning?"

"Yes."

"You promise?"

That weary smile appeared again. "Wild horses couldn't keep me away."

"Why don't I go with you?" Caden asked.

Nick's face brightened. "Would you like to do that?"

"It would beat sleeping on the couch," he joked.

Autumn felt her husband's gaze on her face and looked up. "Is that okay with you?" he asked.

"Of course."

"Then grab your stuff," he told Caden, who sprang into action.

Once Caden had his bag packed, Nick hesitated at the door. "I'll come by to take everyone to breakfast in the morning, okay?"

"Okay," Taylor said.

Autumn squeezed her mother's hand again. "Sure. See you then."

34

Autumn had to wear sunglasses to breakfast. Her eyes were so swollen from crying that she didn't want anyone to see them. She pretended to be pleased that her husband was back, since her children *were* pleased and she thought she should be, too. She was relieved that he was safe, at least, but she was so torn by what his return would mean that the best she could do was act the part of a happy wife until more genuine feeling returned.

Nick watched her closely, flashing a ready smile whenever she returned his gaze. His eyes said, "Remember me? Remember what we used to have? It could be that way again." She knew he was determined to save his family, to try to make up for what'd happened by being so nice she couldn't fault him. He claimed he still loved her, that getting back to her was all he could think about during those long months in captivity, and she felt so sorry for what he'd suffered that she couldn't be the one to destroy the future he'd relied on to pull him through. She didn't want her children to have to endure any more trauma, either.

"Your mother tells me that you're going to finish high school by homeschooling," he said to Taylor.

He'd taken them to Elvira's Country Café, a relatively new

place that was doing quite well, judging by the breakfast crowd. Taylor stirred a bite of the French toast she'd ordered in a puddle of syrup but didn't look up. "I know you can't be happy about the pregnancy, Dad. I'm sorry that you're finally back and that's what you have to come home to."

He reached out to touch her arm. "It's okay, honey. I know you didn't mean for this to happen. It couldn't have been easy for you after I went missing. I'm not blaming you. As a matter of fact, I feel it's partially my fault, which is why I'm more than happy to help your mother take care of the baby while you go to college."

Caden must've told him what she and Quinn had been planning, so Nick was letting everyone know that he was willing to step into the same role. Autumn supposed she should be glad. She guessed he might even be willing to move to Sable Beach— at last. She'd been begging him for years, but he loved Tampa and his career had always been too important to him, even after they inherited the money and they could've made the move.

Taylor glanced over at her. Autumn's heart was pounding deep and loud, like a bass drum. She could feel the reverberations all the way to her fingertips, but she was grateful no one else seemed able to tell. She curved her lips into what she hoped was a pleasant smile, but she feared it had come off rather feeble when she saw the look of compassion that entered her daughter's eyes. "That's nice of you, Dad. Thank you," Taylor mumbled and stuffed that syrup-soaked bite of French toast into her mouth.

Caden cleared his throat. "So you're okay with moving here?"

Nick still had a whole plateful of food. He didn't seem to have much of an appetite, either. He kept cutting and moving his pancakes around but not eating them. "Sure. I mean, whatever's best for the rest of you. I can see why Taylor wouldn't be happy to return to Tampa. And with your grandmother opening a coffee shop in the bookstore and your mother hoping to help with that, maybe this is a better place for us to be, for the time being. You told me last night that you're willing to change schools. If you can do that, I guess I could work remotely for a while."

The men in the family would sacrifice for the women, but it hadn't been like that when Quinn was part of the picture. It'd been new and fresh and exciting. Autumn got the impression that even Caden hadn't minded the changes. He'd become close to the twins, so he had people he cared about here, too.

"Yeah, I think staying is probably good," Caden said. "I've already registered for school and everything."

"So…will we live in the new house?" Taylor sounded as though she couldn't imagine it, and Autumn felt the same.

"We could," Nick said. "It sounds like a nice one."

Autumn stared at her plate. She'd picked that house out with Quinn. It was his Realtor friend who'd told him it was about to go on the market, so they were able to get in the first day. It didn't seem right that she would now move into it with another man.

"It's a great house," Caden said. "Right on the beach."

Autumn couldn't force down another bite. She set her fork by her plate and concentrated on sipping her coffee. The acid in the coffee was probably partially responsible for the way her stomach was twisting and burning, but the warmth of just holding it in her hands was soothing. The restaurant had the air-conditioning turned so low she was freezing despite the heat and humidity outside.

"Maybe we could go see it today," Nick said.

Autumn didn't know what to say. She thought they should just move back to Tampa. It would be too hard to run into Quinn around town. She didn't think she could bear it. But before she could decide on what to say to get out of showing Nick the house, a shadow fell over their table, blocking the bright light from the many windows, and she looked up to see Mrs. Vizii glaring at her in a bright red hat. "You're with another man *al-*

ready?" she said. "What, did Quinn cheat on you like I said he would?"

Autumn felt her jaw harden, but she refused to embarrass her family by making a scene. "This happens to be my husband, Mrs. Vizii," she said politely, suppressing her anger. "He's back."

"I can see that." She propped a hand on one of her broad hips. "Did you know what your wife was up to while you were gone?"

"Whoever you are, we have enough problems," Nick said. "Please, just mind your own business and move along."

"I'm going," she said but looked at Autumn before she took a single step. "You should consider yourself lucky," she added. "Quinn isn't half the man you think he is."

That wasn't true. To Autumn, Quinn was everything a man should be. The way he treated his parents and her and the kids... Even how he'd treated Sarah after she stabbed him—standing up for her in court the way he had, asking for mental help instead of incarceration. Sarah was the one who'd failed their marriage, not Quinn. But Autumn couldn't defend him the way she wanted to without making what Nick was going through even worse. She told herself to just ignore the old lady, so it surprised her when Taylor spoke up instead.

"Then you don't know Quinn the way we do," she said softly.

As soon as Sierra picked up the phone, Taylor plugged one ear so that she could hear above the large truck rumbling past. "It's me."

"You're done with breakfast?"

She began pacing along the covered sidewalk in front of the bookstore, head bowed, phone pressed tightly to her ear. "Yeah."

"How'd it go?"

"It was awkward," she said as she stared down the street in the direction of Mimi's house and the beach. "Why couldn't my dad have come back two months ago? Then everything would be different."

"I'm sorry."

"I know."

"What does his return mean for—for whether you'll be staying?"

"Who can say? Everything is up in the air now. My dad acts as though he'd be willing to move here, even though he never wanted to do it before, but now I don't think my mom wants to stay."

"I can understand why. What about Quinn? They were so happy together."

"My mom and dad were happy, too," she said, feeling immediately defensive. But *she'd* been the one to defend Quinn in the restaurant when that old biddy marched up to their table and was so rude, so she couldn't fault Sierra. She liked Quinn as much as anyone.

"This sucks," Sierra said. "I mean… I'm glad your dad's back. I know how much you missed him, but this could change everything."

"You'll like my dad once you get to know him," she said hopefully.

"It's not about that. Have you mentioned me yet?"

"I haven't. But I'm guessing my mother has."

"You think she's told him that we're more than friends?"

"She told him about the baby, so why not that?"

"What did he say about the baby?"

"Just that he'd help my mom babysit while I'm in college."

"In other words, he'll take Quinn's place."

"Quinn took his place first." When that same defensiveness welled up again, Sierra fell silent.

"I'm sorry, Sierra," Taylor said as she pivoted to head back toward the bookstore. "I don't mean to take this out on you. I'm just…confused."

"It was my bad. I turn into a smartass when I feel threatened. I don't want to lose you."

"No matter what happens, you will always be my first love."

"That already sounds like goodbye."

Caden came out of the bookstore. With the way his shoulders were rounded and he had his hands shoved in his pockets, Taylor knew he wasn't his normal, happy-go-lucky self. "Listen, I'll have to call you back later," she said to Sierra.

"No problem. I understand."

Contrary to what she'd just said, Taylor knew Sierra was upset. But she had to deal with her family first. She pressed the end button and looked up at her brother. "What's wrong?"

"Everything. I thought we'd all be so happy if only Dad could come home."

She sighed as she put her phone in her pocket. "A lot has changed in two years."

"Yeah. Mom found another man," he said glumly.

"Mom and Dad just…need to spend more time together, get to know each other again."

Mimi stepped out of the store. "Is everything okay?"

"Yeah. We're fine," Taylor said and waited for her to go back in before speaking again. "I hate to tell you this, but… I've made a decision."

"What's that?"

"Even if you guys go back to Tampa, I'm staying here." She felt strangely empowered just saying it. Her decision would have consequences—not all of them pleasant—but she was going to take control of her own life.

"I guessed you'd say that. But what happens after the baby is born? How will you go to college?"

"I don't know. Maybe I'll have to take online classes."

"That isn't the life Mom wants for you."

"I liked what we had set up better, too, Caden. I'm going to need her. But I'm not going back to Tampa."

Ignoring all the activity on the beach, as well as the afternoon heat, Quinn sat in the spot where he and Autumn had made love and stared out to sea. He was supposed to be at the restaurant, but he couldn't stay focused on what he was doing at work. First, he'd dropped a pan of scalding water and nearly burned the feet of one of their waitresses. Then he cut his finger so deeply while chopping vegetables that his father insisted he go have someone take a look at it.

Mike thought he was driving to a med center right now to get stitches, but Quinn had just duct-taped the cut closed and headed to the beach, hoping that having a chance to be alone and gather his thoughts might help him get a better grip on his emotions.

He'd fallen hard for Autumn, had assumed he'd finally have the wife and family he'd always wanted—and been totally blindsided. Who would've believed that after nearly two years without a single word to his family, Nick would show up out of the blue?

He wondered how Autumn was feeling about the situation, how much she'd told Nick about them and if Nick was surprised that she'd gotten involved with the boy she'd given her virginity to in a tree house when she was in high school.

She'd once said they'd laughed about that through the years. It probably wasn't so funny anymore.

He managed a smile as one of the patrons of The Daily Catch recognized him and said hello. He would've waved, but he had his hand cradled in his lap, a towel wrapped around it so that no one could see the blood seeping out from under his makeshift bandage.

Autumn had to be even more blown away that Nick was back than he was, he thought after the customer was gone. But…was she happy about it? She had to be, didn't she? *How* happy? Would they just drive off into the sunset and leave him to put the pieces of his life back together after it had collided so hard with hers?

What else could they do?

Quinn wished he still had a chance with her, but she wouldn't break up her family, even if she would rather be with him. What they'd had was intense and wonderful—euphoric, at times—but it had been short-lived, probably too short to put him in any kind of position, except that of the guy who was going to lose her.

"Fuck," he muttered as the picture of what he wanted for his future blurred together in his mind and drained away.

His phone kept going off—his father trying to see how his finger was, no doubt. He appreciated the concern, but he couldn't talk to either of his parents right now. He needed some space.

When his phone signaled yet another text, he decided to let his dad know that everything was fine.

But the message wasn't from his father; it was from Autumn.

Can we talk today? Maybe after you get off work?

He considered pretending he was at the restaurant, as she expected. He felt a little silly that he couldn't even work. But wondering what was going on in her mind was eating him up inside. If he had the chance to talk to her sooner rather than later, he was going to take it.

I'm at the beach. Are you free?

She didn't respond immediately. He watched all the people who were playing in the surf and the sand or just sunbathing around him, while remembering that first morning, when he and Autumn had gone swimming and she'd let him remove her bikini top. He'd thought he'd been through a lot with Sarah, and he had. His marriage had been a nightmare, especially at the end. But this was, in ways, worse, because he could only accept what Autumn decided. He couldn't fight for her as he wanted to, not without making things worse for her and her kids.

Finally, he heard his phone buzz.

I'm on my way.

It took fifteen minutes before he spotted her walking toward him wearing a pair of shorts, a tank top, flip-flops, a large-brimmed hat and sunglasses. He wanted to get up and walk toward her—rush to her, actually—but he could tell just by her body language that he'd guessed correctly. She was going to stay with Nick.

The hard thing was that he couldn't even blame her. It would be the best thing for her kids.

He turned his attention back to the sea and kept it there, even when she sat down beside him.

"You've got your work clothes on, and it's like a hundred and fifty degrees out here," she said. "What are you doing?"

"Just thinking."

She indicated the towel wrapped around his hand. "What happened?"

"Nothing big. It's just a scratch."

"Let me see it," she said.

He shook his head. "You can't see it. I taped it closed."

"Do you need stitches?"

"No, I'll be fine."

"You're sure."

He wasn't sure of anything, but that had much more to do with her than his hand. "Of course. It's not a big deal."

She sighed as she gazed out to sea. "I'm sorry, Quinn," she said. "I'm so—" her voice broke "—sorry."

"I know," he said. "You tried to tell me Nick could come back. It's my fault for assuming he wouldn't."

"I quit believing it, too," she admitted as a tear ran down her cheek.

"I love you," he said, suddenly unable to hold the words back. "I know I've never told you that before. Seems a little crazy that I would feel that strongly when we haven't been together very long. But it's true. For what it's worth, I love you."

She wiped that tear before it could fall from her chin. "I know," she said. "I love you, too."

"Is there no way?" He knew the answer before he asked that question, but he couldn't help himself.

She shook her head. "Nick's a good husband, a good father. And he's been through hell, through no fault of his own. How can I leave him?"

Quinn didn't have an answer for that. "Okay," he said. "I understand."

"I want you to know that...this summer has been the best summer of my life," she said. "I'll always remember it—remember *you*."

He sucked in a deep breath to help mitigate the sting of what was happening and so that he'd have the strength to do what he knew he should do: release her. "I won't be able to forget you, either. But... I want you to let go of whatever you feel for me and give Nick everything you gave him before. Although it kills me to lose you—" he had to clear his throat to be able to keep speaking "—I want you to be happy more than anything else, and I know that's what it will take. So don't worry about me, okay? I'll be fine."

Fresh tears appeared, and she sniffed. "We'll be going back to Tampa soon."

His throat grew even tighter. "You've already made that decision?"

"He doesn't know it yet. But going back is the only way I can do this. I can't stay here where...where you are, so that will be my only stipulation to...to picking up where we left off."

He closed his eyes. This was going exactly as he'd thought it would. "What about Taylor?"

"She can homeschool there as well as here."

"She'll be willing to leave Sierra?"

"She won't like it, but..."

"Right. Well...tell the kids I'm happy for them."

"I will," she said, and covered a sob as she got up and walked away.

35

Autumn sat in the kitchen with her mother at five o'clock in the morning. It was still dark outside. Even the birds weren't chirping quite yet, but she, Caden and Nick were going to drive home today. The car was already packed, and she planned to wake Nick and Caden soon so they could get an early start—it was a long way. But first she was going to enjoy these last few minutes with her mother.

"What a summer," her mother commented, sipping the coffee she'd made for them.

Autumn turned her mug around and around without lifting it. She didn't seem to have much of an appetite anymore. "No kidding."

"Everything hit at once, but you weathered it beautifully," she said.

"Not so beautifully," Autumn argued. "I feel like I've been dragged behind a horse."

"Emotionally, you have."

"How are things going with Tammy?" They'd discussed having her meet Tammy, and Autumn was interested, but it wasn't something she'd been willing to take on in the middle of everything else. They were hoping to plan a rendezvous—just the three of them—in Nashville once Autumn felt she had her life on track again.

"Good. I'm enjoying her."

"She's determined not to let Nora back into her life?"

"One hundred percent, or I couldn't have anything to do with her."

"You trust her?"

"I do. Her mother wouldn't have gone to all that trouble to try to find me if she felt she had an easier way. That must've cost her several thousand dollars, and we know she doesn't have much."

"Did you ever find out where she got that money?"

"Tammy says she must've gotten it from her brother. He's the only one who could or would help her."

"So how often are you talking to Tammy these days?"

"I've only spoken to her a few times, but she's texted me quite a bit. I think she's excited to have reconnected, and she's anxious to meet you."

"Does she know what's going on with me?"

Mary nodded. "I told her. I hope you don't mind."

"No. It's not a secret. Everyone in Sable Beach knows."

"The people in this town do love to gossip."

"And Mrs. Vizii is happy to lead the pack now that they're talking about someone other than her daughter."

"She's immature and frank to the point of rudeness sometimes, but it's just because she's hurting." She leaned to one side, apparently checking to see if Caden was still asleep, and lowered her voice. "Are you sure you're doing the right thing—going back to Tampa?"

Autumn knew her mother was really asking if she was doing the right thing staying with Nick. "If going back isn't the right thing, what could be?" she responded, lowering her voice, too.

"It's got to be hard for you to leave Taylor behind."

It made her sad that her daughter's high school career had

come to an early end, before all the fun activities she would've participated in as a senior—especially graduation. But Autumn understood that staying was indeed the best thing for her. At least she hoped it was, and that she and Sierra would be able to take care of the baby on their own, at least until they got their diplomas and would be willing to move back to Tampa or do something else. Mary said she'd help and so would Laurie, if it came to babysitting here and there, but leaving her daughter behind was one of the most difficult things Autumn would ever do.

But so was leaving Quinn.

"Taylor made a good case for staying," she said. "And I know you'll be here to take care of her, like you've always taken care of me."

Mary smiled and reached over to cover her hand. "I'm glad you trust me with her—because I *will* take good care of her. But I'm so worried about you. I don't think you've slept a wink since Nick came home, have you?"

Autumn twisted around to check for herself that her son was asleep. "It's been an adjustment," she said, speaking euphemistically, just in case. "But don't worry. I'll stay in close touch, and I'll come back often. Nick agreed that I can come home whenever I want."

"Was that part of your *deal*?" she asked wryly.

No doubt her mother had been able to tell how strained things were between them. Nick was sleeping in her bed again—it seemed too cruel to relegate him to a motel when he hadn't done anything wrong; and it upset their children—but she hadn't been able to make love to him yet. As long as she "snapped back" to the wife she'd been, he seemed eager to forgive and forget Quinn, which was partly why he was pressing her to resume sexual relations. He needed the reassurance it would provide, so she was counting on the physical aspect of their relationship being easier for her once they got away from Sable Beach and were back in their own house. "With time," she kept telling him, but she was nowhere near ready. Her heart and her body still longed for Quinn. It had only been a week since she'd spoken to him on the beach, however. She had to give herself more time.

"This will be the best thing for Caden," she said. "It's so hard to change schools when you're in high school."

"Seemed to me, he was okay with it."

"But his water polo…"

"Right. I remember."

Autumn pushed her cup away. "Mother, you're not making this any easier."

"I appreciate Nick, honey. I'm grateful for all he's done. But I don't see how it can work. You can't tell your heart who to love."

"I loved him once. I can love him again," she insisted. "I mean, I still do love him—in many ways."

Her mother studied her for several long seconds. "No matter what, just know that I admire the kind of character you have and that I'm proud of you."

"Thanks." Autumn knew Mary wasn't convinced, but she was afraid to discuss it any longer for fear she'd wind up letting Nick and her kids down when she was trying so hard not to do that.

"I'll get Taylor up so she can say goodbye."

"I'll go get Nick," Autumn said.

"So…how are you doing?" Mary asked, her voice slightly tinny because she was coming through FaceTime on Autumn's iPad.

Autumn wanted to tell her mother that she was doing great, but this had been the hardest three weeks of her life. "Caden is enjoying school. I think it was good that we came back—for his sake."

"I'm happy to hear that. But I didn't ask about Caden."

Autumn took a sip of her coffee. It had grown cold while she'd sat at the kitchen table, staring off into space, yet she couldn't summon the energy to get up and pour herself a fresh cup. She was just glad to be alone—at last—so that she didn't have to smile and pretend to be okay. "I know."

"It's that bad?"

She shifted her chair so that she could see Chris's painting of the little girl carrying a stack of books while leaving a bookstore with her mother and missed Sable Beach more than ever. "I keep telling myself it'll get better."

"But…"

"It hasn't so far."

"What's going on?"

"Nothing I can point to. Nick has been home a lot, of course. Trying to acclimate and get reacquainted with me and Caden. He's been…kind, supportive, understanding and yet…"

"And yet, you're still not connecting like you did before?"

She sighed as she thought back over the past several days. She'd finally given in and had sex with him. She felt too bad turning him away when he wanted to be with her so badly. She'd also thought it might help erase Quinn from her mind. She was desperate to get back to the wife and mother she used to be, so they could be happy as a family again and move on.

But afterward, as soon as Nick fell asleep, she'd slipped into the bathroom and cried. They'd made love a couple of times since, but it was always a challenge for her—very mechanical and harder each time. "Not yet. But that's understandable, isn't it? I mean, he was gone for so long, and…and I'd just gotten over him when he returned."

"You're talking much more frankly than you have so far," Mary said. "Either you're getting desperate, or he's not at home."

It was both, but she didn't want to admit the desperation. "He's not at home. He left for work an hour ago." *Thank God.* With Caden at school and Nick at his new office, she finally had the chance to sink into a chair and just…try to recoup.

"I thought there wasn't anything left of his practice. I remember you had to box up his office and bring everything home when his lease ran up."

"It didn't make sense to extend if I couldn't find him. But he's rented a new office, and he went there today to contact his former clients and try to get his practice going again."

"Picking up after almost two years in a prison cell must be so hard."

"He says it's better than still being stuck in Ukraine," she said and managed a feeble smile for Nick's attempt to make light of it. She admired his resilience, recognized how hard he was trying to get back to his old self and wanted things to work between them. It was difficult enough that Taylor was away from the family and pregnant at seventeen. They didn't need a separation or a divorce on top of that.

But Autumn couldn't get her heart on board. It didn't seem to understand the urgency of falling in love with Nick again and remained stubbornly loyal to Quinn. "How's Taylor?"

"Happy. Doing well."

"She called me after her doctor's appointment yesterday, crying."

"Because…"

"She didn't like the exam."

"Those exams are pretty invasive, but we've all had them. Well, most women, anyway."

"You never had any neonatal exams. I can't believe you had me without any outside help."

"I'm just glad you survived. I think of that night often and realize what a miracle it was."

"Have you heard anything else from Nora?"

"No, I told you I blocked her."

"She could call the store."

"At which point I would contact the police and get a restraining order against her."

Autumn took another sip of her coffee. "How's it going with Tammy?"

"We've been using Skype so that we can see each other, and we talk almost every day. It's fun. I shipped her some of your spaghetti sauce, and she loved it. She can't wait to meet you."

They were going to run low on spaghetti sauce this year. What with Nick's return, she hadn't finished her summer the way she usually did. Instead, they'd given away any produce they couldn't eat. "I'm anxious to meet her, too."

"Then why not take a break, now that Caden's in school, and come back? You could see Taylor and meet Tammy at the same time. Tammy's offered to come here, so that we don't have to go to her."

"And you're okay with that? With having her come to your house?"

"It's taken me some time to build that trust, but yeah."

Autumn wanted to agree right away. But...could she go back without breaking down and seeing Quinn?

Picking up her cell phone, she navigated to her messages and, where her mother wouldn't be able to see, scrolled to his name. He'd left her alone since she'd said goodbye to him on the beach, hadn't even tried to call. He was doing his best to respect her wishes. The only thing she'd received from him since she'd left Sable Beach was one simple text message. It had come in yesterday, almost as if he knew how hard she was struggling, and was just a simple heart emoji.

Tears gathered behind her eyes as she stared at it, and even though she knew she shouldn't—that it was the worst possible thing she could do given the situation—she couldn't help texting him back that same emoji.

"Autumn?" her mother said.

"What?"

"Do you want to come meet Tammy?"

She set her phone down. "When?"

"In two weeks?"

Now that the possibility of a visit had been raised, she wanted to come even sooner—today—but she could hold out that long, couldn't she? "Okay."

"Should I schedule your flight?" Her mother sounded relieved.

"No, I have to talk to Nick about it first. Then I'll make the arrangements."

"I can't wait," her mother said. "I hope he's okay with it."

Autumn knew he would probably want to come with her, but she was going to ask him to stay so one of them would be home with Caden. Returning to the place where she grew up, to the sand and the sea and the bird with just one eye, not to mention the bookstore, Aunt Laurie, her mother and Taylor, sounded like a welcome break if not a much-needed escape. Maybe if she went back alone, she could get her feet underneath her again and wouldn't feel as though she'd left such a huge chunk of herself behind. By leaving Nick in Tampa, she might realize just how much she loved him, and when she came home, be able to give him her whole heart, as he deserved.

That was what she told herself as she finished the conversation with her mother.

But she knew, if she happened to see Quinn, the opposite could also prove to be true.

Autumn could hear Nick getting into the cupboards behind her as she waited at the kitchen table for the Skype session she had scheduled with her mother. He'd worked a few days over the past couple of weeks, but not anywhere close to full-time, like she'd expected when he leased the new office. She'd anticipated having hours and hours to herself while planting her fall garden and cleaning the house, had been counting on the solitude.

But he would hardly let her out of his sight. And the more days and weeks that passed, the more possessive he got. He even made a few comments that led her to believe, if he did leave the house, he secretly checked up on her when he got back by going through her phone and computer.

There was nothing for him to find, of course. Except for that one exchange of heart emojis, she and Quinn hadn't communicated since she left him on the beach. She could easily have deleted their whole chain of texts, so that Nick wouldn't be able to scroll through them even if he tried. But she couldn't bring herself to give them up. Those texts were all she had left of Quinn. Sometimes, when Nick did go to work, she reread them.

She didn't know whether Nick ever snooped on her or not, but whenever she tried to tell him to back off a little, that she needed more space, they got into an argument. That was exactly what'd happened when she'd said she wanted to go back to Sable Beach to meet Tammy. He'd said she could go as long as he went with her—that it wouldn't be wise for them to separate so soon—and because she didn't want to pull Caden out of school during the first month, she'd decided to stay home.

"I've been through enough. I'm not going to lose you on top of everything else," Nick told her, over and over.

She bit back a sigh as she opened the Skype app on her computer and tried to put her husband and her marriage out of her mind. Tammy was staying with her mother in Sable Beach. She was about to meet her half sister for the first time, and she didn't want to be dwelling on her problems when she did.

Almost immediately, an electronic pop sounded, and her mother appeared on the screen. Punctual, as usual. "There you are. All set?"

"I am."

Nick leaned over her shoulder. "Hi, Mom. Where's Taylor?"

"She's at Sierra's," Mary said. "Because we're telling her and Caden that Tammy is an old childhood friend of mine, I figured it would be better to do this when she wasn't around."

Autumn had an aunt that was really a friend and a friend who was really a half sister. But it was more important to cut Jeff and Nora out of their narrative than to get all the labels right.

"Of course," Nick said. "I can't wait to meet her."

"Good, because she's right here." Mary turned the computer so they could see the woman sitting next to her.

"Ta-da!" Tammy said, doing spirit fingers and laughing. "As you can probably tell, I'm nervous but excited."

"Tammy, this is Autumn," Mary said, even though it wasn't necessary.

Autumn studied her half sister, looking for similarities. They had the same coloring, but Tammy wore her hair very short and stylish, and she had big dimples that appeared when she smiled. Autumn thought she was quite attractive. "My mother has told me so much about you."

"She's told me a great deal about you, too," Tammy said. "She's very proud of you. And your daughter is just beautiful."

Autumn pulled the computer closer. "Thank you. I miss her." She spoke to Taylor every day, but it was still hard.

"I bet you do."

They visited for the next hour, and Nick stayed for the whole thing, constantly inserting himself into the conversation. Autumn wished he'd let her enjoy this on her own, but she supposed it was only natural he'd be interested. He was Tammy's brother-in-law, after all.

Luckily, before her mother and Tammy signed off, Caden texted to say he'd forgotten his PE shoes, and Nick agreed to take them over. The way Nick had been acting lately, she was surprised he didn't demand that she hang up and go with him. She knew he felt threatened by anything that had to do with Sable Beach—was terrified that something might draw her back there.

"Your husband seems like a nice man," Tammy said after he was gone.

Autumn wanted to tell them both how badly she was struggling, but she feared acknowledging it would only make it worse. So she said, "He is," and left it at that.

"I'm sorry for what you've been through, what with his disappearance."

"Thank you. We all have our trials." She certainly hadn't suffered anything worse than her mother or Tammy.

"I guess that's true."

"Next time you come to Sable Beach, I'll come, too," Autumn said. "I wish I was there now."

"So do we," her mother said.

They talked a little longer, and after they hung up, Autumn put on her gardening gloves and went outside. She was determined to hang on to the good feeling she had from Tammy—how much she liked her half sister and how much her mother seemed to like her, too—and think of nothing else.

But it wasn't ten minutes later that she had to take off her gloves to dig her phone out of her pocket. Her mother was calling back.

"Hello?"

"I'm sorry to bother you again," Mary said. "But..."

"What is it?" Autumn asked, instantly concerned, because she could hear tears in her mother's voice. "What's happened?"

"Quinn's mother just died."

Quinn spotted her immediately. Autumn was at the funeral. Taylor, Sierra and Mary were with her, but he didn't see Nick or Caden. Were they still in Tampa? Had she come alone?

Suddenly feeling strangled by his tie, he closed his eyes and took a deep breath. What was already going to be a difficult two hours had just gotten worse. While he appreciated the fact that she would come to his mother's funeral, she had no idea how hard it had been for him when she went back to Nick. Seeing her again just brought back all the desire he'd felt before.

"Autumn's here," his father muttered. "Did you see?"

"I did."

"Why do you think she came?"

"Just to be nice," he said. What else could it be? She'd already moved to Tampa, had been there for six weeks—the longest six weeks of Quinn's life. When she'd sent him that heart emoji three weeks ago, he'd felt a burst of hope, thought maybe she'd change her mind. He'd wanted to call her and tell her how badly he missed her. But he knew he couldn't. If she was going to come back to him, she had to do it on her own.

So he'd waited. And waited. And nothing had happened.

The pastor approached the pulpit and everyone sat down. Quinn heard the words of the eulogy. He even got up and said a few things himself. But he felt so disconnected from everything. It was almost as if he was outside his own body, watching what went on.

This will soon be over, he kept telling himself. It wouldn't last forever.

But the loss—of both the women he loved—would.

Taylor was glad she'd stayed in Sable Beach. She wasn't tempted to go to Tampa, but it was hard to be separated from her family. If not for the pregnancy, she would've made a different decision, especially since her father had been missing for so long. But having a baby changed everything.

She was starting to show, could barely button her shorts and pants even though she hadn't gained much weight yet. She was relieved she didn't have to face anyone she knew in Tampa as her waist thickened. She hadn't told any of them, other than Oliver, that she was pregnant, doubted she ever would. Danielle and the other kids were surprised she hadn't come home, but she'd painted Sable Beach as such a great place to live that they'd let it go at that. She was leaving her childhood behind and moving on—and although it was scary and new, it was sort of exciting, too.

She'd been looking forward to seeing her parents. But when Autumn arrived yesterday, she'd shown up without Nick, even though he'd initially said he'd be coming with her, and her smile no longer reached her eyes. She talked, even laughed at the appropriate times, but she seemed...hollow inside.

"She's depressed," Sierra had said when Taylor mentioned it to her on the phone late last night.

"Because of Quinn?"

"Maybe. How would you feel if you had to give me up and go back to your old boyfriend in Tampa?"

"It's not the same thing," Taylor argued. "My parents never broke up."

"They were apart for almost two years. Anyway, I don't know if it's because of Quinn, but she's definitely unhappy. I could tell the second I saw her at dinner."

Taylor hadn't wanted to hear that. Now that her father was home, she wanted her parents to stay together and be happy. But she knew Sierra was right. Caden had told Taylor about the many arguments their parents were having and how difficult it was at home. He'd said their mother had a hard time getting out of bed, and when she did, she walked around in her pajamas for most of the day.

As soon as Taylor had shared *that* with Sierra, Sierra had freaked out. "That isn't right," she'd insisted. "You need to do something. You don't want her to end up like *my* mother, do you?"

Taylor didn't think Autumn would ever take her own life, but just in case she was feeling that bad, Taylor watched her extra closely at the funeral. Her mother had lost weight. She was skinnier than Taylor had ever seen her. She didn't seem to be interested in food—had barely touched what was on her plate last night.

Sierra claimed that was another sign of depression.

Her mother caught her staring and gave her one of those fake smiles. Autumn was pretending that everything was okay, but Taylor could tell it wasn't. Taylor had texted Caden before bed last night to see why their father hadn't come, and he'd said that Autumn had tearfully admitted that she needed a break.

When Taylor looked across the room at Quinn, she saw a similar, empty expression on his face. His mother had just died, so she expected him to be sad. But he'd been this way since Autumn left. They both seemed like shells of their former selves. Taylor liked Quinn. He was still nice to her if she ever happened to see him. But she could tell he wasn't the same after her mother left, either.

The pastor was talking about what a wonderful life Mrs. Vanderbilt had lived when Taylor leaned over to whisper in Sierra's ear. "I have to do it, don't I."

Sierra knew what she was talking about, didn't even have to ask. "*I* would."

"But...what about my father?"

"I wouldn't want her to stay with me if she didn't love me anymore, would you?" Sierra replied.

She wouldn't, no. But it was easy to say that when she wasn't the one who was hurting. Nick had already been through so much. Taylor didn't want to make it worse. And yet...

Mimi leaned around Autumn to give her a scowl that said she shouldn't be talking, so Taylor fell silent. But she continued to study her mother and Quinn. Even at the graveside, when they lowered the coffin, they kept glancing at each other but then quickly looking away.

As soon as it was over, Autumn said, "Well, we'd better get going." But Taylor couldn't take it anymore. She told Sierra and Mimi that they'd meet them at the car and pulled her mother aside.

"Is something wrong?" Autumn asked.

"You're not a very good actor," she replied. "That's what's wrong."

"I don't know what you're talking about."

"You're only staying with Dad because of Caden and me."

"That's not all of it—" she started, but Taylor cut her off.

"We'll be fine, Mom. Mimi once told me that I have to live my truth. I think you need the same advice."

"But your father—"

"He's already lost you, hasn't he? In all the ways that count?"

When tears welled up in her mother's eyes, Taylor felt like crying, too. "If Quinn makes you happy, you owe it to yourself to grab hold of that happiness," she said and walked away. If her mother followed her to the car and then went back to Tampa, Taylor told herself she'd let it go. At least she'd said her piece. She couldn't push Autumn any further. Even though what she said was true, she felt too guilty supporting a divorce.

But her mother didn't come. When Taylor reached the car, she looked back to see Autumn staring after her. And a second later, she pivoted and walked right back to the grave.

Almost everyone had left the cemetery. As Autumn returned, she could see Mike off to one side, speaking to Jimmy Pollard, the young pastor who'd performed the services. And she could see Quinn staring down at his mother's casket as if he couldn't quite believe she was gone.

He looked so forlorn. Watching Beth go through all those treatments and then pass away in spite of how brutal they were must've been a nightmare, and yet he'd shouldered it all so well. Gave up his job and moved home to help them. Supported them any way he could.

Autumn had walked through the line and offered her condolences to him and his father earlier, just like everyone else at the funeral, but when Quinn had greeted her, he hadn't even taken her hand. He'd merely nodded and thanked her politely. Then he'd looked to the next person in line.

She hated that he was suffering. The fact that she couldn't

even breathe when she thought she might be part of the cause was how she knew that she couldn't allow it to continue. Taylor was right. It didn't matter how hard she tried to make herself love Nick, how long she forced herself to stay in Tampa, their marriage wasn't going to work.

Because her heart was right here with Quinn, in Sable Beach.

Mike spotted her first. He mumbled something to Quinn as he walked past him on the way to his truck, which he climbed into and then waited.

She started to approach Quinn, but he shook his head. "Don't," he said without looking up. "It'll only make this harder."

She stopped. "I'm sorry. I'm *so* sorry."

"I know. It's not your fault. It's not anyone's fault. It's just the way things are, and I need to accept it. But having you back, wishing I could pull you into my arms, that's—that's twisting me up inside. I'm not strong enough. Not today."

She knew the ramifications of what she was about to do would be big. Taylor understood. Caden might, too. But she and Nick would have to figure out how to split their assets and share their children. She didn't want to do that. But if she couldn't love Nick, was she really doing him any favors by staying with him?

Ignoring what Quinn had said, she approached him, anyway.

"Autumn," he warned, his voice a bit rougher. "Stop. Go away."

"I won't stop," she said. "And I won't go away. Because I can't."

He watched her warily as she drew closer. "What do you want from me?"

"I want everything from you," she said simply. "But I'm willing to give you everything I have in return."

He seemed doubly uncertain. "What are you saying?"

She took hold of his hand and drew it to her cheek. "I've never loved anyone the way I love you. That's what I'm saying. And I can't quit loving you no matter how hard I try. So I'm coming back, and I'm never going to leave you again."

His mouth fell open. "And Nick?"

"I'll have to tell him the truth, too."

"That you want me. That you've come back to me, and you're staying."

"Yes. Exactly that."

His Adam's apple bobbed as he swallowed, and she thought she saw the sparkle of tears in his eyes just before he gathered her in his arms and buried his face in her hair. "We'll make it as easy as possible on everyone," he said when he could speak.

"Yes, we will. But what we want matters, too." She leaned back to look up into his face. "Do you think we can still get our house?"

He laughed as he held her tightly again. "I don't care where we live, as long as I've got you."

★ ★ ★ ★ ★

Questions for Discussion

1. The story follows three main female points of view—Mary, Autumn and Taylor. Were you more interested in one of their stories over the others'? Whose, and why?

2. Could you identify with any one character over the others, and why?

3. What did you think of Mary/Bailey's history? Have you heard about stories like this in the news, and what do you make of them?

4. Did you feel Mary should form a connection with Tammy, or should she have left that whole part of her past behind?

5. Did you feel as though Mary should've been open to forgiving Nora? Why or why not? Did you see what was coming with that part of the story before it happened?

6. Taylor faces a lot of big life changes for a seventeen-year-old throughout the course of one summer. What did you

find most compelling about her storyline? How would you have reacted as her mother?

7. What did you think of Autumn's decision in the end? Did you agree with what—and who—she chose? Why or why not?

8. Did you have a favorite scene in the novel? What was it? Why was it your favorite?

9. If you were to cast the movie version of *The Bookstore on the Beach*, who would you choose to play each character?

A Conversation with the Author

What inspired you to write *The Bookstore on the Beach*?

I wanted to write a big, beefy escapist read—something I would love to devour while sitting on a beach somewhere. Because I'd already written about three sisters in *One Perfect Summer*, I thought it would be a nice change to write about three generations of women—a grandmother, a mother and a daughter.

Did you identify with any of the main characters? Who, and how?

I probably identified with Autumn the most, because I'm also in that "between" stage where I'm dealing with both parents and children. I couldn't help sympathizing with the difficult challenges she faces—and I enjoyed watching her fall in love again, especially with her first crush. I love second-chance-at-love stories.

Where did you get the idea for Mary's backstory?

I live in Northern California, where there was a lot of news coverage of the Jaycee Dugard abduction once she escaped. I was horrified by what I read—that a child could be held captive for so long, even bear her captor's children while his wife was also living in the house. So much of Mary's backstory is based on what Jaycee Dugard endured.

Do you have a favorite character in the book? Who is it, and why?

I'm in love with Quinn—and I hope, after finishing this story, you'll be in love with him, too.

How did you decide on the bookstore setting for the story? Are you a big reader?

A bookstore holds such promise for me. The content of all those volumes yet to be explored is magical, so just walking into one is a pleasure. Actually owning one would be a dream come true. So I was able to pretend to own a bookstore—one that's set on the beach and looks just the way I'd like mine to look—through the pages of this novel.

What was the most challenging part of writing this book? What was the most enjoyable?

Each character is facing at least one life-changing decision. While I found their conflicts and reactions interesting to explore (the most enjoyable aspect), I also knew I'd set a pretty ambitious goal for myself, weaving these three stories together so that they were cohesive and each scene built on the last (the most challenging aspect).

Can you describe your writing process? Do you tend to outline first or dive right in and figure out the details as you go along?

If I outline in advance, I feel as though I've already told the story, and the actual writing becomes drudgery to me. I have to be surprised right along with the reader. Then I'm excited to get to work each day, and the story feels fresh and holds the emotional tension that makes my work so enjoyable for me. It also prevents me from giving away certain elements too soon. (Can you tell I'm not very good at keeping secrets? Ha!)

Can you tell us anything about what you're working on next?

I'm hard at work on *When I Found You*, a romance, which is the latest addition to my Silver Springs series, and I'm having such a wonderful time. This book involves two characters from my Whiskey Creek series—one of them has moved to Silver Springs—and it's wonderful to work with them again. While those who haven't read my Whiskey Creek series won't even realize that these characters come from a previous series, I will also get to finish a plotline that many of my readers have been waiting years to get back to, so I think it's going to be a win all around.